FURY

Salman Rushdie is the author of seven previous novels – *Grimus*, *Midnight's Children*, *Shame*, *The Satanic Verses*, *Haroun and the Sea of Stories*, *The Moor's Last Sigh* and *The Ground Beneath Her Feet* – and one work of short stories entitled *East, West*. He has also published three works of non-fiction – *The Jaguar Smile*, *Imaginary Homelands*, *The Wizard of Oz* – and, as co-editor, *The Vintage Book of Indian Writing*.

He has received many awards for his writing including the European Union's Aristeion Prize for Literature. He is a fellow of the Royal Society of Literature and Commandeur des Arts et des Lettres. In 1993 *Midnight's Children* was adjudged the 'Booker of Bookers', the best novel to have won the Booker Prize in its first 25 years.

ALSO BY SALMAN RUSHDIE

Fiction

Grimus
Midnight's Children
Shame
The Satanic Verses
Haroun and the Sea of Stories
East, West
The Moor's Last Sigh
The Ground Beneath Her Feet

Non Fiction

The Jaguar Smile
Imaginary Homelands
The Wizard of Oz

Screenplay

Midnight's Children

Anthology

The Vintage Book of Indian Writing (co-editor)

Salman Rushdie

FURY

A Novel

VINTAGE

Published by Vintage 2002

2 4 6 8 10 9 7 5 3 1

First published in Great Britain in 2001 by Jonathan Cape

Vintage
Random House, 20 Vauxhall Bridge Road, London SW1V 2SA

Random House Australia (Pty) Limited
20 Alfred Street, Milsons Point, Sydney
New South Wales 2061, Australia

Random House New Zealand Limited
18 Poland Road, Glenfield, Auckland 10, New Zealand

Random House (Pty) Limited
Endulini, 5A Jubilee Road, Parktown 2193, South Africa

The Random House Group Limited Reg. No. 954009
www.randomhouse.co.uk

Grateful acknowledgement is made to the following for permission to reprint previously published material:

'The Motorcycle Song' by Arlo Guthrie © 1967, 1969 (renewed) by APPLESEED MUSIC, INC. All rights reserved. Used by permission.

'I'm on Fire' by Bruce Springsteen. Copyright © 1984 by Bruce Springsteen (ASCAP). Reprinted by permission.

'The Donkey Song'. Words and music by Irving Burgie and William Attaway. Copyright © 1955; renewed 1983 Cherry Lane Music Publishing Company, Inc (ASCAP), Lord Burgess Music Publishing Company (ASCAP) and Dream Works Songs (ASCAP). Worldwide Rights for Lord Burgess Music Publishing Company and Dream Works Songs administered by Cherry Lane Music Publishing Company, Inc. International copyright secured. All rights reserved.

A CIP catalogue record for this book
is available from the British Library

ISBN 0 099 42186 0

Papers used by Random House are natural, recyclable products made from wood grown in sustainable forests. The manufacturing processes conform to the environmental regulations of the country of origin

Printed and bound in Great Britain by
Bookmarque Ltd, Croydon, Surrey

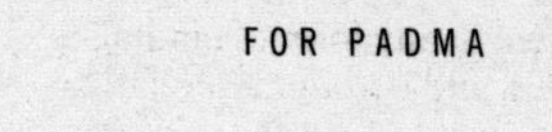

FOR PADMA

PART ONE

1

Professor Malik Solanka, retired historian of ideas, irascible dollmaker, and since his recent fifty-fifth birthday celibate and solitary by his own (much criticized) choice, in his silvered years found himself living in a golden age. Outside his window a long, humid summer, the first hot season of the third millennium, baked and perspired. The city boiled with money. Rents and property values had never been higher, and in the garment industry it was widely held that fashion had never been so fashionable. New restaurants opened every hour. Stores, dealerships, galleries struggled to satisfy the skyrocketing demand for ever more recherché produce: limited-edition olive oils, three-hundred-dollar corkscrews, customized Humvees, the latest anti-virus software, escort services featuring contortionists and twins, video installations, outsider art, featherlight shawls made from the chin-fluff of extinct mountain goats. So many people were doing up their apartments that supplies of high-grade fixtures and fittings were at a premium. There were waiting lists for baths, doorknobs, imported hardwoods, antiqued fireplaces, bidets, marble slabs. In spite of the recent falls in the value of the Nasdaq index and the value of Amazon stock, the new technology had the city by the ears: the talk was still of start-ups, IPOs, interactivity, the unimaginable future that had just begun to begin. The future was a casino, and everyone was gambling, and everyone expected to win.

On Professor Solanka's street, well-heeled white youths lounged in baggy garments on roseate stoops, stylishly simulating indigence while they waited for the billionairedom that would surely be along sometime soon. There was a tall, green-eyed young woman with steeply slanting Central European cheekbones who particularly caught his sexually abstinent but still roving eye. Her spiky strawberry-blonde hair stuck out clown-fashion from under a black D'Angelo *Voodoo* baseball cap, her lips were full and sardonic, and she giggled rudely behind a perfunctory palm as old-world, dandyish, cane-twirling little Solly Solanka in straw Panama hat and cream linen suit went by on his afternoon walk. Solly: the college identity he'd never cared for but had not entirely managed to lose.

"Hey, sir? Sir, excuse me?" The blonde was calling out to him, in imperious tones that insisted on a reply. Her satraps became watchful, like a Praetorian guard. She was breaking a rule of big-city life, breaking it brazenly, sure of her power, confident of her turf and posse, fearing nothing. This was just pretty-girl chutzpah; no big deal. Professor Solanka paused and turned to face the lounging goddess of the threshold, who proceeded, unnervingly, to interview him. "You walk a lot. I mean, five or six times a day, I see you walking someplace. I'm sitting here, I see you come, I see you go, but there's no dog, and it's not like you come back with lady friends or produce. Also, the hours are strange, it can't be that you're going to a job. So I'm asking myself, Why is he always out walking alone? There's a guy with a lump of concrete hitting women on the head across town, maybe you heard that, but if I thought you were a weirdo, I wouldn't be talking to you. And you have a British accent, which makes you interesting too, right. A few times there we even followed you, but you weren't going anywhere, just wandering, just covering ground. I got the impression you were looking for something, and it crossed my mind to ask you what that might be. Just being friendly, sir, just being neighbourly. You're kind of a mystery. To me you are, anyhow."

Sudden anger rose in him. "What I'm looking for," he barked, "is to be left in peace." His voice trembled with a rage far bigger than her intrusion merited, the rage which shocked him whenever it coursed through his nervous system, like a flood. Hearing his vehemence, the young woman recoiled, retreating into silence.

"Man," said the largest, most protective of the Praetorian guard, her lover, no doubt, and her peroxide-blond centurion, "for an apostle of peace you sure are filled up with war."

She reminded him of someone, but he couldn't remember whom, and the little failure of memory, the "senior moment", nagged at him infuriatingly. Luckily she wasn't there any more, no one was, when he returned from the Caribbean carnival damp-hatted and soaked through after being caught unprepared by a squall of hard, hot rain. Passing the Congregation Shearith Israel on Central Park West (a white whale of a building with a triangular pediment supported by four count 'em four massive Corinthian columns), Professor Solanka scurrying through the downpour remembered the newly bat-mitzvahed thirteen-year-old girl he'd glimpsed through the side door, waiting knife in hand for the ceremony of the blessing of the bread. No religion offers a ceremony of the Counting of the Blessings, mused Professor Solanka: you'd think the Anglicans, at least, would have come up with one of those. The girl's face glowed through the gathered gloom, its young round features utterly confident of achieving the highest expectations. Yes, a blessed time, if you cared to use words like "blessed"; which Solanka, a sceptic, did not.

On nearby Amsterdam Avenue there was a summer block party, a street market, doing good business in spite of the showers. Professor Solanka surmised that in the greater part of the planet the goods piled high on these cut-price barrows would have filled the shelves and display cabinets of the most exclusive little boutiques and upper-echelon department stores. In all of India, China, Africa, and much of the southern American continent, those who had the leisure and wallet for fashion—or more simply, in the poorer latitudes, for the mere acquisition of things—would have killed for the street merchandise of Manhattan, as also for the cast-off clothing and soft furnishings to be found in the opulent thrift stores, the reject china and designer-label bargains to be found in downtown discount emporia. America insulted the rest of the planet, thought Malik Solanka in his old-fashioned way, by treating such bounty with the shoulder-shrugging casualness of the inequitably wealthy. But New York in this time of plenty had become the object and goal of the world's concupiscence and lust, and the "insult" only made the rest of the planet more desirous than ever. On Central Park West the horse-drawn carriages moved up and down. The jingling of the bells on the harnesses sounded like cash in hand.

The season's hit movie portrayed the decadence of Caesar Joaquin Phoenix's imperial Rome, in which honour and dignity, not to mention life-and-death actions and distractions, were to be found only in the computer-regenerated illusion of the great gladiatorial arena, the Flavian Amphitheatre or Colosseum. In New York, too, there were circuses as well as bread: a musical about lovable lions, a bike race on Fifth, Springsteen at the Garden with a song about the forty-one police gunshots that killed innocent Amadou Diallo, the police union's threat to boycott the Boss's concert, Hillary *vs.* Rudy, a cardinal's funeral, a movie about lovable dinosaurs, the motorcades of two largely interchangeable and certainly unlovable presidential candidates (Gush, Bore), Hillary *vs.* Rick, the lightning storms that hit the Springsteen concert and Shea Stadium, a cardinal's inauguration, a cartoon about lovable British chickens, and even a literary festival; plus a series of "exuberant" parades celebrating the city's many ethnic, national and sexual subcultures and ending (sometimes) in knifings and assaults on (usually) women. Professor Solanka, who thought of himself as egalitarian by nature and a born-and-bred metropolitan of the countryside-is-for-cows persuasion, on parade days strolled sweatily cheek by jowl among his fellow citizens.

One Sunday he rubbed shoulders with slim-hipped gay-pride prancers, the next weekend he got jiggy beside a big-assed Puerto Rican girl wearing her national flag as a bra. He didn't feel intruded upon amid these multitudes; to the contrary. There was a satisfying anonymity in the crowds, an absence of intrusion. Nobody here was interested in his mysteries. Everyone was here to lose themselves. Such was the unarticulated magic of the masses, and these days losing himself was just about Professor Solanka's only purpose in life. This particular rainy weekend there was a calypso beat in the air, not the mere Harry Belafonte Jamaica-farewells and jackass-songs of Solanka's somewhat guiltily fond memory (*"Now I tell you in a positive way / don' tie me donkey down dere / 'cause me donkey will jump and bray / don' tie me donkey down dere!"*), but the true satirical music of the Jamaican troubadour-polemicists, Banana Bird, Cool Runnings, Yellowbelly, live in Bryant Park and on shoulder-high boomboxes up and down Broadway.

When he got home from the parade, however, Professor Solanka was seized by melancholy, his usual secret sadness, which he sublimated into the public sphere. Something was amiss with the world. The optimistic peace-and-love philosophy of his youth having given him up, he no longer knew how to reconcile himself to an increasingly phoney (he loathed, in this context, the otherwise excellent word "virtual") reality. Questions of power preyed on his mind. While the overheated citizenry was eating these many varieties of lotus, who knew what the city's rulers were getting away with—not the Giulianis and Safirs, who responded so contemptibly to the complaints of abused women until amateur videos of the incidents showed up on the evening news, not these crude glove-puppets, but the high ones who were always there, forever feeding their insatiable desires, seeking out newness, devouring beauty, and always, always wanting more? The never encountered but ever present kings of the world—godless Malik Solanka avoided crediting these human phantoms with the gift of omnipresence—the petulant, lethal Caesars, as his friend Rhinehart would say, the Bolingbrokes cold of soul, the tribunes with their hands up the mayor's and police commissioner's Coriolanuses . . . Professor Solanka shuddered faintly at this last image. He knew himself well enough to be conscious of the broad scarlet streak of vulgarity in his character; still, the crude pun shocked him when he thought of it.

Puppet-masters were making us all jump and bray, Malik Solanka fretted. While we marionettes dance, who is yanking our strings?

The phone was ringing as he came through his front door, the rain still dripping off his hat brim. He answered it snappishly, snatching off its base the cordless unit in the apartment's entrance hall. "Yes, what, please?" His wife's voice arrived in his ear via a cable on the Atlantic bed, or maybe in these days when everything was changing it was a satellite high above the ocean, he couldn't be sure. In these days when the age of pulse was giving way to the age of tone. When the epoch of analogue (which was to say also of the richness of language, of *analogy*) was giving way to the digital era, the final victory of the numerate over the literate. He had always loved her voice. Fifteen years ago in London he had telephoned Morgen Franz, a publishing friend who by chance was away from his desk, and Eleanor Masters, passing by, had picked up the clamouring instrument; they had never met but ended up talking for an hour. A week later they dined at her place, neither of them alluding to the inappropriateness of so intimate a venue for a first date. A decade and a half of togetherness ensued. So, he fell in love with her voice before the rest of her. This had always been their favourite story about each other; now, of course, in love's brutal aftermath, when memory was reinvented as pain, when voices on the phone were all they had left, it had become one of the saddest. Professor Solanka listened to the sound of Eleanor's voice and with some distaste imagined it being broken up into little parcels of digitized information, her low lovely voice first consumed and then regurgitated by a mainframe computer probably located someplace like Hyderabad-Deccan. What is the digital equivalent of lovely? he wondered. What are the digits that encode beauty, the number-fingers that enclose, transform, transmit, decode, and somehow, in the process, fail to trap or choke the soul of it? Not because of the technology but in spite of it, beauty, that ghost, that treasure, passes undiminished through the new machines.

"Malik. *Solly.*" (This, to annoy him.) "You're not listening. You've gone off inside your head on one of your riffs and the plain fact that your son is ill hasn't even registered. The plain fact that I have to wake up every morning and listen to him asking—unbearably asking—why his father isn't home hasn't registered. Not to mention the plainest fact of all, namely that without a shred of a reason or a scrap of credible explanation you walked out on us, you went off across an ocean and betrayed all those who need and love you most, who still do, damn you, in spite of everything." It was only a cough, the boy didn't have anything life-threatening, but she was right; Professor Solanka had withdrawn into himself. In this small telephonic matter as in the greater business of their life once together and now apart, their marriage once considered indissoluble, the best partnership any of their friends had ever witnessed; and of their joint parenthood of Asmaan Solanka, now an improbably beautiful and gentle-natured three-year-old, the miraculously yellow-haired product of dark-haired parents, whom they had named so celestially (*Asmaan,* n., m., *lit.* the sky, but also *fig.* paradise) because he was the only heaven in which they could both wholeheartedly and unreservedly believe.

Professor Solanka apologized to his wife for his distractedness, whereupon she wept, a loud honking noise that squeezed at his heart, for he was by no means a heartless man. He waited silently for her to stop. When she did, he spoke in his most mandarin manner, denying himself—denying *her*—the slightest hint of emotion. "I accept that what I have done must feel inexplicable to you. I am remembering, however, what you yourself taught me about the importance of the inexplicable"—here she hung up on him, but he finished the sentence anyway—"in, ah, Shakespeare." Which unheard conclusion conjured up the vision of his wife in the nude, of Eleanor Masters fifteen years ago in her long-haired, twenty-five-year-old glory lying naked with her head in his lap and a battered *Complete Works,* bound in blue leather, face down across her bush. Such had been the indecorous but sweetly swift conclusion of that first dinner. He had brought the wine, three expensive bottles of Tignanello Antinori (three! Evidence of a seducer's excessiveness there), while she had roasted a lamb shank for him and also served, to accompany the cumin-scented meat, a salad of fresh flowers. She wore a short black dress and walked lightly, and barefoot, through a flat much influenced by Bloomsbury Group design and craftwork, and boasting a caged parrot who imitated her laugh: a big laugh for so delicate a woman. His first and last blind date, she turned out to be fully the equal of her voice; not only beautiful but smart, somehow both confident and vulnerable, and a great cook. After eating many nasturtiums and drinking copiously of his Tuscan red, she began to explain her doctoral thesis (they were sitting on the floor of her living room by now, lounging on a handmade rug woven by Cressida Bell), but kisses interrupted her, for Professor Solanka had fallen tenderly, like a lamb, in love. They would happily argue, during their long good years, about which of them had made the first move, she always hotly (but with bright eyes) denying that she could ever have been so forward, he insisting—while knowing it to be untrue—that she had "thrown herself at him".

"Do you want to hear this stuff or not?" Yes, he'd nodded, his hand caressing one small, finely wrought breast. She put her hand over his and launched into her argument. Her proposition was that at the heart of each of the great tragedies were unanswerable questions about love, and, to make sense of the plays, we must each attempt to explicate these inexplicables in our own way. Why did Hamlet, loving his dead father, interminably delay his revenge while, loved by Ophelia, he destroyed her instead? Why did Lear, loving Cordelia best of his daughters, fail to hear the love in her opening-scene honesty and so fall prey to her sisters' unlovingness; and why was Macbeth, a man's man who loved his king and country, so easily led by the erotic but loveless Lady M. towards an evil throne of blood? Professor Solanka in New York, still absently holding the cordless telephone in his hand, recalled with awe naked

Eleanor's erect nipple beneath his moving fingers; also her extraordinary answer to the problem of Othello, which for her was not the "motiveless malignity" of Iago but rather the Moor's lack of emotional intelligence, "Othello's incredible stupidity about love, the moronic scale of the jealousy which leads him to murder his allegedly beloved wife on the flimsiest of evidence." This was Eleanor's solution: "*Othello doesn't love Desdemona.* The idea just popped into my head one day. A real lightbulb moment for me. He says he does, but it can't be true. Because if he loves her, the murder makes no sense. For me, Desdemona is Othello's trophy wife, his most valuable and status-giving possession, the physical proof of his risen standing in a white man's world. You see? He loves that *about* her, but not *her.* Othello himself, obviously, is not a black man but a 'Moor': an Arab, a Muslim, his name probably a Latinization of the Arabic Attallah or Ataullah. So he's not a creature of the Christian world of sin and redemption but rather of the Islamic moral universe, whose polarities are honour and shame. Desdemona's death is an 'honour killing'. She didn't have to be guilty. The accusation was enough. The attack on her virtue was incompatible with Othello's honour. That's why he didn't listen to her, or give her the benefit of the doubt, or forgive her, or do anything a man who loved a woman might have done. Othello loves only himself, himself as lover and leader, what Racine, a more inflated writer, would have called his *flamme,* his *gloire.* She's not even a person to him. He has reified her. She's his Oscar-Barbie statuette. His doll. At least that's what I argued, and they gave me the doctorate, perhaps just as a prize for brazenness, for my sheer gall." She took a big gulp of the Tignanello, then arched her back and put both arms around his neck and pulled him down to her. Tragedy vanished from their thoughts.

These many years later, Professor Solanka stood under a hot shower, warming himself after his soaked ramble with the calypso revellers and feeling like a pompous dope. To quote Eleanor's thesis against her was a cruelty he might easily have spared her. What was he thinking of, giving himself and his paltry actions these high Shakespearean airs? Did he truly dare to set himself beside the Moor of Venice and King Lear, to liken his humble mysteries to theirs? Such vanity was surely a more than adequate ground for divorce. He should call her back and tell her that, by way of apology. But that, too, would strike the wrong note. Eleanor didn't want a divorce. Even now, she wanted him back. "You know perfectly well," she had told him more than once, "that if you decided to give this up, this stupidity of yours, everything would be fine. It would be so fine. I can't bear it that you won't."

And this was the wife he had left! If she had a failing, it was that she didn't give blow jobs. (His own eccentricity was that he hated having the top of his head touched during the act of love.) If she had a failing, it was that she had so acute a sense of smell that she made him feel as if he stank the place up. (As a result, however, he had begun to wash more often.) If she had a failing, it was that she bought things without ever asking what they cost, an extraordinary trait in a woman who did not, as the British say, come from money. If she had a failing, it was that she had grown accustomed to being kept, and could spend more money on Christmas than half the population earned in a year. If she had a failing, it was that her mother-love blinded her to the rest of humanity's desires, including, to be blunt, Professor Solanka's. If she had a failing, it was that she wanted more children. That she wanted nothing else. Not all the gold of Araby.

No, she was faultless: the tenderest, most attentive of lovers, the most extraordinary mother, charismatic and imaginative, the easiest and most rewarding of companions, not a big talker but a good one (reference that first phone call), and a connoisseur not just of food and drink but of human character, too. To be smiled on by Eleanor Masters Solanka was to feel subtly, pleasingly complimented. Her friendship was a pat on the back. And if she spent freely, what of it? The Solankas were unexpectedly well-off, thanks to the almost shocking worldwide popularity of a female doll with a cheeky grin and the cocky insouciance that was just beginning to be called "attitude", and of whom Asmaan Solanka, born eight years later, uncannily looked like the fair-haired, dark-eyed, sweeter-natured flesh-and-blood embodiment. Though he was very much a boy, preoccupied by giant diggers, steamrollers, rocket ships and railway engines, and captivated by the I-think-I-can-I-think-I-can-I-thought-I-could-I-thought-I-could determination of Casey Jones, the indomitable circus-hauling little engine in *Dumbo,* Asmaan was constantly, infuriatingly, taken for a girl, probably because of his long-eyelashed beauty, but possibly also because he reminded people of his father's earlier creation. The doll's name was Little Brain.

2

Professor Solanka in the late 1980s despaired of the academic life, its narrowness, infighting and ultimate provincialism. "The grave yawns for us all, but for college dons it yawns with boredom," he proclaimed to Eleanor, adding, unnecessarily as things turned out, "Prepare for poverty." Then to the consternation of his fellows, but with his wife's unqualified approval, he resigned his tenured position at King's, Cambridge—where he had been enquiring into the development of the idea of the state's responsibility to and for its citizens, and of the parallel and sometimes contradictory idea of the sovereign self—and moved to London (Highbury Hill, within shouting distance of the Arsenal Stadium). Soon afterwards he plunged into, yes, television; which drew down much predictably envious scorn, especially when the BBC commissioned him to develop a late-night series of popular history-of-philosophy programmes whose protagonists would be Professor Solanka's notorious collection of outsize egghead dolls, all made by himself.

This was simply too much. What had been a tolerable eccentricity in a respected colleague became intolerable folly in a craven defector, and *The Adventures of Little Brain* was unanimously derided, before it was ever screened, by "intellos" both great and small. Then it aired, and within a season, to general astonishment and the knockers' chagrin, grew from a sophisticated coterie's secret pleasure into a cult classic with a satisfyingly youthful and rapidly expanding fan base, until at last it was handed the accolade of being moved into the coveted slot after the main evening news. Here it blossomed into a full-blooded prime-time hit.

It was well known at King's that in Amsterdam in his middle twenties Malik Solanka—in the city to speak on religion and politics at a left-leaning institute funded by Fabergé money—visited the Rijksmuseum and was entranced by that great treasure-trove's displays of meticulously period-furnished doll's houses, those unique descriptions of the interior life of Holland down the ages. They were open-fronted, as if bombs had knocked away their façades; or like little theatres, which he completed by being there. He was their fourth wall. He began to see everything in Amsterdam as if miniaturized: his own hotel on the Herengracht, the Anne Frank house, the impossibly good-looking Surinamese women. It was a trick of the mind to see human life made small, reduced to doll size. Young Solanka approved of the results. A little modesty about the scale of human endeavour was to be desired. Once you had thrown that switch in your head, the hard thing was to see in the old way. Small was beautiful, as Schumacher had just then begun to say.

Day after day, Malik visited the Rijksmuseum doll's houses. Never before in his life had he thought of making anything with his hands. Now his head was full of chisels and glue, rags and needles, scissors and paste. He envisioned wallpaper and soft furnishings, dreamed bedsheets, designed bathroom fixtures. After a few visits, however, he became clear that mere houses would not be enough for him. His imaginary environments must be peopled. Without people there was no point. The Dutch doll's houses, for all their intricacy and beauty, and in spite of their ability to furnish and decorate his imagination, finally made him think of the end of the world, some strange cataclysm in which property had remained undamaged while all breathing creatures had been destroyed. (This was some years before the invention of that ultimate revenge of the inanimate upon the living, the neutron bomb.) After he had this idea, the place began to revolt him. He started imagining back rooms in the museum filled with giant heaps of the miniature dead: birds, animals, children, servants, actors, ladies, lords. One day he walked out of the great museum and never went back to Amsterdam again.

On his return to Cambridge he immediately started to construct microcosms of his own. From the beginning his doll's houses were the products of an idiosyncratic personal vision. They were fanciful at first, even fabulist; science-fiction plunges into the mind of the future instead of the past, which had already and unimprovably been captured by the miniaturist masters of the Netherlands. This sci-fi phase didn't last long. Solanka soon learned the value of working, like the great matadors, closer to the bull; that is, using the material of his own life and immediate surroundings and, by the alchemy of art, making it strange. His insight, which Eleanor would have called a "lightbulb moment", eventually led to a series of "Great Minds" dolls, often arranged in little tableaux—Bertrand Russell being clubbed by policemen at a wartime pacifist rally, Kierkegaard going to the opera for the interval so that his friends didn't think he was working too hard, Machiavelli being subjected to the excruciating torture known as the *strappado,* Socrates drinking his inevitable hemlock, and Solanka's favourite, a two-faced, four-armed Galileo: one face muttered the truth under its breath, while one pair of arms, hidden in the folds of his garments, secreted a little model of the earth spinning around the sun; the other face, downcast and penitent under the stern gaze of the men in the red frocks, publicly recanted its knowledge, while a copy of the Bible was tightly, devoutly clutched by the second pair of arms. Years later, when Solanka quit the academy, these dolls would go to work for him. These, and the questing knowledge-seeker he created to be their television interrogator and the audience's surrogate, the female time-travelling doll Little Brain, who afterwards became a star and sold in large numbers around the world. Little Brain, his hip, fashion-conscious, but still idealistic Candide, his Valiant-for-Truth in urban-guerrilla threads, his spiky-haired girl-Basho journeying, mendicant bowl in hand, far into the Deep North of Japan.

Little Brain was smart, sassy, unafraid, genuinely interested in the deep information, in the getting of good-quality wisdom; not so much a disciple as an agent provocateur with a time machine, she goaded the great minds of the ages into surprising revelations. For example, the favourite fiction writer of the seventeenth-century heretic Baruch Spinoza turned out to be P. G. Wodehouse, an astonishing coincidence, because of course the favourite philosopher of the immortal shimmying butler Reginald Jeeves was Spinoza. (Spinoza who cut our strings, who allowed God to retire from the post of divine marionettist and believed that revelation was an event not above human history but inside it. Spinoza who never wore unsuitable shirts or ties.) The Great Minds in *The Adventures of Little Brain* could be time-hoppers, too. The Iberian Arab thinker Averroës, like his Jewish counterpart Maimonides, was a huge Yankees fan.

Little Brain went too far just once. In her interview with Galileo Galilei, she, in the beer-swilling, trash-talking fashion of the new ladettes, offered the great man her own nobody-fucks-with-me point of view on his troubles. "Man, I wouldn't have taken that stuff lying down," she leaned towards him and fervently said. "If some pope had tried to get me to lie, I'd have started a fucking revolution, me. I'd have set his house on fire. I'd have burned his fucking city down." Well, the bad language got toned down—to "freaking"—at an early stage of production, but that wasn't the problem. Arson at the Vatican was too much for the bosses of the airwaves to bear and Little Brain suffered, for the first time, the numbing indignities of censorship. And could do nothing about it except, perhaps, to mutter the truth along with Galileo: it does too move. I would too let it all go up in flames . . .

Rewind to Cambridge. Even "Solly" Solanka's first efforts—his space stations and podlike domestic structures for assembly on the moon—displayed qualities of originality and imagination which, in the loud dinner-table opinion of a French Lit specialist who was working on Voltaire, were "refreshingly absent" from his scholarly work. The quip raised a big laugh from everyone within earshot.

"Refreshingly absent." This is the Oxbridge way of speech, this easy, bantering offer of insults which are simultaneously not at all serious and in deadly earnest. Professor Solanka never grew accustomed to the barbs, often received terrible injuries from them, always pretended he saw the funny side, never once saw it. Oddly, this was something he had in common with his Voltairean assailant, the alarmingly named Krysztof Waterford-Wajda, known as Dubdub, with whom he had in fact forged the most unlikely of friendships. Waterford-Wajda, like Solanka, had gotten the hang of the expected conversational style under the pressure of their ferocious peer group, but he too remained uncomfortable with it. Solanka knew this, and so didn't hold "refreshingly absent" against him. The laughter of the listeners, however, he never forgot.

Dubdub was jovial, Old Etonian, loaded, half-Hurlingham Club deb's delight, half-Polish glowerer, the son of a self-made man, a stocky immigrant glazier who looked, talked and drank like a backstreet fighter, made his bundle in double glazing, and married amazingly well, to the horror of the country-house set ("Sophie Waterford's married a Pole!"). Dubdub had floppy-haired Rupert Brooke good looks marred by a lantern jaw, a wardrobe full of loud tweed jackets, a drum kit, a fast car, no girlfriend. At a freshers' ball in his first term, emancipated young sixties women refused his invitations to dance, prompting him to cry out, plaintively, "Why are all the girls in Cambridge so rude?" To which some heartless Andrée or Sharon replied, "Because most of the men are like you." In the dinner line, hooray-Henry playfully, he offered another young beauty his sausage. To which she, this deadpan Sabrina, this Nicki used to blowing off unwanted admirers, without turning a hair retorted sweetly, "Oh, but there are some animals I simply never eat."

It has to be admitted that Solanka himself had been guilty of needling Dubdub more than once. On their joint graduation day in the liberated summer of 1966, when gowned and elated and hemmed in by parents on the college front lawn they were allowing themselves to dream the future, innocent Dubdub astonishingly announced his intention of becoming a novelist. "Like Kafka perhaps," he mused, grinning that big upper-class grin, his mother's hockey-captain grin which no shadow of pain, poverty or doubt had ever darkened and which sat so incongruously below his paternal inheritance, the beetling, dark eyebrows reminiscent of untranslatable privations endured by his ancestors in the unglamorous town of Łodz. "*In the Rat Hole. Construction of a Machine Without a Purpose. Fury.* That sort of thing."

Solanka restrained his mirth, charitably telling himself that in the conflict between that smile and those eyebrows, between silver-spoon England and tin-cup Poland, between this glowing six-foot Cruella de Vil fashion plate of a mother and that squat, flat-faced tank of a father, there might indeed be room for a writer to germinate and flourish. Who could say? These might even be the right breeding conditions for that unlikely hybrid, an English Kafka.

"Or, alternatively," Dubdub pondered, "one could go in for the more commercial stuff. *Valley of the Dollybirds.* Or there's the happy medium, halfway between the highbrow and the dross. Most people are middlebrow, Solly, don't argue. They want a little stimulation but not too blasted much. Also, by the by, not too blasted long. None of your great doorstops, your Tolstoy, your Proust. Short books that don't give you a headache. The great classics retold—briefly—as pulp fiction. *Othello* updated as *The Moor Murders.* What do you say to that?"

That did it. Lubricated by the Waterford-Wajdas' vintage champagne—neither of his own parents had seen fit to travel from Bombay to attend his graduation, and Dubdub had generously insisted on pouring him a glass, and refilling it frequently—Solanka erupted into an impassioned protest against Krysztof's absurd proposals, pleading earnestly that the world be spared the literary outpourings of Waterford-Wajda, author. "Please, no obscurely menacing country-house sagas: *Brideshead* in the style of *The Castle. Metamorphosis at Blandings.* Oh, have mercy. Even more, regarding sex romps, restrain yourself. You're more Alex Portnoy than Jackie Susann, who said, remember, that she admired Mr Roth's talent but wouldn't want to shake his hand. Above all, from your blockbuster classics, desist. *The Cordelia Conundrum*? *The Elsinore Uncertainty*? Oh, oh, oh."

After several minutes of such friendly-unfriendly teasing, Dubdub good-naturedly relented: "Well, p'raps I'll be a film director instead. We're just off to the South of France. They probably need film directors down there."

Malik Solanka had always had a soft spot for goofy Dubdub, in part because of his ability to say things like this, but also because of the fundamentally good and open heart concealed beneath all the posh hee-haw. Also, he owed him. At the Market Hill hostel of King's College on a cold fall night in 1963, the eighteen-year-old Solanka had needed rescuing. He had spent his whole first day at college in a state of wild, overweening funk, unable to get out of bed, seeing demons. The future was like an open mouth waiting to devour him as Kronos had devoured his children, and the past—Solanka's links with his family were badly eroded—the past was a broken pot. Only this intolerable present remained, in which he found he couldn't function at all. Far easier to stay in bed and pull up the covers. In his characterless modern room of Norwegian wood and steel-frame windows he barricaded himself against whatever was next in store. There were voices at the door; he didn't answer. Footsteps came and went. At seven P.M., however, a voice unlike any other—louder, plummier, and utterly confident of a reply—shouted out, "Anyone in there mislaid a bloody great trunk with some funny wog name on it?" And Solanka, to his own surprise, spoke up. So the day of terror, of suspended animation, ended and his university years began. Dubdub's appalling voice, like a prince's kiss, had broken the evil spell.

Solanka's worldly goods had been delivered by mistake to the college's hostel on Peas Hill. Krys—he hadn't yet become Dubdub—found a cart, helped Solanka haul the trunk on to it and steer it to its proper home, then dragged the trunk's hapless owner off for a beer and dinner in the college hall. Later they sat side by side in that hall listening to the dazzlingly shiny Provost of King's tell them they were at Cambridge for "three things—intellect! Intellect! Intellect!" And that in the years ahead they would learn most, more than in any supervision or lecture hall, from the time they spent "in one another's rooms, fertilizing one another". Waterford-Wajda's unignorable bray—"HA, ha, ha, HA"—shattered the stunned silence that followed this remark. Solanka loved him for that irreverent guffaw.

Dubdub did not become a novelist or a film director. He did his research, got his doctorate, was eventually offered a fellowship, and snapped it up with the grateful look of a man who has just settled forever the whole question of the rest of his life. In that expression Solanka glimpsed the Dubdub behind the golden-boy mask, the young man desperate to escape from the privileged world into which he had been born. Solanka tried inventing for him, by way of explanation, a hollow socialite of a mother and a boorish brute of a father, but his imagination failed him; the parents he had actually met were perfectly pleasant and seemed to love their son a great deal. Yet Waterford-Wajda had certainly been desperate, and even spoke, when drunk, of the King's fellowship as a "blasted lifeline, the only thing I've got". This, when by anyone's ordinary standards he had so much. The fast car, the drum kit, the family spread in Roehampton, the trust fund, the *Tatler*ish connections. Solanka, in a failure of sympathy he later much regretted, told Dubdub not to roll about so much in the mud of self-pity. Dubdub stiffened, nodded, gave a hard laugh—"HA-ha-ha-HA"—and did not speak of personal matters again for many years.

The question of Dubdub's intellectual capacity remained, for many of his colleagues, unanswerable: the Dubdub Conundrum. He seemed so foolish so often—a nickname that never caught on, because it was too unkind even for Cambridge men, was Pooh, after the immortal Bear of Little Brain—yet his academic performance won him much preferment. The thesis on Voltaire that got him his doctorate and provided the launchpad for his later fame read like a defence of Pangloss—both of that imaginary worthy's initial Leibnizian over-optimism and of his later espousal of fenced-in quietism. This ran so profoundly counter to the dystopic, collectivist, politically engagé current of the times in which he wrote it as to be, for Solanka as for others, quite seriously shocking. Dubdub gave an annual series of lectures called "*Cultiver Son Jardin*". Few lectures at Cambridge—Pevsner's, Leavis's, no others—had attracted comparable crowds. The young (or, to be exact, the younger, because Dubdub for all his fogeyish attire had by no means done with his youth) came to heckle and boo but left more quietly and thoughtfully, seduced by his deep sweetness of nature, by that same blue-eyed innocence and concomitant certainty of being heard that had roused Malik Solanka from his first-day funk.

Times change. One morning in the mid-seventies, Solanka slipped in at the back of his friend's lecture hall. What impressed him now was the toughness of what Dubdub was saying and the way in which his strongly contrasting, almost Pythonesque twittishness defused it. If you looked at him you saw a tweedy fop, hopelessly out of touch with what was then still being called the zeitgeist. But if you listened, you heard something very different: an enveloping Beckettian bleakness. "Expect nothing, don't you know," Dubdub told them, leftist radicals and beaded hairies alike, waving a crumbling copy of *Candide*. "That's what the good book says. There will be no improvement in the way life is. Dreadful news, I know, but there you have it. This is as good as it gets. The perfectibility of man is just, as you might say, God's bad joke."

Ten years earlier, when various utopias, Marxist, hippyish, seemed just around the corner, when economic prosperity and full employment allowed the intelligent young to indulge their brilliant, idiotic fantasies of dropout or revolutionary Erewhons, he might have been lynched, or at least heckled into silence. But this was the England in the aftermath of the miners' strike and the three-day week, a cracked England in the image of Lucky's great soliloquy in *Godot*, in which man in brief was seen to shrink and dwindle, and that golden moment of optimism, when the best of all possible worlds seemed just around the bend, was fading fast. Dubdub's Stoical take on Pangloss—rejoice in the world, warts and all, because it's all you've got, and rejoicing and despair are therefore interchangeable terms—was rapidly coming into its own.

Solanka himself was affected by it. As he struggled to formulate his thoughts on the perennial problem of authority and the individual, he sometimes heard Dubdub's voice egging him on. These were statist times, and it was in part Waterford-Wajda who allowed him not to run with the crowd. The state couldn't make you happy, Dubdub whispered in his ear, it couldn't make you good or heal a broken heart. The state ran schools, but could it teach your children to love reading, or was that your job? There was a National Health Service, but what could it do about the high percentage of people who went to their doctors when they didn't need to? There was state housing, sure, but neighbourliness was not a government issue. Solanka's first book, a small volume called *What We Need*, an account of the shifting attitudes in European history toward the state-*vs.*-individual problem, was attacked from both ends of the political spectrum and later described as one of the "pre/texts" of what came to be called Thatcherism. Professor Solanka, who loathed Margaret Thatcher, guiltily conceded the partial truth of what felt like an accusation. Thatcherite Conservatism was the counterculture gone wrong: it shared his generation's mistrust of the institutions of power and used their language of opposition to destroy the old power-blocs—to give the power not to the people, whatever that meant, but to a web of fat-cat cronies. This was trickle-up economics, and it was the sixties' fault. Such reflections contributed greatly to Professor Solanka's decision to quit the world of thought.

By the late 1970s Krysztof Waterford-Wajda was a bit of a star. Academics had become charismatic. The victory of science, when physics would become the new metaphysics, and microbiology, not philosophy, would grapple with the great question of what it is to be human, was as yet a little way off; literary criticism was the glamour act, and its titans strode from continent to continent in seven-league boots to strut upon an ever larger international stage. Dubdub travelled the world with personal wind effects ruffling his tousled, prematurely silvery locks, even indoors, like Peter Sellers in *The Magic Christian.* Sometimes he was mistaken by eager delegates for the mighty Frenchman Jacques Derrida, but this honour he would wave away with an English self-deprecating smile, while his Polish eyebrows frowned at the insult.

This was the period in which the two great industries of the future were being born. The industry of culture would in the coming decades replace that of ideology, becoming "primary" in the way that economics used to be, and spawn a whole new *nomenklatura* of cultural commissars, a new breed of apparatchiks engaged in great ministries of definition, exclusion, revision and persecution, and a dialectic based on the new dualism of defence and offence. And if culture was the world's new secularism, then its new religion was fame, and the industry—or, better, the church—of celebrity would give meaningful work to a new *ecclesia*, a proselytizing mission designed to conquer this new frontier, building its glitzy celluloid vehicles and its cathode-ray rockets, developing new fuels out of gossip, flying the Chosen Ones to the stars. And to fulfil the darker requirements of the new faith, there were occasional human sacrifices, and steep, wing-burning falls.

Dubdub was an early Icarus-like flameout. Solanka saw little of him in his golden years. Life separates us with its apparently casual happenstance, and when one day we shake our heads as if waking from a reverie, our friends have become strangers and can't be retrieved: "Does nobody here know poor Rip van Winkle?" we ask plaintively, and nobody, any longer, does. So it was with the two old college pals. Dubdub was mostly in America now, some sort of a chair had been invented for him at Princeton, and there were phone calls back and forth at first, then Christmas and birthday cards, then silence. Until, one balmy Cambridge summer evening in 1984, when the old place was its most perfectly storybook self, an American woman knocked on the oak, the outer door of Professor Solanka's rooms—formerly occupied by E. M. Forster—on "A" staircase, above the students' bar. Her name was Perry Pincus; she was small-boned, dark, big-breasted, sexy, young, but fortunately not young enough to be a student. All these things quickly made a good impression on Solanka's melancholy consciousness. He was recovering from the end of a first, childless marriage, and Eleanor Masters was some way in the future. "Krysztof and I got to Cambridge yesterday," Perry Pincus said. "We're at the Garden House. Or, *I'm* at the Garden House. He's in Addenbrooke's. Last night he cut his wrists. He's been very depressed. He asked for you. Can I get a drink?"

She came in and took in her surroundings appreciatively. The houses, little and largeish, and the humanoid figures sitting everywhere, tiny figures in the houses, of course, but also others outside them, on Professor Solanka's furniture, in the corners of his rooms, soft and hard figures, male and female, also both largeish and small. Perry Pincus was carefully—if heavily—painted, her eyelids weighed down by heavy black eyelash extensions, and she wore full sex-kitten battle dress, a short tight outfit, stiletto heels. Not the customary attire of a woman whose lover has just attempted suicide, but she made no excuses for herself. Perry Pincus was a young Eng Lit person who liked to fuck the stars of her increasingly uncloistered world. As a devotee of the casual encounter, consequences (wives, suicides) were not her thing. Yet she was bright, lively, and like all of us believed herself to be an acceptable person, even, perhaps, a good one. After her first shot of vodka—Professor Solanka always kept a bottle in the freezer—she said, matter-of-factly, "It's clinical depression. I don't know what to do. He's sweet, but I'm no good at sticking by men in trouble. I'm not the nurse type. I like a take-charge guy." After two shots she said, "I think he was a virgin when he met me. Is that even possible? He didn't admit it, of course. Said back home he was quite a catch. That turns out to be true, financially speaking, but I'm not the money-grubbing type." After three shots she said, "All he ever wanted was to get a b.j. or, alternatively, fuck me in the ass. Which was okay, you know, whatever. I get a lot of that. It's one of my looks: boy-with-tits. It gets the sexually confused guys. Trust me on this. I know." After four shots, she said, "Talking of sexually confused, Professor, great *dolls*."

He decided he was hungry, but not this hungry, and gently coaxed her downstairs onto King's Parade and into a taxi. She stared at him through the window with smudged eyes and a puzzled expression, then leaned back, closed her eyes, faintly shrugged. *Whatever.* Afterwards he learned that in her own way Perry "Pinch-ass" was famous on the global literary circuit. You could be famous for anything nowadays, and she was.

The next morning he visited Dubdub, not in the main hospital, but in a good-looking old brick building standing in green, leafy grounds a little way down Trumpington Road: like a country house for the hopeless. Dubdub stood at a window smoking a cigarette, wearing crisp, wide-striped pyjamas under what looked like his old school dressing-gown, a worn, stained thing that was perhaps playing the part of a security blanket. His wrists were bandaged. He looked heavier, older, but that goddamn society smile was still there, still on parade. Professor Solanka thought that if his own genes had sentenced him to wear such a mask every day of his life, he'd have been in here with bandaged wrists long ago.

"Dutch elm disease," Dubdub said, pointing to the stumps of trees. "Frightful business. The elms of old England, lost and gone." *Lorst and gorn.* Professor Solanka said nothing. He hadn't come to talk about trees. Dubdub turned towards him, got the point. "Expect nothing and you won't be disappointed, eh," he murmured, looking boyishly shamefaced. "Should've listened to my own lectures." Still Solanka didn't answer. Then, for the first time in many years, Dubdub put aside the Old Etonian act. "It's to do with suffering," he said flatly. "Why do we all suffer so. Why is there so much of it. Why can't you ever stop it. You can build dikes, but it always comes oozing through, and then one day the dikes just give way. And it's not just me. I mean, it is me, but it's everyone. It's you, too. Why does it go on and on? It's killing us. I mean, me. It's killing me."

"This sounds a little abstract," Professor Solanka ventured, gently.

"Yes, well." That was definitely a snap. The deflector shields were back in place. "Sorry not to come up to scratch. Trouble with being a Bear of Little Brain."

"Please," Professor Solanka asked. "Just tell me."

"That's the worst part," Dubdub said. "There's nothing to tell. No direct or proximate cause. You just wake up one day and you aren't a part of your life. You know this. Your life doesn't belong to you. Your body is not, I don't know how to make you feel the force of this, *yours*. There's just life, living itself. You don't have it. You don't have anything to do with it. That's all. It doesn't sound like much, but believe me. It's like when you hypnotize someone and persuade them there's a big pile of mattresses outside their window. They no longer see a reason not to jump."

"I remember it, or a lesser version of it," Professor Solanka assented, thinking of that night in Market Hill long ago. "And you were the one who snapped me out of it. Now it's for me to do the same for you." The other shook his head. "This isn't something you just snap out of, I'm afraid." The attention he'd been getting, the celebrity status, had greatly aggravated Dubdub's existential crisis. The more he became a Personality, the less like a person he felt. Finally he had decided on a retreat back into the cloisters of traditional academe. No more of all that globe-trotting *Magic Christian* Derridada! No more *performance*. Energized by his new resolve, he had flown back to Cambridge with the literary groupie Perry Pincus, an unashamed sexual butterfly, actually believing he could set up house with her and build a stable life around the relationship. That's how far gone he was.

Krysztof Waterford-Wajda would survive three further suicide attempts. Then, just one month before Professor Solanka metaphorically took his own life, saying goodbye to everyone and everything he held dear and striking out for America with a spiky-haired doll in his arms—

a special, early-period limited edition of Little Brain in bad condition, the clothes ripped, the body damaged—Dubdub dropped dead. Three arteries had been badly clogged. A simple bypass operation could have saved him, but he refused it and, like an English elm, fell. Which perhaps, if one were searching for such explanations, helped trigger Professor Solanka's metamorphosis. Professor Solanka, remembering his dead friend in New York, realized that he had followed Dubdub in so many things: in some of his thinking, yes, but also into *le monde médiatique,* into America, into crisis.

Perry Pincus had been one of the first to intuit the link between them. She had returned to her native San Diego and now taught, in a local college, the work of some of the critics and writers whom she had carnally known. Pincus 101, she called it, brazen as ever, in one of the annual Happy Holidays messages she never failed to send Professor Solanka. "It's my personal greatest-hits collection, my Top Twenty," she wrote, adding, a little cuttingly, "You're not in it, Professor. I can't walk around in a man's work if I don't know which entrance he prefers." Her season's greetings were invariably accompanied, incomprehensibly, by the gift of a soft toy—a platypus, a walrus, a polar bear. Eleanor had always been much amused by the annual parcels from California. "Because you wouldn't fuck her," Professor Solanka was informed by his wife, "she can't think of you as a lover. So she's trying to become your mother instead. How does it feel to be Perry Pinch-ass's little boy?"

3

In his comfortable Upper West Side sublet, a handsome, high-ceilinged, first- and second-floor duplex boasting majestic oak panelling and a library that spoke highly of the owners, Professor Malik Solanka nursed a glass of red Geyserville zinfandel and mourned. The decision to leave had been wholly his; still, he grieved for his old life. Whatever Eleanor said on the phone, the break was almost certainly irreparable. Solanka had never thought of himself as a bolter or quitter, yet he had shed more skins than a snake. Country, family and not one wife but two had been left in his wake. Also, now, a child. Maybe the mistake was to see his latest exit as unusual. The harsh reality was perhaps that he was acting not against nature but according to its dictates. When he stood naked before the unvarnished mirror of truth, this was what he was really like.

Yet, like Perry Pincus, he believed himself to be a good person. Women believed it too. Sensing in him a ferocity of commitment that was rarely found in modern men, women had often allowed themselves to fall in love with him, surprising themselves—these wised-up, cautious women!—by the speed with which they charged outwards into the really deep emotional water. And he didn't let them down. He was kind, understanding, generous, clever, funny, grown-up, and the sex was good, it was always good. This is forever, they thought, because they could see him thinking it too; they felt loved, treasured, safe. He told them—each of his women in turn—that friendship was what he had instead of family ties, and, more than friendship, love. That sounded right. So they dropped their defences and relaxed into all the good stuff, and never saw the hidden twisting in him, the dreadful torque of his doubt, until the day he snapped and the alien burst out of his stomach, baring multiple rows of teeth. They never saw the end coming until it hit them. His first wife, Sara, the one with the graphic verbal gift, put it thus: "It felt like an axe-murder."

"Your trouble is," Sara incandescently said near the end of their last quarrel, "that you're really only in love with those fucking dolls. The world in inanimate miniature is just about all you can handle. The world you can make, unmake and manipulate, filled with women who don't answer back, women you don't have to fuck. Or are you making them with cunts now, wooden cunts, rubber cunts, fucking inflatable cunts that squeak like balloons as you slide in and out; do you have a life-size fuck-dolly harem hidden in a shed somewhere, is that what they'll find when one day you're arrested for raping and chopping up some golden-haired eight-year-old, some poor fucking living doll you played with and then threw away? They'll find her shoe in a hedge and there'll be descriptions of a minivan on TV and I'll be watching and you won't be home and I'll think, Jesus, I know that van, it's the one he carries his fucking toys around in when he goes to his perverts' I'll-show-you-my-dolly-if-you'll-show-me-yours reunions. I'll be the wife who never knew a thing. I'll be the fucking cow-faced wife on TV forced to defend you just to defend myself, my own unimaginable stupidity, because after all, I chose you."

Life is fury, he'd thought. Fury—sexual, Oedipal, political, magical, brutal—drives us to our finest heights and coarsest depths. Out of *furia* comes creation, inspiration, originality, passion, but also violence, pain, pure unafraid destruction, the giving and receiving of blows from which we never recover. The Furies pursue us; Shiva dances his furious dance to create and also to destroy. But never mind about gods! Sara ranting at him represented the human spirit in its purest, least socialized form. This is what we are, what we civilize ourselves to disguise—the terrifying human animal in us, the exalted, transcendent, self-destructive, untrammelled lord of creation. We raise each other to the heights of joy. We tear each other limb from fucking limb.

Her name was Lear, Sara Jane Lear, some sort of distant relative of the writer and watercolourist, but there wasn't a trace of antic Edward's immortal nonsense in her. *How pleasant to know Sara Lear, who remembers such volumes of stuff! Some folks think her awfully queer, but I find her pleasant enough.* The revised verse didn't raise the ghost of a smile. "Imagine how many times people have recited those exact words to me and you'll excuse me for not being impressed." She was a year or so his senior and was writing a thesis on Joyce and the French *nouveau roman.* In her second-floor flat on Chesterton Road, "love"—which in retrospect looked more like fear, a mutual clutching at the lifebelt of the other while drowning in twentysomething loneliness—made him plough his way twice through *Finnegans Wake.* Also the dour pages of Sarraute, Robbe-Grillet and Butor. When he looked up miserably from the great heaps of their slow, obscure sentences, he found her watching him from the other armchair, turning in his direction that angular devil-mask of a face, beautiful but sly. Sly-eyed lady of the Fenlands. He couldn't read her expression. It might have been contempt.

They married too quickly for thought and felt trapped by the mistake almost immediately. Yet they stayed together for several miserable years. Afterwards, when he told the story of his life to Eleanor Masters, Solanka cast his first wife as the one with the exit strategies, the player most likely to resign the game. "She gave up early on everything she desired most. Before she found out she wasn't up to it." Sara had been the outstanding university actress of her generation but had left it there, forever leaving behind the greasepaint and the crowd without a word of regret. Later she would also abandon her thesis and get a job in advertising, emerging from the chrysalis of her bluestocking wardrobe and spreading gorgeous butterfly wings.

This was soon after their marriage ended. When Solanka found out about it he was briefly furious. All that effortful reading for nothing! And not only reading. "Thanks to her," he raged at Eleanor, "I saw *L'Année dernière à Marienbad* three times in one day. We spent a whole weekend working out that damn matchstick game they play. 'You won't win, you know.'—'It's not a game if you can't lose.'—'Oh, I can lose, but I never do.' That game. Thanks to her it's still stuck in my head, but she's buggered off to the universe of if you've got it flaunt it. I'm stuck here in the blasted *couloirs* of French fiction and she's in a Jil Sander power suit in a forty-ninth-floor corner office on Sixth Avenue, pulling down, I have no doubt, some major bucks."

"Yes, but for the record, *you* dumped *her,*" Eleanor pointed out. "You found the next one and traded Sara in: left her cold and flat. You should never have married her, obviously, which is your only excuse. That's the great unanswerable question about love posed by your Queen Lear: what on earth were you thinking of? Also, you got yours when the next one, the Wagnerian Valkyrie with the Harley, threw you over for which composer was it?" She knew the answer perfectly well, but it was a story they both enjoyed. "Fucking Rummenigge." Solanka grinned, calming down. "She worked as an assistant on one of his three-orchestras-and-a-Sherman-tank efforts and afterwards he sent her a telegram. *Kindly refrain from all sexual intercourse until we can examine the deep bond that evidently lies between us.* And the next day a one-way ticket to Munich, and she disappeared into the Black Forest for years. She wasn't happy, though," he added. "Didn't know when she was well-off, you see." When Solanka left Eleanor, she added a bitter postscript to these reflections. "Actually, I'd like to hear their sides of these stories," she said during one difficult telephone call. "Maybe you were just a cold-hearted bastard from the start."

* * *

Malik Solanka, strolling alone towards a late-night Kieslowski double bill at the Lincoln Plaza, tried to imagine his own life as a *Dekalog* movie. A Short Film About Desertion. Which Commandments could his story be said to illustrate or, as the Kieslowski scholar who introduced last week's episodes preferred, interrogate? There were many Commandments against the sins of improper commission. Covetousness, adultery, lust, these things were anathematized. But where were the laws against sins of improper omission? Thou Shalt Not Be an Absentee Father. Cometh to Thinkst of It, Thou Shalt Not Walk Out of Thy Life Without a Fucking Good Reason, Buster, and What You've Put Up So Far Doesn't Even Come Close. What Dost Thou Think? Thou Canst Do Any Goddamn Thing Thou Wantest? Who the Fuck Dost Thou Imagine Thou Ist: Hugh Hefner? The Dalai Lama? Donald Trump? At What the Sam Hill Art Thou Playing? Huh, bub? *Huh???*

Sara Lear was probably right here in town, he suddenly thought. She would be in her late fifties now, a big shot with a booming portfolio, the secret booking numbers for Pastis and Nobu, and a weekend place south of the highway in, ah, Amagansett. Thank heavens there was no need to track her down, look her up, congratulate her on her life choices. How she would have crowed! For they had lived long enough to witness the absolute victory of advertising. Back in the seventies, when Sara gave up the serious life for the frivolous, working in ad-land had been slightly shameful. You confessed it to your friends with lowered voice and downcast eyes. Advertising was a confidence trick, a cheat, the notorious enemy of promise. It was—a horrible thought in that era—nakedly capitalist. Selling things was *low.* Now everyone—eminent writers, great painters, architects, politicians—wanted to be in on the act. Reformed alcoholics plugged booze. Everybody, as well as everything, was for sale. Advertisements had become colossi, clambering like Kong up the walls of buildings. What was more, they were loved. When he was watching TV, Solanka still turned the sound down at commercial breaks, but everyone else, he was sure, turned it up. The girls in the ads—Esther, Bridget, Elizabeth, Halle, Gisele, Tyra, Isis, Aphrodite, Kate—were more desirable than the actresses in the shows in between; hell, the *guys* in the ads—Mark Vanderloo, Marcus Schenkenberg, Marcus Aurelius, Marc Antony, Marky Mark—were more desirable than the actresses in the shows. And as well as presenting the dream of an ideally beautiful America in which all women were babes and all men were Marks, after doing the basic work of selling pizza and SUVs and I Can't Believe It's Not Butter, beyond money management and the new ditditdit of the dotcoms, the commercials soothed America's pain, its head pain, its gas pain, its heartache, its loneliness, the pain of babyhood and old age, of being a parent and of being a child, the pain of manhood and women's pain, the pain of success and that of failure, the good pain of the athlete and the bad pain of the guilty, the anguish of loneliness and of ignorance, the needle-sharp torment of the cities and the dull, mad ache of the empty plains, the pain of wanting without knowing what was wanted, the agony of the howling void within each watching, semi-conscious self. No wonder advertising was popular. It made things better. It showed you the road. It wasn't a part of the problem. It solved things.

As a matter of fact, there was a copywriter living in Professor Solanka's building. He wore red suspenders and Hathaway shirts and even smoked a pipe. He had introduced himself that very afternoon by the mailboxes in the vestibule, holding a set of rolled-up layouts. (What was it about Solanka's solitude, the professor silently asked himself, that apparently obliged his neighbours to disturb it?) "Mark Skywalker, from the planet Tatooine."

Whatever, as Perry Pincus would have said. Solanka was uninterested in this bow-tied, bespectacled, markedly un-Jedi-knight-like young man, and as a former science-fiction buff despised the lowbrow space opera of the *Star Wars* cycle. But he had already learned not to argue with self-invention in New York. He had learned, also, when giving his own name to omit the "Professor". Learning annoyed people, and formality was a form of pulling rank. This was the country of the diminutive. Even the stores and eating places got friendly fast. Right around the corner he could find Andy's, Bennie's, Josie's, Gabriela's, Vinnie's, Freddie & Pepper's. The country of reserve, of the understatement and the unsaid, he had left behind, and a good thing too, on the whole. At Hana's (medical supplies) you could walk right in and buy a MASTECTOMY BRA. The unsayable was right there in the window in red letters a foot high. So, anyway, "Solly Solanka," he replied, neutrally, surprising himself by using the disliked nickname; whereupon Skywalker frowned. "Are you a landsman?" Solanka was unfamiliar with the term, and said as much, apologetically. "Oh, then you're not." Skywalker nodded. "I thought, because of Solly, maybe. Also, excuse me, something about the nose." The meaning of the unknown word quickly became clear from context and raised an interesting question, which Solanka refrained from asking: so, they had Jews on Tatooine?

"You're British, right," Skywalker went on. (Solanka didn't get into the postcolonial, migrational niceties.) "Mila told me. Do me a favour. Take a look at these." Mila was presumably the young empress of the street. Solanka noted without pleasure the euphony of their naming: Mila, Malik. When the young woman discovered this, she would no doubt be unable to resist mentioning it to him. He would be forced to point out the obvious, namely that sounds were not meanings, and this was a mere interlingual echo from which nothing, certainly not a human connection, need follow. The young adman had unrolled the layouts and spread them on the hall table. "I want to get your honest opinion," Skywalker explained. "It's a corporate-image campaign." The layouts showed double-page-spread images of famous city skylines at sunset. Solanka gestured vaguely, not knowing how to respond. "The copy line," Skywalker prompted. "Is it okay?" All the pictures bore the same heading. THE SUN NEVER SETS ON AMERICAN EXPRESS INTERNATIONAL BANKING CORPORATION. "Good. It's good," Solanka said, not knowing if it was in fact good, average or terrible. Presumably there was always an American Express office open somewhere in the world, so the statement was probably true, though why would it be useful to an individual in, say, London to know that the banks were still open in Los Angeles? All this he kept to himself, and looked, he hoped, judicious and approving. But Skywalker evidently wanted more. "As a Britisher," he probed, "you're saying the British won't be insulted?"

This was a genuine puzzlement. "Because of the British empire, I mean. On which the sun never sets. There's no offence intended. That's what I want to be sure of. That the line doesn't come across as an insult to your country's glorious past." Professor Solanka felt huge irritation rise up in his breast. He experienced a strong desire to screech at this fellow with the damnfool alias, to call him names and perhaps actually smack him across the face with an open hand. It took an effort to restrain himself, and in a level voice to reassure earnest young Mark in his David Ogilvy-clone outfit that even the most red-faced colonels in England were unlikely to be upset by his banal formulation. Then he hurried into his apartment, shut the door with his heart pounding, leaned against the wall, closed his eyes, gasped and shook. Yes, this was the other side of the coin of his new hi-how-you-doin', up-front, in-your-face, MASTECTOMY BRA environment: this new cultural hypersensitivity, this almost pathological fear of giving offence. Okay, he knew that, everybody knew it, that wasn't the point. The point was, where was all this anger coming from? Why was he being caught off guard, time and again, by surges of rage that almost overwhelmed his will?

He took a cold shower. Then for two hours he lay in his darkened bedroom with both air conditioner and ceiling fan working flat-out to battle the heat and humidity. Controlling his breathing helped, and he also used visualization techniques to relax. He imagined the anger as a physical object, a soft dark throbbing lump, and mentally drew a red triangle around it. Then he slowly made the triangle smaller until the lump disappeared. This worked. His heartbeat returned to normal. He switched on the bedroom television, a whirring and clanking old monster of a set dating from an earlier generation of technology, and watched El Duque on the mound, his amazing, hyperbolic action. The pitcher coiled himself up until his knee almost touched his nose, then unwound like a whip. Even in this erratic, almost panicky season in the Bronx, Hernández inspired calm.

Professor Solanka made the mistake of flipping briefly to CNN, where it was all Elián, all the time. Professor Solanka was nauseated by people's eternal need for totems. A little boy had been rescued from a rubber ring in the sea, his mother drowned, and at once the religious hysteria had begun. The dead mother became almost a Marian figure and there were posters reading ELIÁN, SAVE US. The cult, born of Miami's necessary demonology—according to which Castro the devil, Hannibal-the-Cannibal Castro, would eat the boy alive, would tear out his immortal soul and munch it down with a few fava beans and a glass of red wine—instantly developed a priesthood as well. The dreadful media-fixated uncle was anointed pope of Eliánismo, and his daughter, poor Marisleysis, with her "nervous exhaustion", was exactly the type who would, any day now, start witnessing the seven-year-old's first miracles. There was even a fisherman involved. And of course apostles, spreading the word: the photographer living in Elián's bedroom, the TV-movie people waving contracts, publishing houses doing likewise, CNN itself and all the other news crews with their uplink dishes and fuzzy mikes. Meanwhile in Cuba, the little boy was being transformed into quite another totem. A dying revolution, a revolution of the old and straggle-bearded, held the child up as proof of its renewed youth. In this version, Elián rising from the waters became an image of the revolution's immortality: a lie. Fidel, that ancient infidel, made interminable speeches wearing an Elián mask.

And for a long time the father, Juan Miguel González, stayed in his home town of Cárdenas and said little. He said he wanted his son back, which was perhaps dignified, and perhaps enough. Pondering what he himself might do if his uncles and cousins were to come between him and Asmaan, Professor Solanka snapped a pencil in half. Then he switched channels back to the ball game, but it was too late. El Duque, himself a Cuban refugee, would not be of Solanka's mind in this. That mind, in which Asmaan Solanka and Elián González blurred and joined, was overheating again, pointing out that in his own case no relatives had needed to get between Solanka and his child. He had achieved the rupture without outside assistance. As the helpless rage mounted in him he used, again, his well-practised techniques of sublimation, and directed the anger outwards, at the ideologically deranged Miami mob, transformed by experience into what they hated most. Their flight from bigotry had turned them into bigots. They screamed at journalists, abused politicians who disagreed with them, shook their fists at passing cars. They spoke of the evils of brainwashing, but their own brains were self-evidently unclean. "Not washing but staining," Solanka found himself actually yelling aloud at the Cuban pitcher on TV. "You people have been brainstained by your lives. And that little boy on a swing with a hundred camera snouts nosing at his confusion: what are you telling him about his dad?"

He had to go through it all over again: the shaking, the pounding, the gasping for air, the shower, the darkness, the breathing, the visualization. No drugs; he had put them off-limits, and he was also avoiding head doctors. The gangster Tony Soprano might be going to a shrink, but fuck him, he was fictional. Professor Solanka had resolved to face his demon by himself. Psychoanalysis and chemistry felt like cheating. If the duel were to be truly won, if the demon that possessed him was to be wrestled to the mat and consigned to hell, it had to be just the two of them going at it, ass naked, without restraint, in a bare-knuckle fight to the death.

It was dark when Malik Solanka deemed himself fit to leave the apartment. Shaken, but putting on a show of jauntiness, he set out for the Kieslowski double bill. If he had been a Vietnam vet or even a reporter who'd seen too much, his behaviour would have been more readily comprehensible. Jack Rhinehart, an American poet and war correspondent he had known for twenty years, if woken by a ringing telephone would, to this day, usually smash the instrument to bits. He couldn't stop himself doing it, and was only half awake when it happened. Jack got through a lot of phones, but he accepted his fate. He was damaged, and thought himself lucky it wasn't worse. But the only war Professor Solanka had been in was life itself, and life had been kind to him. He had money and what most people thought of as an ideal family. Both his wife and child were exceptional. Yet he had sat in his kitchen in the middle of the night with murder on the brain; actual murder, not the metaphorical kind. He'd even brought a carving knife upstairs and stood for a terrible, dumb minute over the body of his sleeping wife. Then he turned away, slept in the spare bedroom, and in the morning packed his bags and caught the first plane to New York without giving a reason. What had happened was beyond reason. He needed to put an ocean, at least an ocean, between himself and what he had almost done. So Ms Mila, the empress of West Seventieth Street, had been closer to the truth than she knew. Than she must ever know.

He was waiting in line at the cinema, lost inside himself. Then a young man's voice started up behind his right ear, disgracefully loud, not caring who listened, telling its story to a companion but also to the whole line, to the city; as if the city cared. To live in Metropolis was to know that the exceptional was as commonplace as diet soda, that abnormality was the popcorn norm: "So finally I called her, and I'm like, hi, Mom, wassup, and she goes, You wanna know who's sitting down to dinner here in Nowheresville, who's right here eating your mother's meatloaf, we've got Santa Claus, that's all. Santa Claus sitting right there at the head of the table where your snake skunk weasel father used to set his motherfuckin' dumb-fuck ass. I swear to God. I mean it's three P.M. and she's already losing it. That's what she said, word for fuckin' word. Santa Claus. And I go, Sure, Mom, and where's Jesus at. And she comes back with, That's *Mister* Jesus Christ to you, young man, and I'll have you know that Mister Jesus *H.* Christ is takin' care of the fish course. So, that was all I could handle, so I'm like, So long, Mom, give the gentlemen my best, have a happy." And alongside the male voice there was a woman's hard, horrified laughter. HA-ha-ha-HA.

At this point in a Woody Allen movie (a part of *Husbands and Wives* had actually been filmed in Solanka's rented apartment) the cinema-goers would have joined in the conversation, taking sides, offering personal anecdotes to rival or surpass the one they had just heard, and finding precedents for the monologue of the angry, crazy mother in late Bergman, in Ozu, in Sirk. In a Woody Allen movie Noam Chomsky or Marshall McLuhan, or maybe nowadays it would be Gurumayi or Deepak Chopra, would have stepped out from behind a potted palm and offered a few words of unctuous, polished commentary. The mother's plight would briefly be the subject of an agonized Woody meditation—was she delusional all day or only at mealtimes? What medication was she on and were its side effects properly labelled on the bottle? What did it mean that she was possibly planning to fool around with not one but two major icons? What would Freud say about this unusual sex triangle? What did this woman's equal need for gift-wrapped possessions and the salvation of her immortal soul tell us about her? What did it tell us about America?

Also, if those were real men in the room with her, who were they? Maybe killers on the run, holing up in this poor bourbon-soaked lady's kitchen? Was she actually in danger? Alternatively, as open-minded thinkers, should we not allow the possibility, at least theoretically, of a genuine double miracle having occurred? In which case, what kind of Christmas present would Jesus ask Santa for? And, okay, so the Son of God was in charge of the tuna, but would there be enough meatloaf to go round?

To all of this Mariel Hemingway would pay careful but vapid attention; then, equally swiftly, it would be forgotten forever. In a Woody Allen movie the scene would have been shot in black and white, that most unreal of processes, which had come to stand for realism, integrity and art. But the world is in colour and is less well scripted than the movies. Malik Solanka turned around sharply, opened his mouth to remonstrate, and found himself looking at Mila and her quarterback centurion of a boyfriend. By thinking of her he had conjured them up.

And behind them stood—leaned, hunched, squatted, posed—the rest of the indolent stoop troop.

They looked gorgeous, Solanka conceded; their daytime Hilfiger uniform had been sloughed off to reveal a very different, preppier style based on Calvin's classic white-and-tan summerwear, and they all wore shades in spite of the hour. There was a commercial playing in the multiplexes in which a group of fashionable vampires—thanks to Buffy on TV, vampires were hot—sat on a dune in their Ray-Bans and waited for the dawn. The one who had forgotten his shades was fried when the sun's rays hit him and his comrades laughed as he exploded, baring their fangs. HA-ha-ha-HA. Perhaps, thought Professor Solanka, Mila & Co. were vampires and he was the fool without the protection. Except, of course, that that would mean he was a vampire too, a refugee from death, able to defy the laws of time. . . . Mila removed her sunglasses and looked him provocatively in the eye, and at once he remembered who it was that she resembled.

"What do you know, it's Mr Garbo, who vants to be alone," the peroxide centurion was saying, nastily, indicating that he was ready for all the trouble creaky old Professor Solanka cared to put his way. But Malik was trapped by Mila's gaze. "Oh, my," he said. "Oh, my, excuse me, it's Little Brain. Excuse me, but it's my doll." The giant centurion found this to be an opaque, and therefore objectionable utterance, and indeed, in Solanka's manner there was something more than surprise; something bilious, almost hostile, something that might have been disgust. "Take it easy, Greta," the big young man said, putting the palm of an enormous hand against Solanka's chest and applying an impressive amount of pressure; Solanka staggered backwards and hit a wall.

But the young woman called off her attack dog. "It's okay, Ed. Eddie, really, it's fine." Just then, mercifully, the line began to move rapidly. Malik Solanka rushed forward into the auditorium and sat down at some distance from the vampire group. As the lights went down he saw those piercing green eyes looking intently at him across the art-house crowd.

4

He stayed out all night, but there was no peace to be found, even when walking through the dead of night, much less in the already bustling hour after the dawn. There was no dead of night. He could not remember his exact route, had the impression of having gone across town and back on or around Broadway, but he could remember the sheer volume of the white and coloured noise. He could remember the noise dancing in abstract shapes before his red-rimmed eyes. The coat of his linen suit weighed heavily, damply, on his shoulders, yet in the name of rectitude, of how things should be done, he kept it on; also his straw Panama hat. The noise of the city increased almost daily, or perhaps it was his sensitivity to that noise which was being turned up to the screaming point. Garbage trucks like giant cockroaches moved through the city, roaring. He was never out of earshot of a siren, an alarm, a large vehicle's reverse-gear bleeps, the beat of some unbearable music.

The hours went by. Kieslowski's characters stayed with him. What were the roots of our actions? Two brothers, estranged from each other and from their dead father, were almost deranged by the power of his priceless stamp collection. A man was told he was impotent and found he could not bear the idea of his loving wife having a sexual future without him. Mysteries drive us all. We only glimpse their veiled faces, but their power pushes us onward, towards darkness. Or into the light.

As he turned into his street, even the buildings began to speak to him in the sonorous manner of the supremely confident, of the rulers of the world. The School of the Blessed Sacrament did its proselytizing in Latin carved in stone. PARENTES CATHOLICOS HORTAMUR UT DILECTAE PROLI SUAE EDUCATIONEM CHRISTIANAM ET CATHOLICAM PROCURANT. The sentiment struck no responsive chord in Solanka. Next door, a more fortune-cookie-ish sentiment inscribed in gilded letters rang out from a mighty DeMille-Assyrian entrance. IF FRATERNAL LOVE HELD ALL MEN BOUND HOW BEAUTIFUL THE WORLD WOULD BE. Three-quarters of a century ago this edifice, garishly handsome in the city's brashest manner, had been dedicated, on the cornerstone, "to Pythianism", without any embarrassment at the clash of Greek and Mesopotamian metaphors. Such plundering and jumbling of the storehouse of yesterday's empires, this melting pot or *métissage* of past power, was the true indicator of present might.

Pytho was the ancient name of Delphi, home of the Python, who wrestled Apollo; and, more famously, of the Delphic Oracle, the Pythia being the prophesying priestess there, a creature of frenzies and ecstasies. Solanka could not imagine that this was the meaning of "Pythian" the builders intended: dedicated to convulsions and epilepsies. Nor could so epic a house be intended for the humble—the grandly, mightily humble—practice of poetry. (Pythian verse is poetry written in the dactylic hexameter.) Some general Apollonian reference was probably intended, Apollo in both his musical and athletic incarnations. From the sixth century Before the Common Era, the Pythian games, one of the great quartet of Panhellenic festivals, had been held in the third year of the Olympic cycle. There were musical contests as well as sporting ones, and the great battle of the god and the snake was also re-created. Maybe some scrap of this would have been known to those who had built this shrine to half-knowledge, this temple dedicated to the belief that ignorance, if backed up by sufficient dollars, became wisdom. The temple of Boobus Apollo.

To the devil with this classical mishmash, Professor Solanka silently exclaimed. For a greater deity was all around him: America, in the highest hour of its hybrid, omnivorous power. America, to which he had come to erase himself. To be free of attachment and so also of anger, fear and pain. Eat me, Professor Solanka silently prayed. Eat me, America, and give me peace.

Across the street from Pythia's phoney Assyrian palace, the city's best simulacrum of a Viennese *Kaffeehaus* was just opening its doors. Here the *Times* and *Herald Tribune* could be found inserted into wooden rails. Solanka went inside, drank strong coffee, and allowed himself to join in this most transient of cities' eternal imitation game. In his now dishevelled linen suit and straw Panama, he could pass for one of the more down-and-out habitués of the Café Hawelka on Dorotheergasse. In New York nobody looked too carefully, and few people's eyes were trained to the old European subtleties. The unstarched collar of the sweat-stained white shirt from Banana Republic, the dusty brown sandals, the straggly badgerish beard (neither carefully clipped nor delicately pomaded) struck no false notes here. Even his name, had he ever been obliged to give it, sounded vaguely *Mitteleuropäische.* What a place, he thought. A city of half-truths and echoes that somehow dominates the earth. And its eyes, emerald green, staring into your heart.

Approaching the counter with its refrigerated display of the great cakes of Austria, he passed over the excellent-looking Sacher *gâteau* and asked, instead, for a piece of Linzertorte, receiving in response a look of perfect Hispanic incomprehension, which obliged him exasperatedly to point. Then finally he was able to sip and read.

The morning papers were full of the publication of the report on the human genome. They were calling it the best version yet of the "bright book of life", a phrase variously used to describe the Bible and the Novel; even though this new brightness was not a book at all but an electronic message posted on the Internet, a code written in four amino acids, and Professor Solanka wasn't good with codes, had never even managed to learn elementary pig Latin, let alone semaphore or the now defunct Morse, apart from what everybody knew. Dit dit dit dah dah dah dit dit dit. *Help.* Or, in Iglatinpay, elp-hay. Everyone was speculating about the miracles that would follow the genome triumph, for example the extra limbs we could decide to grow for ourselves to solve the problem of how at a buffet dinner to hold a plate and a wine-glass and eat at the same time; but to Malik the only two certainties were, first, that whatever discoveries were made would come too late to be of any use to him and, second, that this book—which changed everything, which transformed the philosophical nature of our being, which contained a quantitative change in our self-knowledge so immense as to be a qualititative change as well—was one he would never be able to read.

While human beings had been excluded from this degree of understanding, they could console themselves that they were all in the same bog of ignorance together. Now that Solanka knew that someone somewhere knew what he would never know, and was additionally quite aware that what was known was vitally important to know, he felt the dull irritation, the slow anger, of the fool. He felt like a drone, or a worker ant. He felt like one of the shuffling thousands in the old movies of Chaplin and Fritz Lang, the faceless ones doomed to break their bodies on society's wheel while knowledge exercised power over them from on high. The new age had new emperors and he would be their slave.

"Sir. *Sir.*" A young woman was standing over him, uncomfortably close, wearing a pencil-thin knee-length navy blue skirt and a smart white blouse. Her fair hair was pulled back severely. "I'm going to ask you to leave, sir." The Hispanic counter staff were tensed, ready to intervene. Professor Solanka was truly perplexed: "What appears to be the trouble, Miss?"

"What is the trouble, sir, not what 'appears', is that you have been using bad language, obscene terms, and so loudly. Speaking the unspeakable, I should say. You have been shouting it out. And now amazingly you ask what is the trouble. Sir, you are the trouble. You will go now, please." At last, he thought even as he was receiving this verbal bum's rush, a moment of genuineness. One Austrian is here, at least. He rose, pulled his lumpy coat around him, and left, tipping his hat, though not her. There was no explanation for the woman's extraordinary speech. When he was still sleeping with Eleanor, she would accuse him of snoring. He would be halfway between wakefulness and sleep and she would push at him and say, Turn on your side. But he was conscious, he wanted to say, he could hear her speak, and therefore, had he been making any sort of noise himself, he would have heard that, too. After a while she gave up persecuting him and he slept soundly. Until the time when once again he didn't. No, not that again, not right now. Right now when, once again, he was conscious, and all manner of noise was in his ears.

As he approached his apartment he saw a workman hanging in a cradle outside his window, doing repairs to the exterior of the building and, in loud, rolling Punjabi, shouting instructions and dirty jokes to his partner smoking a beedi on the sidewalk below. Malik Solanka at once telephoned his landlords the Jays, wealthy organic farmers who spent summers upstate with their fruits and vegetables, and made emphatic complaints. This brutish din was intolerable. The lease stated clearly that the work would be not only external but quiet. Furthermore, the toilet didn't work properly; small pieces of fecal matter bobbed back up after he flushed. In the mood he was in, this caused him a degree of distress disproportionate to the problem, and he spoke vehemently of his feelings to Mr Simon Jay, the gentle, bemused owner of the apartment, who had lived there happily for thirty years with his wife, Ada, had raised his children in these rooms, toilet-trained them on these very water closets, and had found every day of his occupancy a simple and unqualified delight. Solanka wasn't interested. A second flushing invariably dealt with the trouble, he conceded, but that was not acceptable. A plumber must come, and soon.

But the plumber, like the Punjabi construction workers, was a talker, an octogenarian named Joseph Schlink. Erect, wiry, with Albert Einstein white hair and Bugs Bunny front teeth, Joseph came through the door impelled by a form of defensive pridefulness to get his retaliation in first. "Don't tell me, eh?, I'm too old you're maybe thinking, or maybe not, mind reading I make no claim on, but a better plumber in the tri-state area you von't find, also fit like a fiddle or I'm no Schlink." The thick, unimproved accent of the transplanted German Jew. "My name amuses you? So laugh. The chentleman, Mr Simon, calls me Kitchen Schlink, to his Mrs Ada I'm also Bathroom Schlink, let zem call me Schlink the Bismarck, it von't bother me, it's a free country, but in my business I haff no use for humour. In Latin, *humor* is a dampness from the eye. This is to quote Heinrich Böll, Nobel Prize nineteen hundred seventy-two. In his line of vork he alleges it's helpful, but in my job it leads to mistakes. No damp eyes on me, eh?, and no chokes in my tool bag. Chust I like to do the vork prompt, receive payment also prompt, you follow me here. Like the *shvartzer* says in the movie, show me the money. After a war spent plugging leaks on a Nazi U-boat, you think I can't fix up your little doofus here?"

An educated plumber with a tale to tell, Solanka realized with a sinking feeling. (He refused the tempting "Schlinking".) This when he was almost too tired to remain upright. The city was teaching him a lesson. There was to be no escape from intrusion, from noise. He had crossed the ocean to separate his life from life. He had come in search of silence and found a loudness greater than the one he left behind. The noise was inside him now. He was afraid to go into the room where the dolls were. Maybe they would begin to speak to him, too. Maybe they would come to life and chatter and gossip and twitter until he had to shut them up once and for all, until he was obliged by the everywhereness of life, by its bloody-minded refusal to back off, by the sheer goddamn unbearable head-bursting volume of the third millennium, to rip off their fucking heads.

Breathe. He did a slow circular breathing exercise. Very well. He would accept the plumber's garrulity as a penance. Dealing with it would be an exercise in humility and self-control. This was a Jewish plumber who had escaped the death camps by going underwater. His skills as a plumber meant the crew had protected him, they hung on to him until the day of their surrender, when he walked free and came to America, leaving behind, or, to put it another way, bringing along his ghosts.

Schlink had told the story a thousand times before, a thousand thousand. Out it came in its set phrases and cadences. "You can chust imagine it. A plumber in a submarine is already a little comic, but on top of that you haff the irony, the *psychologische* complexity. I don't haff to spell it out. But I stand before you. I haff liffed my life. I haff kept, eh?, my appointment."

A novelistic life, Solanka was forced to concede. Filmic, too. A life that could be a successful mid-budget feature film. Dustin Hoffman maybe as the plumber, and as the U-boat captain, who? Klaus Maria Brandauer, Rutger Hauer. But probably both parts would go to younger actors whose names Malik didn't know. Even this was fading with the years, the movie knowledge in which he had always taken such pride. "You should write this down and register it," he told Schlink, speaking too loudly. "It's as they say high-concept. *U-571* meets *Schindler's List.* Maybe a double-edged comedy like Benigni's. No, tougher than Benigni's. Call it *Jewboat.*" Schlink stiffened; and, before giving his full, injured attention to the toilet, turned on Solanka his mournful, disgusted gaze. "No *humour,*" he said. "As I haff already told you. I am sorry to say that you are a disrespectful man."

And in the kitchen downstairs, the Polish cleaner Wisława had arrived. She came with the sublet, refused to do the ironing, left cobwebs untouched in corners, and after she left you could make a line in the dust on the mantelpiece. On the plus side she had a pleasant temperament and a big, gummy smile. However, if you gave her half a chance, or even if you didn't, she too would plunge into narrative. The dangerous, unsuppressable power of the tale. Wisława, a devout Catholic, had had her faith profoundly shaken by an ostensibly true story told by her husband who got it from his uncle who got it from a trusted friend who knew the person concerned, a certain Ryszard, who was for many years the personal driver of the Pope, this of course before he was elected to the Holy See. When it was time for that election, Ryszard the chauffeur drove the future pope all the way across Europe, a Europe standing on the very hinge of history, on the cusp of great changes. Ah, the comradeship of the two men, the simple human pleasures and annoyances of such a long journey! And then they arrived in the Holy City, the man of the cloth was walled up with his peers and the driver waited. At last the white smoke was seen, the cry of *habemus papam* was raised, and then there was a cardinal all in red, descending an enormous, wide flight of yellow stone steps slowly, and crabwise, like a character in a Fellini movie, and right at the bottom of the steps waited the smoky little car and its excited driver. The cardinal came mopping his brow and puffing up to the driver's window, which Ryszard had wound down in anticipation of the news. And so the cardinal was able to deliver the personal message of the new, the Polish pope:

"You're fired."

Solanka, not a Catholic, not a believer, not much interested in the story even if true, not remotely convinced that it was true, not anxious to referee the cleaner's wrestling match with the imp of doubt who presently had her immortal soul in a stranglehold, would have preferred not to speak to Wisława at all, would have wished her to glide around the apartment rendering it spotless and habitable, leaving the laundry done, pressed and folded. But in spite of the expenditure of over eight thousand dollars a month on the sublet, cleaner included, fate had dealt him a pretty much unplayable hand. On the topic of Wisława's imperiled reservation in heaven, he most earnestly did not wish to comment; yet she returned to the theme constantly. "How to kiss the ring of a

Holy Father like that one, he is of my own people, but O God, to send a cardinal, and just like that, so lightly, to give the sack. And if not the Holy Father, then how his priests, and if not the priests, then how confession and absolution, and here are opening below my feets the iron gates of Hell."

Professor Solanka, his fuse shortening, grew daily more tempted to say something unkind. Paradise, he considered telling Wisława, was a place to which only the coolest and highest in New York possessed the secret number. As a gesture to the democratic spirit a few ordinary mortals were allowed in, too; they would arrive wearing properly reverential expressions, the expressions of those who know that they have truly, just this once, lucked out. The wide-eyed thrilledness of this bridge-and-tunnel mob would add to the jaded satisfaction of the in-crowd, and of course of the Proprietor himself. It was extremely improbable, however, the laws of supply and demand being what they were, that Wisława would turn out to be one of the fortunate few in the public seats, the sun-kissed bleachers of eternity.

This and much else Solanka restrained himself from saying. Instead he pointed out cobwebs and dust, to be answered only by that gummy smile and a gesture of Krakóvian incomprehension. "I work for Mrs Jay long time." This answer dealt, in Wisława's view, with all complaints. After the second week Solanka gave up asking, wiped down the mantels himself, got rid of the cobwebs, and took his shirts to the good Chinese laundry just around the corner on Columbus. But her soul, her non-existent soul, continued intermittently to insist on his pastoral, his uncaring care.

Solanka's head began to spin lightly. Sleep-deprived, wild of thought, he headed for his bedroom. Behind him through the thick, humid air he could hear his dolls, alive now and jabbering behind their closed door, each loudly telling the other his or her "back-story", the tale of how she or he came to be. The imaginary tale, which he, Solanka, had made up for each of them. If a doll had no back-story, its market value was low. And as with dolls so with human beings. This was what we brought with us on our journey across oceans, beyond frontiers, through life: our little storehouse of anecdote and what-happened-next, our private once-upon-a-time. We were our stories, and when we died, if we were very lucky, our immortality would be in another such tale.

This was the great truth against which Malik Solanka had set his face. It was precisely his back-story that he wanted to destroy. Never mind where he came from or who, when little Malik could barely walk, had deserted his mother and so given him permission, years later, to do the same. To the devil with stepfathers and pushes on the top of a young boy's head and dressing up and weak mothers and guilty Desdemonas and the whole useless baggage of blood and tribe. He had come to America as so many before him to receive the benison of being Ellis Islanded, of starting over. Give me a name, America, make of me a Buzz or Chip or Spike. Bathe me in amnesia and clothe me in your powerful unknowing. Enlist me in your J. Crew and hand me my mouse-ears! No longer a historian but a man without histories let me be. I'll rip my lying mother tongue out of my throat and speak your broken English instead. Scan me, digitize me, beam me up. If the past is the sick old Earth, then, America, be my flying saucer. Fly me to the rim of space. The moon's not far enough.

But still through the ill-fitting bedroom window the stories came pouring in. What would Saul and Gayfryd—"she became the Stanley Cup of trophy wives when trophy wives were as common as Porsches"—do now that they were down to their last $40 or $50 million? . . . And hurray, Muffie Potter Ashton's pregnant! . . . And wasn't that Paloma Huffington de Woody getting friendly with S. J. "Yitzhak" Perelman on Gibson's Beach, Sagaponack? . . . And did you hear about Griffin and his great big beautiful Dahl? . . . What, Nina's planning to launch a *perfume*? But, my dear, she's so over, she's starting to smell like *roadkill*. . . . And Meg and Dennis, just moved to Splitsville, are squabbling over who gets not just the CD collection but the *guru*. . . . Which big-name Hollywood actress has been whispering that a new young star's elevation has Sapphic origins involving a major studio boss? . . .

And have you *read* Karen's latest, *Thin Thighs for Life*? . . . And Lotus, coolest of niteries, nixed O. J. Simpson's birthday bash! Only in America, kids, only in America!

With his hands over his ears, and still wearing his ruined linen suit, Professor Solanka slept.

5

The telephone woke him at noon. Jack Rhinehart, the phone-smasher, invited Professor Solanka over to watch the Holland-Yugoslavia Euro 2000 quarter final on Pay-Per-View. Malik accepted, surprising them both. "Glad to get you out of that mole hole," Rhinehart said. "But if you plan to root for the Serbs, stay home." Solanka felt refreshed today: less burdened, and, yes, in need of a friend. Even in these days of his retreat, he still had such needs. A holy man up a Himalaya could do without football on TV. Solanka was not so pure of heart. He shed the slept-in suit, showered, dressed quickly and rode downtown. When he climbed out of the cab at Rhinehart's building, a woman in shades rushed into it, jostling him, and he had, for the second time in as many days, the unsettling feeling that the stranger was someone he knew. In the elevator he identified her: the squeeze-me-and-I-talk doll-woman whose name was the contemporary byword for tacky infidelity, Our Lady of the Thong. "Oh Jesus, Monica," Rhinehart said. "I run into her all the time. Around here it used to be Naomi Campbell, Courtney Love, Angelina Jolie. Now it's Minnie Mouth. There goes the neighbourhood, right?"

Rhinehart had been trying to get divorced for years, but his wife had made it her life's work to deny him. They had been a beautiful, perfectly contrasted ebony-and-ivory couple, she long, languid, pale, he equally long, but a pitch-black African-American, and a hyperactive one at that, a hunter, fisherman, weekend driver of very fast cars, marathon runner, gym rat, tennis player, and, lately, thanks to the rise of Tiger Woods, an obsessive golfer too. From the earliest days of their marriage Solanka had wondered how a man with so much energy would handle a woman with so little. They had married splashily in London—Rhinehart had for most of his war years preferred to base himself outside America—and, in a ceramic-and-mosaic palazzo rented for the occasion from a charity that ran it as a halfway house for the mentally troubled, Malik Solanka had made a best-man's speech whose tone was spectacularly misjudged—at one point, doing his then-celebrated W. C. Fields impression, he compared the risks of the union to those of "jumping out of an airplane from twenty thousand feet and trying to land on a bale of hay"—but prophetically apt. Like most of their circle, however, he had underestimated Bronisława Rhinehart in one essential respect: she had the sticking power of a leech.

(At least there were no children, Solanka thought when his, everybody's, misgivings about the union proved justified. He thought of Asmaan on the telephone. "Where've you gone, Daddy, are you here?" He thought of himself long ago. At least Rhinehart didn't have to deal with that, the slow deep pain of a child.)

Rhinehart had done her wrong, no denying that. His response to marriage had been to begin an affair, and his response to the difficulty of maintaining a clandestine relationship had been to initiate another one, and when both his mistresses insisted that he regularize his life, when they both insisted on occupying pole position on the grid of his personal auto rally, he at once managed to find room for yet another woman in his noisy, overcrowded bed. Minnie Mouth was perhaps not such an inappropriate local icon. After a few years of this, and a move from Holland Park to the West Village, Bronisława—what was it with all these Poles who kept cropping up in various positions?—moved out of the apartment on Hudson Street and used the courts to force Rhinehart to maintain her in high style in a junior suite at a tony Upper East Side hotel, with major credit card spending power. Instead of divorcing him, she told him sweetly, she intended to make the rest of his life a misery, and bleed him slowly dry. "And don't run out of money, honey," she advised. "Because then I'll have to come after what you really like."

What Rhinehart really liked was food and drink. He owned a little saltbox cottage in the Springs with, at the back of the garden, a shed that he'd equipped as a wine-storage facility and insured for considerably more money than the cottage, in which the most valuable object was the six-burner Viking range. Rhinehart these days was a turbocharged gastronome, his freezer full of the carcasses of dead birds awaiting their reduction—their elevation!—to *jus.* In his refrigerator the delicacies of the earth jostled for space: larks' tongues, emus' testicles, dinosaurs' eggs. Yet when, at his friend's wedding, Solanka had spoken to Rhinehart's mother and sister of the exquisite pleasures of dining at Jack's table, he had bewildered and amazed them both. "Jack, cook? *This* Jack?" asked his mother, disbelievingly pointing at her son. "Jack I know couldn't open a can of beans less'n I showed him how to hold the can opener." "Jack *I* know," his sister added, "couldn't boil a pan of water without burnin' it up." "Jack *I* know," his mother concluded, definitively, "couldn't find the *kitchen* without a seein'-eye dog leadin' the way."

This same Jack could now hold his own with the great chefs of the world, and Solanka marvelled, once again, at the human capacity for automorphosis, the transformation of the self, which Americans claimed as their own special, defining characteristic. It wasn't. Americans were always labelling things with the America logo: American Dream, American Buffalo, American Graffiti, American Psycho, American Tune. But everyone else had such things too, and in the rest of the world the addition of a nationalist prefix didn't seem to add much meaning. English Psycho, Indian Graffiti, Australian Buffalo, Egyptian

Dream, Chilean Tune. America's need to make things American, to own them, thought Solanka, was the mark of an odd insecurity. Also, of course, and more prosaically, capitalist.

Bronisława's threat to Rhinehart's booze hoard found its mark. He gave up visiting war zones and began to write, instead, lucrative profiles of the super-powerful, super-famous and super-rich for their weekly and monthly magazines of choice: chronicling their loves, their deals, their wild children, their personal tragedies, their tell-all maids, their murders, their surgeries, their good works, their evil secrets, their games, their feuds, their sexual practices, their meanness, their generosity, their groomers, their walkers, their cars. Then he gave up writing poetry and turned his hand, instead, to novels set in the same world, the unreal world that ruled the real one. He often compared his subject to that of the Roman Suetonius. "These are the lives of today's Caesars in their Palaces," he'd taken to telling Malik Solanka and anyone else who was prepared to listen. "They sleep with their sisters, murder their mothers, make their horses into senators. It's mayhem in there, in the Palaces. But guess what? If you're outside, if you're the mob in the street, if, that is, you're us, all you see is that the Palaces are the Palaces, all the money and power is in there, an' when dey snaps dey fingers, boy, de planet it start jumpin'." (It was Rhinehart's habit from time to time to slip into an Eddie Murphy-meets-Br'er Rabbit manner, for emphasis or fun.) "Now that I'm writing about this billionairess in a coma or those moneyed kids who iced their parents, now that I'm on this diamond beat, I'm seeing more of the truth of things than I did in fucking Desert Storm or some Sniper's Alley doorway in Sarajevo, and believe me it's just as easy, easier even, to step on a fucking land mine and get yourself blown to bits."

These days, whenever Professor Solanka heard his friend deliver a version of this not infrequent speech, he detected a strengthening note of insincerity. Jack had gone to war—as a noted young radical journalist of colour with a distinguished record of investigating American racism and a consequent string of powerful enemies—nursing many of the same fears expressed a generation earlier by the young Cassius Clay: most afraid, that is, of the bullet in the back, of death by what was not then known as "friendly fire". In the years that followed, however, Jack witnessed, over and over again, the tragic gift of his species for ignoring the notion of ethnic solidarity: the brutalities of blacks against blacks, Arabs against Arabs, Serbs against Bosnians and Croats. Ex-Yugo, Iran-Iraq, Rwanda, Eritrea, Afghanistan. The exterminations in Timor, the communal massacres in Meerut and Assam, the endless colour-blind cataclysm of the earth. Somewhere in those years he became capable of close friendships with his white colleagues from the USA. His label changed. He stopped hyphenating himself and became, simply, an American.

Solanka, who was sensitive to the undertones of such rebrandings, understood that for Jack there was much disappointment involved in this transformation, even much anger directed at what white racists would eagerly have called "his own kind", and that such anger turns all too easily against the angry party. Jack stayed away from America, married a white woman, and moved in *bien-pensant* circles in which race was "not an issue": that is, almost everyone was white. Back in New York, separated from Bronisława, he continued to date what he called "the daughters of Paleface". The joke couldn't hide the truth. These days Jack was more or less the only black man Jack knew, and Solanka was probably the only brown one. Rhinehart had crossed a line.

And now, perhaps, was crossing another one. Jack's new line of work gave him an all-access pass to the Palaces, and he loved it. He wrote about this gilded milieu with waspish venom, he tore it apart for its crassness, its blindness, its mindlessness, its depthless surfaceness, but the invitations from the Warren Redstones and Ross Buffetts, from the Schuylers and Muybridges and Van Burens and Kleins, from Ivana Opalberg-Speedvogel and Marlalee Booken Candell, just kept on coming, because the guy was hooked and they knew it. He was their house nigger and it suited them to keep him around, as, Solanka suspected, a sort of pet. "Jack Rhinehart" was a usefully non–black specific name, carrying none of the ghetto connotations of a Tupac, Vondie, Anfernee, or Rah'schied (these were days of innovative naming and creative orthography in the African-American community). In the Palaces, people were not named in this way. Men were not called Biggie or Hammer or Shaquille or Snoop or Dre, nor were women named Pepa or LeftEye or D:Neece. No Kunta Kintes or Shaznays in America's golden halls; where, however, a man might be nicknamed Stash or Club by way of a sexual compliment, and the women might be Blaine or Brooke or Horne, and anything you wanted was probably simmering between satin sheets just behind the door of that bedroom suite over there, the one with the door standing ever so slightly ajar.

Yes, women, of course. Women were Rhinehart's addiction and Achilles' heel, and this was the Valley of the Dollybirds. No: it was the mountain, the Everest of the Dollybirds, the fabled Dollybird Horn of Plenty. Send these women his way, the Christies and Christys and Kristens and Chrystèles, the giantesses about whom most of the planet was busy fantasizing, with whom even Castro and Mandela were happy to pose, and Rhinehart would lie down (or sit up) and beg. Behind the infinite layers of Rhinehart's cool was this ignoble fact: he had been seduced, and his desire to be accepted into this white man's club was the dark secret he could not confess to anyone, perhaps not even to himself. And these are the secrets from which the anger comes. In this dark bed the seeds of fury grow. And although Jack's act was armour-plated, although his mask never slipped, Solanka was sure he could see, in his friend's blazing eyes, the self-loathing fire of his rage. It took him a long while to concede that Jack's suppressed fury was the mirror of his own.

Rhinehart's annual income was currently in the median-to-upper range of the six-figure bracket, but he claimed, only half jokingly, to be frequently pressed for cash. Bronisława had exhausted three judges and four lawyers, discovering on her journey a Jarndyce-like gift—even, Solanka thought, an Indian genius—for legal obstruction and delay. Of this she had become (perhaps literally) insanely proud. She had learned how to twist and thicken the plot. As a practising Catholic, she initially announced that she wouldn't sue Rhinehart for divorce even though he was the devil in disguise. The devil, she explained to her attorneys, was short, white, wore a green frock coat, a pigtail, and high-heeled slippers, and strongly resembled the philosopher Immanuel Kant. But he was capable of taking any form, a column of smoke, a reflection in a mirror, or a long, black, frenziedly energetic husband. "My revenge on Satan," she told the bemused lawyers, "will be to keep him the prisoner of my ring." In New York, where the legal grounds for divorce were few and rigorously defined and the no-fault split didn't exist, Rhinehart's case against his wife was weak. He tried persuasion, bribery, threats. She stood firm and brought no suit. Eventually he did begin a court action, against which she brilliantly and determinedly offered a stupendous, almost mystical inaction. The ferocity of her passive resistance would have impressed, probably, Gandhi. She got away with a decade-long sequence of psychological and physical "breakdowns" that the cheesiest daytime soap would have found excessive, and had been in contempt of court forty-seven times, without ever going to jail, because of Rhinehart's unwillingness to ask the court to act against her. So in his middle forties he was still paying for the sins of his middle thirties. Meanwhile he continued to be promiscuous, and to praise the city for its bounty. "For a single man with a few bucks in the bank and an inclination to party, this little piece of real estate stolen from those Mannahattoes is the happy hunting grounds, no less."

But he wasn't single. And in eleven years he could surely have, for example, moved across the state border to Connecticut, where no-fault divorce did exist, or found the six or so weeks required to establish legal residence in Nevada and cut this Gordian knot. This he had not done. Once, in his cups, he had confided to Solanka that for all the city's generosity in providing the grateful male with multiple-choice options in dating, there was a snag. "They all want the big words," he protested. "They want forever, serious, heavy, long-term. If it's not grand passion, it's not happening. This is why they're so lonely. There aren't enough men to go around, but they won't shop if they can't buy. They aren't open to the concept of the rental, the time share. They're fucked-up, man. They're looking for real estate in a market that's crazily high, but they know it'll be going even higher soon." In this version of the truth, Rhinehart's incomplete divorce bought him breathing space, lebensraum. Women would try him out, for he was beautiful and charming, and, until they got sick of the endlessness of it, would wait.

There was also, however, another possible reading of the situation. Up where Rhinehart now mostly lived, on the Big Rock Candy Mountain, the Diamond as Big as the Ritz, he was literally outclassed and, the moment he fell into the trap of wanting what was on offer up there on Olympus, also out of his depth. He was, remember, their toy, and while girls will play with toys, they don't marry them. So maybe being half-married, stuck in this endlessly divorcing condition, was also a way for Rhinehart to kid himself. In reality there probably wasn't much of a line forming to wait for him. Single, and ageing—he had turned forty now—he was almost out of time. Almost—the killer word for any ambitious ladykiller—ineligible.

Malik Solanka, a decade and a half older than Jack Rhinehart and a dozen dozen times more inhibited, had often watched and listened with envious wonder as Rhinehart went about his life's business in so unshamedly male a manner. The combat zones, the women, the dangerous sports, the life of a man of deeds. Even the now-abandoned poetry had been of the virile Ted Hughes school. Often Solanka had felt that in spite of his seniority in years, it was Rhinehart who was the master and he the student. A mere maker of dolls must bow his head before a wind surfer, a sky diver, a bungee jumper, a rock climber, a man whose idea of fun it was to go to Hunter College twice a week and run up and down forty flights of stairs. Being a boy—but this was getting too close to his forbidden, obliterated back-story—was a skill Malik Solanka had not been allowed to acquire in full.

Patrick Kluivert scored for the Dutch, and both Solanka and Rhinehart jumped to their feet, waving bottles of Mexican beer and shouting. Then the doorbell rang and Rhinehart said, without preamble, "Oh, by the way, I think I'm in love. I invited her to join us. Hope that's okay." This was not an original line. Traditionally it signalled the arrival of what Rhinehart would very privately call the new waitress. What followed, however, was new. "She's one of yours," Rhinehart said over his shoulder as he got up to open the door. "Indian diaspora. One hundred years of servitude. In the eighteen nineties her ancestors went as indentured labourers to work in what's-its-name. Lilliput-Blefuscu. Now they run the sugarcane production and the economy would fall apart without them, but you know how it is wherever Indians go. People don't like them. Dey works too hard and dey keeps to deyself and dey acts so dang uppity. Ask anyone. Ask Idi Amin."

On the television the Dutch were playing sublime football, but the match had suddenly become an irrelevance. Malik Solanka was thinking that the woman who had just entered Rhinehart's living room was by some distance the most beautiful Indian woman—the most beautiful *woman*—he had ever seen. Compared to the intoxicating effect of her presence, the bottle of Dos Equis in his left hand was wholly alcohol free. Other women in the world were just under six feet tall, with waist-length black hair, he supposed; and no doubt such smoky eyes were also to be found elsewhere, as also other lips as richly cushioned, other necks as slender, other legs as interminably long. On other women, too, there might be breasts like these. So what? In the words of an idiotic song from the fifties, "Bernardine", sung in one of his raunchier moments by his mother's favourite recording artist, the Christian conservative Pat Boone: "Your separate parts are not unknown / but the way you assemble 'em's all your own." Exactly, thought Professor Solanka, drowning. Just exactly so.

Down the upper part of the woman's right arm there was an eight-inch-long herringbone-pattern scar. When she saw him looking at it, she at once crossed her arms and put her left hand over the injury, not understanding that it made her more beautiful, that it perfected her beauty by adding an essential imperfection. By showing that she could be injured, that such astonishing loveliness could be broken in an instant, the cicatrice only emphasized what was there, and made one cherish it—my goodness, Solanka thought, what a word to use about a stranger!—all the more.

Extreme physical beauty draws all available light towards itself, becomes a shining beacon in an otherwise darkened world. Why would one peer into the encircling gloom when one could look at this kindly flame? Why talk, eat, sleep, work when such effulgence was on display? Why do anything but look, for the rest of one's paltry life? *Lumen de lumine.* Staring into the sidereal unreality of her beauty, which wheeled in the room like a galaxy on fire, he was thinking that if he had been able to wish his ideal woman into being, if he'd had a magic lamp to rub, this would have been what he'd have wished for. And, at the same time, while he was mentally congratulating Rhinehart for breaking away at last from the many daughters of Paleface, he was also imagining himself with this dark Venus, he was allowing his own, closed heart to open, and so remembering once again what he spent much of his life trying to forget: the size of the crater within him, the hole left by his break with his recent and remote past, which, just perhaps, the love of such a woman could fill. Ancient, secret pain welled up in him, pleading to be healed.

"Yeah, sorry 'bout that, buddy" came Rhinehart's tickled drawl from the far side of the universe. "She hits most people that way. Can't help it. Doesn't know how to switch it off. Neela, meet my celibate pal Malik. He's given up women forever, as you can plainly see." Jack was enjoying himself, Solanka noted. He forced himself back into the real world. "Lucky for all of us that I have," he finally said, pushing his mouth into some sort of smile. "Otherwise, I'd have to fight you for her." Here's that old euphony again, he thought: Neela, Mila. Desire is coming after me, and giving me warnings in rhyme.

She worked as a producer with one of the better independents, and specialized in documentary programming for television. Right now she was planning a project that would take her back to her roots. Things back home in Lilliput-Blefuscu were not good, Neela explained. People in the West thought of it as a South Sea paradise, a place for honeymoons and other trysts, but there was trouble brewing. Relations between the Indo-Lilliputians and the indigenous, ethnic "Elbee" community—which still made up a majority of the population, but only just—were deteriorating fast. To highlight the issues, New York representatives of the opposing factions had both arranged to hold parades on the same upcoming Sunday. These manifestations would be small but fervent. The two march routes were to be widely separated, but it was still a good bet that there would be some angry clashes. Neela herself was determined to march. As she talked about the worsening political turbulence in her tiny patch of the antipodes, Professor Solanka saw the hot blood rising in her. This conflict was not a small matter for beautiful Neela. She was still connected to her origins, and Solanka almost envied her for it. Jack Rhinehart was saying, boyishly, "Great! We'll all go! Sure we will! You'll march for your people, Malik, right? Well, you'll march for Neela, anyhow." Rhinehart's tone was light: a miscalculation. Solanka saw Neela stiffen and frown. This wasn't to be treated as a game. "Yes," Solanka said, looking her in the eyes. "I'll march."

They settled down to watch the game. More goals came: six in all for the Netherlands, a late, irrelevant consolation strike for Yugoslavia. Neela, too, was glad the Dutch had done well. She saw their black players, uncompetitively but also without false modesty, as her near equals in gorgeousness. "The Surinamese," she said, unknowingly echoing the thoughts of the young Malik Solanka in Amsterdam all those years ago, "are the living proof of the value of mixing up the races. Look at them. Edgar Davids, Kluivert, Rijkaard in the dugout, and, in the good old days, Ruud. The great Gullit. All of them, *métèques.* Stir all the races together and you get the most beautiful people in the world. I want to go," she added, to nobody in particular, "soon, to Surinam." She sprawled across the settee, throwing one long, leather-clad leg over the arm, and dislodged the day's *Post.* It fell to the floor at Solanka's feet, and his eye was caught by the headline: CONCRETE KILLER STRIKES AGAIN. And below, in smaller type: *Who Was the Man in the Panama Hat?* Everything changed at once; darkness rushed in through the open window, blinding him. His little rush of excitement, good humour and lust drained away. He felt himself trembling, and rose quickly to his feet. "I have to leave," he said. "What, the final whistle blows and you're out of here? Malik, friend, that just plain ain't polite." But Solanka only shook his head at Rhinehart and headed out through the door, fast. Behind him he heard Neela talking about the *Post* headline; she'd picked up the paper as he left. "*Bastard.* This stuff is supposed to have stopped, it's supposed to be safe now, right," she was saying. "But, shit, it's never over. Here we go again."

6

"Islam will cleanse this street of godless motherfucker bad drivers," the taxi driver screamed at a rival motorist. "Islam will purify this whole city of Jew pimp assholes like you and your whore roadhog of a Jew wife too." All the way up Tenth Avenue the curses continued. "Infidel fucker of your underage sister, the inferno of Allah awaits you and your unholy wreck of a motorcar as well." "Unclean offspring of a shit-eating pig, try that again and the victorious jihad will crush your balls in its unforgiving fist." Malik Solanka, listening in to the explosive, village-accented Urdu, was briefly distracted from his own inner turmoil by the driver's venom. ALI MAJNU said the card. Majnu meant *beloved.* This particular Beloved looked twenty-five or less, a nice handsome boy, tall and skinny, with a sexy John Travolta quiff, and here he was living in New York, with a steady job; what had so comprehensively gotten his goat?

Solanka silently answered his own question. When one is too young to have accumulated the bruises of one's own experience, one can choose to put on, like a hair shirt, the sufferings of one's world. In this case, as the Middle East peace process staggered onward and the outgoing American president, hungry for a breakthrough to buff up his tarnished legacy, was urging Barak and Arafat to a Camp David summit conference, Tenth Avenue was perhaps being blamed for the continued sufferings of Palestine. Beloved Ali was Indian or Pakistani, but, no doubt out of some misguided collectivist spirit of paranoiac pan-Islamic solidarity, he blamed all New York road users for the tribulations of the Muslim world. In between curses, he spoke to his mother's brother on the radio—"Yes, Uncle. Yes, carefully, of course, Uncle. Yes, the car costs money. No, Uncle. Yes, courteously, always, Uncle, trust me. Yes, best policy. I know"—and also asked Solanka, sheepishly, for directions. It was the boy's first day at work in the mean streets, and he was scared witless. Solanka, himself in a state of high agitation, treated Beloved gently but did say, as he alighted at Verdi Square, "Maybe a little less of the blue language, okay, Ali Majnu? Tone it down. Some customers might be offended. Even those who don't understand."

The boy looked at him blankly. "I, sir? Swearing, sir? When?" This was odd. "All the way," Solanka explained. "At everyone within shouting distance. Motherfucker, Jew, the usual repertoire. *Urdu,*" he added, in Urdu, to make things clear, *"meri madri zaban hai."* Urdu is my mother tongue. Beloved blushed, deeply, the colour spreading all the way to his collar line, and met Solanka's gaze with bewildered, innocent dark eyes. "Sahib, if you heard it, then it must be so. But, sir, you see, I am not aware." Solanka lost patience, turned to go. "It doesn't matter," he said. "Road rage. You were carried away. It's not important." As he walked off along Broadway, Beloved Ali shouted after him, needily, asking to be understood: "It means nothing, sahib. Me, I don't even go to the mosque. God bless America, okay? It's just words."

Yes, and words are not deeds, Solanka allowed, moving off fretfully. Though words can become deeds. If said in the right place and at the right time, they can move mountains and change the world. Also, uh-huh, not knowing what you're doing—separating deeds from the words that define them—was apparently becoming an acceptable excuse. To say "I didn't mean it" was to erase meaning from your misdeeds, at least in the opinion of the Beloved Alis of the world. Could that be so? Obviously, no. No, it simply could not. Many people would say that even a genuine act of repentance could not atone for a crime, much less this unexplained blankness—an infinitely lesser excuse, a mere assertion of ignorance that wouldn't even register on any scale of regret. Shockingly, Solanka recognized himself in foolish young Ali Majnu: the vehemence as well as the blanks in the record. He did not, however, excuse himself. At Jack Rhinehart's apartment, before the poleaxing arrival of Neela Mahendra had changed the subject, he had been attempting, while concealing the depth of his perturbation, to confess to Rhinehart something of his fear about the terrorist anger that kept taking him hostage. Jack, absorbed in the football game, nodded absently. "You must know you've always had a short fuse," he said. "I mean, you are aware of that, right? You're conscious of the number of times you've rung people up to apologize—the number of times you've rung *me* up—the morning after some little wine-lubricated explosion of yours? The Collected Apologies of Malik Solanka. I always thought that would make a fine book. Repetitive, maybe, but with rich comic delights."

Some years back, the Solankas had vacationed at the cottage in the Springs with Rhinehart and his "waitress" of the moment, a petite Southern belle—from Lookout Mountain, Tennessee, scene of the Civil War's "Battle above the Clouds"—who was a dead ringer for the cartoon sexpot Betty Boop and to whom Rhinehart referred affectionately as Roscoe, after Lookout Mountain's only living celebrity, the heavy-serving tennis player Roscoe Tanner, in spite of her evident hatred of the nickname. The cottage was small and it was necessary to spend as much time as possible away from it. One night after a protracted, men-only drinking session at an East Hampton watering hole, Solanka had insisted on driving back during a heavy downpour. A period of dumbstruck terror ensued. Then Rhinehart said, as mildly as he could, "Malik, in America we drive on the other side of the road." Solanka had blown up and, incensed at the disrespect being shown to his driving skills, had stopped the car and actually forced Rhinehart to walk home in the drenching rain. "That was one of your best apologies," Jack now reminded him. "Particularly because the next morning you couldn't remember doing anything wrong at all."

"Yes," Solanka murmured, "but now I'm having the blackouts without the booze. And the anger events are on a completely different scale." The noise of the TV crowd surged as he spoke, demanding Rhinehart's attention, and the confession passed unheard. "Oh, and," Rhinehart resumed moments later, "you can't not know how hard your friends try to avoid certain subjects in your company. U.S. policy in Central America, for example. U.S. policy in Southeast Asia. Actually, the U.S.A. in general has been pretty much an off-limits topic for years, so don't think I wasn't tickled when you decided to relocate yo' ass in the bosom of the Great Satan hisself." Yes, but, Solanka wanted to say, rising to the bait, what's wrong is wrong, and because of the immense goddamn *power* of America, the immense fucking *seduction* of America, those bastards in charge get away with . . . "There you go, you see," Rhinehart pointed at him, chuckling. "Just swellin' up fit to bust. Bright red, then purple, then almost black. A heart attack waiting to happen. You know what we call it when it happens? Getting Solankered. Malik's China syndrome. It's an honest to God fuckin' meltdown. I mean, mah fren', *I'm* the man who actually *done gone* to these places and brought back the bad news, but that don't stop you from tellin' me off 'bout it, on account of my citizenship, which in yo' mad eyes makes me *'sponsible* for de mighty evil dat keep gettin' done in mah po' name."

No fool like an old fool. So he and Beloved Ali were really the same after all, Solanka humbly thought. Just a few slight surface differences of vocabulary and education. No: he was worse, because Beloved was just a boy on his first day in a new job, while he, Solanka, was becoming something awful and perhaps uncontrollable. The bitter irony was that his old habits of combativeness, this evidently comic intemperateness of his, would blind even his friends to the great change in kind, the hideous deterioration, that was now taking place. This time there really was a wolf coming and nobody, not even Jack, was listening to his cries. "And furthermore," Rhinehart carolled gaily, "remember when you ejected, oh, what's his name from your house for *misquoting Philip Larkin*? Man! So *you've* been getting snappy with the neighbours? Whoo-ee. Hold the front page."

How could Malik Solanka speak to his mirthful friend of the abnegation of the self: how to say, America is the great devourer, and so I have come to America to be devoured? How could he say, I am a knife in the dark; I endanger those I love?

Solanka's hands itched. Even his skin was betraying him. He, whose baby-bottom skin had always caused women to marvel and to tease him for having led a life of cosseted ease, had begun to suffer from uncomfortable raw irruptions along his hairline and, most awkwardly of all, on both hands. The skin reddened, puckered and broke. So far he had not visited a dermatologist. Before walking out on Eleanor, a lifetime eczema sufferer, he had raided her medicine box and brought away two thick tubes of hydrocortisone ointment. At the local Duane Reade he bought a jumbo-sized bottle of industrial-strength moisturizer and resigned himself to using it several times a day. Professor Solanka did not have a high opinion of doctors. Accordingly, he self-medicated, and itched.

It was the age of science, but medical science was still in the hands of primitives and oafs. The main thing you learned from doctors was how little they knew. In the paper yesterday there had been a story about a doctor who had accidentally removed a woman's healthy breast. He was "reprimanded". It was such an everyday story that it only made a deep inside page. This was the sort of thing doctors did: the wrong kidney, the wrong lung, the wrong eye, the wrong baby. Doctors did wrong. It was just barely news.

The news: it was right there in his hand. After getting out of Beloved Ali's cab he'd picked up a copy of the *News* and the *Post,* then had taken an erratic route home, walking fast, as if trying to escape something. . . . Ellen DeGeneres, posters proclaimed, was coming soon to the Beacon Theatre. Solanka grimaced. She'd be singing her theme song, of course: *Where the hormones, there moan I.* And the room would be full of women hollering, "Ellen, we love you," and in the midst of her set of deeply so-so material the comedienne would pause, lower her head, put her hand on her heart, and say how moved she was to have become a symbol of their pain. Praise me, thank you, thank you, praise me some more, hey, look, Anne, we're an icon!, wow!, it's so *humbling.* . . . Science was making extraordinary discoveries, Professor Solanka thought. Scientists in London believed they had identified the medial insula, a part of the brain associated with "gut feelings", and also that part of the anterior cingulate that was linked to euphoria, as the locations of love. Also, British and German scientists now claimed that the frontal lateral cortex was responsible for intelligence. The blood flow in this region increased when tested volunteers were called upon to solve complicated puzzles. *Tell me where is fancy bred? / I' the heart or i' the head?* And where in the brain, wild-hearted Solanka only half rhetorically asked himself, is the seat of stupidity? Eh, scientists of the world? In what insula or cortex does the blood flow increase when one shouts "I love you" at a total fucking stranger? And how about hypocrisy? Let's get to the interesting stuff here . . .

He shook his head. You're avoiding the issue, Professor. You're dancing all around it when what you have to do is stare it down, look it right in the face. Let's get to anger, okay? Let's get to the goddamn fury that actually kills. Tell me, where is murder bred? Malik Solanka, clutching his newspaper, hurtled east along Seventy-second Street, scattering pedestrians. On Columbus he made a left and half-ran another dozen distraught blocks or so before coming to a halt. Even the stores hereabouts had Indian names: Bombay, Pondicherry. Everything conspired to remind him of what he was trying to forget—of, that is, home, the idea of home in general and his own home life in particular. In not Pondicherry but, yes, it cannot be denied, Bombay. He went into a Mexican-themed bar with a high *Zagat*'s rating, ordered a shot of tequila, and another, and then, finally, it was time for the dead.

This one, last night's corpse, and the two before. These were their names. Saskia "Sky" Schuyler, today's big picture, and her predecessors Lauren "Ren" Muybridge Klein and Belinda "Bindy" Booken Candell. These were their ages: nineteen, twenty, nineteen. These were their photographs. Look at their smiles: these were the smiles of power. A lump of concrete put out those lights. These were not poor girls, but they're penniless now.

She was something, Sky was. Five-foot-nine, stacked, spoke six languages, reminded everyone of Christie Brinkley as the Uptown Girl, loved big hats and high fashion, could've walked for anyone—Jean-Paul, Donatella, Dries had all *begged* her, Tom Ford had gone down on his *knees,* but she was just too "naturally shy"—this was code for naturally upper-crust, too much a member of that old-money snobberia that thought of couturiers as tailors and runway models as just one small step better than whores—and, besides, there was her scholarship at Juilliard. Just last weekend she was in a hurry to get out to Southampton, needed something to wear, no time to choose, so she rang her great pal the high-end designer Imelda Poushine, asked her to just send over the whole collection, and messengered back, in return, a personal check for four count 'em four hundred thousand dollars.

Yes, says Imelda in Rush & Molloy, the check cleared two days ago. She was a great girl, a living doll, but business is business, I guess. We'll all miss her *dreadfully.* Yes, it'll be at the family plot, right there in the best part, right across from Jimmy Stewart. Everybody's going. *Big* security operation. I hear they decided to lay her to rest in the wedding gown. *So* honoured. She'll look beautiful, but that girl would've looked beautiful in rags, believe me. Yes, I'll be dressing her. Are you kidding? My *privilege.* It's an open-casket situation. They've booked the best: Sally H. for the hair, Rafael for the makeup, Herb for the photographs. Sky's the limit, I guess, no pun intended. Her mother's handling it all. That woman is made of iron. Not a tear. Just fifty herself and drop dead gor, excuse me, don't print that, okay. No pun intended.

The inheritors disinherited, the masters made victims: that was the angle. All that wasted training! For Saskia at nineteen was not only a linguist, pianist and dedicated fashionista; she was also already an expert horsewoman, an archer with hopes of making the Sydney Olympic team, a long-distance swimmer, a fabulous dancer, a great cook, a happy weekend painter, a bel canto singer, a hostess in her mother's grand manner, and, to judge by the openly worldly sensuality of her newspaper smile, skilled, too, in other arts to which the tabloid press was utterly devoted but whereof it dared not speak freely in such a context. The papers contented themselves with printing photographs of Saskia's handsome beau, the polo player Bradley Marsalis III, of whom all regular readers knew at least this: that his teammates called him Horse, in honour of the way he was hung.

A stone from a Lost Boy's slingshot had felled the beautiful Wendy Bird. Make that birds: for what was said of Sky Schuyler applied equally to Bindy Candell and Ren Klein. All three were beautiful, all three long and blonde and formidably accomplished. If the financial future of their great families rested in the hands of their superlatively confident brothers, then these young women had been reared to take charge of the personae of their clans—their style, their class. Their image. Looking at their stunned menfolk now, it was easy to gauge the size of their loss. We boys can take care of business, said the silent grieving faces of the families, but our girls make us who we are. We are the boat and they are the ocean. We are the vehicle, they're the motion. Who, now, will tell us how to be? And there was fear too: who'll be next? Of all the ripe girls given to us to pluck from their branches like the golden apples of the sun, who's next for the fatal worm?

A living doll. These young women were born to be trophies, fully accessorized Oscar-Barbies, to use Eleanor Masters Solanka's phrase. It was obvious that the young men of their class were reacting to the three deaths exactly as if some coveted medallions, some golden bowls or silver cups, had been stolen from their clubhouse plinths. A secret society of gilded young men calling itself the S&M, which stood, it was suggested, for Single & Male, was reportedly planning a midnight gathering to mourn the loss of its members' much-loved main squeezes.

"Horse" Marsalis, Anders "Stash" Andriessen—the Candell girl's restaurateur Eurohunk—and Lauren Klein's good-time guy Keith Medford ("Club") would lead the mourners. As the S&M was a secret society, all its members flatly denied its existence and refused to verify the rumours that the mourning ceremonies would climax with mixed-sex war-painted naked dancing and skinny-dipping on a private Vineyard beach, at which time candidates for the vacancies in the big guys' beds would be intimately auditioned.

All three dead girls, and their living sisters, thus conformed to Eleanor's definition of Desdemonas. They were property. And now there was a murderous Othello on the loose—in this case, perhaps, destroying what he could not possess, because that very non-possession insulted his honour. Not for their infidelity but for their uninterest was he killing them in this Y2K revision of the play. Or perhaps he broke them simply to reveal their lack of humanity, their breakability. Their dollness. For these had been—yes!—android women, dolls of the modern age, mechanized, computerized, not the simple effigies of bygone nurseries but fully realized avatars of human beings.

In its origin, the doll was not a thing in itself but a representation. Long before the earliest rag dolls and golliwogs, human beings had made dolls as portraits of particular children and adults, too. It was always a mistake to let others possess the doll of yourself; who owned your doll owned a crucial piece of you. The extreme expression of this idea was of course the voodoo doll, the doll you could stick pins in to hurt the one it represented, the doll whose neck you could wring to kill a living being, at a distance, as effectively as a Muslim cook deals with a chicken. Then came mass production, and the link between man and doll was broken; dolls became themselves and clones of themselves. They became reproductions, assembly-line versions, characterless, uniform. In the present day, all that was changing again. Solanka's own bank balance owed everything to the desire of modern people to own dolls with not just personality but individuality. His dolls had tales to tell.

But now living women wanted to be doll-like, to cross the frontier and look like toys. Now the doll was the original, the woman the representation. These living dolls, these stringless marionettes, were not just "dolled up" on the outside. Behind their high-style exteriors, beneath that perfectly lucent skin, they were so stuffed full of behavioural chips, so thoroughly programmed for action, so perfectly groomed and wardrobed, that there was no room left in them for messy humanity. Sky, Bindy and Ren thus represented the final step in the transformation of the cultural history of the doll. Having conspired in their own dehumanization, they ended up as mere totems of their class, the class that ran America, which in turn ran the world, so that an attack on them was also, if you cared to see it that way, an attack on the great American empire, the Pax Americana, itself. . . . A dead body on a street, thought Malik Solanka, coming down to earth, looks a lot like a broken doll.

. . . Oh, who even thought like this any more, other than himself? Was there anyone else left in America with such ugly, misconceived notions in his head? If you'd asked these young women, these tall confident beauties on their way to summa cum laude college degrees and glamorous yachting weekends, these Princesses of the Now, with their limo services and charity work and mile-a-minute lives and tame, adoring superheroes striving to win their favour, they would have told you they were free, freer than any women in any country in any time, and they belonged to no man, whether father or lover or boss. They were nobody's dolls, but their own women, playing with their own appearance, their own sexuality, their own stories: the first generation of young women to be truly in control, in thrall neither to the old patriarchy nor to the man-hating hard-line feminism that had battered at Bluebeard's gate. They could be businesswomen and flirts, profound and superficial, serious and light, and they would make those decisions for themselves. They had it all—emancipation, sex appeal, cash—and they loved it. And then somebody came and took it away from them by hitting them hard on the back of their heads, the first blow to knock them out and the rest to finish them off. So, who killed them? If it was dehumanization you were interested in, the murderer was your man. Not they themselves but he, the Concrete Killer, had dehumanized them. Professor Malik Solanka, tears running down his face as he sat hunched over his tequila on a bar stool, buried his head in his hands.

Saskia Schuyler had lived in a many-roomed but low-ceilinged apartment in what she called "the ugliest building on Madison Avenue", a blue brick monstrosity opposite the Armani store, whose "only good point", in Sky's opinion, was that she could call the store and have them hold dresses up to the window so that she could check them out through binoculars. She hated the apartment, her parents' former Manhattan pied-à-terre. The Schuylers lived mostly out of town, on a gated estate set in rolling landscape near Chappaqua, New York, and spent much time complaining about the Clintons' purchase of a house in their home town. Sky, said Bradley Marsalis, liked to reassure her parents that Hillary wouldn't be there long. "If she wins, she'll be off to D.C. and the Senate, and if she loses, she'll leave even faster." Meanwhile, Sky wanted to sell up on Madison and move to Tribeca, but the co-op board had three times turned down the purchasers she had found. On the subject of the board, Sky was vociferous. "It's full of lacquered old dames covered in tight shiny fabric, like overstuffed sofas, and I guess if you want to get in, you have to look like furniture too." The building did have a twenty-four-hour doorman service, however, and the night-duty doorman, old Abe Green, reported that on the date in question Miss Schuyler, "lookin' like a million dollars" after a big night out at a music-awards gala ("Horse" had industry connections), got home around one-thirty. She parted at the door from a plainly reluctant Mr Marsalis—"Boy, did he look pissed," Green noted—and walked unhappily to the elevator. Green rode up with her. "To make her smile, I told her, Too bad you only live on the fifth, miss, otherwise I could enjoy lookin' at you a little longer." Fifteen minutes later she buzzed for the elevator again. "Everything okay, miss?" Abe asked her. "Oh, I guess so. Yeah, sure, Abe," she said. "Sure." Then she walked out by herself, still in her party finery, and never came back. Her body was found a long way downtown, near the entrance to the Midtown Tunnel. A study of the last hours of Lauren Klein and Bindy Candell showed that they, too, had come home late, refused entry to their boyfriends, and gone out again shortly afterwards. As if these girls had turned Life away, then set out to keep their assignations with Death.

Saskia, Lauren and Belinda had not been robbed. Their finger rings, earrings, chokers and upper-arm bracelets were all found to be in place. Nor had they been sexually assaulted. No motive for the murders had emerged, but all three boyfriends raised the possibility of a stalker. In the days before their deaths, all the dead women had mentioned seeing a Panama-hatted stranger "lurking oddly". "It's like Sky was executed," a sombre, cigar-smoking Brad Marsalis told the press at a photo-op and Q-and-A at a hotel suite in Vineyard Haven. "It's like somebody sentenced her to death and carried out that sentence in, like, cold blood."

7

The news of Solanka's split from Eleanor had sent shock waves through their circle. Each marriage that breaks interrogates those that continue to hold. Malik Solanka was conscious of having initiated a chain reaction of spoken and unspoken questions at breakfast tables across the city, and in bedrooms, and in other cities too: Are we still good? Okay, how good? Are there things you're not telling me? Am I going to wake up one day and you'll say something that makes me realize I've been sharing my bed with a stranger? How will tomorrow rewrite yesterday, how will next week unmake the past five, ten, fifteen years? Are you bored? Is it my fault? Are you weaker than I thought? Is it him? Is it her? Is it the sex? The children? Do you want to fix it? Is there anything to fix? Do you love me? Do you still love me? Do I still, oh Jesus Jesus, love you?

These agonies, for which his friends inevitably held him responsible to some unspecified degree, returned to him as echoes. In spite of his emphatic embargo, Eleanor was handing out his Manhattan phone number to anyone who wanted it. Men, more than women, seemed moved to call up and reprove. Morgen Franz, the post-hippie Buddhist publisher whose telephone Eleanor had answered all those years ago, was first in line. Morgen was Californian and had taken refuge from that fact in Bloomsbury, but never shaken off his slow Haight-Ashbury drawl. "I'm not happy about this, man," he'd called Malik to reveal, his vowels even more elongated than usual to emphasize his pain. "And what's more, I don't know anyone who is. I don't know why you did this, man, and because you're neither a dope nor a shit, I'm sure you'll have your reasons, I'm sure you will, you know?, and they'll be good reasons, too, man, I have no doubt of it, I mean what can I tell you, I love you, you know?, I love you both, but right now I have to say I feel a lot of anger toward you." Solanka could visualize his friend's reddened, short-bearded face, his small deep-set eyes blinking fiercely for emphasis. Franz was legendarily laid-back—"nobody's cooler than the Morg," that was his catchphrase—so this heated climax came as a jolt. Solanka, however, stayed cold, and allowed himself to express his own feelings truthfully and irrevocably.

"Six, seven, eight years ago," he said, "Lin used to call Eleanor in tears because you refused to have a child with her, and you know what?, you had your reasons, you had your deep disenchantment with the human race to deal with every day, and on children, as on Philadelphia, you took the Fields position. And, Morgen, I 'felt a lot of anger toward you' in those days myself. I saw Lin settling for cats instead of babies and I didn't like it and guess what? I never called you to scold you or to ask what was the relevant Buddhist teaching on the subject, because I decided it was none of my damn business what went on between you and your wife. That it was your private affair, given that you weren't actually beating her up, or given, anyway, that it was merely her spirit you were breaking, not her body. So do me a favour and bugger off. This is not your story. It's mine." And there it went, their old friendship, eight or was it nine Christmas Days spent in turn at each other's homes, the Trivial Pursuit, the charades, the love. Lin Franz called him the next morning to tell him that what he had said was unforgivable. "Please know," she added, in her whisper-soft, overly formal Vietnamese-American English, "that your desertion of Eleanor has only served to bring Morgen and I even closer together. And Eleanor is a strong woman, and will pick up the reins of her life soon, when she has mourned. We will all go on without you, Malik, and you will be the poorer for having excluded us from your life. I am sorry for you."

A knife held over the sleeping figures of your wife and child cannot be mentioned to anyone, much less explained. Such a knife represents a crime far worse than the substitution of a long-haired feline for a mewling babe. And Solanka had no answer to the hows and whys of this appalling, enigmatic event. *Is this a dagger which I see before me, the handle towards my hand?* There he had simply been, like guilty Macbeth, and the weapon too was simply there, impossible to wish away or to edit out of the image afterwards. That he had not plunged the knife into sleeping hearts did not make him innocent. To hold the knife so and to stand thus was more than enough. Guilty, guilty! Even as he spoke his stern, friendship-breaking words to his old friend, Malik Solanka had been starkly aware of their hypocrisy, and he received Lin's subsequent rebuke without comment. He had surrendered all his rights to protest when he ran his thumb along the Sabatier blade, testing its sharpness in the dark. This knife was his story now, and he had come to America to write it.

No! In despair, to *unwrite* it. Not to be but to un-be. He had flown to the land of self-creation, the home of Mark Skywalker the Jedi copywriter in red suspenders, the country whose paradigmatic modern fiction was the story of a man who remade himself—his past, his present, his shirts, even his name—for love; and here, in this place from whose narratives he was all but disconnected, he intended to attempt the first phase of such a restructuring, namely—he deliberately now applied to himself the same sort of mechanical imagery that he had so callously used against the dead women—the complete erasure, or "master deletion", of the old program. Somewhere in the existing software there was a bug, a potentially lethal flaw. Nothing less than the unselfing of the self would do. If he could cleanse the whole machine, then maybe the bug, too, would end up in the trash. After that, he could perhaps begin to construct a new man. He fully saw that this was a fantastic, unrealistic ambition, if intended seriously, literally, instead of in-a-manner-of-speaking; nevertheless, literally was how he meant it, no matter how unhinged that might sound. For what was the alternative? Confession, fear, separation, policemen, head doctors, Broadmoor, shame, divorce, jail? The steps down into that inferno seemed inexorable. And the worse inferno he would leave behind, the burning blade turning forever in the mind's eye of his growing son.

He had conceived, in that instant, an almost religious belief in the power of flight. Flight would save others from him, and him from himself. He would go where he was not known and wash himself in that unknowing. A memory from forbidden Bombay peremptorily insisted on his attention: the memory of the day in 1955 when Mr Venkat—the big-deal banker whose son Chandra was the ten-year-old Malik's best friend—became a *sanyasi* on his sixtieth birthday and abandoned his family forever, wearing no more than a Gandhian loincloth, with a long wooden staff in one hand and a begging bowl in the other. Malik had always liked Mr Venkat, who would tease him by asking him to pronounce, very quickly, his full, polysyllabically tumbling South Indian name: Balasubramanyam Venkataraghavan. "Come on, boy, faster," he'd coax Malik as his childish tongue stumbled over the syllables. "Don't you wish you had a name as magnificent as this?"

Malik Solanka lived in a second-floor apartment in a building called Noor Ville on Methwold's Estate off Warden Road. The Venkats occupied the other apartment on that floor, and gave every indication of being a happy family: one, in fact, that Malik envied every day of his life. Now both apartment doors stood open, and children crowded wide-eyed and grave around stricken adults as Mr Venkat took his leave of his old life forever. From the depths of the Venkats' apartment came the noise of a crackly seventy-eight: a song by the Ink Spots, Mr Venkat's favourite group. The spectacle of Mrs Venkat crying her eyes out on his mother's shoulder hit little Malik Solanka hard. As the banker turned to go,

Malik suddenly called out to him. "Balasubramanyam Venkataraghavan!" And then, saying it faster and louder, until he was simultaneously gabbling and screaming: "Balasubramanyamvenkataraghavanbalasubramanyamvenkataraghavan*balasubramanyamvenkataraghavan*BALASUBRAMANYAMVENKATAR GHAVAN!"

The banker paused gravely. He was a small, bony man, kind-faced, bright-eyed. "That is very well said, and the speed is impressive too," he commented. "And because you have repeated it five times without a mistake, I will answer five questions, if you wish to ask them."

Where are you going? "I am going in search of knowledge and if possible of peace." Why aren't you wearing your office suit? "Because I have given up my employment." Why is Mrs Venkat crying? "That is a question for her." When are you coming back? "This step, Malik, is once and for all." What about Chandra? "He will understand one day." Don't you care about us any more? "That is the sixth question. Over the limit. Be a good child now. Be a good friend to your friend." Malik Solanka remembered his mother trying, after Mr Venkat went away down the hill, to explain the philosophy of the *sanyasi,* of a man's decision to give up all possessions and worldly connections, severing himself from life, in order to come closer to the Divine before it was time to die. Mr Venkat had left his affairs in good order; his family would be well provided for. But he would never return. Malik did not understand most of what he was being told, but he had a vivid comprehension of what Chandra meant when, later that day, he broke his father's old Ink Spots records and shouted: "I hate knowledge! And peace, too. I really hate peace *a lot.*"

When a man without faith mimicked the choices of the faithful, the result was likely to be both vulgar and inept. Professor Malik Solanka donned no loincloth, picked up no begging bowl. Instead of surrendering himself to the fortune of the street and the charity of strangers, he flew business class to JFK, checked briefly into the Lowell, called a real estate broker, and speedily lucked out, finding himself this commodious West Side sublet. Instead of heading for Manaus, Alice Springs or

Vladivostok, he had landed himself in a city in which he was not completely unknown, which was not completely unknown to him, in which he could speak the language and find his way around and understand, up to a point, the customs of the natives. He had acted without thinking, had been strapped into his airline seat before he allowed himself to reflect; then he'd simply accepted the imperfect choice his reflexes had made, agreed to proceed down the unlikely road on to which his feet, without prompting, had turned. A *sanyasi* in New York, a *sanyasi* with a duplex and credit card, was a contradiction in terms. Very well. He would be that contradiction and, in spite of his oxymoronic nature, pursue his goal. He too was in search of a quietus, of peace. So, his old self must somehow be cancelled, put away for good. It must not rise up like a spectre from the tomb to claim him at some future point, dragging him down into the sepulchre of the past. And if he failed, then he failed, but one did not contemplate what lay beyond failure while one was still trying to succeed. After all, Jay Gatsby, the highest bouncer of them all, failed too in the end, but lived out, before he crashed, that brilliant, brittle, gold-hatted, exemplary American life.

He awoke in his bed—fully dressed, again, with strong drink on his breath—without knowing how or when he'd reached it. With consciousness came fear of himself. Another night unaccounted for. Another blank snowstorm in the videotape. But as before there was no blood on his hands or clothes, no weapon on his person, not so much as a concrete lump. He lurched upright, grabbed the zapper and found the tail end of the local news on TV. Nothing about a Concrete Killer or a Panama Hat Man or a privileged beauty done to death. No breaking of a living doll. He fell back across the bed, breathing hard and fast. Then, kicking off his street shoes, he pulled the covers over his aching head.

He recognized this funk. Long ago in a Cambridge hostel he had been unable to rise and face his new undergraduate existence. Now as then, panic and demons rushed in at him from every side. He was vulnerable to demons. He heard their bat-wings flapping by his ears, felt their goblin fingers twining around his ankles to pull him down to that hell in which he didn't believe but which kept cropping up in his language, in his emotions, in the part of him that was not his to control. That growing part of him that was running wild, out of his feeble hands . . . where was Krysztof Waterford-Wajda when he needed him? Come on, Dubdub, knock at the door and pull me away from the edge of the yawning Pit.—But Dubdub didn't return from beyond Heaven's door to knock.

This wasn't it, Solanka told himself feverishly. This wasn't the story that had brought him all this way! Not this Jekyll and Hyde melodrama, a saga of a lower order entirely. There was no Gothic strain in the architecture of his life, no mad scientist's laboratory, no bubbling retorts, no gulped potion of demonic metamorphosis. Yet the fear, the funk, would not leave him. He drew the covers down more tightly over his head. He could smell the street on his clothes. There was no evidence linking him to any crime. Nor was he under investigation for anything at all. How many men, in an average Manhattan summer, wore Panama hats? Hundreds, at least? Why, then, was he tormenting himself so? Because if the knife was possible, so was this. And then the circumstances: three failures of nocturnal memory, three dead women. This was the conjunction that required his silence as absolutely as the knife in the dark but which he could not hide from himself. Also that stream of obscenities unknowingly spoken in Café Mozart. Not enough for any court to convict, but he was his own judge, and the jury was out.

Blearily, he dialled a number and waited through the interminable mechanized-voice preliminaries to receive his voice mail. *You have—one!—new message.—The following—one!—new message—has NOT been heard.—First message.* Then came Eleanor's voice, with which long ago he fell in love. "Malik, you say you want to forget yourself. I say you have already forgotten yourself. You say you don't want to be ruled by your anger. I say your anger has never ruled you more. I remember you though you have forgotten me. I remember you before that doll screwed up our lives: you used to be interested in everything. I loved that. I remember your gaiety, your terrible singing, your funny voices. You taught me to love cricket; now I want Asmaan to love it too. I remember your longing to know, of human beings, the best that we are capable of, but also to look without illusions at the worst. I remember your love of life, of our son, and of me. You abandoned us, but we have not abandoned you. Come home, darling. Please come home." Naked, courageous, heart-tearing stuff. But here was another gap. When had he spoken to Eleanor of anger and forgetting? Perhaps he had come home drunk and wanted to explain himself. Maybe he had left her a message, to which this was her answer. And she, as ever, had heard much more than he had said. Had heard, in short, his fear.

He made himself get up, stripped and showered. He was brewing coffee in the kitchen when he realized that the apartment was empty. Yet it was one of Wisława's days. Why wasn't she here? Solanka dialled her number. "Yes?" It was her voice all right. "Wisława?" he demanded. "Professor Solanka. Aren't you supposed to be working today?" There was a long pause. "Professor?" said Wisława's voice, sounding timid and small. "You do not remember?" He felt his body temperature dropping rapidly. "What? Remember what?" Now Wisława's voice grew tearful. "Professor, you fire me. You fire me, for what? For nothing. Of course you remember. And the words. Such words from an educated man, I never heard. After this, it's over for me. Even now that you call to ask me, I cannot return." Somebody spoke behind her, another woman's voice, and Wisława rallied, to add with considerable determination. "However, cost of my work is included in your contract. Since you fire me unjustly I will continue to receive this. I have spoken to landlord and they are agree. I think they will speak also to you. You know, I work for Mrs Jay long time." Malik Solanka put the receiver down without another word.

You're fired. As if in a movie. The red-skirted cardinal descends the golden steps to deliver the pope's adieu. The driver, a woman, waits in her little car, and when the cruel messenger leans into her window, he wears Solanka's face.

The city was being sprayed with the pesticide Anvil. Several birds, mostly from the Staten Island wetlands, had died of West Nile virus, and the mayor was taking no chances. Everyone was on high mosquito alert. Stay indoors at dusk! Wear long sleeves! During spraying, close all windows and turn all air-conditioning units off! Such interventionist radicalism, although not a single human being had contracted the illness since the beginning of the new millennium. (Later, a few cases were reported; but no deaths.) The timorousness of Americans in the face of the unknown, their overcompensation, had always made Europeans laugh. "A car backfires in Paris," Eleanor Solanka—even Eleanor, the least bitchy of human beings—liked to say, "and the next day a million Americans cancel their holidays."

Solanka had forgotten about the spraying, had walked for hours through the falling invisible poison. For a moment he considered blaming the pesticide for his memory loss. Asthmatics were having convulsions, lobsters were said to be dying by the thousand, environmentalists were squawking; why shouldn't he? But his natural fairness prevented him from going down this route. The source of his problems was likely to be of existential rather than chemical origin.

If you heard it, good Wisława, then it must be so. But you see, I was not aware . . . Aspects of his behaviour had been escaping from his control. If he were to seek professional help, no doubt a breakdown of some sort would be diagnosed. (If he were Bronisława Rhinehart, he would gladly take that diagnosis home with him and then start looking for somebody to sue.) It struck him with great force that a breakdown of some sort was precisely what he had been inviting all along. All those rhapsodies about wishing to be unmade! So now that certain chronological segments of himself had ceased to be in touch with others—now that he had literally dis-integrated in time—why was he so shocked? Be careful what you wish for, Malik. Remember W. W. Jacobs. The story of the monkey's paw.

He had come to New York as the Land Surveyor came to the Castle: in ambivalence, in extremis, and in unrealistic hope. He had found his billet, a more comfortable one than the poor Surveyor's, and ever since then had been roaming the streets, looking for a way in, telling himself that the great World-City could heal him, a city child, if he could only find the gateway to its magic, invisible, hybrid heart. This mystical proposition had clearly altered the continuum around him. Things appeared to proceed by logic, according to the laws of psychological verisimilitude and the deep inner coherences of metropolitan life, but in fact all was mystery. But perhaps his was not the only identity to be coming apart at the seams. Behind the façade of this age of gold, this time of plenty, the contradictions and impoverishment of the Western human individual, or let's say the human self in America, were deepening and widening. Perhaps that wider disintegration was also to be made visible in this city of fiery, jewelled garments and secret ash, in this time of public hedonism and private fear.

A change of direction was required. The story you finished was perhaps never the one you began. Yes! He would take charge of his life anew, binding his breaking selves together. Those changes in himself that he sought, he himself would initiate and make them. No more of this miasmic, absent drift. How had he ever persuaded himself that this money-mad burg would rescue him all by itself, this Gotham in which Jokers and Penguins were running riot with no Batman (or even Robin) to frustrate their schemes, this Metropolis built of Kryptonite in which no Superman dared set foot, where wealth was mistaken for riches and the joy of possession for happiness, where people lived such polished lives that the great rough truths of raw existence had been rubbed and buffed away, and in which human souls had wandered so separately for so long that they barely remembered how to touch; this city whose fabled electricity powered the electric fences that were being erected between men and men, and men and women, too? Rome did not fall because her armies weakened but because Romans forgot what being a Roman meant. Might this new Rome actually be more provincial than its provinces; might these new Romans have forgotten what and how to value, or had they never known? Were all empires so undeserving, or was this one particularly crass? Was nobody in all this bustling endeavour and material plenitude engaged, any longer, on the deep quarry-work of the mind and heart? O Dream-America, was civilization's quest to end in obesity and trivia, at Roy Rogers and Planet Hollywood, in *USA Today* and on E!; or in million-dollar-game-show greed or fly-on-the-wall voyeurism; or in the eternal confessional booth of Ricki and Oprah and Jerry, whose guests murdered each other after the show; or in a spurt of gross-out dumb-and-dumber comedies designed for young people who sat in darkness howling their ignorance at the silver screen; or even at the unattainable tables of Jean-Georges Vongerichten and Alain Ducasse? What of the search for the hidden keys that unlock the doors of exaltation? Who demolished the City on the Hill and put in its place a row of electric chairs, those dealers in death's democracy, where everyone, the innocent, the mentally deficient, the guilty, could come to die side by side? Who paved Paradise and put up a parking lot? Who settled for George W. Gush's boredom and Al Bore's gush? Who let Charlton Heston out of his cage and then asked why children were getting shot? What, America, of the Grail? O ye Yankee Galahads, ye Hoosier Lancelots, O Parsifals of the stockyards, what of the Table Round? He felt a flood bursting in him and did not hold it back. Yes, it had seduced him, America; yes, its brilliance aroused him, and its vast potency too, and he was compromised by this seduction. What he opposed in it he must also attack in himself. It made him want what it promised and eternally withheld. Everyone was an American now, or at least Americanized: Indians, Iranians, Uzbeks, Japanese, Lilliputians, all. America was the world's playing field, its rule book, umpire and ball. Even anti-Americanism was Americanism in disguise, conceding, as it did, that America was the only game in town and the matter of America the only business at hand; and so, like everyone, Malik Solanka now walked its high corridors cap in hand, a supplicant at its feast; but that did not mean he could not look it in the eye.

Arthur had fallen, Excalibur was lost, and dark Mordred was king. Beside him on the throne of Camelot sat the queen, his sister, the witch Morgan le Fay.

Professor Malik Solanka prided himself on being a practical man. Deft with his hands, he could thread a needle, mend his own clothes, iron a dress shirt. For a time, when he first began to make his philosophy dolls, he had apprenticed himself to a Cambridge tailor and learned to cut the clothes his pint-sized thinkers would wear; also the street-fashion knockoffs he created for Little Brain. Wisława or no, he knew how to keep his living quarters clean. Henceforth he would apply the same principles of good housekeeping to his inner life as well.

He set off along Seventieth Street with the Chinese cleaners' purple laundry bag slung over his right shoulder. Turning onto Columbus, he overheard the following soliloquy. "You remember my ex-wife, Erin. Tess's mom. Yeah, the actress; these days she does mainly commercials. So guess what? We're seeing each other again. Pretty weird, huh. After two years of thinking she was the enemy, and five more of better but still tricky relations! I started inviting her to come over sometimes with Tess. Tess likes her mom to be around, to tell the truth. And then one night. Yeah, it was one of those Then One Night things. There was a point at which I went over and sat down next to her on the settee instead of staying in my usual chair way over across the other side of the room. You know, my desire for her never went away, it just got buried under a heap of other stuff, a whole heap of anger, to tell the truth, and so now it all just poured out, boom! An ocean of it. To tell the truth the seven years had backed up a whole load of it, desire, that is, and maybe the anger made it even more intense, so it was amazingly bigger than it used to be. But so here's the thing. I walk over to the settee and what happens, happens, and afterwards she says, 'You know, when you came over to me, I didn't know if you were going to hit me or kiss me.' I guess I didn't know either until I reached the settee. To tell the truth."

All this spoken into the air at high volume by a gangling, frizz-haired Art Garfunkel-y man in his forties, out walking a brindled dog.

It was a moment before Solanka saw the cell-phone headset through the halo of ginger hair. These days we all come across like rummies or crackpots, Solanka thought, confiding our secrets to the wind as we stroll along. Here was a striking example of the disintegrated contemporary reality that was preoccupying him. Dog-walking Art, existing for the moment only in the Telephone Continuum—lingering in the sound of silence—was quite unaware that in the alternative, or Seventieth Street Continuum, he was revealing his deepest intimacies to strangers. This about New York Professor Solanka liked a lot—this sense of being crowded out by other people's stories, of walking like a phantom through a city that was in the middle of a story which didn't need him as a character. And the man's ambivalence to his wife, Solanka thought: for wife, read America. And maybe I'm still walking over to the settee.

The day's newspapers brought unexpected comfort. He must have turned on the TV too late to hear the day's main developments in the Sky-Ren-Bindy murder investigation. Now with lifting heart he read that the team of detectives—three precincts had joined forces on this inquiry—had hauled the three beaux in for questioning. They had later been released, and no charges had been filed for the moment, but the detectives' demeanour had been grave and the young men had been warned not to head off in a hurry for any Riviera yachts or South-east Asian beaches. Unnamed sources close to the investigation said that the "Mr Panama Hat" theory was being heavily discounted, which clearly implied that the suspect boyfriends were thought to have cooked up the mysterious stalker between them. Stash, Horse and Club looked, in the photos, like three very scared young men. Press comment, wasting no time, instantly linked the unsolved triple murder to the Nicole Brown Simpson killing and the death of little JonBenét Ramsey. "In such cases," one editorial concluded, "it's wisest to keep the search pretty close to home."

* * *

"Can I talk to you?" When he got back to the apartment, giddy with relief, Mila was waiting for him on the stoop, sans entourage, but holding in her arms a half-life-size Little Brain doll. The transformation in her manner was startling. Gone was the street-goddess swagger, the queen-of-the-world attitude. This was a shy, gawky young woman with stars in her green eyes. "What you said at the movies. Are you, it has to be you, right? You're *that* Professor Solanka? 'Little Brain created by Prof. Malik Solanka.' You brought her into being, you gave her life. Oh, wow. I even have all the videotapes of *Adventures,* and for my twenty-first birthday my dad went to a dealer and bought me the first-draft script of the Galileo episode, you know, before they made you cut all the blasphemy out?, that's like my most treasured possession. Okay, please say I'm right, because otherwise I'm making such a fool of myself my cool is totally blown forever. Well, it's pretty blown anyway, you have no idea what Eddie and the guys thought of me coming over here with a *doll,* for Chrissake." Solanka's natural defences, already lowered on account of his lightened heart, were overwhelmed by such extreme passion. "Yes," he conceded. "Yes, that's me." She screamed at the top of her voice, leaping high in the air about three inches away from his face. "No way!" she then hooted, unable to stop hopping up and down. "Oh my *God.* I have to tell you, Professor: you totally *rock.* And your L.B., this little lady right here, has been my like total *obsession* for most of the last ten *years.* I watch every move she makes. And as you spotted, she's only the *basis* and *inspiration* for my whole current *personal style.*" She stuck a hand out. "Mila. Mila Milo. Don't laugh. It was Milosevic originally, but my dad wanted something everyone could say. I mean, this is America, right? Make it easy. Mee-la My-lo." Stretching the vowels out exaggeratedly, she pulled a face, then grinned. "Sounds like, I don't know, *farm fertilizer.* Or maybe *cereal.*"

He felt the old anger surge in him as she spoke, the huge, unassuaged Little Brain anger that had remained unexpressed, inexpressible, all these years. This was the anger that had led directly to the episode of the knife. . . . He made an immense effort and forced it down. This was the first day of his new phase. Today there would be no red mist, no obscene tirade, no fury-induced memory blackout. Today he would face the demon and wrestle it to the mat. Breathe, he told himself. Breathe.

Mila was looking worried. "Professor? Are you okay?" He nodded rapidly, yes, yes. And briefly said: "Come inside, please. I want to tell you a story."

PART TWO

8

His earliest dolls, the little characters he had made, when younger, to populate the houses he'd designed, were painstakingly whittled out of soft whitewoods, clothes and all, and afterwards painted, the clothing in vivid colours and the faces full of tiny but significant details: here a woman's cheek swollen to hint at toothache, there a fan crow's feet at the corners of some jolly fellow's eyes. Since those distant beginnings he had lost interest in the houses, while the people he made had grown in stature and psychological complexity. Nowadays they started out as clay figurines. Clay, of which God, who didn't exist, made man, who did. Such was the paradox of human life: its creator was fictional, but life itself was a fact.

He thought of them as people. When he was bringing them into being, they were as real to him as anyone else he knew. Once he had created them, however, once he knew their stories, he was happy to let them go their own way: other hands could manipulate them for the television camera, other craftsmen could cast and replicate them. The character and the story were all he cared about. The rest was just playing with toys.

The only one of his creations with whom he fell in love—the only one he didn't want anyone else to handle—would break his heart. This was, of course, Little Brain: first a doll, later a puppet, then an animated cartoon, and afterwards an actress, or, at various other times, a talk-show host, gymnast, ballerina or supermodel, in a Little Brain outfit. Her first, late-night, series, of which nobody expected much, had been made more or less exactly as Malik Solanka desired. In that time-travelling quest programme, "L.B." was the disciple, while the philosophers she met were the real heroes. After the move to prime time, however, the channel's executives soon weighed in. The original format was deemed much too highbrow. Little Brain was the star, and the new show had to be built around her, it was decreed. Instead of travelling constantly, she needed a location and a cast of recurring characters to play off. She needed a love interest, or better still a series of suitors, which would allow the hottest young male actors of the time to guest-star on the show and wouldn't tie her down. Above all, she needed comedy: smart comedy, brainy comedy, yes, but there must definitely be a great many laughs. Probably even a laugh track. Writers could, would, be provided to work with Solanka to develop his hit idea for the mass audience that would now come into contact with it. This was what he wanted, wasn't it—to move into the mainstream? If an idea didn't develop, it died. These were the facts of televisual life.

Thus Little Brain moved to Brain Street in Brainville, with a whole family and neighbourhood posse of Brains: she had an older brother called Little Big Brain, there was a science laboratory down the street called the Brain Drain, and even a laconic cowboy movie star neighbour (John Brayne). It was painful stuff, but the lower the comedy stooped, the higher the ratings soared. *Brain Street* wiped out the memory of *The Adventures of Little Brain* in a minute and settled in for a long, lucrative run. At a certain point Malik Solanka bowed to the inevitable and walked off the programme. But he kept his credit on the show, ensured that his "moral rights" in his creation were protected, and negotiated a healthy share of the merchandising income. He couldn't watch the show any longer. But Little Brain gave every indication of being happy to see him go.

She had outgrown her creator—literally; she was life-size now, and several inches taller than Solanka—and was making her own way in the world. Like Hawkeye or Sherlock Holmes or Jeeves, she had transcended the work that created her, had attained the fiction's version of freedom. She now endorsed products on television, opened supermarkets, gave after-dinner speeches, emceed gong shows. By the time *Brain Street* had run its course she was a fully-fledged television personality. She got her own talk show, made guest appearances in new hit comedies, appeared on the catwalk for Vivienne Westwood, and was attacked, for demeaning women, by Andrea Dworkin—"smart women don't have to be dolls"—and, for emasculating men, by Karl Lagerfeld ("what true man wants a woman with a bigger shall I say *vocabulary* than his own?"). Both critics then immediately agreed, for high consultancy fees, to join the concept group behind "L.B.", a team known at the BBC as the Little Brains Trust. Little Brain's bubblegum-poppy debut movie *Brainwave* was a rare false step, and flopped badly, but the first volume of her memoirs (!) went straight to the top of the Amazon bestseller charts as soon as it was announced, months before it was even published, clocking up over a quarter of a million sales in pre-orders alone, from hysterical fans who were determined to be first in line. After publication it broke all records; a second, third and fourth volume followed, one per year, and sold, at the most conservative estimate, over fifty million copies worldwide.

She had become the Maya Angelou of the doll world, as relentless an autobiographer as that other caged bird, her life the model for millions of young people—its humble beginnings, its years of struggle, its triumphant overcomings; and, O, her dauntlessness in the face of poverty and cruelty! O, her joy when Fate chose her to be one of its Elect!—among whom West Seventieth Street's own empress of cool, Mila Milo, was proud to be numbered. (Her unlived life! Solanka thought. Her fictive history, part Dungeons & Dragons fairy tale, part dirt-poor ghetto saga, and all ghostwritten for her by anonymous persons of phantom talent! This was not the life he had imagined for her; this had nothing to do with the back-story he had dreamed up for his pride and joy. This L.B. was an impostor, with the wrong history, the wrong dialogue, the wrong personality, the wrong wardrobe, the wrong *brain.* Somewhere in medialand there was a Château d'If in which the real Little Brain was being held captive. Somewhere there was a Doll in an Iron Mask.)

The extraordinary thing about her fan base was its catholicity: boys dug her as much as girls, adults as much as children. She crossed all boundaries of language, race and class. She became, variously, her admirers' ideal lover or confidante or goal. Her first book of memoirs was originally placed by the Amazon people in the *non-fiction* lists. The decision to move it, and the subsequent volumes, across into the world of make-believe was resisted by both readers and staff. Little Brain, they argued, was no longer a simulacrum. She was a phenomenon. The fairy's wand had touched her, and she was real.

All this Malik Solanka witnessed from a distance with growing horror. This creature of his own imagining, born of his best self and purest endeavour, was turning before his eyes into the kind of monster of tawdry celebrity he most profoundly abhorred. His original and now obliterated Little Brain had been genuinely smart, able to hold her own with Erasmus or Schopenhauer. She had been beautiful and sharp-tongued, but she had swum in the sea of ideas, living the life of the mind. This revised edition, over which he had long ago lost creative control, had the intellect of a slightly over-average chimpanzee. Day by day she became a creature of the entertainment microverse, her music videos—yes, she was a recording artist now!—out-raunching Madonna's, her appearances at premieres out-Hurleying every starlet who ever trod the red carpet in a dangerous frock. She was a video game and a cover girl, and this, remember, in her personal appearance mode at least, was essentially a woman whose own head was completely concealed inside the iconic doll's. Yet many aspirants to stardom vied for the role, even though the Little Brains Trust—which had become too big for the BBC to hold on to, and had broken away to become a booming independent business, projected to break the billion-dollar barrier some day soon—insisted on utter confidentiality; the names of the women who brought Little Brain to life were never revealed, though rumours abounded, and the paparazzi of Europe and America, bringing their own special expertise to bear, claimed to be able to identify this actress or that model by those other, non-facial attributes which Little Brain so proudly put on display.

Astonishingly, the glamour-puss transformation lost latex-headed Little Brain no fans, but brought her a new legion of adult male admirers. She had become unstoppable, giving press conferences at which she spoke of setting up her own film production company, launching her own magazine in which beauty hints, lifestyle advice, and cutting-edge contemporary culture would all receive the special Little Brain treatment, and even going nationwide, in the U.S.A., on cable television. There would be a Broadway show—she was in discussion with all the major players in the musical game, dear Tim and dear Elton and dear Cameron and of course dear, dear Andrew—and a new, big-budget movie was also planned. This would not repeat the corny teeny-bopper mistakes of the first but grow "organically" out of the zillion-selling memoirs. "Little Brain is not some plastic-fantastic Barbie Spice," she told the world—she had started speaking of herself in the third person—"and the new film will be very human, and quality all the way. Marty, Bobby, Brad, Gwynnie, Meg, Julia, Tom and Nic are all interested; also Jenny, Puffy, Maddy, Robbie, Mick: I guess everybody these days wants a Little Brain."

The ballooning triumph of Little Brain inevitably occasioned much comment and analysis. Her admirers were jeered at for their lowbrow obsession, but at once eminent theatre folk came forward to speak of the ancient tradition of mask theatre, its origins in Greece and Japan. "The actor in the mask is liberated from her normality, her everydayness. Her body acquires remarkable new freedoms. The mask dictates all this. The mask acts." Professor Solanka remained aloof, refusing all invitations to discuss his out-of-control creation. The money, however, he was unable to refuse. Royalties continued to pour into his bank account. He was compromised by greed, and the compromise sealed his lips. Contractually bound not to attack the goose that laid the golden eggs, he had to bottle up his thoughts and, in keeping his own counsel, filled up with the bitter bile of his many discontents. With every new media initiative spearheaded by the character he had once delineated with such sprightliness and care, his impotent fury grew.

In *Hello!* magazine, Little Brain—for a reported seven-figure fee—allowed readers an intimate look at her beautiful country home, which was, apparently, an old Queen Anne pile not far from the Prince of Wales in Gloucestershire, and Malik Solanka, whose original inspiration had been the Rijksmuseum doll's houses, was thunderstruck by the effrontery of this latest inversion. So now the big houses would belong to these uppity dolls, while most of the human race still lived in cramped accommodation? The wrongness—in his view the moral bankruptcy—of this particular development alarmed him profoundly; still, far from bankrupted himself, he held his tongue and took the dirty money. For ten years, as "Art Garfunkel" might have said into his mouthpiece, he had backed up a whole heap of self-loathing and rage. Fury stood above him like a cresting Hokusai wave. Little Brain was his delinquent child grown into a rampaging giantess, who now stood for everything he despised and trampled beneath her giant feet all the high principles he had brought her into being to extol; including, evidently, his own.

The L.B. phenomenon had seen off the 1990s and showed no sign of running out of steam in the new millennium. Malik Solanka was forced to admit a terrible truth. He hated Little Brain.

Meanwhile, nothing to which he turned his hand was bearing much fruit. He continued to approach the newly successful British claymation companies with characters and storylines but was told, kindly and unkindly, that his concepts weren't of the moment. In a young person's business, he had become something much worse than merely older: he was old-fashioned. At a meeting to discuss his proposal for a feature-length claymation life of Niccolò Machiavelli, he did his best to speak the new language of commercialism. The film would, of course, use anthropomorphic animals to represent human originals. "This really has everything," he awkwardly enthused. "The golden age of Florence! The Medicis in their splendour—cool clay aristocats! Simonetta Vespussy, the most beautiful cat in the world, being immortalized by that young hound Barkicelli. The Birth of Feline Venus! The Rite of Pussy Spring! Meanwhile Amerigo Vespussy, that old sea lion, her uncle, sails off to discover America! Savona-Roland the Rat Monk ignites the Bonfire of the Vanities! And at the heart of it all, a mouse. Not just any old Mickey, though: this is the mouse who invented realpolitik, the brilliant mouse playwright, the distinguished public rodent, the republican mouse who survived being tortured by the cruel cat prince and dreamed in exile of a day of glorious return . . ." He was interrupted unceremoniously by an executive from the money people, a plump boy who could not have been more than twenty-three years old. "Florence is great," he said. "No question. I love that. And Niccolò, what did you call him?, Mousiavelli sounds . . . possible. But what you have here—this treatment—let me put it like this. It just doesn't *deserve* Florence. Maybe, yeah?, it's not a good time right now for the Renaissance in plasticine."

He could go back to writing books, he thought, but soon found that his heart wasn't in it. The inexorability of happenstance, the way events have of deflecting you from your course, had corrupted him and left him good for nothing. His old life had left him forever and the new world he'd created had slipped through his fingers too. He was James Mason, a falling star, drinking hard, drowning in defeats, and that damn doll was flying high in the Judy Garland role. With Pinocchio, Geppetto's troubles ended when the blasted puppet became a real, live boy; with Little Brain, as with Galatea, that's when they began. Professor Solanka in drunken wrath issued anathemas against his ungrateful Frankendoll: Out of my sight let her go! Begone, unnatural child. Lo, I know you not.

You shall not bear my name. Never send to ask for me, nor never seek my blessing. And call me father no more.

Out she went from his home in all her versions—the sketches, maquettes, tableaux, the infinite proliferation of her in all her myriad versions, paper, cloth, wood, plastic, animation cell, videotape, film; and with her, inevitably, went a once-precious version of himself. He hadn't been able to bear to perform the act of expulsion personally. Eleanor agreed to take on the task. Eleanor, who could see the crisis mounting—the red cracks in the eyes of the man she loved, the alcohol, the rudderless wandering—said in her gentle, efficient way, "Just go out for the day and leave it to me." Her own career in publishing was on hold, Asmaan being all the career she needed for the moment, but she had been a high flier and was greatly in demand. This, too, she concealed from him, though he wasn't a fool, and knew what it meant when Morgen Franz and others rang to speak to her and stayed on the phone, coaxing, for thirty minutes at a time. She was wanted, he understood that, everyone was wanted except him, but at least he could have this paltry revenge; he could not want something too, even if it was only that two-faced creature, that traitress, that, that, doll.

So he left home on the agreed day, stamping over Hampstead Heath at high speed—they lived in a capacious, double-fronted house on Willow Road and had always both rejoiced in having the Heath, North London's treasure, its lung, just outside their door—and in his absence Eleanor had everything properly packed and taken away to a long-term storage facility. He'd have preferred the whole caboodle to end up at the Highbury garbage dump, but on this, too, he compromised. Eleanor had insisted. She had strong archival instincts and, needing her to take charge of the project, he waved a hand at her strictures as if at a mosquito, and didn't argue. He walked for hours, allowing the Heath's cool music to soothe his savage breast, the quiet heart-rhythms of its slow paths and trees, and, later in the day, the sweet strings of a summer concert in the grounds of the Iveagh Bequest. When he got back, Little Brain was gone. Or, almost gone. For, unknown to Eleanor, one doll had been locked away in a cupboard in Solanka's study. And there she remained.

The house felt emptied when he returned, voided, the way a house feels after the death of a child. Solanka felt as if he had suddenly aged by twenty or thirty years; as if, divorced from the best work of his youthful enthusiasms, he at last stood face-to-face with ruthless Time. Waterford-Wajda had spoken of such a feeling at Addenbrooke's years ago. "Life becomes very, I don't know, finite. You realize you don't have anything, you belong nowhere, you're just using things for a while. The inanimate world laughs at you: you'll be going soon, but it will be staying on. Not very profound, Solly, it's Pooh Bear philosophy, I know, but it rips you to pieces all the same." This wasn't just the death of a child, Solanka was thinking: more like a killing. Kronos devouring his daughter. He was the murderer of his fictional offspring: not flesh of his flesh but dream of his dream. There was, however, a living child still awake, overexcited by the day's events: the arrival of the moving van, the packers, the steady come and go of boxes. "I was helping, Daddy," eager Asmaan greeted his father. "I helped send Little Brain away." He was bad at compound consonants, saying *b* for *br:* Little B'ain. That's about right, Solanka thought. She became the bane of my life. "Yes," he answered absently. "Well done." But Asmaan had more on his mind. "Why did she have to go away, Daddy? Mummy said you wanted her to go away." Oh, Mummy said, did she. Thanks, Mummy. He glared at Eleanor, who shrugged. "Really, I didn't know what to tell him. This one's for you."

On children's television, in comic books, and in audio versions of her legendary memoirs, Little Brain's protean persona had reached out and captured the hearts of children even younger than Asmaan Solanka. Three was not too young to fall in love with this most universally appealing of contemporary icons. "L.B." could be driven out of the house on Willow Road, but could she be expelled from the imagination of her creator's child? "I want her back," Asmaan said emphatically. Back was *bat.* "I want Little B'ain." The pastoral symphony of

Hampstead Heath gave way to the jangling discords of family life. Solanka felt the clouds gathering around him once again. "It was just time for her to go," he said, and picked up Asmaan, who wriggled hard against him, responding unconsciously, as children do, to his father's bad mood. "No! Put me down! Put me down!" He was exhausted and cranky and so was Solanka. "I want to watch a video," he demanded. *Viduwo.* "I want to watch a Little B'ain viduwo." Malik Solanka, unbalanced by the impact of the absence of the Little Brain archive, of her exile to some Doll-Elba, some Black Sea town, such as Ovid's barren Tomis, for unwanted, used-up toys, had been plunged quite unexpectedly into a condition resembling deep mourning and received his son's end-of-day petulance as an unacceptable provocation. "It's too late. Behave yourself," he snapped, and Asmaan, in return, crouched down on the front-room rug and produced his latest trick: a burst of impressively convincing crocodile tears. Solanka, no less childishly than his son, and without the excuse of being three years old, rounded on Eleanor. "I suppose this is your way of punishing me," he said. "If you didn't want to get rid of the stuff, why not just say so. Why use him. I should have known I'd come back to trouble. To some manipulative crap like this."

"Please don't let him hear you talking to me that way," she said, scooping Asmaan into her arms. "He understands everything." Solanka noted that the boy suffered himself to be taken off to bed by his mother without the slightest wriggle, nuzzling into Eleanor's long neck. "As a matter of fact," she went on levelly, "after doing this entire day's work for you, I thought, stupidly as it turns out, that we might use it as the moment for a new beginning. I took a leg of lamb out of the freezer and rubbed it with cumin, I called the flower shop, oh God this is so silly, and had them deliver nasturtiums. And you'll find three bottles of Tignanello on the kitchen table. One for pleasure, two for too much, three for bed. Perhaps you remember that. It's your line. But I'm sure you can't be bothered any more to have a romantic candlelit supper with your boring, no-longer-young wife."

They had been drifting apart, she into the engulfing, full-time experience of first-time motherhood, which fulfilled her so deeply and which she was so eager to repeat, he into that fog of failure and self-disgust which was thickened, more and more, by drink. Yet the marriage had not broken, thanks in large measure to Eleanor's generous heart, and to Asmaan. Asmaan, who loved books and could be read to for hours; Asmaan on his garden swing, asking Malik to twist him around and around so that he could untwist in a high-speed counter-clockwise blur; Asmaan riding on his father's shoulders, ducking his head under doorways ("I'm being very careful, Daddy!"); Asmaan chasing and being chased, Asmaan hiding under bedclothes and piles of pillows; Asmaan attempting to sing "Rock Around the Clock"—*rot around the tot*—most of all, perhaps, Asmaan bouncing. He loved to bounce on his parents' bed, with his soft toys cheering him on. "Look at me," he'd cry—look was *loot*—"I'm bouncing very well! I'm bouncing higher and higher!"

He was the young incarnation of their old high-bouncing love. When their child was flooding their lives with delight, Eleanor and Malik Solanka could take refuge in a fantasy of undamaged familial contentment. At other times, however, the cracks were becoming ever easier to see. She found his self-absorbed misery, his constant railing against imagined slights, duller and more of a strain than she was ever cruel enough to show; while he, locked into his downward spiral, accused her of ignoring him and his concerns. In bed, whispering so as not to wake Asmaan sleeping on a mattress on the floor beside them, she complained that Malik never initiated sex; he retorted that she had lost interest in sex entirely except at the baby-making time of the month. And at that time of the month, routinely, they fought: yes, no, please, I can't, why not, because I don't want to, but I need it so badly, well, I don't need it at all, but I don't want this lovely little boy to be an only child like me, and I don't want to be a father again at my age, I'll already be over seventy before Asmaan is twenty years old. And then tears and anger and, as often as not, a night for Solanka in the guest bedroom.

Advice to husbands, he thought bitterly: make sure the spare room is comfortable, because sooner or later, pal, that's your room.

Eleanor was waiting tensely by the stairs for his reply to her invitation to a night of peace and love. Time passed in slow beats, arriving at a hinge moment. He could, if he had the wit and desire, accept her invitation, and then, yes, a good evening would follow: delicious food, and, if at this age three bottles of Tignanello didn't send him straight to sleep, then no doubt the lovemaking would be up to the old high standard. But now there was a worm in Paradise, and he failed the test. "You're ovulating, I suppose," he said, and she jerked her face away from him as if he'd slapped her. "No," she lied, and then, giving in to the inevitable, "Oh, all right, yes. But can't we just, oh, I wish you could see how desperately, oh, to hell with it, what's the use." She carried Asmaan away, unable to hold back her tears. "I'm going to go to sleep, too, when I put him to bed, okay?" she said, weeping angrily. "Do what you like. Just don't leave the lamb in the fucking Aga. Take it out and throw it in the fucking bin."

As Asmaan went upstairs in his mother's arms, Solanka heard the worry in his tired young voice. "Daddy's not cross," Asmaan said, reassuring himself, wanting to be reassured. Cross was *toss.* "Daddy doesn't want to send me away."

Alone in the kitchen, Professor Malik Solanka began to drink. The wine was as good and as powerful as ever, but he wasn't drinking for pleasure. Steadily, he worked his way through the bottles, and as he did, the demons came crawling out through the several orifices of his body, sliding down his nose and out through his ears, dribbling and squeezing through every opening they could find. By the bottom of the first bottle they were dancing on his eyeballs, his fingernails, they had wrapped their rough lapping tongues around his throat, their spears were jabbing at his genitals, and all he could hear was their scarlet song of shrill, most horrid hate. He had come through self-pity now and entered a terrible, blaming anger, and by the bottom of the second bottle, as his head slopped about on his neck, the demons were kissing him with their forked tongues and their tails were wrapped around his penis, rubbing and squeezing, and as he listened to their dirty talk, the unforgivable blame for what he had become had begun to settle on the woman upstairs, she who was nearest to hand, the traitress who had refused to destroy his enemy, his nemesis, the doll, she who had poured the poison of Little Brain into the brain of his child, turning the son against the father, she who had destroyed the peace of his home life by preferring the uncreated child of her obsession to her actually existing husband, she, his wife, his betrayer, his one great foe. The third bottle fell, half unfinished, across the kitchen table that she had so lovingly set for dinner *à deux,* using her mother's old lace tablecloth and the best cutlery and a pair of long-stemmed red Bohemian wineglasses, and as the red fluid spilled across the old lace, he remembered that he'd forgotten the damn lamb, and when he opened the Aga door, the smoke poured out and set off the smoke detector in the ceiling, and the screaming of the alarm was the laughter of the demons, and to stop it STOP IT he had to get the step stool and climb up on unsteady wine-dark legs to take the battery pack out of the damn fool thing, okay, okay, but even when he'd done that without breaking his goddamn neck, the demons went right on laughing their screaming laughter, and the room was still full of smoke, goddamn her, couldn't she even have done this one small thing, and what would it take to stop the screaming in his head, this screaming like a knife, like a knife in his brain in his ear in his eye in his stomach in his heart in his soul, couldn't the bitch just have taken the meat out and put it right there, on the carving board next to the sharpening steel, the long fork and the knife, the carving knife, the knife.

It was a big house and the smoke alarm had not woken Eleanor or Asmaan, who was already in her bed, Malik's bed. Fat lot of use that alarm system turned out to be, huh. And here he was standing above them in the dark and here in his hand was the carving knife, and there was no alarm system to warn them against him, was there, Eleanor lying on her back with her mouth slightly open and a low burr of a snore rumbling in her nose, Asmaan on his side, curled tightly into her, sleeping the pure deep sleep of innocence and trust. Asmaan murmured inaudibly in his sleep and the sound of his faint voice broke through the demons' shrieking and brought his father to his senses. Before him lay his only child, the one living being under this roof who still knew that the world was a place of wonders and life was sweet and the present moment was everything and the future was infinite and didn't need to be thought about, while the past was useless and fortunately gone for good and he, a child wrapped in the soft sorcerer's cloak of childhood, was loved beyond words, and safe. Malik Solanka panicked. What was he doing standing over these two sleepers with a, with a, knife, he wasn't the sort of person who would do a thing like this, you read about those persons every day in the yellow press, coarse men and sly women who slaughtered their babies and ate their grandmothers, cold serial murderers and tormented paedophiles and unashamed sexual abusers and wicked stepfathers and dumb violent Neanderthal apes and all the world's ill-educated uncivilized brutes, and those were other persons entirely, no persons of that nature resided in this house, ergo he, Professor Malik Solanka formerly of King's College in the University of Cambridge, he of all people could not be in here holding in his drunken hand a savage instrument of death. Q.E.D. And anyway, I never was any good with the meat, Eleanor. It was always you who carved.

The doll, he thought with a belching, vinous start. Of course! That satanic doll was to blame. He had sent all the avatars of the she-devil out of the house, but one remained. That had been his mistake. She had crawled out of her cupboard and down through his nose and given him the carving knife and sent him to do her bloody work. But he knew where she was hiding. She couldn't hide from him. Professor Solanka turned and left the bedroom, knife in hand, muttering, and if Eleanor opened her eyes after he'd gone, he did not know it; if she had watched his retreating back and knew and judged him, it must be for her to say.

It had grown dark outside on West Seventieth Street. Little Brain was on his lap as he finished speaking. Its garments were slashed and torn and you could see where the knife had made deep incisions in its body. "Even after I stabbed her, as you see, I couldn't leave her behind. All the way to America I held her body in my arms." Mila's own doll silently interrogated its damaged twin. "Now you've heard everything, which is a great deal more than you wanted," Solanka said. "You know how this thing has ruined my life." Mila Milo's green eyes were on fire. She came over and caught up both his hands between her own. "I don't believe it," she said. "Your life isn't ruined. And these—come on, Professor!—these are just *dolls*."

9

"There's a look you sometimes get that reminds me of my father before he died," Mila Milo said, blithely unaware of how that sentence might be received by its subject. "Kind of indistinct, like a picture where the photographer's hand shook a little? Like Robin Williams in that movie where he's always out of focus. I once asked Dad what it meant and he said it was the look of a person who had spent too much time around other human beings. The human race is a life sentence, he said, it's a rough confinement, and sometimes we all need to break out of jail. He was a writer, a poet mostly but a novelist also, you won't have heard of him, but in Serbo-Croat he's considered pretty good. More than pretty good, actually, quite amazing, one of the best of the best. *Nobelisablé,* as the French say, but he never got it. Didn't live long enough, I guess. Still. Take it from me. He was good. The depth of his connection to the natural world, his feeling for the ancients, for folklore: he was one of a kind. Hobgoblins jumping in and out of flowers, I teased him. The flower inside the goblin would be better, he answered. The memory of a pure shining river that lingers in Satan's heart. You have to understand that religion was important for him. He lived in cities mostly, but his soul was in the hills. An old soul, people called him. But he was young at heart, too, you know? He really was. A barrel of monkeys. Most of the time. I don't know how he managed it. They never let up on him, they kept messing with his head. We lived in Paris for years after he got out from under Tito, I attended the American School there until I was eight, nearly nine, my mom unfortunately passed when I was three, three and a half, breast cancer, what can you do, it just killed her real fast and real painfully, may she rest in peace. Anyway, so he would get letters from home and I would open them for him and there, stamped on the front page of a letter from I don't know his *sister* or someone was a big official stamp saying, *This letter has not been censored.* HA! In the mid-eighties I came with him to New York to attend the big PEN conference, the famous one when there were all those parties, one at the Temple of Dendur in the Metropolitan and another at Saul and Gayfryd Steinberg's apartment, and nobody could decide which was grander, and Norman Mailer invited George Shultz to speak at the Public Library and so the South Africans boycotted the event because he was, like, pro-apartheid, and Shultz's security people wouldn't let Bellow in because he'd forgotten his invitation, so that made him a possible terrorist, until Mailer vouched for him, Bellow must have liked *that*! and then the women writers protested because the platform speakers were mostly men, and either Susan Sontag or Nadine Gordimer scolded them because, she said, Nadine or Susan, I forget, literature isn't an equal opportunity employer. And Cynthia Ozick I think it was accused Bruno Kreisky of being an anti-Semite even though he was a, a Jew and b, the European politician who'd taken in the most Russian-Jewish refugees, and all this because he'd had a meeting with Arafat, one meeting, so that makes Ehud Barak and Clinton *really* anti-Semitic, right?, I mean it's going to be Jew-Haters International down there at Camp David. And anyway Dad spoke, too, the conference had some grand title like 'The Imagination of the Writer Versus the Imagination of the State', and after somebody, I've forgotten,

Breytenbach or Oz, someone like that, said that the state had no imagination, Dad said that on the contrary, not only did it have an imagination, it also had a sense of humour, and he would give an example of a joke by the state, and then he told the story of the letter that had not been censored, and I sat there in the audience feeling so proud because everybody laughed and after all I was the one who opened the letter. I went with him to every session, are you kidding?, I was crazy for writers, I'd been a writer's daughter all my life and books to me were like the greatest thing, and it was so cool because they let me sit in on everything even though I was only small. It was so great to see my dad finally with his like peers and getting so much respect, and besides, here were all these names walking around attached to the real people they belonged to, Donald Barthelme, Günter Grass, Czeslaw Milosz, Grace Paley, John Updike, everyone. But at the end my father had that look on his face, the one like the one on yours, and he left me with Aunt Kitty from Chelsea, not my real aunt, she and Dad had a thing for about five minutes—you should have seen him with women, he was this big sexy guy with huge hands and a thick moustache like I guess Stalin, and he would look women in the eye and start talking about animals in heat, wolves, for instance, and that was it, they were gone. I swear to God these ladies would actually make a line, he'd go up to his hotel room and they'd form right up outside, a real honest to goodness line, the greatest women you can imagine, just weak at the knees with lust; and it's lucky I liked to read a lot, and also there was American TV to watch for once, so I was okay in the other room, I was fine, though a lot of times I wanted to go out and ask those women waiting around for it to be their turn, like, don't you have something better to do, you know?, it's only his pecker for Chrissakes, get a life. Yeah, I used to shock a lot of people, I grew up fast I guess because it was always my dad and me, always him and me against the world. So anyway I guess he liked Aunt Kitty, she must've passed the audition, because her prize was she got to look after me for two weeks while Dad went off with two professors to walk in I think the Appalachians; hill walking was what he liked to do to get rid of his people overdoses, and he always came back looking different, kind of clearer, you know? I called it his Moses look. Down from the mountain, you know, with the Dekalog. Only in Dad's case, usually, poetry. Anyhow, long story short, about five minutes after he got back from schmoozing with the profs on a mountainside, he was offered a post at Columbia University and we moved to New York permanently. Which I loved, sure, but he was like I said a country person and a dyed-in-the-wool European person, too, so it was harder for him. Still, he was used to working with what there was, used to handling whatever life sent his way. Okay, he drank like a real Yugoslav and he smoked about a hundred a day and he had a bad heart, he knew he was never going to be an old man, but he had made a decision about his life. You know, like in *The Nigger of the Narcissus.* I must live until I die. And that's what he did, he did great work and had great sex and smoked great cigarettes and drank great liquor and then the damn war started and out of nowhere he turned into this person I didn't know, this, I guess, Serb. Listen, he despised the guy he called the other Milosevic, he hated having the same name, and that's really why he changed it, if you want the truth. To separate Milo the poet from Milosevic the fascist gangster pig. But after it all went crazy out there in getting-to-be-ex-Yugo, he got all worked up about the demonization of the Serbs, even though he agreed with most of the analysis of what Milosevic was doing in Croatia and going to do in Bosnia, his heart was just inflamed by the anti-Serb stuff, and in some mad moment he decided it was his duty to go back and be the moral conscience of the place, you know, like Stephen Dedalus, to forge in the smithy of his soul et cetera et cetera or some Serb Solzhenitsyn. I told him to cut it out, who was Solzhenitsyn anyway but this crazy old coot in Vermont dreaming of being a prophet back in Mother Russia, but when he got home nobody was listening to his same old song, that's definitely not the route you want to go, Dad, for you it's women and cigarettes and booze and mountains and work work work, the idea was to let that stuff kill you, right, the plan was to stay away from Milosevic and his killers, not to mention bombs. But he didn't listen to me, and instead of sticking to the game plan he caught a plane back there, into the fury. That's what I started out to say, Professor, don't talk to me about fury, I know what it can do. America, because of its omnipotence, is full of fear; it fears the fury of the world and renames it envy, or so my dad used to say. They think we want to be them, he'd say after a few hits of hooch, but really we're just mad as hell and don't want to take it any more. See, he knew about fury. But then he set aside what he knew and behaved like a damn fool. Because about five minutes after he landed in Belgrade—or maybe it was five hours or five days or five weeks, who, like, *cares*?—the fury blew him to pieces and there wasn't enough of him found to collect up and put in a box. So, yeah, Professor, and you're mad about a doll. Well, excuse *me.*"

The weather had changed. The heat of early summer had given way to a disturbed, patternless time. There were many clouds and too much rain, and days of morning heat that abruptly turned cold after lunch, sending shivers through the girls in their summer dresses and the bare-torsoed rollerbladers in the park, with those mysterious leather belts strapped tightly across their chests, like self-imposed penances, just below their pectoral muscles. In the faces of his fellow citizens Professor Solanka discerned new bewilderments; the things on which they had relied, summery summers, cheap gasoline, the pitching arms of David Cone and yes, even Orlando Hernández, these things had begun to let them down. A Concorde crashed in France, and people imagined they saw a part of their own dreams of the future, the future in which they too would break through the barriers that held them back, the imaginary future of their own limitlessness, going up in those awful flames.

This golden age, too, must end, Solanka thought, as do all such periods in the human chronicle. Maybe this truth was just beginning to slide into people's consciousness, like the drizzle trickling down inside the upturned collars of their raincoats, like a dagger slipping through the gaps in their armour-plated confidence. In an election year, America's confidence was political currency. Its existence could not be denied; the incumbents took credit for it, their opponents refused them that credit, calling the boom an act of God or else of Alan Greenspan of the Federal Reserve. But our nature is our nature and uncertainty is at the heart of what we are, uncertainty per se, in and of itself, the sense that nothing is written in stone, everything crumbles. As Marx was probably still saying out there in the junkyard of ideas, the intellectual St Helena to which he had been exiled, all that is solid melts into air. In a public climate of such daily-trumpeted assurance, where did our fears go to hide? On what did they feed? On ourselves, perhaps, Solanka thought. While the greenback was all-powerful and America bestrode the world, psychological disorders and aberrations of all sorts were having a field day back home. Under the self-satisfied rhetoric of this repackaged, homogenized America, this America with the twenty-two million new jobs and the highest home-owning rate in history, this balanced-budget, low-deficit, stock-owning Mall America, people were stressed-out, cracking up, and talking about it all day long in superstrings of moronic cliché. Among the young, the inheritors of plenty, the problem was most acute. Mila, with her ultra-precocious Parisian upbringing, often referred scornfully to the confusion of her contemporaries. Everybody was scared, she said, everybody she knew, however good their façade, was quaking inside, and it didn't make any difference that everybody was rich. Between the sexes the trouble was worst of all. "Guys don't really know how or when or where to touch girls any more, and girls can barely tell the difference between desire and assault, flirtation and offensiveness, love and sexual abuse." When everything and everyone you touch turns instantly to gold, as King Midas learned in the other classic be-careful-what-you-wish-for fable, you end up not being able to touch anything, or anyone, at all.

Mila had changed too of late, but in her case the transformation was, in Professor Solanka's opinion, a vast improvement on the feckless chick, still playing at teen queenery in her twenties, that she'd been pretending to be. To hold on to her beautiful Eddie, the college sports hero—whom she described to Solanka as "not the brightest bulb, but a dear heart" and to whom a brainy, cultured woman would no doubt be a threat and a turnoff—she had dimmed her own light. Not entirely, it had to be said: after all, she had somehow managed to lure the boyfriend and the rest of the guys into a Kieslowski double bill, which meant either that they weren't as dumb as they looked or that she had even greater powers of persuasion than Solanka already suspected.

Day by day, she unfurled before Malik's astonished eyes into a young woman of wit and competence. She took to visiting him at all hours: either early, to force him to eat breakfast—it was his habit not to eat until the evening, a custom that she termed "plain barbaric, and *so* bad for you", and so under her tutelage he began to learn the mysteries of oatmeal and bran, and to consume, with his fresh coffee, at least one piece of daily matutinal fruit—or else in the steamy afternoon hours traditionally reserved for illicit love affairs. However, love was apparently not on her mind. She engaged him in simpler pleasures: green tea with honey, strolls in the park, shopping expeditions—"Professor, the situation is critical; we have to take *immediate* and *drastic* measures to get you some wearable clothes"—and even a visit to the Planetarium. As he stood with her in the middle of the Big Bang, hatless, casually attired, newly and springily shod in the first pair of sneakers he'd bought in thirty years, and feeling as if she were his parent and he a boy of Asmaan's age—well, perhaps just a little older—she turned to him, bent down a little, for in her heels she was at least six inches taller than he, and actually took his face in her hands. "Here you are, Professor, at the very beginning of things. Looking good, too. Cheer up, for Chrissake! It's good to make a new start." All around them a new cycle of Time was being initiated. This was how everything had begun: boom! Things flew apart. The centre did not hold. But the birth of the universe was a feel-good metaphor. What followed it was not mere Yeatsian anarchy. Look, matter clumped with other matter, the primal soup grew lumpy. Then came stars, planets, single-cell organisms, fish, journalists, dinosaurs, lawyers, mammals. Life, life. Yes, Finnegan, begin again, Malik Solanka thought. Finn MacCool, sleep no more, sucking your mighty thumb. Finnegan, wake.

She also came to talk, as if moved by a deep need for reciprocity. She spoke at these times with an almost frightening directness and speed, pulling no punches; yet the purpose of her soliloquies was not pugilism but friendship. Solanka, receiving her words in their intended spirit, was much soothed. From her conversation he frequently learned much of importance, picking up wisdom on the fly, so to speak; there were unregarded nuggets of pleasure lying about everywhere, like discarded toys, in the corners of her talk. This, for instance, while she explained why an earlier boyfriend had dumped her, a fact she plainly found as improbable as did Solanka: "He was filthy rich and I wasn't." She shrugged. "It was a problem for him. I mean, I was already in my twenties and I didn't have my unit." Unit? Solanka had been told—by Jack Rhinehart—that the word was used in certain masculinist American circles to refer to the male genitalia, but presumably Mila had not been given the heave-ho for lacking these. Mila defined the term as if speaking to a slow but likeable child, using that careful, idiot's-guide voice into which Solanka had heard her occasionally lapse when talking to her Eddie. "A unit, Professor, is one hundred million dollars." Solanka was dazed by the revelatory beauty of this fact. A century of big ones: the contemporary price of admission to the United States' Elysian fields. Such was the life of the young in the America of the incipient third millennium. That a girl of exceptional beauty and high intelligence could be deemed unsuitable for so fiscally precise a reason, Solanka told Mila gravely, only showed that American standards in matters of the heart, or at least in the mating game, had risen even higher than real-estate prices. "Word, Professor," Mila replied. Then they both burst into a laughter that Solanka had not heard emerging from his own mouth in an eternity. The unfettered laughter of youth.

He understood that she had made him one of her projects. Mila's special thing turned out to be the collection and repair of damaged people. She was up front about this when he asked her. "It's what I can do. I fix people up. Some people do up houses. I renovate people." So in her eyes he was like an old mansion, or at least like this old Upper West Side duplex he had sublet, this handsome space that hadn't been spruced up since, probably, the sixties and had begun to look a bit tragic; inside and out, she said, it was time for a whole new look. "As long as you don't hang any cradle full of noisy, foulmouthed, beedi-smoking Punjabi decorators on my frontage," he concurred. (The construction workers had, mercifully, done their work and left; only the characteristic din of the city street remained. Even this racket, however, seemed more muted than before.)

Her friends, the vampire stoop troop, were also unveiled by her for Solanka's benefit, becoming a little more than mere attitudes. She had worked on them, too, and was proud of her—of their—achievements. "It took time—they actually liked their schoolboy eyewear and ugh corduroy. But now I am privileged to lead the most fashion-forward geek posse in New York, and when I say geek, Professor, I mean genius. These kids are the coolest, and when I say cool I mean hot. The Filipino who sent out the I Love You virus? Forget it. That was amateur night; this is major league. If these babies wanted to hit Gates with a virus, you can bet he'd sneeze for *years.* You see before you the kind of surfer boys and girls the Evil Emperor is really scared of, disguised as Gen X slackers for their own safety, to conceal them from the Empire's Darths, Vader the Black and Maul the Red 'n' Horny. Or, right, you don't like *Star Wars,* so then these are like hobbits I'm hiding from Sauron the Dark Lord and his Ringwraiths. Frodo, Bilbo, Sam Gamgee, the whole Fellowship of the Ring. Until the time comes and we take him down and burn his power in Mount Doom. Don't think I'm kidding. Why should Gates fear the competitors he has, he's beaten them already: they're just serfs. He's got them cold. What gives him nightmares is that some kid will come out of a cold-water walk-up someplace with the next big thing, the thing that makes him yesterday's papers. Obsolete. That's why he keeps buying people like us out, he's ready to lose a few million now so that he won't lose his billions tomorrow. Yeah, I'm with the law courts, tear that palace down, break it in half, can't happen too soon for me. But in the meanwhile we've got big plans of our own. Me? Call me Yoda. Backwards I speak. Upside down I think. Inside out can I turn you. Strong with you think you the Force is? Strongest in me it moves. Seriously," she concluded, dropping the rubber-puppet voice, "I'm just management. And at this point sales and marketing and publicity also. Keep it lean and mean, right? What you call my vampires? They're the creative artists. Webspyder.net. We're designing sites right now for Steve Martin, Al Pacino, Melissa Etheridge, Warren Beatty, Christina Ricci and Will Smith. Yeah. *And* Dennis Rodman. And Marion Jones and Christina Aguilera and Jennifer Lopez and Todd Solondz and 'N Sync. Big business? We're in there. Con Ed, Verizon, British Telecom, Nokia, Canal Plus, if it's in communication, we're in communication wit' *it.* You want highbrow? These are the guys whose phones're ringing off the hook from like Robert Wilson and the Thalia Theatre of Hamburg and Robert Lepage. I'm telling you: they're out there. It's frontier law today, Professor, and this here's the Hole-in-the-Wall Gang. Butch, Sundance, the whole Wild Bunch. Me, I play house mother. And run the front of house."

So he had misjudged them, and they were whiz kids; except for Eddie. They were the stormtroopers of the technologized future about which he had such profound misgivings; except, again, for Eddie. But then Eddie Ford had been Mila's most ambitious project "until you came along. Also," she said, "you and Eddie have more in common than you think."

Eddie had a throwing arm that had brought him far from his origins in Nowheresville, all the way to Columbia, in fact, all the way to Mila Milo's bed, one of the most sought-after pieces of real estate in Manhattan; but in the end it doesn't matter how far you can throw the football. You can't throw away the past, and in that past, back home in Nowheresville, Nix., Eddie's young life had been freighted with tragedy. The characters were sketched out for Solanka by Mila, whose solemnity imbued them with something close to Greek stature. Here was Eddie's uncle Raymond, the hero back from Vietnam, who skulked for years in a Unabomberish cottage in the pine-wooded mountains above town, believing himself unfit for human company on account of his damaged soul. Ray Ford was prone to violent rages, which could be triggered even in those remote altitudes by a backfiring truck in the valley below, a falling tree, or birdsong. And here was Ray's "snake skunk weasel" of a brother, Eddie's mechanic father, Tobe, cheap cardplayer, cheaper drunk, an asshole whose act of betrayal would cripple all their lives. And here finally was Eddie's mom, Judy Carver, who in those days hadn't started keeping company with Santa and Jesus and who out of the goodness of her heart had gone up into the mountains every week since the early seventies, until, fifteen years later, when little Eddie was ten years old, she coaxed the mountain man down into town.

Eddie was in awe of his shaggy, odorous uncle, and more than a little afraid of him; yet his childhood trips up to Ray's place were the highlights of his life experience and formed his most vivid memories, "better than the movies," he said. (Judy had started taking him along after his fifth birthday, hoping to tempt Ray back into the world by showing him the future, trusting in Eddie's good nature to win the wild man's heart.) On their way up the mountain Judy would sing old Arlo Guthrie songs and young Eddie would sing right along: *"It was late last night the other day, I thought I'd go up and see Ray, So I went up and I saw Ray, There was only one thing Ray could say, was, I don't want a pickle, Just want to ride on my motorsickle . . ."* But this Ray wasn't that Ray. This Ray didn't own a Harley hog and there wasn't no Alice with or without a restaurant. This Ray lived on beans and roots and probably bugs and germs, Eddie reckoned, and on snakes caught in his bare hands and eagles pulled out of the sky. This Ray was gimpy and had teeth like rotting wood and breath that could knock you flat at a dozen paces. And yet this was the Ray in whom Judy Carver Ford could still see the sweet boy who went to war, the boy who could twist the silver paper inside cigarette packs into free-standing human figures and whittle pine into portraits of girls, which he'd give them in return for a kiss. (Dolls, Malik Solanka marvelled. No escape from their old voodoo. Here was another goddamn dollmaker's tale. And another *sanyasi,* too. That was what Mila had meant. A truer *sanyasi* than I, his withdrawal from society made in proper ascetic fashion. But like me in that he wanted to lose himself because of his fear of what lay beneath, what might bubble up at any moment and lay waste to the undeserving world.) Judy had once kissed Raymond herself, before making her bad mistake and settling for Tobe, whose bad back saved him from the draft, from whose bad character nobody could save her; except, she thought, Ray. If Ray came down from his fastness maybe that would be a sign, and things would change, and the brothers could go fishing and bowling, and Tobe would clean up his act, and then maybe she'd get some peace. And at long last Ray Ford did come, scrubbed and shaved and wearing a clean shirt, so spruced up that Eddie didn't recognize him when he walked through the door. Judy had made her signature celebration dinner, the same feast of meatloaf and tuna that she afterwards offered to Messrs Christmas and Christ, and for a while there everything went well; not too much talking, but that was okay, everybody was getting used to being in the house with everybody else.

Over ice cream, Uncle Ray spoke up. Judy hadn't been the only woman to visit him up in the woods. "There's been somebody else," he said, with difficulty. "Woman name of Hatty, Carole Hatty, knows there's a few of us scattered about them woods, and from the goodness of her heart she come up to visit with us 'n bring clothes 'n pie 'n stuff, even though there's mad bastards up there'd take an axe to anythin' came within ten feet, man, woman, child, or rabid dog." As he talked about the woman, Uncle Ray began to colour and shift in his seat. Judy said, "She important to you, Raymond? You want us to ask her over?" Whereupon the snake skunk weasel across the kitchen table began to slap his thigh and laugh, a loud drunk snake skunk weasel traitor's laugh, he laughed till he cried, then jumped up, knocking over his chair, and said, "Oo, Carole Hatty. Carole Easy-Over from the Big Dipper

Diner on Hopper Street? *That* Carole Hatty? *Woo.* Man, I never knowed she need so much sugar she come up your way lookin' for more. Hell, Ray, you been outa touch. Us boys, we bin bangin' li'l Carole regular, since she was fifteen years old and beggin'." Now Ray looked over at little Eddie, a horrible empty look, and even at ten Eddie could understand its meaning, could feel how deeply his Uncle Ray had been stabbed in the back, because Raymond Ford in his own way had been saying that he had come down from his hilltop redoubt not only for the love of family—the love of Eddie, the look said—but also for what he thought of as a good woman's love; after the long angry years he had come in the hope of having his heart healed by these things, and what Tobe Ford had done was to puncture both those balloons, to stab him twice in the heart with a single blow.

Well, the big man stood up himself after Tobe finished talking and Judy started shrieking at both of them and trying to get Eddie behind her at the same time because the snake skunk weasel her husband had a small pistol in his hand and it was pointed at his brother's heart. "Now, then, Raymond," said old Tobe, grinning, "let's be rememberin' what the good book say on the subject of brotherly love." Ray Ford walked out of the house and Judy was so scared she started singing *"Late last night I heard the screen door slam"*, and at that Tobe left too, saying he didn't have to take the crap being handed down around here, she could take her attitude and stick it where the sun don't shine, you hear me, Jude? Don't judge me, bitch, you're only my fuckin' wife, and if you don't care for your husband's remarks, why don't you just go suck old loony Raymond's dick. Tobe went out to play cards over at the Corrigan body shop, where he worked, and before morning came, Carole Hatty had been found in an alley with a broken neck, dead, and Raymond Ford was in the junkyard full of rusting autos at the back of the Corrigan lot, with a single gunshot wound in his heart and no sign of a weapon anywhere. That was when the snake skunk weasel took off, just never came home from the card game, and even though the word on Tobias Ford, armed and dangerous, was put out in five states, nobody ever found a trace of him. Eddie's mother was of the opinion that the bastard had really been a snake in disguise all along, and after what he'd done he simply slipped out of his human skin, just shucked it off and it crumbled to dust the moment he let it go, and one more snake wouldn't get any attention around Nowheresville, where the houses of the Lord were full of rattlers and diamondbacks and those were just the ministers. Let him go, she said, if I'd a knowed I was marryin' a serpent I'd a drunk poison before sayin' my Christian vows.

Judy took comfort in her growing collection of quarts of Jack and Jim, but after what happened had happened, Eddie Ford just clammed up, hardly spoke twenty words a day. Like his uncle, but without leaving town, he had sequestered himself from the world, had locked himself away inside his own body, and as he grew he concentrated all the immense energies of that newly puissant frame on throwing the football, throwing it harder and faster than a football had ever been thrown in Nowheresville, as if by hurling it clean into outer space he could save himself from the curse of his blood, as if a touchdown pass were the same thing as freedom. And finally he threw himself as far as Mila, who rescued him from his demons, coaxing him out of his internal exile, taking for her own pleasure the beautiful body that he had made his prison cell and in return giving him back companionship, community, the world.

Everywhere you looked, thought Professor Malik Solanka, the fury was in the air. Everywhere you listened you heard the beating of the dark goddesses' wings. Tisiphone, Alecto, Megaera: the ancient Greeks were so afraid of these, their most ferocious deities, that they didn't even dare to speak their real name. To use that name, *Erinnyes,* Furies, might very well be to call down upon yourself those ladies' lethal wrath. Therefore, and with deep irony, they called the enraged trinity "the good-tempered ones": *Eumenides.* The euphemistic name did not, alas, result in much of an improvement in the goddesses' permanent bad mood.

* * *

At first he tried to resist thinking of Mila as Little Brain come alive: and not Little Brain the hollow media re-creation at that, not Little Brain the traitress, the lobotomized baby doll of *Brain Street* and beyond, but her forgotten original, the lost L.B. of his first imagining, the star of *Adventures of Little Brain.* At first he told himself it would be wrong to do this to Mila, to dollify her thus, but then—he argued back against himself—had she not done it to herself, had she not by her own admission made early-period Little Brain her model and inspiration? Was she not quite plainly presenting herself to him in the role of the True One he had lost? She was, he now knew, a very bright young woman indeed; she must have foreseen how her performance would be received. Yes! Deliberately, to save him, she was offering him that mystery which—she had somehow divined—would answer his deepest, though never articulated, need. Shyly, then, Solanka began to allow himself to see her as his creation, given life by some unlooked-for miracle and caring for him, now, as might the daughter he'd never had. Then a slip of the tongue let out his secret, but Mila seemed not at all put out. Instead she smiled a private little smile—a smile that, Solanka was obliged to concede, was full of a strange erotic pleasure, in which there was something of the patient angler's satisfaction at the bait being finally taken, and something, too, of the prompter's hidden joy when a much repeated cue is picked up at the last—and, instead of correcting him, she replied as if he had used her right name and not the doll's. Malik Solanka flushed hotly, overcome by an almost incestuous shame, and stammeringly tried to apologize; whereupon she came up close, until her breasts moved against his shirt and he could feel the breath from her lips brushing against his, and murmured, "Professor, call me whatever you like. If it makes you feel good, please know that it's good with me." So they sank daily deeper into fantasy. Alone in his apartment in the rainy afternoons of that ruined summer, they played out their little father-and-daughter game. Mila Milo began quite deliberately to be the doll for him, to dress more and more precisely in the doll's original sartorial image and to act out for a much-aroused Solanka a series of scenarios derived from the early shows. He might play the part of Machiavelli, Marx or, most often, Galileo, while she would be, oh, exactly what he wanted her to be; would sit by his chair and press his feet while he delivered himself of the wisdom of the great sages of the world; and after a little time at his feet, she might move up to his aching lap, though they would make sure, without a word being said, that a plump cushion was always placed between her body and his, so that if he, who had sworn to lie with no woman, responded to her presence there as might another, less forsworn man, then she need never know it, they need never mention it, and he need never be obliged to admit the occasional spilling weakness of his body. Like Gandhi performing his *brahmacharya* "experiments with truth", when the wives of his friends lay with him at night to enable him to test the mastery of mind over limb, he preserved the outward form of high propriety; and so did she, so did she.

10

Asmaan twisted in him like a knife: Asmaan in the morning, proud of performing his natural functions to a high standard before an applauding—if unashamedly biased—audience of two. Asmaan in his daytime incarnations as motorbike rider, tent dweller, sandbox emperor, good eater, bad eater, singing star, star having tantrums, fireman, spaceman, Batman. Asmaan after dinner, in his one permitted video hour, watching endless reruns of Disney movies. *Robin Hood* was popular, with its absurd "Notting Ham", which featured a singing C&W rooster, cheap rip-offs of Baloo and Kaa from *The Jungle Book,* unadulterated American accents all over Sherwood Forest, and the frequently uttered, if previously little known, Disney Olde Englishe cry of "Oo-de-lally!" *Toy Story,* however, was banned. "It's got a stary boy in it." *Stary* was scary, and the boy was frightening because he treated his toys badly. This betrayal of love terrified Asmaan. He identified with the toys, not their owner. The toys were like the boy's children, and his maltreatment of them was, in Asmaan's three-year-old moral universe, a crime too hideous to contemplate. (As was death. In Asmaan's revisionist reading of *Peter Pan,* Captain Hook escaped the crocodile every time.) And after video-Asmaan came evening-Asmaan, Asmaan in the bath suffering Eleanor to brush his teeth and announcing preemptively, "We're not washing my hair today." Asmaan, finally, going to sleep holding his father's hand.

The boy had taken to telephoning Solanka without regard to the five-hour time difference. Eleanor had programmed the New York number into the Willow Road kitchen phone's speed-dial system; all Asmaan had to do was push a single button. Hello, Daddy came his transatlantic voice (this first call had been at five A.M.): I had a nice time at the part, Daddy. *Park, Asmaan,* sleepy Solanka tried to teach his son. *Say park.* Part. Where are you, Daddy, are you at home? Are you not coming back? I should have put you in the car, Daddy, I should have taken you to the sings. *Swings. Say swings.* I should have taken you to the sa-wings, Daddy. Morgen pushed me higher and higher. Are you binging me a peasant? *Say bringing, Asmaan. Say present. You can do it.* Are you ba-ringing me a pa-resent, Daddy? What's inside it? Will I like it very much? Daddy, you not going away any more. I won't let you. I had an ice team in the part. Morgen bought it. It was very nice. *Ice cream, Asmaan. Say ice cream.* Ice ta-ream.

Eleanor came on to the line. "I'm sorry, he came downstairs and pushed the button all by himself. I'm afraid I didn't wake up." Oh, that's okay, Solanka replied, and there followed a long silence. Then Eleanor unsteadily said, "Malik, I just don't know what's going on. I'm falling apart here. Can't we, if you don't want to come to London I could get on a, I could leave Asmaan with his grandma and we could sit down and try to work this thing, whatever it is, oh God I don't even know what it *is*!, couldn't we work it out? Or do you just hate me now, do I all of a sudden disgust you for some reason? Is there someone else? There must be, mustn't there? Who is it? For God's sake tell me, at least that would make sense, and then I could just be fucking furious with you instead of going slowly out of my mind."

The truth was that her voice still lacked any trace of real wrath. Yet he had abandoned her without a word, Solanka thought: surely her grief would turn, sooner or later, to rage? Perhaps she would let her solicitor express it for her, unleashing against him the cold rage of the law. But he could not see her as a second Bronisława Rhinehart. There was simply no vindictiveness in her nature. But for there to be so little anger: that was inhuman, even a little frightening. Or, alternatively, proof of what everybody was thinking and what Morgen and afterwards Lin Franz had put into words: that she was the better person of the two of them, too good for him, and, once she had recovered from the pain, would be better off without him. None of which would be any comfort to her right now, or to the child to whose arms he did not dare—for the sake of the boy's safety—to return.

For he knew he had not shaken the Furies off. A low, simmering, disconnected anger continued to seep and flow deep within him, threatening to rise up without warning in a mighty volcanic burst; as if it were its own master, as if he were merely the receptacle, the host, and it, the fury, were the sentient, controlling being. In spite of all the apparently necromantic strides of science these were prosaic times, in which everything was deemed capable of explication and comprehension; and throughout his life Professor Solanka, the Malik Solanka who had latterly become conscious of the inexplicable within himself, had been firmly of the prosaic party, the party of reason and science in its original and broadest meaning: *scientia,* knowledge. Yet even in these microscopically observed and interminably explicated days, what was bubbling inside him defied all explanations. There is that within us, he was being forced to concede, which is capricious and for which the language of explanation is inappropriate. We are made of shadow as well as light, of heat as well as dust. Naturalism, the philosophy of the visible, cannot capture us, for we exceed. We fear this in ourselves, our boundary-breaking, rule-disproving, shape-shifting, transgressive, trespassing shadow-self, the true ghost in our machine. Not in the afterlife, or in any improbably immortal sphere, but here on earth the spirit escapes the chains of what we know ourselves to be. It may rise in wrath, inflamed by its captivity, and lay reason's world to waste.

What was true of him, he found himself thinking once again, might also be true to some degree of everyone. The whole world was burning on a shorter fuse. There was a knife twisting in every gut, a scourge for every back. We were all grievously provoked. Explosions were heard on every side. Human life was now lived in the moment before the fury, when the anger grew, or the moment during—the fury's hour, the time of the beast set free—or in the ruined aftermath of a great violence, when the fury ebbed and chaos abated, until the tide began, once again, to turn. Craters—in cities, in deserts, in nations, in the heart—had become commonplace. People snarled and cowered in the rubble of their own misdeeds.

In spite of all Mila Milo's ministrations (or, often, because of them) Professor Solanka still needed, on his frequent insomniac nights, to still his boiling thoughts by walking the city streets for hours, even in the rain. They were digging up Amsterdam Avenue, the sidewalk as well as the pavement, just a couple of blocks away (some days it seemed as if they were digging up the whole town), and one night as he was out walking through a medium to heavy downpour past the untidily fenced off hole he stubbed his toe on something and burst into a three-minute tirade of invective, at the end of which an admiring voice came from beneath an oilcloth in a doorway, "Man, sure learned some new vocabulary tonight." Solanka looked down to see what had bruised his foot, and there, lying on the sidewalk, was a broken lump of concrete paving-stone; upon seeing which he broke into an ungainly limping run, fleeing that concrete lump like a guilty man leaving the scene of a crime.

Ever since the investigation of the three society killings had focused on the three rich boys, he had felt lighter of spirit, but in his heart of hearts he had not yet fully exonerated himself. He followed reports of the investigation with care. There had still been no arrests and no confessions, and the news media were growing restive; the possibility of an upper-crust serial killer was juicily enticing, and the N.Y.P.D.'s failure to crack the case was all the more frustrating as a result. Give those swanky no-goodniks the third degree! One of them must break! An unappetizing lynch-mob atmosphere was generated by this kind of speculative commentary, of which there was much to be found. Solanka's attention was captured by the one possible new lead. Mr Panama Hat had been replaced in the unsolved mystery's dramatis personae by an even stranger group of characters. People in fancy-dress Disney costumes had been sighted near each of the three murder scenes: a Goofy near Lauren Klein's corpse, a Buzz Lightyear near the body of Belinda Booken Candell, and where Saskia Schuyler lay a passerby had spotted a red fox in Lincoln green: Robin Hood himself, tormentor of the bad old Sheriff of Notting Ham, and now also eluding the Sheriffs of Manhattan. Oo-de-lally! Detectives admitted that a significant connection between the three sightings was impossible to establish for sure, but the coincidence was certainly striking—Halloween being many months away—and they were keeping it very much in mind.

In the minds of children, Solanka thought, the creatures of the imagined world—characters from books or videos or songs—actually felt more solidly real than did most living people, parents excepted. As we grew, the balance shifted and fiction was relegated to the separate reality, the world apart in which we were taught that it belonged. Yet here was macabre proof of fiction's ability to cross that supposedly impermeable frontier. Asmaan's world—Disney World—was trespassing in New York and murdering the city's young women. And one or more very scary boys were concealed somewhere in this video, too.

At least there had been no more Concrete Killer murders for a while. Also, and for this Solanka did give Mila credit, he was drinking a good deal less, and as a result there had been no more amnesiac stupors: he no longer woke up in his street clothes with terrible unanswerable questions in his aching head. There were even moments when, as he fell under Mila's spell, he had come close, for the first time in months, to something very like happiness. And yet the dark goddesses still hovered over him, dripping their malevolence into his heart.

While Mila was with him, in that wood-panelled space in which, even when thunderstorms darkened the sky, they no longer troubled to switch on any electric lights, he was held within the magic circle of her charm; but as soon as she left, the noises in his head began again. The murmuring, the beating of black wings. After his first dawn phone conversation with Asmaan and Eleanor, as the knife twisted in him, the murmurs turned for the first time against Mila, his angel of mercy, his living doll.

This was her face in the half-light, its knife-edge planes moving comfortably against his half-unbuttoned shirt, the short, erect, red-gold hair brushing the underside of his chin. The re-enactments of old TV shows had stopped, a pretence whose purpose had been served. These days, in the slow darkened afternoons, they barely spoke, and when they did, it was no longer of philosophy. Sometimes for an instant her tongue lapped at his breast. Everybody needs a doll to play with, she whispered. Professor, you poor angry man, it's been so long. Shh, there's no hurry, take your time, I'm not going anywhere, nobody's going to disturb us, I'm here for you. Let it go. You don't need it any more, all that rage. You just need to remember how to play. These were her long fingers, with their blood-red nails, finding their way, by the smallest of daily increments, further inside his shirt.

Her physical memory was extraordinary. Each time she visited him, she could take up exactly the position on his cushioned lap that she had reached at the end of her last visit. The placing of her head and hands, the tightness with which her body curled into itself, the exact weight with which she leaned against him: her high-precision remembering, and infinitesimal adjustment, of these variables were themselves prodigiously arousing sexual acts. For the veils were falling away from their play, as Mila showed Professor Solanka with each (daily more explicit) touch. The effect on Professor Solanka of Mila's strengthening caresses was electric all right, at his age and in his situation in life he had not looked to receive such benison ever again. Yes, she had turned his head, had set out to do so while pretending to be doing nothing of the sort, and now he was deeply enmeshed in her web. The queen webspyder, mistress of the whole webspyder posse, had him in her net.

Then there was another change. Just as he had let slip a doll's name, accidentally or under the pressure of a barely conscious desire, so one afternoon she too let a forbidden word pass her lips. At once that shuttered and darkened sitting room had been magically flooded with lurid, revelatory light, and Professor Malik Solanka knew Mila Milo's backstory. It was always my dad and me, she had said it herself, always him and me against the world. There it was in her own undisguised words. She had laid it right out in front of Solanka and he had been too blind (or too unwilling?) to see what she had so openly and unashamedly shown. But as Solanka looked at her in the aftermath of her "slip of the tongue"—which he was already more than half convinced had been no slip, for this was a woman of formidable self-control, to whom accidents most likely never happened—those sharp and somehow cryptic facial planes, those slanting eyes, that face which was most closed when it looked most open, that wise little private smile, at last revealed their secrets.

Papi, she had said. That treacherous diminutive, that freighted term of endearment meant for a dead man's ear, had served as the open-sesame to her lightless childhood cave. There sat the widowed poet and his precocious child. There was a cushion on his lap and she, year after year, curling and uncurling, moving against him, kissing dry his tears of shame. This was the heart of her, the daughter who sought to compensate her father for the loss of the woman he loved, no doubt in part to assuage her own loss by clinging to the parent who remained, but also to supplant that woman in this man's affections, to fill the forbidden, vacated maternal space more fully than it had been filled by her dead mother, for he must need her, must need living Mila, more than he had ever needed his wife; she would show him new depths of needing, until he wanted her more than he had known he could want any woman's touch. This father—after his own experience of Mila's powers, Solanka was utterly sure of what had happened—was slowly wooed by his child, seduced millimetre by millimetre into the undiscovered country, towards his never-discovered crime. Here was the great writer, *l'écrivain nobelisablé,* the conscience of his people, suffering those appallingly knowledgeable little hands to move at the buttons of his shirt, and at some point allowing the unallowable, crossing the frontier from which there can be no return, and beginning, tormentedly but eagerly, too, to participate. Thus was a religious man brought forever into mortal sin, forced by desire to renounce his God and sign the Devil's treaty, while the burgeoning girl, his demon child, the goblin in the heart of the flower, whispered the vertiginous faith-murdering words that sucked him down: this isn't happening unless we say it is, and we don't say it is, do we, Papi, so it's not. And because nothing was happening, nothing was wrong. The dead poet had entered that world of fantasy where everything is always safe, where the crocodile never catches Hook and a little boy never grows tired of his toys. So Malik Solanka saw his mistress's real self unveiled, and said, "This is an echo, isn't it, Mila, a reprise. You sang this song once before." And immediately, silently corrected himself. No, don't flatter yourself. Not just once. You are by no means the first.

Shh, she said, laying a finger across his lips. Shh, Papi, no. Nothing happened then and it's not happening now. Her second use of the incriminating nickname had a new, pleading quality to it. She needed this, needed him to allow it. The spider was caught in her own necrophiliac web, dependent on men like Solanka to raise her lover very, very slowly from the dead. Thank the God who doesn't exist that I have no daughters, Malik Solanka thought. Then misery choked him. No daughter, and I have also lost my son. Elián the Icon has gone home to Cárdenas, Cuba, with his papa but I can't go home to my boy. Mila's lips were against his neck now, moving over his Adam's apple, and he felt a gentle suction. The pain ebbed; and something more, too, was taken. His words were being removed from him. She was drawing them out and swallowing them and he would never be able to say them again, the words describing the thing that was not, that the spider-sorceress in her black majesty would never permit to be.

And what if, Solanka wildly conjectured, she was feeding off his fury? What if she was hungriest for what he feared most, the goblin anger within? For she was driven by fury also, he knew that, by the wild imperative fury of her hidden need. At that moment of revelation Solanka could easily have believed that this beautiful, accursed girl, whose weight was moving with such suggestive languor on his lap, whose fingertips touched his chest hair as faintly as a summer breeze and whose lips were working softly at his throat, might actually be the very incarnation of a Fury, one of the three deadly sisters, the scourges of mankind. Fury was their divine nature and boiling human wrath their favourite food. He could have persuaded himself that behind her low whispers, beneath her unfailingly even-tempered tones, he could hear the Erinnyes' shrieks.

Another page of her back-story revealed itself to him. Here was the poet Milo with his weak heart. This gifted, driven man had ignored all medical advice and continued, with an almost ludicrous excessiveness, to drink, smoke and womanize. His daughter had offered an explanation of Conradian grandeur for this behaviour: life must be lived until it can be lived no more. But as Solanka's eyes opened he saw a different picture of the poet, a portrait of the artist fleeing into excess from grievous sin, from what he must have daily believed to be his soul's death, its condemnation for all eternity to the most agonizing circle of Hell. Then came that last journey, Papi Milo's suicidal flight towards his murderous namesake. This, too, now conveyed to Malik Solanka something other than Mila had made it mean. Fleeing one evil, Milo had gone to face what he thought of as the lesser peril. Escaping the consuming Fury, his daughter, he ran towards his full, unabbreviated name, towards himself. Mila, thought Solanka, you probably drove your maddened father to his death. And what, now, might you have in store for me?

He knew one frightening answer to that. At least one veil still hung between them, over not her story but his. He had known from the first minute of this illicit liaison that he was playing with fire, that everything he had driven deep down within himself was being stirred, the seals were being broken one by one, and that the past, which had almost destroyed him once before, might yet be given a second chance to finish the job. Between this new, unlooked-for story and that old, suppressed tale the unarticulated resonances echoed. This question of dollification and its. The matter of allowing oneself to be. Of having no choice but. Of the slavery of childhood when. Of need: this one's that one's most inexorable. Of the power of doctors to. Of the child's impotence in the face of. Of the innocence of children in. Of the child's guilt, its fault, its most grievous fault. Above all the matter of sentences that must never be completed, because to complete them would release the fury, and the crater of that explosion would consume everything at hand.

Oh, weakness, weakness! He still couldn't refuse her. Even knowing her as he now did, even understanding her true capabilities and intuiting his possible peril, he couldn't send her away. A mortal who makes love to a goddess is doomed, but once chosen cannot avoid his fate. She continued to visit him, all dolled up, just the way he wanted her, and every day there was progress. The polar ice-cap was melting. Soon the level of the ocean would rise too high and they would surely drown.

When he left the apartment nowadays he felt like an ancient sleeper, rising. Outside, in America, everything was too bright, too loud, too strange. The city had come out in a rash of painfully punning cows. At Lincoln Center Solanka ran into Moozart and Moodama Butterfly. Outside the Beacon Theatre a trio of horned and uddered divas had taken up residence: Whitney Mooston, Mooriah Cowrey and Bette Midler (the Bovine Miss M). Bewildered by this infestation of paronomasticating livestock, Professor Solanka suddenly felt like a visitor from Lilliput-Blefuscu or the moon or, to be straightforward, London. He was alienated, too, by the postage stamps, by the monthly, rather than quarterly, payment of gas, electricity and telephone bills, by the unknown brands of candy in the stores (Twinkies, Ho Hos, Ring Pops), by the words "candy" and "stores", by the armed policemen on the streets, by the anonymous faces in magazines, faces that all Americans somehow recognized at once, by the indecipherable words of popular songs which American ears could apparently make out without strain, by the end-loaded pronunciation of names like Far*rar,* Har*rell,* Can*dell,* by the broadly spoken *e*'s that turned *expression* into *axprassion, I'll get the check* into *I'll gat the chack;* by, in short, the sheer immensity of his ignorance of the engulfing mêlée of ordinary American life. Little Brain's memoirs filled bookstore windows here as well as in Britain, but that brought him no joy. The successful writers of the moment were unknown to him. Eggers, Pilcher: they sounded like they belonged on a restaurant menu, not a bestseller list.

Eddie Ford was often to be seen sitting alone on the neighbouring stoop as Professor Solanka returned home—the webspyders were evidently busy with their nets—and in the banked fire of the blond centurion's slow-burn gaze Malik Solanka imagined he saw the belated beginnings of suspicion. Nothing was said between them, however. They nodded at each other briefly and left it at that. Then Malik entered his panelled retreat and waited for his deity to come. He took up his place in the large leather armchair that had become their preferred place of ease and set upon his lap the red velvet cushion with which, thus far, he had continued to protect what remained of his heavily compromised modesty. He closed his eyes and listened to the ticking of the mantelpiece's antique carriage clock. And at some point Mila came soundlessly in—he had given her a set of keys—and what was to be done, what she insisted was not being done at all, was quietly done.

In that charmed space, during Mila's visits, almost complete silence remained the norm. There were murmurs and whispers but no more. However, in the last quarter hour or so before she left, after she briskly leapt off his lap, smoothed her dress, and brought them both a glass of cranberry juice or a cup of green tea, and while she adjusted herself for the outside world, Solanka could offer her, if he so desired, his hypotheses on the country whose codes he was trying to unlock.

For example, Professor Solanka's as-yet-unpublished theory on the differing attitudes towards oral sex in the United States and England—this aria being prompted by the president's inane decision to start apologizing yet again for what he should always have crisply said was nobody else's business—got a sympathetic hearing from the young woman snuggled down on his lap. "In England," he explained in his most straitlaced style, "the heterosexual b.j. is almost never offered or received before full, penetrative coitus has taken place, and sometimes not even then. It's considered a sign of deep intimacy. Also a sexual reward for good behaviour. It's *rare.* Whereas in America, with your well-established tradition of teenage, ah, 'makeouts' in the backs of various iconic automobiles, 'giving head', to use the technical term, precedes 'full' missionary-position sex more often than not; indeed, it's the most common way for young girls to preserve their virginity while keeping their sweethearts satisfied.

"In short, an acceptable alternative to fucking. Thus, when Clinton affirms that he had never had sex with that woman, Moonica, the Bovine Ms L., everyone in England thinks he's a pink-faced liar, whereas the whole of teen (and much of pre- and post-teen) America understands that he's telling the truth, as culturally defined in these United States. Oral sex is precisely *not sex.* It's what enables young girls to come home and with their hands on their hearts tell their parents—hell, it probably enabled you to tell your father—that you hadn't 'done it'. So Slick Willy, Billy the Clint, has just been parroting what any red-blooded American teenager would have said. Arrested development? Okay, probably so, but this was why the impeachment of the president failed."

"I see what you mean." Mila Milo nodded when he was done, and returned to his side, in an unexpected and overwhelming escalation of their end-of-afternoon routine, to remove the red velvet cushion from his helpless lap.

That evening, encouraged by whispering Mila, he returned with new fire to his old craft. There's so much inside you, waiting, she had said. I can feel it, you're bursting with it. Here, here. Put it into your work, Papi. The *furia.* Okay? Make sad dolls if you're sad, mad dolls if you're mad. Professor Solanka's new badass dolls. We need a tribe of dolls like that. Dolls that say something. You can do it. I know you can, because you made Little Brain. Make me dolls that come from her neighbourhood—from that wild place in your heart. The place that isn't a little middle-aged guy under a pile of old clothes. This place. The place for me. Blow me away, Papi. Make me forget her! Make adult dolls, R-rated, NC-17 dolls. I'm not a kid any more, right? Make me dolls I want to play with now.

He understood at last what Mila did for her webspyders other than dress them more fashionably than they could manage for themselves. The word "muse" was attached sooner or later to almost all beautiful women seen with gifted men, and no self-respecting, Chinese-fan-twirling leader of fashion would currently be seen dead without one, but most such women were more amusement than muse. The true muse was a treasure beyond price, and Mila, Solanka discovered, was capable of being genuinely inspiring. Just moments after her potent urgings, Solanka's ideas, so long congealed and dammed, began to burn and flow. He went out shopping and came home with crayons, paper, clay, wood, knives. Now his days would be full, and most of his nights as well. Now, when he awoke fully dressed, the street smell would not be on his clothes, nor would the odour of strong drink foul his breath. He would awake at his workbench with the tools of his trade in his hand. New figurines would be watching him through mischievous, glittering eyes. A new world was forming in him, and he had Mila to thank for the divine afflatus: the breath of life.

Joy and relief coursed through him in long uncontrollable shudders. Like that other shudder at the end of Mila's last visit, when the cushion came off his lap. The ending he had waited for like the addict he had become. Inspiration also soothed another, growing trouble in him. He had begun to entertain fears about Mila, to hypothesize a great, dangerous selfishness in her, an overarching ambition that made her see others, himself included, as mere stepping-stones on her own journey to the stars. Did those brilliant boys really need her? Solanka had begun to wonder. (And came close to the next question: *Do I?*) He had glimpsed a possible new incarnation of his living doll—in which Mila was Circe, and at her feet sat her oinking swine—but now he pushed that dark vision aside; also its even more ferocious companion, the vision of Mila as Fury, as Tisiphone, Alecto or Megaera come down to earth in a cloak of sumptuous flesh. Mila had justified herself. She had provided the spur that had sent him back to work.

On the cover of a leather-bound notebook he scribbled the words "Professor Kronos's Amazing No-Strings Puppet Kings". And then added: "Or, Revolt of the Living Dolls". And then, "Or, Lives of the Puppet Caesars". Then he crossed out everything except the two words "Puppet Kings", opened the notebook, and in a great rush began to write the back-story of the demented genius who would be his anti-hero.

Akasz Kronos, the great, amoral cyberneticist of the Rijk, he began, *created the Puppet Kings in response to the terminal crisis of the Rijk civilization, but, on account of the deep and unimprovable flaw in his character that made him unable to consider the issue of the general good, intended them to guarantee nobody's survival or fortune but his own.*

Jack Rhinehart rang the next afternoon, sounding wired. "Malik, wassup. You still living like a guru in an ice cave? Or a castaway on *Big Brother Is Not Watching You*? Or does news from the outside world still reach you from time to time.—You heard the one about the Buddhist monk in the bar? He goes up to the Tom Cruise clone with the cocktail shaker and says, 'Make me one with everything.'—Listen: you know a broad by the name of Lear? Claims to have been your *wife.* Seems to me *nobody* deserves as much bad luck as being married to *that* honey. She's like one hundred and ten years old, and ornery as a cut snake. Oh, and on the subject of wives? I'm divorced. It turned out to be easy. I just gave her everything."

Everything really was everything, he amplified: the cottage in the Springs, the fabled wine shack, and several hundreds of thousands of dollars. "And this is all right with you?" Solanka asked, astonished. "*Yeah,* yeah," Rhinehart gabbled. "You should have seen Bronnie. Jaw on the *floor.* Grabbed the offer so fast I thought she'd herniate. So, can you believe it, she's *gone.* She's *toast.* It's Neela, man. I don't know how to say this, but she eased something in me. She made it all okay." His voice became boyish-conspiratorial. "Have you ever seen anyone *actually stop traffic*? I mean one hundred percent without question *arrest the motion of motor vehicles* just by being around? She has that power. She climbs out of a cab and five cars and two fire trucks screech to a halt. Also, walking into lampposts. I never believed it happened outside of Mack Sennett slapstick two-reelers. Now I see guys do it every day. Sometimes, in restaurants," Rhinehart confided, bubbling with glee, "I'd ask her to walk to the women's room and back, just so I could watch the men at the other tables get whiplash injuries. Can you imagine, Malik, my regrettably celibate friend, what it was like to be with *that*? I mean, *every night*?"

"You always did have an ugly turn of phrase," Solanka said, wincing. He changed the subject. "About Sara? Talk about rising from the grave. What cemetery did you find her in?" "Oh, the usual," Rhinehart replied tightly. "Southampton." His ex-wife, Solanka learned, had at the age of fifty married one of the richest men in America, the cattle-feed tycoon Lester Schofield III, now aged ninety-two, and on her recent, fifty-seventh, birthday had instituted divorce proceedings on the grounds of Schofield's adultery with Ondine, a Brazilian runway model of twenty-three. "Schofield made his billion by working out that what's left of a grape after making grape juice would make a great dinner for a cow," Rhinehart said, and moved into his most exaggerated Uncle Remus manner. "And now yo' ole lady she done had de same idea. She puttin' de big squeeze on *him,* I reckon. Gwine en' up bein' dat well-fed heifer hersel'." All over the Eastern seaboard, it seemed, the young were climbing on to the laps of the old, offering the dying the poisoned chalice of themselves and causing nine kinds of havoc. Marriages and fortunes were foundering daily on these young rocks. "Miz Sara gave an interview," Rhinehart told Solanka, much too merrily, "in which she announced her intention of chopping up her husband into three equal parts, planting one on each of his major properties, and then spending a third of the year with each, to express her appreciation for his love. You lucky to 'scape old Sara when you were po', boy. Dat Bride of Wildenstein? Dat Miz Patricia Duff? Dey doan' even come close in de Divo'ce 'Lympics. Dis lady get de gol' medal, sho' nuff. Perfesser, she done read her *Shakespeare.*" There were rumours that the whole thing was a cynical sting operation—that, in short, Sara Lear Schofield had put the Brazilian swan up to it—but no proof of any such conspiracy had been found.

What was the matter with Rhinehart? If he was as deeply satisfied as he claimed, both with his own divorce and with *l'affaire* Neela, why was he veering at such breakneck speed between sexual crudity—which, in fact, was very much not his usual style—and this clumsy Sara Lear material? "Jack," Solanka asked his friend, "you really are okay, right? Because if . . ." "I'm fine," Jack interrupted in his most stretched, brittle voice. "Hey, Malik? Dis here's Br'er Jack, girlfrien'. *Bawn an' bred in a briar patch.* Chill."

Neela Mahendra called an hour later. "Do you remember? We met during that football game. The Dutch thrashing Serbia." "They still call it Yugoslavia in football circles," Solanka said, "on account of Montenegro. But yes, of course I remember. You're not that easy to forget." She didn't even acknowledge the compliment, receiving such flattery as a minimum: her merest due. "Can we meet? It's about Jack. I need to talk to someone. It's important." She meant immediately, was used to men abandoning, when she beckoned, whatever plans they had made. "I'm across the park from you," she said. "Can we meet outside the Metropolitan Museum in let's say half an hour?" Solanka, already worried about his friend's well-being, more worried as a result of this phone call, and—yes, very well!—unable to resist the summons from gorgeous Neela, got up to go, even though these had become his day's most precious hours: Mila's time. He put on a light overcoat—it was a dry but overcast and unseasonably cool day—and opened the apartment's front door. Mila stood there with his spare key in her hand. "Oh," she said, seeing the coat. "Oh. Okay." In that first instant, when she'd been taken by surprise, before she had time to gather herself, he glimpsed her face naked, so to speak. What was there, without question, was disappointed hunger. The vulpine hunger of an animal denied its—he tried not to think the word, but it forced its way in—its prey.

"I'll be back soon," he said lamely, but she had recovered her composure now, and shrugged. "No big deal." They went through the outside door of the building together and he walked rapidly away from her, towards Columbus Avenue, not looking around, knowing that she'd be with Eddie on the neighbouring stoop, angrily sticking a thirsty tongue down his bemused, delighted throat. There were posters everywhere for *The Cell,* the new Jennifer Lopez movie. In it, Lopez was miniaturized and injected into the brain of a serial killer. It sounded like a remake of *Fantastic Voyage,* starring Raquel Welch, but so what? Nobody remembered the original. Everything's a copy, an echo of the past, thought Professor Solanka. A song for Jennifer: We're living in a retro world and I am a retrograde girl.

11

"In the future, sure theen', they don't listen no more to this type talk radio. Or, jou know wha' I theen'? Porhap' the radio weel listen to *oss.* We'll be like the entortainmon' and the machines weel be the audien', an' own the station, and we all like work for them."—"Yo, lissen up. Dunno what jive sci-fi crap ol' Speedy Gonzalez there was handin' out. Sound to me like he rent *The Matrix* too many times. Where I'm sittin' the future plain ain't arrive. Ever'thin' look the same. I mean the exact same shinola goin' down all over. Ever'body in the same accommodation, gettin' the same education, doin' the same recreation, lookin' for the same . . . ploymentation. Check it out. We gettin' the same bills, datin' the same girls, goin' to the same jails; gettin' paid bad, laid bad 'n' made bad, am I right? That would be cor-recto, señor. And *my* radio? It come wit' a on-off switch, daddy-o, and I turn that sucker off anytime I choose."—"Boy, does he don' get eet. That guy jus' now, he don' get eet so bad he won't see eet comin' till eet sittin' on his face. Jou better wise up, hermano. They got machine now eat food for fuel, jou hear that? No more gasoline. Eat human food like jou an' me. Pizza, chili dog, tuna melt, whatev'. Pretty soon Mr Machine gonna be takin' a table in a restauran'. Gonna be, like, gimme the bes' booth. Now jou tell me what's the differen'? If eet eatin', eet alive, I say. The future here, man, right now, jou better watch jou butt. Pretty soon Mr Live Machine gonna be comin' for that employmentation jou talkin' 'bout, maybe for jour pretty girlfrien' too."—"Hey, hey, my paranoid Latino friend, Ricky Ricardo, I missed the name, but slow down, Desi, okay? This here's not that communist Cuba you escaped from in yo' rubber boat an' got sanctuary in the land of the free . . ." "Don' insul' me, please, now. I'm sayin' please, because I was raise polite, no? The brother here, how he's call, Señor Cleef Hoxtaboo' or Mr No Good from the 'Hood, maybe hees mother never tol' heem right, but we goin' out live on air here, we talkin' to the whole metro region, less keep eet clean."—"Can I get in here? Excuse me? I'm listening to all this?, and I'm thinking, they have electronically generated TV presenters now?, and there's dead actors selling motor vehicles?, Steve McQueen in that car?, so I'm more with our Cuban friend?, the technology scares me? And so in the future?, like, will anyone even be thinking about our like needs? I'm an actress?, I work mainly in commercials?, and there's this big SAG strike?, and for months now I can't earn a dollar?, and it doesn't stop one single spot going on air?, because they can get Lara Croft?, Jar Jar Binks?, they can get Gable or Bogey or Marilyn or Max Headroom or HAL from *2001*?"—"I'm going to interrupt, ma'am, because we're out of time and this is something I know a lot of people feel strongly about. Can't blame cutting-edge technological innovation for the fix your union's got you in. You chose socialism, union made your bed, now you're lying in it. My personal take on the future? You can't turn back the clock, so go with the flow and ride the tide. Be the new thing. Seize the day. From sea to shining sea."

Sitting on the steps of the great museum, caught in a sudden burst of slanting, golden afternoon sunlight, scanning the *Times* while he waited for Neela, Professor Malik Solanka felt more than ever like a refugee in a small boat, caught between surging tides: reason and unreason, war and peace, the future and the past. Or like a boy in a rubber ring who watched his mother slip under the black water and drown. And after the terror and the thirst and the sunburn there was the noise, the incessant adversarial buzz of voices on a taxi driver's radio, drowning his own inner voice, making thought impossible, or choice, or peace. How to defeat the demons of the past when the demons of the future were all around him in full cry? The past was rising up; it could not be denied. As well as Sara Lear, here in the TV listings was Krysztof Waterford-Wajda's little Ms Pinch-ass back from the dead. Perry Pincus—she must be, what, forty by now—had written a tell-all book about her years as the eggheads' premier groupie, *Men with Pens,* and Charlie Rose was talking to her about it this very night. Oh poor Dub-dub, Malik Solanka thought. This is the girl you wanted to settle down with, and now she's going to dance on your grave. If tonight it's Charlie—"Tell me what sort of qualms this project gave you, Perry; as an intellectual yourself, you must have had serious misgivings. Say how you overcame those scruples"—then tomorrow it'll be Howard Stern: "Chicks dig writers. But then, a lot of writers dug this chick." Halloween, Walpurgisnacht, did indeed seem to be early this year. The witches were gathering for their sabbat.

Yet another story was being half told behind his back; another stranger's fairy tale of the city poured into his defenceless ear. "Yeah, it went great, honey. No, no problems, I'm en route to the trustees' meeting, that's why I'm calling you on my mo-fo. Conscious all the time, but doped-up, sure. So, *semi*-conscious. Yeah, the knife comes right at your eyeball, but the chemical assistance makes you think it's a feather. No, no bruising, and let me tell you it's amazing what my visual world now contains. Amazing grace, yeah, good one. Was blind but now I see. Really. Look at all this stuff out here. I've been missing so much. Well, think about it. He really is the laser king. I asked around a lot as you know and the same name kept coming up. A little dryness is all, but that goes away in a few weeks, he says. Okay, love ya. I'll be home late. What can you do. Don't wait up." And of course he turned round, of course he saw that the young woman was not alone, a man was nuzzling at her even as she flipped her "mo-fo" shut. She, gladly allowing herself to be nuzzled, met Solanka's eye; and, seeing herself caught in her lie, beamed guiltily, and shrugged. What can you do, as she had said on the phone. The heart has its reasons, and we are all the servants of love.

Twenty minutes to ten in London. Asmaan would be asleep. Five and a half hours later in India. Turn the watch upside down in London and you got the time in the town of Malik Solanka's birth, the Forbidden City by the Arabian Sea. That, too, was coming back. The thought filled him with dread: of what, driven by his long-sealed-away fury, he might become. Even after all these years it defined him, had not lost any of its power over him. And if he finished the sentences of that untold tale? . . . That question must be for another day. He shook his head. Neela was late. Solanka put down his newspaper, pulled a piece of wood and a Swiss Army knife out of an overcoat pocket, and began, with complete absorption, to whittle.

"Who is he?" Neela Mahendra's shadow fell across him. The sun was behind her, and in silhouette she looked even taller than he remembered. "He's an artist," Solanka replied. "The most dangerous man in the world." She dusted off a spot on the museum steps and sat down beside him. "I don't believe you," she said. "I know a lot of dangerous men, and none of them ever created a credible work of art. Also, trust me, not a single one of them was made of wood." They sat there in silence for a while, he whittling, she simply still, offering the world the gift of her being in it. Afterwards Malik Solanka, remembering their first moments alone together, would dwell particularly on the silence and stillness, on how easy that had been. "I fell in love with you when you weren't saying a word," he told her. "How was I to know you were the most talkative woman on earth? I know a lot of talkative women and, trust me, compared to you, every single one of them was made of wood."

After a few minutes he put the half-finished figure away and apologized for being so distracted. "No apology required," she said. "Work is work." They got up to make their way down the great flight of steps towards the park, and as she rose, a man slipped on the step above her and rolled heavily and painfully down a dozen or more steps, narrowly missing Neela on his way down; his fall was broken by a group of schoolgirls sitting screaming in his way. Professor Solanka recognized the man as the one who had been necking so enthusiastically with the mobile-phone prevaricator. He looked around for Ms Mo-Fo, and after a moment spotted her storming off uptown on foot, hailing off-duty cabs that ignored her angry arm.

Neela was wearing a knee-length mustard-coloured scarf dress in silk. Her black hair was twisted up into a tight chignon and her long arms were bare. A cab stopped and expelled its passenger just in case she needed a ride. A hot dog vendor offered her anything she wanted, free of charge: "Just eat it here, lady, so I can watch you do it." Experiencing for the first time the effect about which Jack Rhinehart had been so vulgarly effusive, Solanka felt as if he were escorting one of the Met's more important possessions down an awestruck Fifth Avenue. No: the masterpiece he was thinking of was at the Louvre. With a light breeze blowing the dress against her body, she looked like the Winged Victory of Samothraki, only with the head on. "Nike," he said aloud, puzzling her. "It's who you remind me of," he clarified. She frowned. "I make you think of sportswear?"

Sportswear was certainly thinking of her. As they turned into the park, a young man in running clothes approached them, rendered positively humble by the force of Neela's beauty. Unable to speak directly to her at first, he addressed himself to Solanka instead. "Sir," he said, "please don't think I'm trying to hit on your daughter, that is, I'm not asking for a date or anything, it's just that she is the most, I had to tell her"—and here at last he did turn towards Neela—"to tell you, you're the most . . ." A great roaring rose in Malik Solanka's breast. It would be good now to tear this young man's tongue out from that vile fleshy mouth. It would be good to see how those muscled arms might look when detached from that highly defined torso. Cut? Ripped? How about if he was cut and ripped into about a million pieces? *How about if I ate his fucking heart?*

He felt Neela Mahendra's hand come to rest lightly on his arm. The fury abated as quickly as it had risen. The phenomenon, his unpredictable temper's rise and fall, had been so rapid that Malik Solanka was left feeling giddy and confused. Had it really happened? Had he really been on the verge of tearing this super-fit fellow limb from limb? And if so, then how had Neela dissipated his anger—the anger to combat which Solanka sometimes had to lie in darkened rooms for hours, doing breathing exercises and visualizing red triangles—by the merest touch? Could a woman's hand really possess such power? And if so (the thought offered itself to him and would not be denied), was this not a woman to keep by his side and cherish for the rest of his haunted life?

He shook his head to clear it of such notions and returned his attention to the unfolding scene. Neela was giving the young runner her most dazzling smile, a smile after receiving which it would be best to die, for the rest of life was sure to be a big letdown. "He isn't my father," she told the smile-blinded wearer of sportswear. "He's my live-in lover." This information struck the poor fellow like a hammer blow; whereupon, to underscore the point, Neela Mahendra planted on the still-befuddled Solanka's unprepared but nevertheless grateful mouth a long, explicit kiss. "And, guess what?" she panted, coming up for air to deliver the coup de grâce. "He's absolutely fantastic in bed."

"What was *that*?" flattered, more than somewhat overcome, Professor Solanka asked her dizzily after the runner had departed, looking as if he were off to disembowel himself with a blunt bamboo stick. She laughed, a great wicked cackle of a noise that made even Mila's raucous laughter seem refined. "I could see you were on the edge of losing it," she said. "And I need you here right now, paying attention, and not in a hospital or jail." Which explained about eighty per cent of it, Solanka thought as his head stopped whirling, but didn't fully translate the meaning of everything she had been doing with her tongue.

Jack! Jack! he reproved himself. The subject for this afternoon was

Rhinehart, his pal, his best buddy, and not his friend's girlfriend's tongue, no matter how long and gymnastic it was. They sat on a bench near the pond, and all around them dog walkers were colliding with trees, Tai Chi practitioners lost their balance, rollerbladers smashed into one another, and people out strolling just walked right into the pond as if they'd forgotten it was there. Neela Mahendra gave no sign of noticing any of this. A man walked past with an ice cream cone, which, owing to his sudden but comprehensive loss of hand-to-mouth co-ordination, completely missed his tongue and instead made contact, messily, with his ear. Another young fellow began, with every appearance of genuine emotion, to weep copiously as he jogged by. Only the middle-aged African-American woman sitting on the next bench (who am I calling middle-aged? She's probably younger than I am, Solanka thought disappointedly) seemed impervious to the Neela factor as she ate her way through a long egg salad hero, advertising her enjoyment of every mouthful with loud *mmm*s and *uh-huh*s. Neela, meanwhile, had eyes only for Professor Malik Solanka. "Surprisingly good kiss, by the way," she said. "Really. First class."

She looked away from him, across the shining water. "It's over between Jack and me," she went on quickly. "Maybe he already told you. It's been over for a while. I know he's your good friend, and you should be a good friend to him at this time, but I can't stay with a man once I lose respect for him." A pause. Solanka said nothing. He was replaying Rhinehart's last phone call and hearing what he had missed: the elegiac note beneath the sexual boasting. The use of the past tense. The loss. He didn't push Neela for the story. Let it come, he thought. It'll be here soon enough. "What do you think about the election?" she asked, making one of the dramatic conversational tacks to which Solanka would soon enough become accustomed. "I'll tell you what I think. I think the American voters owe it to the rest of the world not to vote for Bush. It's their duty. I'll tell you what I hate," she added. "I hate when people say there's no difference between the candidates. That Gush-and-Bore stuff is getting so *old*. It makes me hopping mad." Not the moment,

Solanka thought, to confess his own guilty secrets. Neela wasn't really expecting a reply, however. "No difference?" she cried. "How about, for example, *geography*? How about, for example, knowing where my poor little homeland is on the damn map of the world?" Malik Solanka remembered that George W. Bush had been ambushed by a journalist's crafty question during a foreign policy Q-and-A one month before the Republican convention: "Given the growing instability of the ethnic situation in Lilliput-Blefuscu, could you just indicate that nation to us on the map? And what was the name of its capital city again?" Two curve balls, two strikes.

"I'll tell you what *Jack* thinks about the election." Neela swerved back to the subject, the colour rising in her face along with her voice. "New Jack, A-list Black-and-White-Ball Truman Capote Rhinehart, he thinks whatever his 'Caesars' in their 'Palaces' want him to think. Jump, Jack, and he'll jump sky-high. Dance for us, Jack, you're such a great dancer, and he'll show them all the obsolete thirty-year-old moves old white people like, he'll swim and hitchhike and walk the dog, he'll do the mash, the funky chicken and the locomotion all night long. Make us laugh, Jack, and he'll tell them jokes like some court jester. You probably know his favourites. 'After the FBI tested Monica's dress, they announced they couldn't make a positive I.D. from the stain, because everybody in Arkansas has the same DNA.' Yeah, they like that one, the Caesars. Vote Republican, Jack, be pro-life, Jack, read the Bible on homosexuals, Jack, and guns don't kill people, ain't that right, Jack, and he goes, yes, ma'am, people kill people. Good dog, Jack. Roll over. Fetch. Sit up and fucking beg. Beg for it, Jack, you ain't gonna get it, but we do like to see a black boy on his knees. Good dog, Jack, run off now and sleep in the kennel out the back. Oh, darling, would you throw Jack a bone, please? He's been so sweet. Yes, she'll do, she's from the South." Oh, so Rhinehart had been a bad boy, Solanka thought, and he guessed that Neela wasn't used to being cheated on at all. She was used to being the Pied Piper, with lines of boys following wherever she was pleased to lead.

She calmed down, slumping back on the bench, and briefly closed her eyes. The woman on the next bench finished her hero, leaned over to Neela, and said, "Oh, dump *that* boy, honey. Cancel *his* ass *today*. You don't need no relationship with nobody's pet poodle." Neela turned to her as if greeting an old friend. "Ma'am," she said, seriously, "you've got milk in your refrigerator with a longer life than that relationship."

"Let's walk now," she commanded, and Solanka rose to his feet. When she was sure they were out of earshot, she said, "Look, I'm pissed at Jack, that's one thing, but I'm scared for him, too. He really needs a true friend, Malik. He's in a pretty bad jam." As Solanka had guessed from his phone call, Rhinehart was depressed, and not only about the collapse of his perishable milk carton of a love affair. The Sara Lear encounter, which had begun as an interview for an article about the power divorces of the age, had rebounded badly against Jack. Sara had taken against him, and her enmity had hit him hard. After the loss of the Springs place to Bronisława, he'd found himself the tiniest of shoe boxes in the middle of a golf course way out towards Montauk Point. "You know his thing for Tiger Woods," Neela said. "Jack's competitive. He won't be happy till Nike—the other Nike, I mean," she said, flushing with undisguised pleasure, "the Nike he hasn't disgusted yet, starts sponsoring his game too, right down to the swoosh on his cap." After Rhinehart's offer for the little house had been accepted by the seller, two things happened in quick succession. On Rhinehart's third visit to the place, to which the broker had handed him the key, the police showed up less than ten minutes after he did and invited him to assume the position. Neighbours had reported an intruder on the property, and he was it. It took him close to an hour to persuade the cops that he wasn't a burglar but a bona fide purchaser. A week later the golf club blackballed his application for membership. Sara's arm was long. Rhinehart, for whom, as he said, "being black's just not the issue any more," had rediscovered, the hard way, that it still was. "There's a club out there that got started so Jews could play golf," Neela said contemptuously. "Those old Wasps can sting. Jack should've known the score. I mean: Tiger Woods may be of mixed race, but he knows his balls are black."

"That's not the worst of it." They had reached Bethesda Fountain. Double takes and slapstick routines continued all around them; they walked on until they reached a grassy slope. "Sit," said Neela. He sat. Neela lowered her voice. "He's become involved with some crazy boys, Malik. God knows why, but he really wants in with them, and they're the dumbest, wildest white boys you could imagine. Did you ever hear of a secret society, it's not even supposed to exist, called the S&M? Even the name's a bad joke. 'Single and Male.' Yeah, right. Those boys are twisted way, way out of shape. It's like that Skull and Crossbones thing they have at Yale?, right?, where they buy up stuff like Hitler's moustache and Casanova's dick?—only this one's not school-specific, and it doesn't collect memorabilia. It collects girls, young ladies with certain interests and skills. You'd be surprised how many, especially if you knew the games they're expected to play, and I'm not talking strip poker now. Zips, nips 'n' clips. Saddles, reins, harnesses, they probably end up looking like the surrey with the fringe on top. Or, you know, lash me with lashes and tie me with strings, these are a few of my favourite things. Rich girls. I swear. Your family owns a horse farm, so you get turned on being treated like a horse? I wouldn't know. So much that's so desirable comes so easy to these kids"—Neela couldn't be more than five years older than the dead girls, Solanka thought—"that nothing turns them on. They have to travel further and further in search of kicks, further from home, further from safety. The wildest places of the world, the wildest chemicals, the wildest sex. That's it, my five-cent Lucy analysis. Bored little rich girls let dumb rich boys do weird stuff to them. Dumb rich boys can't believe their luck."

Solanka reflected about Neela's use of the word "kids" to describe what were, after all, members of her own generation. The word seemed honest in her mouth. Compared to, say, Mila—Mila, his own guilty secret—this was an adult woman. Mila had her charms, but they had their roots in a childlike wantonness, a greedy whimsicality born of this same crisis of dulled response, this same need to go to extremes, beyond extremes, in order to find what she needed in the way of arousal. When forbidden fruit has been your daily diet, what do you do for thrills? Lucky Mila, Solanka thought. Her rich boyfriend hadn't understood what he might have done with her, and had let her go. If these other rich boys had ever heard about her, how far she was willing to go, what taboos she was willing to ignore, she could have been their goddess, the child-woman queen of their hidden cult. She could have ended up in the Midtown Tunnel with a smashed-in skull. "The affectless at play," Solanka said aloud. "A tragedy of insulation. The unexamined life of the folks who've got their units." He had to explain that, and was happy to hear her laugh again. "No wonder so many of those horny gorillas—those Stashes, Clubs and Horses—want in, no?" Neela sighed. "The question is, why does Jack?"

Professor Malik Solanka felt his stomach tighten. "Jack's a member of this S&M thing?" he asked. "But aren't these the men . . ."—"He's not a member yet," she butted in, driven by her need to share her terrible burden. "But he's hammering on the door, begging to be let in, the stupid bastard. And that's after the evil shit in the press. Once I knew that, I couldn't stay with him. I'll tell you something that wasn't in any of the papers," she added, dropping her voice even further. "Those three dead girls? They weren't raped, they weren't robbed, right? But something was done to them, and that's what really links the three crimes, only the police don't want it in the papers because of the copycat problem." Solanka was beginning to be genuinely frightened. "What happened to them?" he asked weakly. Neela covered her eyes with her hands. "They were scalped," she whispered, and wept.

To be scalped was to remain a trophy even in death. And because rarity created value, a dead girl's scalp in your pocket—O most gruesome of mysteries!—might actually possess greater cachet than would be conferred by the same girl, alive and breathing, on your arm at a glamorous ball, or even as a willing partner in whatever sexual antics you cared to devise. The scalp was a signifier of domination, and to remove it, to see such a relic as desirable, was to value the signifier above the signified. The girls, Solanka in his revolted horror began to understand, had actually been worth more to their murderers dead than alive.

Neela was convinced of the three boyfriends' guilt; convinced, too, that Jack knew a great deal more than he was telling anyone, even her. "It's like heroin," she said, drying her eyes. "He's in so deep he doesn't know how to get out, doesn't *want* to get out, even though staying in there will destroy him. My worry is, what is he ready to do, and who is he ready to do it to? Was *I* being lined up for those assholes' delectation, or what? As for the killings, who knows why? Maybe their little sex games went too far. Maybe it's some insane sex and power thing those rich boys have. Some blood-brother manhood shit. Fuck the girl and kill her, and do it so damn cleverly that you get away with it. I don't know. Maybe I'm just expressing class resentment here. Maybe I've just watched too many movies. *Compulsion. Rope.* You know? 'Why do such a thing?' 'Because we can.' Because they want to prove what little Caesars they are. How above and beyond they are, how exalted, godlike. The law can't touch them. It's such murderous *crap,* but Mr Lapdog Rhinehart just goes on being loyal. 'You don't know jack shit about them, Neela, they're decent enough young men.' Bullshit. He's so blind, he can't see that they'll take him down with them when they go, or, worse still, maybe they're setting him up. He'll take the fall for them and go to the chair singing their praises. Jack Shit. Good name for that weak little fuck. Right at this moment, that's about what he means to me."

"Why are you so sure of this?" Solanka asked her. "I'm sorry, but you're sounding a little wild yourself. Those three men were questioned, but they haven't been arrested. And as I understand it, each of them has a solid alibi for the time his girlfriend died. Witnesses, et cetera. One was seen in a bar, and so on, I forget." His heart was beating hard. For what felt like forever, he had been accusing himself of these crimes. Knowing the disorder in his own heart, the bubbling incoherent storm, he had linked it to the disorder of the city, and come close to declaring himself guilty. Now, it seemed, exoneration was at hand, but the price of his innocence just might be his good friend's guilt. A great turbulence was churning in his stomach, making him nauseous. "And the scalping business," he forced himself to ask. "Where on earth did you hear a thing like that?"

"Oh God," she wailed, letting the worst thing come out into the open at last. "I was tidying his fucking wardrobe. God knows why. I *never* do chores like that for a man. Get a housekeeper, you know? That's not what I'm *for.* I really dug him, I guess for about five minutes there I allowed myself . . . so anyway, I was clearing up for him, and I found, I found." Tears again. Solanka put his hand on her arm now, and she moved against him, hugged him hard, and sobbed. "Goofy," she said. "I found all three of them. The fucking man-sized fancy-dress costumes. Goofy and Robin Hood and Buzz."

She had confronted Rhinehart and he had blustered, badly. Yes, for a joke, Marsalis, Andriessen and Medford would dress up in these outfits and spy on their girlfriends from a distance. Okay, yes, maybe it was a joke in poor taste, but it didn't make them killers. And they hadn't worn the outfits on the nights of the murders, that was nonsense: garbled reporting. But they were afraid, wouldn't you be, and had asked Jack to help. "He went on and on protesting their innocence, denying that his precious club is a front organization for the lewd practices of the privileged class." Neela had refused to let the subject drop. "I set out everything I knew, half knew, intuited and suspected, piled it all up in front of him and told him I wasn't going to let up until he'd said what there was to say." Finally he'd panicked and cried out, "You think I'm the kind of man who goes out at night and cuts off the tops of women's heads?" When she'd asked him what *that* meant, he'd looked scared to death, and claimed he'd read it in the paper. The swish of the tomahawk. The victorious warrior's taking of the spoils. But she had gone on-line to examine the archives of every paper in the Manhattan area, and she knew. "It's not there."

Neela had dressed for beauty, not for warmth, and the afternoon had lost its glow. Solanka took off his coat and put it over her trembling shoulders. All around them in the park the colours were fading. The world became a place of blacks and greys. Women's clothes—unusually for New York, it had been a season of bright colours—faded to monochrome. Under a gunmetal sky, the green leached out of the spreading trees. Neela needed to get out of this suddenly ghostly environment. "Let's get a drink," she proposed, getting up, and in the same instant was off in long strides. "There's a hotel bar that's okay on Seventy-seventh," and Solanka hurried after her, ignoring the now familiar shocks and catastrophes she was leaving, like hurricane damage, in her wake.

She had been born "in the mid-seventies" in Mildendo, the capital of Lilliput-Blefuscu, where her family still lived. They were *girmityas,* descendants of one of the original migrants—her great-grandfather—who had signed an indenture agreement, a *girmit,* back in 1834, the year after the abolition of slavery. Biju Mahendra, from the little Indian village of Titlipur, had travelled with his brothers all the way to this double speck in the remote South Pacific. The Mahendras had gone to work in Blefuscu, the more fertile of the two islands, and the centre of the sugar industry. "As an Indo-Lilly," she said over her second cosmopolitan, "my childhood bogeyman was the Coolumber, who was big and white and spoke not in words but in numbers and would eat little girls at night if they didn't do their homework and wash their private parts. As I grew up I learned that the 'coolumbers' were the sugarcane labourers' overseers. The particular one in my family's story was a white man called Mr Huge—Hughes, really, I suppose—who was 'a devil from Tasmania', and to whom my great-grandfather and great-uncles were no more than numbers on the list he read out every morning. My ancestors were numbers, the children of numbers. Only the indigenous Elbees were called by their true last names. It took us three generations to retrieve our family names from this numerical tyranny. By then, obviously, things between the Elbees and us had gone badly wrong. 'We eat veggies,' my grandmother used to say, 'but those Elbee fatsos eat human meat.' In fact there is a history of cannibalism in Lilliput-Blefuscu. They are offended when you point this out, but it's just so. And for us the very presence of meat in the kitchen was a defilement. Long pork sounded like the devil's own food."

Words for drink played a distressingly big part in her back-story. In the matter of grog, yaqona, kava, beer, as in little else, the Indo-Lilliputians and Elbees were as one; both communities suffered from alcoholism and the problems associated with it. Her own father was a big boozer, and she had been glad to escape him. There were very few scholarships to America available in Lilliput-Blefuscu, but she won one of them, and fell for New York at once, as did everybody who needed, and found here, a home away from home among other wanderers who needed exactly the same thing: a haven in which to spread their wings. Yet her roots pulled at her, and she suffered badly from what she called "the guilt of relief". She had escaped her drunkard of a father, but her mother and sisters had not. And to her community's cause, too, she remained passionately attached. "The parades are on Sunday," she said, ordering a third cosmopolitan. "Will you come with me?" And Solanka—it was Thursday already—inevitably agreed.

"The Elbees say we are greedy and want everything and will chase them out of their own land. We say they are lazy and if it wasn't for us they would sit around doing nothing and starve. They say that the only end of a soft-boiled egg to break is the little one. Whereas we—or at least those of us who eat eggs—are the Big Endians, from Big Endia." She cackled again, tickled by her own joke. "Trouble is coming soon." It was a question, as so many things were, of the land. Even though the Indo-Lilliputians on Blefuscu now did all the farming, were responsible for most of the country's exports, and therefore earned most of the foreign exchange, even though they had prospered and cared for their own, building their own schools and hospitals, still the land on which all this stood was owned by the "indigenous" Elbees. "I hate that word, 'indigenous', " Neela cried. "I'm fourth-generation Indo-Lilly. So I'm indigenous too." The Elbees feared a coup—a revolutionary land grab by the Indo-Lillys, to whom the Elbee constitution still denied the right to own real estate on either island; the Big Endians, for their part, feared the same thing in reverse. They were afraid that when their hundred-year leases expired in the course of the coming decade, the Elbees would simply take back the now valuable farmland for themselves, leaving the Indians, who had developed it, with nothing.

But there was a complication, which Neela, in spite of her ethnic loyalty and three quick cosmopolitans, was honest enough to admit. "This isn't just a question of ethnic antagonism or even of who owns what," she said. "The Elbee culture really is different, and I can see why they are afraid. They're collectivists. The land isn't held by individual landowners but by the Elbee chiefs in trust for the whole Elbee people. And then we Big Endia-wallahs come along with our good business practice, entrepreneurial acumen, free-market mercantilism and profit mentality. And the world speaks our language now, not theirs. It is the age of numbers, isn't it? So we are numbers and the Elbees are words. We are mathematics and they are poetry. We are winning and they are losing: and so of course they're afraid of us, it's like the struggle inside human nature itself, between what's mechanical and utilitarian in us and the part that loves and dreams. We all fear that the cold, machine-like thing in human nature will destroy our magic and song. So the battle between the Indo-Lillys and the Elbees is also the battle of the human spirit and, damn it, with my heart I'm probably on the other side. But my people are my people and justice is justice and after you've worked your butts off for four generations and you're still treated like second-class citizens, you've got a right to be angry. If it comes to it I'll go back. I'll fight alongside them if I have to, shoulder to shoulder. I'm not kidding, I really will." He believed her. And was thinking: how is it that, in the company of this impassioned woman I barely know, I feel so completely at ease?

The scar was the legacy of a bad car accident on the interstate near Albany; she had almost lost her arm. Neela by her own admission drove "like a maharani". It was up to other road users to keep out of her imperious, supra-legal way. In areas where she and her car became known—Blefuscu, or the environs of her smart New England college—motorists, when they saw Neela Mahendra coming, would often abandon their vehicles and run. After a series of small dings and near misses, she experienced the very unfunny Big One. Her survival was a miracle (and a close thing); the preservation of her heartbreaking beauty was an even greater astonishment. "I'll take the scar," she said. "I'm lucky to have it. And it's a reminder of something I shouldn't forget."

In New York, fortunately, it was unnecessary for her to drive. Her regal attitude—"my mother always told me I was a queen, and I believed her"—meant she preferred to be driven anyway, although she was also a terrible backseat driver, full of yelps and gasps. Her rapid success in television production enabled her to afford a car service, whose drivers quickly grew used to her frequent cries of fear. She had no sense of direction, either, and so—remarkably for a New Yorker—never knew where anything was. Her favourite stores, her preferred restaurants and nightclubs, the location of the recording studios and cutting rooms she regularly used: they could have been anywhere. "Where the car stops is where they are," she told Solanka over the fourth cocktail, all wide-eyed innocence. "It's amazing. They're always right there. Right outside the door."

Pleasure is the sweetest drug. Neela Mahendra leaned into him in their black leather booth and said, "I'm having so much fun. I never realized how easy it would be around you, you looked like such a stuffed shirt at Jack's place, watching that stupid game." Her head tilted towards his shoulder. Her hair was down now, and from where he was sitting it veiled much of her face. She let the back of her right hand move slowly against the back of his left hand. "Sometimes, when I drink too much, she comes out to play, the other one, and then there's nothing I can do. She takes charge and that's that." Solanka was lost. She took his hand in hers and kissed the fingertips, sealing their unspoken compact. "You have scars, too," she said, "but you never talk about them. I tell you all my secrets and you don't say one single word. I think, why does this man never talk about his child? Yes, of course Jack told me, you think I didn't ask? Asmaan, Eleanor, that much I know. If I had a little boy, I'd talk about him all the time. You apparently don't even carry his photograph. I think, this man left his wife of many years, the mother of his son, and even his friend doesn't know why. I think, he looks like a good man, a kind man, not a brute, so there must be a good reason, maybe if I open up to him he'll tell me, but, baba, you just keep mum. And then I think, here is this Indian man, Indian from India, not Indo-Lilly like me, a son of the mother country, but apparently that also is a forbidden topic. Born in Bombay, but on the place of his birth he is silent. What are his family circumstances? Brothers, sisters? Parents dead or alive? Nobody knows. Does he ever go back to visit? Seems like not. No interest. Why? The answer must be: more scars. Malik, I think you've been in more accidents than me, and maybe you were even more badly hurt somewhere along the line. But if you don't talk, what can I do? I have nothing to say to you. I can only say, here I am, and if human beings can't save you then nothing can. That's all I'm saying. Talk, don't talk, it's up to you. I'm having a good time and anyway now the other one is here, so shut up, I don't know why men always have to talk so much when it's obvious that words are not the thing required. Not required right now at all."

12

LET THE FITTEST SURVIVE: THE COMING OF THE PUPPET KINGS

Akasz Kronos, the great, cynical cyberneticist of the Rijk, created the Puppet Kings in response to the terminal crisis of the Rijk civilization, but on account of the flaw in his character that made him unable to consider the general good, he used them to guarantee nobody's survival or fortune but his own. In those days the polar ice-caps of Galileo-1, the Rijk's home planet, were in the last stages of melting (a large stretch of open sea had been sighted at the North Pole) and no matter how high the dikes were built, the moment was not far off when the glory of the Rijk, that highest of cultures set in the lowest of lands, which was just then enjoying the richest and most prolonged golden age in its history, would be washed away.

The Rijk fell into decline. Their *artists* put down their brushes for good, for how could art—which relied, like good wine, on the judgement of posterity—be created once posterity had been cancelled? *Science* failed the challenge as well. The Galileo solar system lay in a "*dark quadrant*" near the rim of our own galaxy, a mysterious area in which few other suns burned, and in spite of their high level of technological achievement, the Rijk had never succeeded in locating an alternative home planet. A cross-section of Rijk society was dispatched, cryogenically frozen, in the *Max-H*, a computer-controlled spacecraft programmed to wake its precious cargo if a suitable planet came within range of its sensors. When this spacecraft malfunctioned and exploded a few thousand miles into space, people lost heart. In that most open, broad-minded and reasonable of societies there now arose a number of fire-and-brimstone *preachers*, who blamed the coming catastrophe on the godlessness of Rijk culture. Many citizens fell under the spell of these new, narrow men. Meanwhile the sea continued to rise. When a dike sprang a leak, the water pushed through with such violence that whole counties were sometimes flooded before repairs were complete. The economy collapsed. Lawlessness increased. People stayed home and waited for the end.

The sole surviving *portrait* of Akasz Kronos shows a man with a full head of long silver hair framing a soft, round, surprisingly boyish face dominated by a wine-dark Cupid's bow of a mouth. He wears a floor-length grey tunic, with gold embroidery at the cuffs and neckline, over a frilled white high-collared shirt: the very picture of the dignified genius. But the eyes are mad. As we peer into the darkness around him, we make out fine white filaments floating from his fingertips. Only after much study do we notice the small bronze-coloured figure of a puppet man at the bottom left of the picture, and even then it takes a while before we realize that the puppet has broken free of the puppeteer's control. The homunculus turns its back on its maker and sets off to forge its own destiny, while Kronos, the abandoned creator, takes leave not only of his creation but of his senses, too.

Professor Kronos was not only a great scientist but an entrepreneur of Machiavellian daring and skill. As the Rijk lands drowned, he quietly moved his centre of operations to the two small mountain-islands that formed the primitive but independent nation of *Baburia*, at the Galileian antipodes. Here he negotiated and signed an advantageous treaty with the local ruler, the *Mogol*. The Baburians would retain ownership of their territory, but

Kronos would be granted long leases over the high mountain pastures, for which he agreed to pay what seemed to the Mogol a very high rent indeed: an annual pair of wooden shoes for every Baburian man, woman and child. In addition, Kronos undertook to guarantee the defence of Baburia against the assault that must certainly come as the Rijk's lands sank below the rising waves. For this he was accorded the title of *National Saviour* and granted *droit de seigneur* over all the islands' new brides. Having come to terms, Kronos proceeded with the creation of the masterpieces that would prove his undoing, the so-called *Monstrous Dynasty of Puppet Caesars*, also known as *Professor Kronos's No-Strings Puppet Kings.*

His own lover, *Zameen*, the legendary beauty of the Rijk and the only scientist whom Kronos regarded as his peer, refused to accompany him to his new antipodean world. Her place was with her people, she said, and she would die with them if that was what destiny decreed. Akasz Kronos abandoned her without a second thought, perhaps preferring the sexual multiplicity available on the other side of the world.

The broken strings in the Kronos portrait are purely metaphorical. The Professor's artificial life-forms were string-free from the start. They walked and talked; they had "*stomachs*", sophisticated fuelling centres that could process ordinary food and drink, with solar-cell *back-up systems* that enabled them to stay alert, and work, for longer hours than any flesh-and-blood human being. They were faster, stronger, smarter—"better", Kronos told them—than their human, antipodean hosts. "You are kings and queens," he taught his creatures. "Carry yourselves well. You are the masters now." He even gave them the power to reproduce themselves. Each cyborg was given his or her own blueprint so that it could, in theory, endlessly re-create itself in its own image. But in the master program Kronos added a *Prime Directive*: whatever order he gave, the cyborgs and their replicas were obliged to obey, even to the point of acquiescing in their own destruction, should he deem that necessary. He dressed them in finery and gave them the illusion of freedom, but they were his slaves. He gave them no names. There were *seven-digit numbers* branded on their wrists, and they were known by these.

No two Kronosian creations were the same. Each was given its own sharply delineated personality traits: the *Aristocratic Philosopher; the Promiscuous Child-Woman; the First, Rich Ex-Wife (a Bitch); the Ageing Groupie; the Pope's Driver; the Underwater Plumber; the Traumatized Quarterback; the Blackballed Golfer; the Three Society Girls; the Playboys; the Golden Child and His Ideal Mother; the Deceitful Publisher; the Angry Professor; the Goddess of Victory* (an exceptionally beautiful cyborg modelled after Kronos's abandoned lover, Zameen of Rijk), *the Runners; the Mo-Fo Woman; the Mo-Fo Man; the Human Spiders; the Woman Who Saw Visions; the Astro-Adman;* even a *Dollmaker*. And as well as characters—strengths, weaknesses, habits, memories, allergies, lusts—he gave them a *value system* by which to live. The greatness of Akasz Kronos, which was also his downfall, may be judged by this: that the virtues and vices he inculcated in his creations were not wholly, or not only, his own. Self-serving, opportunistic, unscrupulous, he nevertheless permitted his cybernetic life-forms a degree of ethical independence. The possibility of idealism was allowed.

Lightness, quickness, exactitude, visibility, multiplicity, consistency: these were the six high Kronosian values, but instead of embedding single definitions of these principles in the cyborgs' default programs, he offered his creations a series of multiple-choice options. Thus "*lightness*" might be defined as "doing lightly what is in reality a heavy duty", that is to say, grace; but it might also be "treating frivolously what is serious", or even "making light of what is grave", that is, amorality. And "*quickness*" could be "doing swiftly whatever is necessary", in other words, efficiency; however, if the emphasis were to be placed on the second part of that phrase, a kind of ruthlessness could result. "*Exactitude*" could tend towards "precision" or "tyranny", "*visibility*" might be "clarity of action" or "attention-seeking", "multiplicity" was capable of being both "open-mindedness" and "duplicity", and "*consistency*", the most important of the six, could mean either "trustworthiness" or "obsessiveness"—the consistency of—we may use our own world's models here, for the sake of easy comparison—Bartleby the Scrivener, who preferred not to, or of Michael Kohlhaas, with his inexorable and world-shattering search for redress. Sancho Panza is consistent in the "reliable" sense of the word, but so, contrariwise, is erratic, fixated, chivalry-maddened Quixote. And note, too, the tragic consistency of the Land Surveyor, eternally yearning towards what he can never attain, or of Ahab in his pursuit of the whale. This is the consistency that destroys the consistent; for the Ahabs perish, while the inconsistent, the Ishmaels, survive. "The fullness of a living self is inexpressible, obscure," Kronos told his mechanical fictions. "In that mystery is freedom, which is what I have given you. In that obscurity is light."

Why did he permit the Puppet Kings such psychological and moral liberty? Perhaps because the scientist and scholar in him could not resist seeing how these new life-forms resolved the battle that rages within all sentient creatures, between light and dark, heart and mind, spirit and machine.

At first the Puppet Kings served Kronos well. They made the shoes that paid for the land leases, tended the livestock and tilled the soil. He had dressed them all in court finery, but their long brocaded skirts and dress uniforms quickly grew soiled and torn, and they made themselves new clothes more suited to their labours. As the ice-caps continued to melt and the water levels rose, they prepared to defend their shrinking new home against the foretold *Rijk attack*. By now they had learned how to modify their own systems without Kronos's help, and they added new skills and aptitudes by the day. One such innovation enabled them to use the local firewater as *flying fuel*. Carrying bottles of the toddy with them in case they wanted topping up, the cyborg air force took flight without any need for airplanes, and caught and destroyed the incoming Rijk craft in *spydernets*, the giant booby-trapped metal webs that they hung across the sky. *Underwater*, too, they laid similar spidery traps (they had modified their "lungs" for submarine use and were therefore able to sabotage and scuttle the entire Rijk fleet from below). The so-called *Battle of the Antipodes* was won, and the skies and seas fell silent. On the far side of Galileo-1, floodwaters engulfed the Rijk. If Akasz Kronos felt any compassion as his countrymen drowned, he did not record it.

After the victory, however, things changed. The Puppet Kings returned from the wars with a new sense of individual worth, even of "rights". To bring them into line, Kronos announced an urgent maintenance-and-repair schedule. Many cyborgs failed to keep their appointments at his workshop, preferring—in the case of those damaged in battle—to live with their disabilities: their malfunctioning servo-mechanisms and partially burned-out circuitry. Groups of the Puppet Kings became secretive, conspiratorial, surly. Kronos suspected that they were meeting covertly to plot against him and heard rumours that at these meetings they addressed one another not by number but by new names, which they had chosen for themselves. He became tyrannical, and when one of the Three Society Girls was insolent to his face, he made an example of her, turning against her his much feared "master blaster", which caused an instant, irreversible deletion of all programs: in other words, cybernetic death.

The execution was counter-productive. Dissension grew more rapidly than before. Many cyborgs went underground, erecting, around their hide-outs, sophisticated anti-surveillance electronic shields, which even Kronos could not easily penetrate, and moving frequently, so that by the time the Professor had broken down one set of defences, the revolutionaries had already disappeared behind the next. We cannot say for sure exactly when the Dollmaker, whom Akasz Kronos had created in his own image and imbued with many of his own characteristics, learned how to override the Prime Directive. But soon after that breakthrough it was Professor Akasz Kronos who disappeared. No longer safe from his creations, he had to go underground while the *Peekay revolution* triumphantly emerged into the daylight to be greeted by the cheers of all the cyborgs in Baburia.

The so-called *last word* from Kronos exists only in the form of an electronic message to his usurper, the cyborg Dollmaker. It is a rambling, incoherent text, self-exculpatory and full of accusations of ingratitude, threats and curses. However, there is good reason to suppose that this text is a forgery, perhaps the work of the Dollmaker himself. The creation of a "mad Kronos", whose sane mirror image he was, suited the cyborg's purposes perfectly; and such is history's appetite for the lurid that this version was widely accepted. (That single portrait of Kronos is notable, as we have remarked, for the scientist's insane eyes.) Lately, the discovery of fragments of Professor Kronos's journals has shed new light on his state of mind. A very different Kronos emerges from these fragments, whose authenticity seems beyond dispute; the handwriting is clearly the Professor's. "The gods, too, murdered the Titans who made them," Kronos writes. "Artificial life here merely mirrors the real thing. For man is born in chains but everywhere seeks to be free. I too once had strings. I loved my puppets, knowing that, like children, they might walk away from me one day. But they cannot leave me behind. I made them with love, and my love is in each one of them, in their circuits and plastics. In their wood." Yet this Kronos, so free from bitterness, seems too good to be true. The Professor, a master of dissimulation, may have been plotting his vengeance behind a screen of fatalism.

After Kronos's disappearance, a PK delegation led by the Dollmaker and his lover, the Goddess of Victory, took the scientist's place at the next annual *Day of the Shoes*, and informed the Mogol that the Professor's contract was to be considered void. Henceforth the "Peekays" and Baburians must live on their twin islands as equals. Before walking out of the Mogol's presence (instead of shuffling out backwards as protocol dictated—a custom that even Kronos had not dared to ignore) the Goddess of Victory threw down the challenge that still reverberates between the two communities: "*Let the fittest survive.*"

A few days later a small, battered amphibious craft landed unnoticed in a forested corner of the northern island of Baburia. Zameen of Rijk had escaped the destruction of her lost civilization and made her way, against overwhelming odds, to the island refuge of the man who had left her to die. Had she come to renew their love or to avenge her abandonment? Was she here as lover or assassin? Her uncanny resemblance to the cyborg Dollmaker's lover, the Goddess of Victory, meant that the Puppet Kings deferred to her without question, believing her to be their new queen. What would happen when the two women confronted each other? How would the Dollmaker react to the "real" version of the woman he loved? How would she, the real woman, react to this mechanical avatar of her former lover? What would the Puppet Kings' new enemies, the antipodeans to whose territory they had now staked so extensive a claim, make of her? How would she deal with them? And what had actually befallen Professor Kronos? If he was dead, how did he die? If alive, how great were his remaining powers? Had he genuinely been overthrown, or was his disappearance some sort of fiendish ploy? So many questions! And behind them, the greatest riddle of all. The Puppet Kings had been offered by Kronos a choice between their original, mechanical selves and some, at least, of the ambiguities of human nature. What would be their choice: wisdom—or fury? Peace—or fury? Love—or fury? The fury of genius, of creation, or of the murderer or tyrant, the wild shrieking fury that must never be named?

The continuing story of the twin goddesses and doubled professors, of Zameen's search for the vanished Akasz Kronos, and of the struggle for power between the two communities of Baburia will be reported on this site in regular bulletins. Click on the links for more PK info or on the icons below for answers to 101 FAQs, access to interactivities, and to see the wide range of *PK merchandise* available for INSTANT shipping NOW. All major credit cards accepted.

13

As a young man in the early 1960s, Malik Solanka had devoured the science fiction novels of what was later recognized as the form's golden age. In flight from his own life's ugly reality, he found in the fantastic—its parables and allegories, but also its flights of pure invention, its loopy, spiralling conceits—a ceaselessly metamorphosing alternative world in which he felt instinctively at home. He subscribed to the legendary magazines, *Amazing* and *F&SF,* bought as many of the yellow-jacketed Victor Gollancz SF series as he could afford, and all but memorized the books of Ray Bradbury, Zenna Henderson, A. E. van Vogt, Clifford D. Simak, Isaac Asimov, Frederik Pohl and C. M. Kornbluth, Stanislaw Lem, James Blish, Philip K. Dick and L. Sprague de Camp. Golden-age science fiction and science fantasy were, in Solanka's view, the best popular vehicle ever devised for the novel of ideas and of metaphysics. At twenty, his favourite work of fiction was a story called "The Nine Billion Names of God", in which a Tibetan monastery set up to count the names of the Almighty—believing this to be the only reason for the existence of the universe—buys a top-of-the-line computer to speed up the process. Hard-bitten industry mavens go to the monastery to help the monks get the great machine up and running. They find the whole idea of listing the names pretty laughable, and worry about how the monks might react when the job's done and the universe goes on going on; so once they've done their work, they sneak quietly away. Later, on a plane home, they calculate that the computer must have finished its work. They look out of the window at the night sky, where—Solanka had never forgotten the last line—"one by one, very quietly, the stars were going out."

To such a reader—and admirer, in the cinema, of the highbrow sci-fi of *Fahrenheit 451* and *Solaris*—George Lucas was a kind of Antichrist and the Spielberg of *Close Encounters* was a kid playing in the grown-ups' sandbox, while the *Terminator* films, and above all the mighty *Blade Runner,* were carriers of the sacred flame. And now it was his own turn. In those unreliable summer days, Professor Malik Solanka would work on the world of the Puppet Kings—the dolls as well as their stories—like a man possessed. The story of the mad scientist Akasz Kronos and his beautiful lover, Zameen, filled his mind. New York faded into the background; or, rather, everything that happened to him in the city—every random encounter, every newspaper he opened, every thought, every feeling, every dream—fed his imagination, as though prefabricated to fit into the structure he had already devised. Real life had started obeying the dictates of fiction, providing precisely the raw material he needed to transmute through the alchemy of his reborn art.

Akasz he got from *aakaash,* Hindi for "sky". Sky as in Asmaan (Urdu), as in poor Sky Schuyler, as in the great sky gods: Ouranos-Varuna, Brahma, Yahweh, Manitou. And Kronos was the Greek, the child-devourer, Time. Zameen was earth, the heavens' opposite, which embraces the sky at the horizon. Akasz he had seen clearly from the first, picturing his whole life's arc. Zameen, though, had surprised him. In this tale of a drowning world he hadn't expected an earth goddess—even one modelled on Neela Mahendra—to take a central role. Yet here she undeniably was, and by showing up she had valuably thickened the plot. Her presence seemed to have been prefigured, even though he hadn't planned for it at all. Neela/Zameen of Rijk/Goddess of Victory: three versions of the same woman filled his thoughts, and he realized that he'd finally found the successor to the famous creation of his youth. "Hello to Neela," he told himself, "and so, at last, farewell to Little Brain."

Which was also to say, farewell to his afternoons with Mila Milo. Mila had felt the change in him at once, intuiting it when she saw him leave for his tryst with Neela on the steps of the Met. She knew what I wanted before I had even dared admit it to myself, Solanka acknowledged. It was probably finished between us there and then. Even if there had been no miracle, even if Neela hadn't so unpredictably chosen me, Mila had seen enough. She has real beauty of her own, and pride, and isn't about to play second fiddle to anyone. He returned to West Seventieth Street after an endlessly surprising night spent with Neela in a hotel room across the park—a night whose biggest surprise was that it was happening at all—and found Mila wrapped ostentatiously around beautiful, stupid Eddie Ford on the stoop next door; Eddie, one of nature's bodyguards, glowing with the joy of having regained guardianship over the only body he gave a damn about. The look Eddie gave Solanka over Mila's shoulder was impressively articulate. It said, Buddy, you don't have access privileges at this address no more; between you and this lady there's now a red velvet rope and your accreditation is so cancelled, you shouldn't even think about stepping in this direction, unless of course you'd like me to clean your teeth, using your spinal column as a brush.

The next afternoon, however, she was at his door. "Take me out somewhere great and expensive. I need to dress up and eat industrial quantities of food." Eating was Mila's normal reaction to misery, drinking her response to anger. Sad was probably better than mad, Solanka mused ungenerously. Easier for him, anyway. To make up for this selfish thought, he called one of the talked-about new places of the moment, a Cuban-themed bar-restaurant in Chelsea named Gio in honour of Doña Gioconda, an elderly diva whose star was shining brightly that Buena Vista summer and in whose languid smoke-trail of a voice all of old Havana came back to swaggering, swaying, seducing, smooching life. Solanka got a table so easily that he commented on the fact to the woman taking the booking. "City's a ghost town righ' now," she agreed distantly. "It's, like, Loserville. See jou at nine P.M."

"You left me and I'm dying," Gioconda sang on the restaurant's sound system as Solanka and Mila came in, "but after three days I will rise again. Don't go to my funeral, sucker, I'll be out dancing with some better man. Resurrection, resurrection, and baby I'll make sure you know when." Mila translated the words for Solanka. "That's perfect," she added. "Are you listening, Malik? Because if I could request a track, this would be it. As they say on the radio, the message is in the words. 'Oh, you thought that you could break me, and it's true that I'm in pieces now, but after three days they will wake me, from a distance you will see me take my bow. Resurrection, resurrection, gettin' a new life any day now.' "

At the bar she downed a mojito fast and ordered another one. Solanka saw that he was in for a rougher ride than anticipated. At the bottom of the second glass she moved to the table, ordered all the most highly spiced dishes on the menu, and let him have it. "You're a lucky man," she told him, plunging into the complimentary guacamole, "because evidently you're an optimist. You have to be, because it's so easy for you to throw things away. Your child, your wife, me, whatever. Only a wild optimist, a stupid brain-dead Pollyanna or Pangloss, throws away what's most precious, what's so rare and satisfies his deepest need, which you know and I know you can't even name or look at without the shutters closed and the lights out, you have to put a cushion on your lap to hide it until somebody comes along who's smart enough to know what to do, somebody whose own unspeakable need just happens to make a perfect fit with your own. And now, now when we've got there, when the defences are down and the pretence is over and we're really in that room that we never allowed ourselves to believe could exist for either of us, the invisible room of our greatest fear—right at the very moment when we discover there's no need to be afraid in that room, we can have whatever we want for as long as we want it, and maybe when we've had our fill we'll wake up and notice that we're real living people, we're not the puppets of our desires but just this woman, this man, and then we can stop the games, open up the shutters, turn out the lights, and step out into the city street hand in hand . . . *this* is when you choose to pick up some whore in the park and for Chrissake get a fucking room. An optimist is a man who gives up an impossible pleasure because he's sure he'll find it again just around the bend. An optimist thinks his dick talks better sense than, oh, never mind. I was going to say, than his girl, meaning, stupidly, me. Me, by the way, I'm a pessimist. My view is that not only does lightning not strike twice, it usually doesn't strike once. So that was it for me, what happened between us, that was really *it,* and you, you just, damn, damn. I could have stayed with you, did you ever work that out? Oh, not for long, just thirty or forty years, more than you've got, probably. Instead, I'll marry Eddie. You know what they say: charity begins at home."

Breathing heavily, she paused and applied herself to the carnival of food that stood before her. Solanka waited; more would soon enough be on the way. He was thinking, You can't marry him, you mustn't, but such advice was no longer his to give. "You're telling yourself what we did was wrong," she said. "I know you. You're using guilt to set yourself free. So now you think you can walk away from me and tell yourself it's the moral thing to do. But what we did wasn't wrong," and here her eyes filled with tears. "Not wrong at all. We were just comforting each other for our terrible feelings of loss. The doll thing was just a way of getting there. What, you really think I fucked my father, you imagine I wriggled my ass on his lap and pushed my nail into his nipple and licked his poor sweet throat? That's what you're telling yourself to give yourself an out, or was that also the in? Was that the turn-on, to be my father's ghost? Professor, you're the one who's sick. I'm telling you again. What we did wasn't wrong. It was play. Serious play, dangerous play, maybe, but play.

I thought you understood that. I thought you might just be that impossible creature, a sexually wise man who could give me a safe place, a place to be free and to set you free, too, a place where we could release all the built-up poison and anger and hurt, just let it go and be free of it, but it turns out, Professor, you're just another fool. You were on Howard Stern today, by the way."

That was a left turn he hadn't expected, a fast swerve against the oncoming emotional traffic. Perry Pincus, he realized with a sudden heaviness. "She made it, then. What did she say?" "Oh," said Mila, speaking through lamb smothered in salsa verde, "she said a mouthful." Mila had an excellent memory and could often replay whole conversations almost verbatim. Her Perry Pincus, which she now gave with as much wounding gusto as a young Bernhardt, a Stockard Channing of the near-at-hand, was therefore, Solanka conceded with sinking heart, likely to be extremely reliable as far as accuracy was concerned. "Sometimes these so-called great male minds are textbook cases of pathetically arrested development," Perry had told Howard and his huge audience. "Take the case of this guy Malik Solanka, *not* a major mind, gave up philosophy and went into television, and I should say right out that he was one of those I never, you know. Not on my résumé. What was his problem, right? *Well.* Let me tell you that this Solanka's whole room, and remember we're talking here about a fellow of King's College, Cambridge, England, was crawling with dolls, and I do mean dolls. Once I noticed that, I couldn't leave fast enough. God forbid he should mistake me for a dolly and poke me in the stomach till I said *Ma-ma.* I was like, excuse me, but I never even liked dolls when I was little, and I'm a girl? What? No, no. Gay I'm comfortable with. Absolutely. I'm from California, Howard. Sure. This wasn't gay. This was . . . goo-goo. It was—what can I tell you?—*icky.* For a gag, I still send the guy soft toys at Christmas. The Coca-Cola polar bear. You got it. He never acknowledges receipt, but guess what? He never sent one back, either. Men. When you know their secrets, it's hard not to laugh."

"I wondered if I should tell you," Mila confided, "but then I thought, screw him, the gloves are off." Doña Gio was still singing, but the screaming of the Furies momentarily drowned her voice. The hungry goddesses were beating around both their heads, feeding on their rage. The Pincus interview roared in him, and Mila's expression changed. "Shh," she said. "Okay, I'm sorry, but will you please stop making that noise? We'll get thrown out of here and I haven't even had dessert yet." It was plain that the roar had escaped into the room. People were looking. The owner-manager, a Raul Julia lookalike, was coming across the room. A glass broke in Malik Solanka's hand. There was a messy, mingled flow of wine and blood. It became necessary to leave. Bandages were produced, a doctor's assistance refused, the check was hurriedly brought forward and settled. Outside, it had begun to rain. Mila's fury abated, trumped by his own. "About the woman on Howard?" she said in the eventual taxi uptown. "She came across as basically an ageing nympho playing kiss and tell. You're an older person, you should know how life is. Loose ends dangling everywhere, and once in a while they snap back and lash you across the face. Let her go. She's nothing to you, hardly ever was, and with the amount of bad karma she's storing up, I don't like her chances. Enough public screaming! Jesus. Sometimes you're scary. Mostly I think you wouldn't hurt a fly and then suddenly you're this Godzilla creature from the black lagoon who looks like he could rip the throat off a Tyrannosaurus Rex. You've got to bring that thing under control, Malik. Wherever it's coming from, you need to send it away."

"Islam will cleanse your soul of dirty anger," the taxi driver interrupted, "and reveal to you the holy wrath that moves mountains." Then he added, switching languages as another car came unacceptably close to his taxicab, "Hey! American man! You are a godless homosexual rapist of your grandmother's pet goat." Solanka began to laugh, the dreadful mirthless laughter of release: hard, painful, racking sobs. "Hello again, Beloved Ali," he coughed. "Good to see you in such top form."

* * *

One week later, Mila somewhat surprisingly called and invited him over "to talk about something else". Her manner was friendly, businesslike, excited. She had bounced back fast, Solanka marvelled, accepting her invitation. It was his first visit to Mila's tiny fourth-floor walk-up, which, he thought, was trying hard to be an all-American apartment but failing badly: posters of Latrell Sprewell and Serena Williams hung uncomfortably on either side of floor-to-ceiling bookshelves groaning with volumes of Serbian and Eastern European literature in the original, and in French and English translation—Kiš, Andrič, Pavić, some of the convention-busting Klokotrizans, and, from the classical period, Obradovic and Vuk Stefanovic Karadzic; also Klima, Kadaré, Nádas, Konrad, Herbert. There was no picture of her father on display; Solanka noted the significant omission. A framed monochrome photograph of a young woman in a belted floral-print frock smiled broadly at Solanka. Mila's mother, looking like Mila's younger sister. "Look how happy she is," Mila said. "That was the last summer before she knew she was sick. I'm now the same exact age she was when she passed, so that's one nightmare less to worry about. I made it across that hurdle. For years I didn't think I would." She wanted to belong to this city, this country at this time, but old European demons were screeching in her ears. In one respect, however, Mila was unreservedly of her American generation. The computer workstation was the room's focal point: the Mac PowerBook, the older desktop Macintosh pushed to the back of the work surface, the scanner, the CD burner, the plug-in audio system, the music sequencer, the back-up Zip drive, the manuals, the shelves of CD-ROMs, DVDs, and much other stuff, which Solanka couldn't easily identify. Even the bed felt like an afterthought. Certainly he would never know its pleasures. She had brought him up here, he understood, to put all that behind them. It was another example of her system of inverted signs. Her dead father was the most important person in her life; therefore, no picture of Dad was visible. Solanka was now to be no more than the professor next door; ergo, invite him into your bedroom for a cup of coffee.

She had clearly prepared a speech and was in a state of high readiness, buzzing with it. Once he had been given his mug of coffee, the obviously planned olive branch was offered. "Because I'm a superior type of human being," Mila said, with a trace of the old humour, "because I can rise above personal tragedy and function on a higher plane, and also because I really think you're great at what you do, I talked to the guys about your new project. The cool science fiction figures you've been coming up with: the mad cyberneticist, the drowning planet idea, the cyborgs versus the lotus-eaters from the other side of the world, the fight to the death between the counterfeit and the real. We'd like to come and talk to you about building a site. There's a whole presentation we have, you can get an idea of what's possible. To tell you just one thing, they've developed a way of compressing video material that gives you close to DVD quality on-line, and within one generation it'll be at least a match. It's ahead of anything you'll get anywhere else. You have no comprehension of the speed of things now, every year is the Stone Age to the year that follows. Just the creative potential, what can be done with an idea now. The best sites are inexhaustible, people come back and back, it's like a world you're giving them to belong to. Sure, you have to get the sales and delivery mechanism right, it has to be easy to buy into what you're offering, and we have a cool pitch on that also. But the point is to make it easy for *you.* You already have the back-story and the characters. Which we love. Then to keep control of the concept, you'll need to put together a master handbook, character-development parameters, storyline do's and don'ts, the laws of your imagined universe. Inside that framework, there are so many brilliant kids who would just love to create all kinds of, you can't even say it, they're inventing whole new media every day. If it works, of course, the old media will come running, books, records, TV, movies, musicals, who knows.

"I love these guys. They're so hungry, they can take an idea and run with it into, like, the fifth dimension, and all you have to do is let them make it happen for you, you're the absolute monarch, nothing happens if you don't want it to; you just sit there and go yes, no, yes, yes, no—

whoa, whoa." She made calming, pressing gestures with both hands. "Hear me out. Will you for Chrissake hear me out, you owe me that much. Malik, I know how unhappy you were—are—about the whole Little Brain saga. This is me, remember? Malik, *I know that.* That's what I'm saying to you here. This time you don't lose control. This time you have a better vehicle than even *existed* when you came up with Little Brain, and you drive it, totally. This is your chance to get right what went wrong before, and if it works, let's not be coy here, the financial upside is very, very strong. We all think this could be huge if it's done right. On Little Brain, by the way, I don't one hundred per cent agree with your position, because as you know I think she's great, and things are changing, the whole concept of ownership as far as ideas is so different now, it's so much more co-operative. You have to be a little more flexible, just a little bit more, okay? Let other people into your magic circle now and then. You're still the magician, but let everyone else play with the wands sometimes. Little Brain? Let her fly, Malik, let her be what she is. She's all grown-up now. Let her go. You can still love her. She's still your child."

She was on her feet, her fingers flying at the laptop, soliciting its aid. Perspiration beaded her lip. The seventh veil falls away, Solanka thought. Fully clothed as Mila was in her daytime sportswear, she stood naked before him at last. *Furia.* This was the self she had never fully shown, Mila as Fury, the world-swallower, the self as pure transformative energy. In this incarnation she was simultaneously terrifying and wonderful. He could never resist a woman when she flowed at him this way, letting her riverine abundance overwhelm him. This is what he looked for in women: to be overpowered, outmatched. This Gangetic, Mississippian inexorability, whose dwindling, he sadly knew, was what had gone wrong in his marriage. Overwhelming doesn't last for ever. No matter how astonishing the initial contact, in the end the beloved astonishes us less. She merely whelms and, even further down the road, underwhelms. But to give up on his need for excess, for the immense thing, the thing that made him feel like a surfer in the snow, riding the crest of an avalanche's leading edge! To say goodbye to that need would also be to accept that he was, in the matter of desire, agreeing to be dead. And when the living agree with themselves to be dead, the dark fury begins. The dark fury of life, refusing to die before its allotted time.

He reached out for Mila. She knocked his arm aside. Her eyes were shining: she had recovered from him already and was resurrected as a queen. "This is what we can be to each other now, Malik. Take it or leave it. If you say no, I don't want to talk to you ever again. But if you come aboard, we'll work our butts off for you and there'll be no hard feelings from me. This new world is my life, Malik, it's the thing of my time, growing as I grow, learning as I learn, becoming as I become. It's where I feel most alive. There, inside the electricity. I told you: you need to learn how to play. Serious play, that's my thing. That's the heart of what's happening, and I know how to do it, and if you can give me the material I need to work with, well, baby, for me that's better than what was waiting under the cushion on your lap. Nice as that was, don't get me wrong. Nice as that undoubtedly was. Okay, I'm done. Don't answer. Go home. Think about it. Let us make the full presentation. It's a big decision. Take it slow. Make it when you're ready. But make it soon."

The computer screen burst into life. Images raced towards him like bazaar traders. This was technology as hustler, peddling its wares, Solanka thought; or, as if in a darkened nightclub, gyrating for him. Laptop as lapdancer. The auxiliary sound system poured high-definition noise over him like golden rain. "I don't need to think about it," he told her. "Let's do it. Let's go."

14

Eleanor rang, and Solanka's emotional bar went up another notch. "You know how to generate love, Malik," his wife told him. "You just don't know what to do with it once it's there." But still no anger in that mellifluous voice. "I was thinking, it was so wonderful being loved by you. I was missing you, I suppose, so I'm glad I found you in. I see us everywhere I go, isn't it stupid, I see us having so many good times. Your son is so special. Everyone who sees him thinks so. Morgen thinks he's the best ever, and you know what Morgen thinks of kids. But he loves Asmaan to bits. Everyone does. And you know, he's always asking, 'What would Daddy say? What would Daddy think?' You're very much in his thoughts. And in mine. So I was only wanting to say, both of us are sending you so much love."

Asmaan took the phone. "I want to talk to Daddy. Hello, Daddy. I've got a stuffed-up nose. That's why I was crying. That's why Olive isn't here." *That's why* was because. *Because Olive isn't here.* Olive was the mother's helper, whom Asmaan adored. "I did a picture for you, Daddy. It's for Mummy and you. I'll show it to you. It has red and lellow and white. I did a picture for Grandpa. Grandpa's dead. That's why he was ill for a long while. Grandma isn't dead yet. She's okay. Maybe she'll die tomorrow. I'm going to be a stoolboy, Daddy. That's why I'm going to a good stool soon. I'm not going tomorrow! No. Another day. It's a nursery stool, anyway. Not a big one. That's why I have to be bigger for the big one. I'm not going there today! Hmm. Have you got a pa-resent, Daddy? Maybe there's a big ephelant inside it. Could be! Probably it's a big ephelant. Well: 'bye!"

At dawn he woke alone in bed, roused by an agony of floorboards on the floor above. Somebody certainly was an early riser up there. All Solanka's senses seemed to be on red alert. His hearing had grown so unnaturally sharp that he could hear the beeps of the upstairs message machine, the water pouring from his neighbour's watering can into her window boxes and pots of indoor flowers. A fly settled on his exposed foot, and he actually leapt out of bed as if touched by a ghost and stood in the middle of the room, naked, foolish, filled with fear. Sleep was impossible. The street was already raucous. He took a long hot shower and read himself the riot act. Mila was right. He had to bring this thing under control. A doctor, he had to go to a doctor and get some proper medication. What was it Rhinehart had called him in jest? A heart attack waiting to happen. Well, delete *heart*. He had become an attack in waiting. His bad temper might have been comical once, but it was no joke now. If he hadn't done anything yet, he might at any moment; if the fury hadn't already led him into the country of the irreversible, it would, he knew it would. He feared himself already, and pretty soon he would have scared off everyone else. He wouldn't need to drop out of the world; it would rush away from him. He would become the person people crossed the road to avoid. What if Neela made him angry? What if in a moment of passion she touched the top of his head?

Here at the outset of the third millennium, medication was readily available to deal with the irruption into the adult self of the outrageous and the inchoate. Once if he'd roared like a warlock in a public place, he might have been burned for a devil or weighted with stones to see if he'd float in the East River, like a witch. Once at the very least he might have been placed in the pillory and pelted with rotten fruit. Now all that was required was to settle one's check rapidly and leave. And every good American knew the names of half a dozen effective mood-management medicaments. This was a nation for which the daily recitation of pharmaceutical brand names—Prozac, Halcion, Seroquil, Numscul, Lobotomine—was like a Zen koan, or the assertion of a kind of screwy patriotism: *I pledge allegiance to the American drug.* So what was happening to him was eminently preventable. Therefore, most people would say, it was his duty to prevent it, so that he could stop being afraid of himself, stop being a danger to others, start walking back towards his life. Towards Asmaan, the Golden Child. Asmaan the sky, who needed his father's sheltering love.

Yes, but the medication was a mist. It was a fog you swallowed that curled around your mind. The medication was a shelf and you had to sit on it while the world went on around you. It was a translucent shower curtain, like the one in *Psycho.* Things grew opaque; no, no, that wasn't right. What became opaque was you. Solanka's scorn for this age of doctors resurfaced. You wanted to be taller? All you had to do was go to the tall doctor and let him put metal extensions into your long bones. For thinner, there was the thin doctor, the pretty doctor for prettier, and so on. Was that all there was? Was that it? Were we just cars now, cars that could take themselves to the mechanic and get themselves fixed up any way they wanted? Customized, with leopard-spotted seats and wraparound sound? Everything in him fought against the mechanization of the human. Wasn't this exactly what his imagined world was being created to confront? What could a head doctor tell him about himself that he didn't already know? Doctors knew nothing. All they wanted was to manage you, to tame you doggy-style or hood you like a hawk. Doctors wanted to push you down on your knees and break them, and once you started using those chemical crutches they handed out, you'd never walk on your own two legs again.

All around him the American self was reconceiving itself in mechanical terms, but was everywhere running out of control. This self talked constantly about itself, barely touching on any other topic. An industry of controllers—witch doctors whose role was to augment and "gap-fill" the work of the already witchy doctors—had arisen to deal with its problems of perfomance. Redefinition was this industry's basic mode of operation. Unhappiness was redefined as physical unfitness, despair as a question of good spinal alignment. Happiness was better food, wiser furniture orientation, deeper breathing technique. Happiness was selfishness. The rudderless self was told to be its own steering mechanism, the rootless self was instructed to root itself in itself while, plainly, continuing to pay for the services of the new guides, the cartographers of the altered states of America. Of course, the old industries of control were still available, still making their own, more familiar cases. The vice-presidential candidate of the Democratic party blamed the movies for the national malaise and praised, by contrast, God. God must move closer to the centre of the country's life. (Closer? Solanka thought. If the Almighty got any closer to the presidency, he'd be living at the end of Pennsylvania Avenue and doing the damn job himself.) George Washington was exhumed to be a soldier for Jesus. No morality without religion, George thundered, standing pale and earthy in his grave, holding his little hatchet. And in Washington's country, the supposedly insufficiently devout citizenry said, when asked, that over ninety per cent of them would vote for a Jew or homosexual for president, but only forty-nine per cent would vote for an atheist. Praise the Lord!

In spite of all the chatter, all the diagnosis, all the new consciousness, the most powerful communications made by this new, much-articulated national self were inarticulate. For the real problem was damage not to the machine but to the desirous heart, and the language of the heart was being lost. An excess of this heart damage was the issue, not muscle tone, not food, neither feng shui nor karma, neither godlessness nor

God. This was the Jitter Bug that made people mad: excess not of commodities but of their dashed and thwarted hopes. Here in Boom America, the real-life manifestation of Keats's fabulous realms of gold, here in the doubloon-heavy pot at the rainbow's end, human expectations were at the highest levels in human history, and so, therefore, were human disappointments. When arsonists lit fires that burned the West, when a man picked up a gun and began killing strangers, when a child picked up a gun and began killing friends, when lumps of concrete smashed the skulls of rich young women, this disappointment for which the word "disappointment" was too weak was the engine driving the killers' tongue-tied expressiveness. This was the only subject: the crushing of dreams in a land where the right to dream was the national ideological cornerstone, the pulverizing cancellation of personal possibility at a time when the future was opening up to reveal vistas of unimaginable, glittering treasures such as no man or woman had ever dreamed of before. In the tormented flames and anguished bullets Malik Solanka heard a crucial, ignored, unanswered, perhaps unanswerable question—the same question, loud and life-shattering as a Munch scream, that he had just asked himself: is this all there is? What, this is *it*? *This* is *it*? People were waking up like Krysztof Waterford-Wajda and realizing that their lives didn't belong to them. Their *bodies* didn't belong to them, and nobody else's bodies belonged to anyone, either. They no longer saw a reason not to shoot.

Those whom the gods would destroy they first make mad. The Furies hovered over Malik Solanka, over New York and America, and shrieked. In the streets below, the traffic, human and inhuman, screamed back its enraged assent.

Showered, a little more settled, Solanka remembered that he still hadn't called Jack. It struck him that he didn't want to. The Jack unveiled by Neela had disappointed and unnerved him, which in itself should not have mattered. Certainly, Jack must have been disappointed in him many times, even put off by his famous "Solankering" temper. Friends should hurdle such obstacles; yet Solanka did not pick up the phone. Why, then, he was a bad friend too; add that to the lengthening charge sheet. Neela stood between them now. That was it. Never mind that she had broken off her relationship with Jack before anything had started between her and Solanka. What mattered was how Jack would see it, and he would see it as treason. And, if he was honest with himself, Solanka silently admitted, he saw it as a betrayal, too.

Moreover, Neela was now also an obstacle between himself and Eleanor. He had left home for one apparent and one underlying reason: the horrifying fact of the knife in the dark, and, beneath the surface of the marriage, the erosion of what had once overwhelmed. Furious and newly kindled desire was hard to give up for that calmer, gentler old flame. "There must be someone else," Eleanor had said; and now there was, there was. Neela Mahendra, the last big emotional gamble of his life. Beyond her, if he lost her as he probably would, he saw a desert, its slow white dunes sliding towards a sandy grave. The dangers of the enterprise, accentuated by the differences in age and background, by the damage in him and the whimsicality in her, were considerable. How does a woman for whom every man hungers decide that one is enough? Near the end of their first night together, she had said, "I wasn't looking for this. I'm not sure I'm ready for it." She meant that it had started feeling so deep so fast that it scared her. "The risk might be too big." He had twisted his mouth a little too sourly. "I wonder which of us," he asked, "is taking the bigger emotional risk." She had had no trouble with that question. "Oh, you are," she said.

Wisława returned to work. Soft-spoken Simon Jay had called Solanka from his farm to say that he and his wife had soothed the angry house cleaner, but a contrite phone call from Solanka would help. Gentle as he was, Mr Jay did not fail to point out that the lease required the apartment to be properly maintained. Solanka gritted his teeth and made the call. "Okay, I come, why not," Wisława had agreed. "You are lucky I am big in the heart." Her work was even less satisfactory than before, but Solanka said nothing. There was an imbalance of power in the apartment. Wisława entered like a queen—like a Goddess of Victory who had cut her strings—and after a few hours of wandering around the duplex like a monarch on a royal progress, waving her duster like a royal kerchief, departed with a contemptuous expression on her bony face. Those who formerly served were now the masters, Solanka thought. As on Galileo-1, so also in New York.

His imagined world absorbed him more and more. He drew furiously, modelled in clay, whittled soft woods; above all, and furiously, he wrote. Mila Milo's troop had begun to treat him with a kind of surprised reverence: who'd have thought, their manner seemed to say, that an old duffer could have come up with stuff as hip as this? Even slow, resentful Eddie went along with the new attitude. Solanka, despised by his own house-cleaner, was much mollified by the young men's respect and grew determined to prove worthy of it. Neela took up his nights, but he worked long hours during the days. Three or four hours of sleep proved to be enough. The blood seemed to pump harder through his veins. This, he thought, wondering at his undeserved good fortune, was renewal. Life had unexpectedly dealt him a strong hand, and he would make the most of it. It was time for a long, concentrated, perhaps even healing, burst of what Mila called serious play.

The back-story of events on Galileo-1 had taken on a proliferating life of its own. Never before had Solanka needed—wanted—to go into such detail. Fiction had him in its grip, and the figurines themselves began to feel secondary: not ends in themselves, but means. He, who had been so dubious about the coming of the brave new electronic world, was swept off his feet by the possibilities offered by the new technology, with its formal preference for lateral leaps and its relative uninterest in linear progression, a bias that had already bred in its users a greater interest in variation than in chronology. This freedom from the clock, from the tyranny of what happened next, was exhilarating, allowing him to develop his ideas in parallel, without worrying about sequence or step-by-step causation. Links were electronic now, not narrative. Everything existed at once. This was, Solanka realized, an exact mirror of the divine experience of time. Until the advent of hyperlinks, only God had been able to see simultaneously into past, present and future alike; human beings were imprisoned in the calendar of their days. Now, however, such omniscience was available to all, at the merest click of a mouse.

On the website, as it came into being, visitors would be able to wander at will between the project's different storylines and themes: Zameen of Rijk's search for Akasz Kronos, Zameen *vs.* the Goddess of Victory, the Tale of Two Dollmakers, Mogol the Baburian, Revolt of the Living Dolls I: The Fall of Kronos, Revolt of the Living Dolls II (This Time It's War), the Humanization of the Machines *vs.* the Mechanization of the Humans, the Battle of the Doubles, Mogol Captures Kronos (or Is It the Dollmaker?), the Recantation of the Dollmaker (or Was It Kronos?), and the grand finale, Revolt of the Living Dolls III: The Fall of the Mogol Empire. Each of these in turn would lead to further pages, plunging ever deeper into the multidimensioned world of the Puppet Kings, offering games to play, video segments to watch, chat rooms to enter and, naturally, things to buy.

Professor Solanka was intoxicated for hours on end by the Puppet Kings' six-pack of ethical dilemmas; was at once fascinated and revolted by the emerging personality of Mogol the Baburian, who turned out to be a competent poet, expert astronomer, passionate cultivator of gardens, but also a soldier of Coriolanus-like blood lust, and the most cruel of princes; and was deliriously entranced by the shadow-play possibilities (intellectual, symbolic, confrontational, mystificational, even sexual) of the two sets of doubles, the encounters between "real" and "real", "real" and "double", "double" and "double", which blissfully demonstrated the dissolution of the frontiers between the categories. He found himself inhabiting a world he greatly preferred to the one outside his window, and thus came to understand what Mila Milo had meant when she said that this was where she felt most alive. Here, inside the electricity, Malik Solanka emerged from the half-life of his Manhattan exile, travelled daily to Galileo-1, and began, once more, to live.

Ever since Little Brain's censored remarks to Galileo Galilei, questions of knowledge and power, surrender and defiance, ends and means, had gnawed at Solanka. "Galileo moments", those dramatic occasions when life asked the living whether they would dangerously stand by the truth or prudently recant it, increasingly seemed to him to lie close to the heart of what it was to be human. *Man, I wouldn't have taken that stuff lying down. I'd have started a fucking revolution, me.* When the possessor of truth was weak and the defender of the lie was strong, was it better to bend before the greater force? Or, by standing firm against it, might one discover a deeper strength in oneself and lay the despot low? When the soldiers of truth launched a thousand ships and burned the topless towers of the lie, should they be seen as liberators or had they, by using their enemy's weapons against him, themselves become the scorned barbarians (or even Baburians) whose houses they had set on fire? What were the limits of tolerance? How far, in the pursuit of the right, could we go before we crossed a line, arrived at the antipodes of ourselves, and became wrong?

Near the climax of the back-story of Galileo-1, Solanka embedded one such defining moment. Akasz Kronos, a fugitive from his own creations, was captured in great old age by the Mogol's soldiers and brought in chains to the Baburian court. By this time the Puppet Kings and the Baburians had been at war for a long generation, locked in a stalemate as debilitating as the Trojan War, and ancient Kronos, as creator of the cyborgs, was blamed for all their deeds. His explanation of his creations' arrival at autonomy was rejected by the Mogol with a snort of disbelief. There followed, in the pages Solanka wrote, a long dispute between the two men on the nature of life itself—life as created by a biological act, and life as brought into being by the imagination and skill of the living. Was life "natural", or could the "unnatural" be said to be alive? Was the imagined world necessarily inferior to the organic one? Kronos was still a creative genius in spite of his downfall and long penurious concealment, and he proudly defended his cyborgs: by every definition of sentient existence, they had grown into fully-fledged life-forms. Like *Homo faber*, they were users of tools; like *Homo sapiens*, they reasoned and engaged in moral debate. They could attend to their ills and reproduce their species, and by shedding him, their maker, they had set themselves free. The Mogol rejected these arguments out of hand. A malfunctioning dishwasher did not become a busboy, he argued. By the same token, a rogue puppet was still a doll, a renegade robot was still a robot. This was not a fit direction for their discussions to take. Rather, it was for Kronos to recant his theories and then provide the Baburian authorities with the technological data required to bring the Peekay machines under control. If he refused, the Mogol added, changing the tenor of the conversation, he would of course be tortured and, if necessary, torn limb from limb.

The "recantation of Kronos", his declaration that machines had no souls whereas man was immortal, was greeted by the deeply religious Baburian people as a mighty victory. Armed with information provided by the broken scientist, the antipodean army created new weapons, which paralysed the cyborgs' neurosystems and rendered them inoperative. (The term "killed" was forbidden; what was not alive could not be dead.) The Peekay forces fled in disarray, and a Baburian victory looked assured. The Dollmaker cyborg himself lay among the fallen. Too egotistical—too "consistent"—to have created any replicas of himself, the Dollmaker was still one of a kind; thus his character was erased with his termination. The only person who could have re-created him was Akasz Kronos, whose fate was obscure. Perhaps the Mogol killed him, even after his abject surrender; or perhaps he was blinded like Tiresias and permitted, by way of further humiliation, to wander the world, begging bowl in hand, "speaking the truth that no man would believe", while from every quarter he heard tales of the collapse of his own great enterprises, of the reduction of the great Kronosian Puppet Kings, the sentient cyborgs from Rijk, the first machines ever to cross the frontier between mechanical entities and living beings, into piles of useless junk. And while nobody would now believe the truth that he had himself denied, he himself had no choice but to accept the reality of the catastrophe that his own cowardice, his lack of moral fortitude, had brought about.

At the eleventh hour, however, the tide turned. The Puppet Kings regrouped under a new, dual leadership. Zameen of Rijk and her cyborg counterpart the Goddess of Victory joined forces, like twin Ranis of Jhansi rising up against imperialist oppression, or like Little Brain in a new, double-trouble incarnation, leading her promised revolution. They used their combined scientific brilliance to build electronic shields against the new Baburian weapons. Then, with Zameen and the Goddess at their head, the Peekay army began a major offensive and invested the Mogol's citadel. Thus began the Siege of Baburia, which would not end for a generation or more . . .

In the world of the imagination, in the creative cosmos that had begun with simple doll-making and then proliferated into this many-armed, multimedia beast, it wasn't necessary to answer questions; far better to find interesting ways of rephrasing them. Nor was it necessary to end the story—indeed, it was vital to the project's long-term prospects that the tale be capable of almost indefinite prolongation, with new adventures and themes being grafted on to it at regular intervals and new characters to sell in doll, toy and robot form. The backstory was a skeleton that periodically grew new bones, the framework for a fictional beast capable of constant metamorphosis, which fed on every scrap it could find: its creator's personal history, scraps of gossip, deep learning, current affairs, high and low culture, and the most nourishing diet of all—namely, the past. The ransacking of the world's storehouse of old stories and ancient histories was entirely legitimate. Few Web users were familiar with the myths, or even the facts, of the past; all that was needed was to give the old material a fresh, contemporary twist. Transmutation was all. The Puppet Kings website went on-line and at once achieved and sustained a high level of "hits". Comments flooded in, and the river of Solanka's imagination was fed from a thousand streams. It began to swell and grow.

Because the work never settled, never stopped being a work in progress but remained in a condition of perpetual revolution, a degree of untidiness was inevitable. The histories of characters and places, even their names, sometimes changed as Solanka's vision of his fictitious universe clarified and sharpened. Certain storyline possibilities turned out to be stronger than he had at first realized, and were greatly amplified. The Zameen/Goddess of Victory strand was the most important of these. In the initial conception, Zameen had simply been a beauty, not a scientist at all. Later, however, when Solanka—prompted, he had to concede, by Mila Milo—understood how important Zameen would be in the story's climactic phase, he went back and added much material to her early life, turning her into Kronos's scientific equal as well as his sexual and moral superior. Other avenues turned out to be blind alleys and were discarded. For example, in an early draft of the back-story, Solanka imagined that the "Galilean" figure captured by the Mogol was the cyborg Dollmaker, not the vanished Akasz Kronos. In this version the Dollmaker's denial of his right to be called a "life-form", his confession of his own inferiority, became a crime against himself and his own race. Later the Dollmaker escaped from his Baburian jailers, and when news of his "recantation" was spread by the Mogol's propaganda machine with the aim of undermining his leadership, the cyborg hotly denied the accusations, announcing that he had not been the prisoner in question, that in fact his human avatar, Kronos, was the real traitor to the truth. Even though he discarded this version, Solanka retained a soft spot for it, and often wondered if he'd been wrong. Eventually, benefiting from the Web's fondness for variora, he added the excised story to the site, as a possible alternate version of the facts.

The names Baburia and Mogol were late additions, too. Mogol of course came from "Mughal", and Babur had been the first of the Mughal emperors. But the Babur of whom Malik Solanka had been thinking wasn't an old dead king. He was the designated leader of the aborted "Indo-Lilly" parade-demonstration in New York, to whom, in Solanka's opinion, Neela Mahendra had paid far too much attention. The parade had started out as a poor affair and ended up as a brawl. At the north-west corner of Washington Square, under the faintly interested scrutiny of assorted cold-drink salesmen, magic tricksters, unicyclists and cutpurses, one hundred or so men and a handful of women of Indian-Lilliputian origin assembled, their numbers augmented by American friends, lovers, spouses, members of the usual left groupuscules, token "solidarity cadres" from other diaspora-Indian communities in Brooklyn and Queens, and the inevitable demonstration tourists. Over a thousand in toto, the organizers claimed; around two hundred and fifty, said the police. The parallel demonstration of the "indigenous" Elbees had been even less well attended, and had shamefacedly dispersed without marching. However, groups of disgruntled and well-lubricated Elbee males had found their way to Washington Square to taunt the Indo-Lilly men and hurl sexual insults at the women. Scuffles broke out; the N.Y.P.D., looking amazed that so tiny an event could have generated such heat, moved in a few beats too late. As the crowd fled the advancing police officers, several quick knifings took place, none of them lethal. Within instants, the square was empty of demonstrators, except for Neela Mahendra, Malik Solanka and a hairless giant, who stood stripped to the waist, holding a megaphone in one hand and in the other a wooden flagstaff bearing the new saffron-and-green flag of the proposed "Republic of Filbistan"—the FILB stood for "Free Indian Lilliput-Blefuscu" and the rest was added on because it sounded like a word from "home". This was Babur, the young political leader who had travelled all the way from his distant islands to address the "rally", and who now looked so forlorn, so shorn of purpose as well as hair, so unexpressed, that Neela Mahendra hastened to his side, leaving Solanka where he stood. When he saw Neela approaching, the young giant let go of the flagstaff, which thumped him on the head as it fell. He staggered but, to his considerable credit, remained upright.

Neela was all solicitude, evidently believing that by giving Babur the full benefit of her beauty she could make up for his long, useless trip. And Babur did indeed brighten, and began, after a few moments, to address Neela as if she were the enormous and politically significant public meeting he had hoped for. He spoke of a Rubicon being crossed, of *no compromise* and *no surrender.* Now that the hard-won constitution had been abrogated and Indo-Lilly participation in the government of Lilliput-Blefuscu so shamefully terminated, he said, only extreme measures would suffice. "Rights are never given by those who have them," he declaimed, "only taken by those in need." Neela's eyes brightened. She mentioned her television project, and Babur nodded gravely, seeing that something might be salvaged from the rubble of the day. "Come," he said, taking her arm. (Solanka noted the ease with which she slipped her arm through her countryman's.) "Come. We must discuss these things for many hours. There is much that needs urgently to be done." Neela left with Babur without a backward glance.

Solanka was still in Washington Square at closing time that night, sitting wretchedly on a bench. As a patrol car was ordering him to leave, his cell phone rang. "I'm really sorry, honey," Neela said. "He was so unhappy, and it is my work, we did need to talk. Anyway, I don't need to explain. You're a smart man. I'm sure you worked it out. You should meet Babur. He's so full of passion it's scary, and after the revolution he may even be president. Oh, can you hold on, honey? It's the other line." She had spoken of the revolution as an inevitability. With a deep rumble of alarm, Solanka, on hold, remembered her own declaration of war. *I'll fight alongside them if I have to, shoulder to shoulder. I'm not kidding, I really will.* He looked at the bloodstains drying on the darkened square, evidence here in New York City of the force of a gathering fury on the far side of the world: a group fury, born of long injustice, beside which his own unpredictable temper was a thing of pathetic insignificance, the indulgence, perhaps, of a privileged individual with too much self-interest. And too much time on his hands. He could not give Neela up to this higher, antipodean rage. Come back, he wanted to say. Come to me, my darling, please don't go. But she was back on the line, and her voice had changed. "It's Jack," she said. "He's dead, his head's been blown off, and there's a confession in his hand." You've seen the headless Winged Victory, Solanka dully thought. You've heard of the Headless Horseman. Give it up for my headless friend Jack Rhinehart, the Wingless, Horseless Defeat.

PART THREE

15

Nothing made sense. Jack's body had been found in the Spassky Grain Building, a Tribeca construction site on the corner of Greenwich and N Moore whose developers had recently come under union fire for employing scab labour. It was a fifteen-minute walk from Jack's Hudson Street apartment, and he had apparently strolled here with a loaded shotgun in his hand, crossed Canal—still busily crowded in spite of the late hour—without attracting attention, then broken into his chosen location, taken an elevator to the fourth floor, positioned himself by a west-facing window with a good view of the moonlit river, placed the snout of the gun in his mouth, pulled the trigger, and fallen to the rough, unfinished floor, dropping the weapon but somehow holding on to the suicide note. He had been drinking heavily: Jack Daniel's and Coke, an absurd drink for an oenophile like Rhinehart. When he was discovered, his suit and shirt were folded neatly on the floor, and he was wearing only his socks and underpants, which, for some reason, or perhaps by chance, were on back to front. He had recently cleaned his teeth.

Neela decided to make a clean breast of it and told the detectives everything she knew—the fancy-dress costumes in Jack's closet, her suspicions, everything. She could have been in trouble, withholding information being a serious offence, but the police had bigger fish to fry, and, besides, the two officers who came to her Bedford Street apartment to interview her and Malik Solanka were having troubles of their own in her presence. They kept breaking pencils and stepping on each other's feet and knocking over ornaments and bursting into simultaneous speech and then falling blushingly silent, to none of which Neela paid the slightest attention. "The point is," she concluded as the two detectives bumped heads in eager agreement, "this so-called suicide smells strongly of fish."

Malik and Neela had known that Jack owned a gun, though they had never seen it. It dated from the black-Hemingway hunting-and-fishing period that had preceded his Tiger Woods phase. Now, like poor Ernest, most feminine of great male American writers, destroyed by his failure to be the phoney, macho Papa-self he had chosen to inhabit, Jack had gone hunting for himself, the biggest game of all. That, at least, was what they were being invited to believe. On closer examination, however, this version of events became less and less convincing. Jack's building had a doorman, who had seen him leave the premises alone at around seven P.M., carrying no bags and dressed for an evening on the town. A second witness, a plump young woman wearing a beret who had been waiting on the sidewalk for a taxi, came forward in response to a police appeal to say that she had seen a man answering to Jack's description getting into a large black sports utility vehicle with smoked windows; through the open door, she had briefly glimpsed at least two other men, with, and she was quite clear on this point, large cigars in their mouths. An identical SUV was seen driving away along Greenwich Street soon after the established time of death. A couple of days later, analysis of the technical data from what was already provisionally being called the crime scene revealed that the damage to the Spassky Grain Building's temporary access door had not been inflicted by Rhinehart's shotgun. No other instrument capable of breaking down the very solid door—wooden, with a reinforcing metal frame—was found on or near his body. Moreover, it was strongly suspected that the damage to the door had not been the means of gaining entry to the premises. Somebody had had a key.

The suicide note itself was instrumental in establishing Jack's innocence. Rhinehart was famous for the polished precision of his prose. He rarely made an error of syntax, and never, never made a spelling mistake. Yet here among his last words were solecisms of the worst kind. "Ever since my war corespondent days," the note read, "I have had a violent streak. Sometimes in the middle of the nite I smash up the phone. Horse, Club and Stash are innocent. I killed their girls bec they wouldnot fuckme, probably bec I was of Color." And finally, heartbreakingly, "Tell Nila I love her. I know I fucked up but I love her true." Malik Solanka, when his turn came to be interviewed by the police, told them emphatically that even though the note was in Jack's strong, unmistakable hand, it could not have been his freely written work. "Either it has been dictated by somebody with a far lower level of language skills than Jack or else he has deliberately dumbed down his style to send us a message. Don't you see? He has even told us his three murderers' names."

When it was established that Keith "Club" Medford, last lover of the late Lauren Klein, was the son of the wealthy developer and unionized workers' bête noire Michael Medford, one of whose companies was handling the conversion of the Spassky Grain Building into a mixture of high-end lofts and townhouse-style residences, and that Keith, who had been asked to plan the project's opening-night party, possessed a set of keys, it became clear that the killers had made an irretrievable mistake. Most murderers were stupid, and a life of privilege was no defence against folly. Even the most expensive schools turned out badly educated dolts, and Marsalis, Andriessen and Medford were semi-literate, arrogant young fools. And murderers, too. Club, faced with the accumulating facts, was the first to confess. His buddies' defences collapsed a few hours later.

Jack Rhinehart was buried in the depths of Queens, thirty-five minutes' drive from the bungalow he'd bought his mother and still-unmarried sister in Douglaston. "A house with a view," he'd joked. "If you go to the end of the yard and lean all the way over to your left, you can just catch a what?, call it a *whisper*, of the Sound." Now his own view would forever be of urban blight. Neela and Solanka got a car to drive them out. The cemetery was cramped, treeless, comfortless, damp. Photographers moved around the small group of mourners like pollution floating at the edges of a dark pond. Solanka had somehow forgotten that there would be media interest in Jack's funeral. The moment the confessions had been made and the story of the S&M Club became the society scandal of the summer, Professor Solanka lost interest in the event's public dimension. He was mourning his friend Jack Rhinehart, the great, brave journalist, who had been sucked down by glamour and wealth. To be seduced by what one loathed was a hard destiny. To lose the woman you loved to your best friend was perhaps even harder. Solanka had been a bad friend to Jack, but then it had been Jack's fate to be betrayed. His secret sexual preferences, which he had never inflicted on Neela Mahendra, but which meant that not even Neela would finally have been enough for him, had led him into bad company. He had been loyal to men who did not merit his loyalty, had persuaded himself of their innocence—and what an effort that must have been for a natural finder-out and muckraker, what delusionary brilliance he must have employed!—and consequently had helped to shield them from the law, and his reward was to be killed by them in a clumsy attempt at scapegoating: to be sacrificed on the altar of their invincible, egomaniacal pride.

A gospel singer had been hired to sing a farewell medley of spirituals and more contemporary material: "Fix Me, Jesus" was followed by Puff Daddy's tribute to Notorious B.I.G., "Every Breath You Take (I'll Be Missing You)"; then came "Rock My Soul (In the Bosom of Abraham)". Rain looked imminent but was holding off. The air was moist, as if full of tears. Here were Jack's mother and sister; also Bronisława

Rhinehart, the ex-wife, looking simultaneously devastated and sexy in a short black dress and high-fashion veil. Solanka nodded at Bronnie, to whom he'd never found anything to say, and muttered empty words at the bereaved. The Rhinehart women didn't look sad; they looked angry. "Jack I know," Jack's mother said briefly, "would've seen through those white boys in nine seconds flat." "Jack I know," his sister added, "didn't need no whips or chains to have himself some fun." They were mad at the man they loved for the scandal but even madder at him for having put himself in harm's way, as if he had done it to hurt them, to leave them with the lifelong pain of their bereavement. "The Jack I know," Solanka said, "was a pretty good man, and if he's anywhere at all right now, I'd say he's happy to be set free from his mistakes." Jack was right there with them, of course. Jack in the box from which he would never rise up. Solanka felt a hand tighten around his heart.

In his grief's eye Solanka pictured Jack stretched out in an upscale loft conversion while the whole world gossiped over his corpse and photographers frothed about. Next to Jack lay the three dead girls. Released from the fear of his own involvement in their deaths, Solanka mourned them too. Here lay Lauren, who had become afraid of what she was capable of doing to others and allowing others to do to her. Bindy and Sky had tried and failed to keep her inside their charmed circle of pleasure and pain, but she had sealed her fate by threatening the club's members with the shame of a public exposé. Here lay Bindy, the first to comprehend that her friend's death had been no random killing but a cold-blooded execution: which comprehension was her own death warrant. And here lay Uptown Sky, game-for-anything sexual athlete Sky, the wildest of the doomed three and the most sexually uninhibited, her masochistic excesses—now meticulously detailed in the delighted press—sometimes alarming even her sadistic lover, Brad the Horse. Sky, who believed herself immortal, who never thought they would come for her, because she was the empress of their world, they followed where she led, and her levels of tolerance, her thresholds, were the highest any of them had ever known. She knew about the murders and was crazily aroused by them, murmured in Marsalis's ears that she had no intention of blowing the whistle on so much man, and whispered to both Stash and Club in turn that she would be happy to stand in for her dead friends in any way they wanted, just name it, baby, it's yours. She also explained to all three men, in separate, luridly retold encounters, that the killings bound them together for life; they had passed the point of no return, and the contract of their love had been signed in her friends' lifeblood. Sky, the vampire queen. She died because her killers were too scared of her sexual fury to let her live.

Three scalped girls. The public talk was of voodoo and fetishism, and above all of the icy ruthlessness of the crimes, but Solanka preferred to ponder the death of the heart. These young girls, so desperately desirous of desire, had only been able to find it at the outside extremes of human sexual behaviour. And these three young men, for whom love had become a question of violence and possession, of doing and being done to, had gone to the frontier between love and death, and their fury had worn it away, the fury they could not articulate, born of what they, who had so much, had never been able to acquire: lessness, ordinariness. Real life.

In a thousand, ten thousand, a hundred thousand horrified conversations buzzing over the dead like stench-seeking flies, the city discussed the murders' most minute details. *They killed one another's girls!* Lauren Klein had been taken out by Medford for one last grand night on the town. She sent him home, as he had planned, because of a quarrel he'd deliberately provoked near the evening's end. A few moments later he phoned her, pretending to have had a car accident just around the corner. She ran out to help him, found his vintage Bentley unmarked and waiting with its door open. *Poor babe. She thought he wanted to apologize.* Annoyed at the deception but not alarmed, she climbed in, and was hit repeatedly on the head by Andriessen and Marsalis, while Medford drank margaritas in a nearby bar, announcing loudly that he was drowning his sorrows because his bitch wouldn't put out, obliging the bartender to ask him to shut up or leave, and making sure his presence would be remembered. *And then the scalping. They must've put down plastic sheeting to make sure the car wasn't stained. And the body thrown like garbage in the street.* The same technique worked on Belinda Candell.

Sky, however, was different. As was her way, she took the initiative, whispering her plans for the night to Bradley Marsalis over their last supper. Not tonight, he said, and she shrugged. "Okay. I'll call Stash or Club and see if they're up for some fun." Furious, insulted, but obliged to stick to the game plan, Brad said goodnight at her lobby door, and phoned her a few minutes later, saying, "Okay, you win, but not here. Meet me at the room." (The room was the soundproofed five-star hotel suite booked year-round by the S&M Club for the use of its noisier members. Bradley Marsalis, it was revealed, had made the booking several days in advance, which went to prove premeditation.) Sky never reached the room. A large black sports utility vehicle pulled up beside her and a voice she recognized said, "Hi, princess. Climb aboard. Horse asked us to give you a little ride."

Twenty, nineteen, nineteen, Solanka counted. Their combined age had been just three years more than his.

And what of Jack Rhinehart, who lived through a dozen wars only to die miserably in Tribeca, who wrote so well on much that mattered and so stylishly on much that didn't, and whose last words were, deliberately or by necessity, both poignant and inane? Jack's story was all out in the open, too. The theft of the shotgun by Horse Marsalis. Jack's invitation to his S&M Club induction ceremony. *You made it, man. You're in.* Even when they arrived at the Spassky Grain Building, Rhinehart had no idea he was close to death. He was probably thinking of the orgy scene in *Eyes Wide Shut,* imagining masked girls naked on podiums, waiting for the sting of his sweet lash. Solanka was weeping now. He heard the killers insist that, as part of the ritual, Rhinehart needed to drink a brimming jug of Jack and Coke, the spoiled kids' tipple, at high speed. He heard them order Jack to strip and reverse his underpants, in the name of club tradition. As if it were being tied around his own eyes,

Solanka felt the blindfold they had used on Jack (and afterwards removed). His tears soaked through the imagined silk. *Okay, Jack, are you ready, this'll blow you away.—What's happening, guys, what's the deal?—Just open your mouth, Jack. Did you clean your teeth like we said? Good job. Say aah, Jack. This'll kill you, doll.* How pathetically easy it had been to lure this good, weak man to his death. How willingly—giving five high, getting five low—he stepped into his own hearse and took his brief last ride. *Lord, rock my soul,* the singer cried. Goodbye, Jack, Solanka said silently to his friend. Go on home. I'll be calling you.

Neela took Malik back to Bedford Street, opened a bottle of red wine, drew the curtains, lit many scented candles, and disrespectfully selected a CD of Bollywood song classics from the fifties and early sixties—music from his forbidden past. This was an aspect of her profound emotional wisdom. In all things pertaining to feeling, Neela Mahendra knew what worked. *Kabhi méri gali aaya karó.* The teasingly romantic song lilted across the darkened room. *Come up and see me sometime.* They hadn't spoken since they left the graveside. She drew him down on to a cushion-strewn rug and laid his head between her breasts, wordlessly reminding him of the continued existence of happiness, even in the midst of grief.

She spoke of her beauty as something a little separate from herself. It had simply "showed up". It wasn't the result of anything she'd done. She took no credit for it, was grateful for the gift she'd been given, took great care of it, but mostly thought of herself as a disembodied entity living behind the eyes of this extraordinary alien, her body: looking out through its large eyes, manipulating its long limbs, not quite able to believe her luck. Her impact on her surroundings—the fallen window cleaners sitting splay-legged on various sidewalks with buckets on their heads, the skidding cars, the danger to cleaver-wielding butchers when she stopped by for meat—was a phenomenon of whose results, for all her apparent unconcern, she was sharply, precisely aware. She could control "the effect" to some degree. "Doesn't know how to switch it off," Jack had said, and that was true, but she could play it down with the help of loose-fitting clothes (which she detested) and wide-brimmed hats (which, as a sun-hater, she adored). More impressively, she could intensify the world's response to her by making fine-tuning adjustments to her stride length, the tilt of her chin, her mouth, her voice. At maximum intensity she threatened to reduce entire precincts to disaster areas, and Solanka had to ask her to stop, not least because of the effect she was having on his own state of body and mind. She liked compliments, described herself as a "high-maintenance girl", and at times was prepared to concede that this compartmentalization of herself into "form" and "content" was a useful fiction. Her description of her sexual being as "the other one" who periodically came out to hunt and would not be denied was a clever ruse, a shy person's way of tricking herself into extroversion. It allowed her to reap the rewards of her exceptional erotic presence without being troubled by the paralysing social awkwardness that had plagued her as a stammering young girl. Too astute to speak directly of the strong sense of right and wrong that quietly informed all her actions, she preferred to quote the cartoon sex bomb Jessica Rabbit. "I'm not bad," she liked demurely to purr. "I'm just drawn that way."

She held him close. The contrast with the Mila liaison was very striking. With Mila, Solanka had allowed himself to sink towards the sickly allure of the unmentionable, the unallowed, whereas when Neela wrapped herself around him the opposite was true, everything became mentionable and was mentioned, everything was allowable and allowed. This was no child-woman, and what he was discovering with her was the adult joy of unforbidden love. He had thought of his addiction to Mila as a weakness; this new bond felt like strength. Mila had accused him of optimism, and she was right. Neela was optimism's justification. And, yes, he was grateful to Mila for finding the key to the doors of his imagination. But if Mila Milo had unlocked the floodgate, Neela Mahendra was the flood.

In Neela's arms Solanka felt himself begin to change, felt the inner demons he feared so much growing weaker by the day, felt unpredictable rage give way to the miraculous predictability of this new love. Pack your bags, Furies, he thought, you no longer reside at this address. If he was right, and the origin of fury lay in life's accumulating disappointments, then he had found the antidote that transformed the poison into its opposite. For *furia* could be ecstasy, too, and Neela's love was the philosopher's stone that made possible the transmuting alchemy. Rage grew out of despair: but Neela was hope fulfilled.

The door to his past remained closed, and she had the grace not to push against it just yet. Her need for a degree of personal and psychological privacy was considerable. After their initial night in a hotel room, she had insisted on using her own bed for their encounters, but made it clear that he wasn't welcome to spend the night. Her sleep was filled with nightmares, yet she didn't want the comfort of his presence. She preferred to battle her dream-figments alone and, at the end of each night's wars, to wake up slowly, and definitely by herself. Having no alternative, Solanka accepted her terms, and began to grow accustomed to fighting off the waves of sleep that habitually rolled over him at lovemaking's end. He told himself that it was better for him this way as well. He was, after all, suddenly a very busy man.

He was learning her better every day, exploring her as if she were a new city in which he had sublet space and where he hoped one day to buy. She wasn't completely at ease with that idea. Like him, she was a creature of moods, and he was becoming her personal meteorologist, predicting her weather, studying the duration of her internal gales and their sideswipe effects, in the form of crashing storms, on the golden beaches of their love. Sometimes she liked being seen in such microscopic detail, loved being understood without speaking, having her needs catered for without having to express them. On other occasions it annoyed her. He would see a cloud on her brow and ask, "What's the matter?" In response she'd look exasperated and say, "Oh, nothing. For Pete's sake! You think you can read my mind, but you're so often so wrong. If there's something to be said, I'll say it. Don't meet trouble halfway." She had invested a great deal of effort in building an image of strength and didn't want the man she loved to see her weaknesses.

Medication, he soon discovered, was an issue for Neela, too, and this was another thing they had in common: that they were determined to beat their demons without entering the valley of the dolls. So when she felt low, when she needed to wrestle with herself, she would retreat from him, wouldn't want to see him or explain why, and he was expected to understand, to be grown-up enough to allow her to be what she needed to be; in short, for perhaps the first time in his life he was being required to act his age. She was a highly strung woman, and sometimes admitted that she must be a nightmare to be around, to which he replied, "Yes, but there are compensations." "I hope they're big," she said, looking genuinely worried. "If they weren't, I'd be pretty stupid, wouldn't I?" He grinned, and she relaxed and moved in close. "That's right," she comforted herself. "And you're not."

She possessed immense physical ease, and was actually happier naked than clothed. More than once he had to remind her to dress when there was a knock at her door. But she wanted to guard some secrets, to protect her mystery. Her frequent withdrawals into herself, her habit of recoiling from being too acutely seen, had to do with this very un-American—this positively English—awareness of the value of reserve. She insisted that it had nothing to do with whether she loved him or not, which she deeply and bewilderingly did. "Look, it's obvious," she replied when he asked why. "You may be very creative with your dolls and websites and all, but as far as I'm concerned, your only function is to get into my bed whenever I tell you and fulfil my every whim." At which imperious dictum Professor Malik Solanka, who had wanted to be a sex object all his life, felt quite absurdly pleased.

After making love, she lit a cigarette and went to sit naked by the window to smoke it, knowing his hatred of tobacco smoke. Lucky neighbours, he thought, but she dismissed such considerations as bourgeois and far beneath her. She returned with a straight face to the question he had asked. "The thing about you," she offered, "is that you've got a heart. This is a rare quality in the contemporary guy. Take Babur: an amazing man, brilliant, really, but totally in love with the revolution. Real people are just counters in his game. With most other guys it's status, money, power, golf, ego. Jack, for example." Solanka hated the laudatory reference to the smooth-bodied flag-bearer of Washington Square, felt a sharp twinge of guilt at being favourably compared to his dead friend, and said so. "You see," she marvelled, "you don't just feel, you can actually talk about it. Wow. Finally, a man worth staying with." Solanka had the feeling that he was being obscurely sent up, but couldn't quite identify the joke. Feeling foolish, he settled for the affection in her voice. Love Potion Number Nine. That was the healing balm.

India was insisted upon everywhere in the Bedford Street apartment, in the overemphasized manner of the diaspora: the *filmi* music, the candles and incense, the Krishna-and-milkmaids calendar, the dhurries on the floor, the Company School painting, the hookah coiled atop a bookcase like a stuffed green snake. Neela's Bombay alter ego, Solanka mused, pulling on his clothes, would probably have gone for a heavily Westernized, Californian-minimalist simplicity . . . but never mind about Bombay. Neela was getting dressed as well, pulling on her most "aerodynamically" body-hugging black outfit, made in some nameless space-age fabric. She needed to go to the office in spite of the late hour. The pre-production period on the Lilliput documentary was almost over, and she would be leaving for the antipodes soon. There was still much to do. Get used to this, Solanka thought. Her need for absence is professional as well as personal. To be with this woman is also to learn to be without her. She tied the laces on her white street flyers—sneakers with flip-out wheels built into the soles—and took off at speed, her long black ponytail flying out behind her as she raced away. Solanka stood on the sidewalk and watched her go. The "effect", he noted as the usual mayhem began, worked almost as well in the dark.

He went to FAO Schwarz and sent Asmaan an elephant by mail. Soon the last vestiges of old fury would have been dispelled by new happiness and he would feel confident enough to re-enter his son's life. To do so, however, he would have to face Eleanor and confront her with the fact she still refused to accept. He would have to bury finality like a knife in her good and loving heart.

He telephoned to tell Asmaan to expect a surprise. Great excitement. "What's inside it? What's it saying? What would Morgen say?" Eleanor and Asmaan had been holidaying in Florence with the Franzes. "There's no beach here. No. There's a river, but I douldn't swim in it. Maybe when I'm bigger I'll come back and swim in it. I wasn't stared, Daddy. That's why Morgen and Lin were shouting." *Scared.* "Mummy wasn't. Mummy wasn't shouting. She said don't be stary, Morgen. Lin's so nice. Mummy's so nice too. That's what I think, anyway. He was being a bit stary. Morgen was. A tiny bit. Was he trying to make me laugh? Probably. Do you know, Daddy? What was he saying? We went to look at statues, but Lin douldn't come. That's why she was trying. She stayed at home. Not our home, but. Ai caramba." This, Solanka understood after a moment, was *I can't remember.* "We stayed there. Yes. It was very good. I had my own room. I like that. I've got a bow and arrow. I like you, Daddy, are you coming home today? Saturday Tuesday? You should. 'Bye."

Eleanor took over. "Yes, it was difficult. But Florence was lovely. How are you?" He thought for a minute. "Fine," he said. "I'm fine." She thought for a minute. "You shouldn't promise him you're coming back if you aren't," she said, angling for information. "What's the matter?" he asked, changing the subject. "What's the matter with *you*?" she replied. That was all it took. He had already heard the telltale wrongness in her voice and she in his. Thrown off balance by what he had just understood, Solanka made the mistake of retreating into Neela's dialogue: "Oh, for Pete's sake! You think you can read my mind, but you're so often so wrong. If there's something to be said, I'll say it. Don't meet trouble halfway." Coming from Neela this had sounded genuine enough, but in his mouth it came across as mere bluster. Eleanor was scornfully amused. "For Pete's sake?" she wanted to know. "As in 'Jeepers creepers', 'Jiminy Cricket', or 'What the heck?' When did you start using Ronald Reagan's lines?" Her manner was sharper, more irritable, non-placatory. Morgen and Lin, Solanka thought. Morgen, who had taken the trouble to ring him up to scold him for abandoning his wife, and whose own wife had informed Solanka that his behaviour had brought her and her husband closer together than ever before. Mm-hm. Morgen and Eleanor and Lin in Florence. *That's why she was trying.* Asmaan's evidence left no doubt. *Because she was crying.* Why was she crying, Morgen? Eleanor? Would you care to fill me in on that? Would you care to explain, Eleanor, why your new lover and his wife were quarrelling in the presence of my son?

The fury was passing from him, but everyone else seemed to be in exceedingly poor humour. Mila was moving. Eddie had hired a van from a company called Van-Go and was uncomplainingly hauling her possessions down from the fourth floor while she stayed in the street smoking a cigarette, drinking Irish whiskey from the bottle, and bitching. Her hair was red now, and spikier than ever: even her head looked angry. "What do you think you're looking at?" she yelled up at Solanka when she spotted him watching her from his second-floor workroom window. "Whatever you want from me, Professor, it's unavailable. Got it? I'm a person engaged to be married and believe me you don't want my fiancé to get mad." Against his better judgement—for she had worked her way through most of the fifth of Jameson's—he went down to the street to talk to her. She was moving to Brooklyn, moving in with Eddie in a small place in Park Slope, and the webspyders had opened up an office there. The Puppet Kings site was fast approaching its launch date, and things were looking good. "Don't worry, Professor," Mila said blurrily. "Business is great. It's just you I can't stand."

Eddie Ford came down the front stairs carrying a computer monitor. When he saw Solanka, he scowled theatrically. This was a scene he had been wanting to play for a long time. "She doesn't want to talk to you, man," he said, setting the monitor down. "Do I make myself plain? Ms Milo has no fuckin' desire to fuckin' converse. You apprehend? You want to see her, call the office and seek a fuckin' business appointment. Send us e-mail. You show up at her fuckin' place of residence, you'll be answerin' to me. You and the lady got no personal relationship no more. You're fuckin' estranged. If you ask me, she's a fuckin' saint to want to do business with you at all. Me, I'm not the saintly type. Me, I just want five minutes. Three hundred seconds alone with you would suffice for my fuckin' needs. Yes, sir. You follow me, Professor? Am I on your frequency? Am I comin' through?" Solanka bowed his head quietly and turned to go. "She told me what you tried on her," Eddie shouted after him. "You're one fuckin' sad and sick old man." And what did she tell you, Eddie, about what she tried on me? Oh, never mind.

"Ah, Professor." In the corridor outside his front door he ran into the plumber, Schlink; or, rather, Schlink was waiting for him, waving a document and bursting with words. "All is good in ze apartment? No toilet problem? So, so. What Schlink fixes stays gefixt." He nodded and smiled furiously. "Maybe you don't remember," he continued. "I vos frank viz you, eh?, my life story I shared viz you for nossink. From zis you made a cruel choke. Maybe a movie, you said, could come from my poor tale. Zis you did not mean. You spoke, I am sure of it, in chest. So grand, Professor, so patronizing, you piece of shit." Solanka was greatly taken aback. "Yes," Schlink emphasized. "I make free to say so. I came here particular to tell you. You see, Professor, I haff followed your advice, zis advice vot to you vos chust a schoopit gag, and sanks Gott, success has blessed my effort. A film deal! See for yourself, here it is in black and white. See here, ze studio name. See here, ze financial aspect. Yes, a comedy, chust imagine. After a lifetime vizout *humour* I vill be played for laughs. Billy Crystal in the title role, he's on board already, he's crazy for it. A sure-fire hit, eh? Lensing soon. Opens next spring. Lotsa buzz. Goes boffo right off. Big opening veekend. Vait and see. Okay, so long, Professor Asshole, and sank you for ze title. *Jewboat.* HA, ha, ha, HA."

16

The inadequate summer closed overnight, like a Broadway flop. The temperature fell like a guillotine; the dollar, however, soared. Everywhere you looked, in gyms, clubs, galleries, offices, on the streets and on the floor of the NYSE, at the city's great sports stadia and entertainment centres, people were readying themselves for the new season, limbering up for action, flexing their bodies, minds and wardrobes, setting themselves on their marks. Showtime on Olympus! The city was a race. Mere rats need not bother to enter this high-intensity competition. This was the main event, the blue riband contest, the world series. This was the master race, whose winners would be as gods. Second place was nowhere: "Loserville." No silver or bronze medals would be struck, and the only rule was victory or bust.

Athletes were all over the airwaves that Olympic fall: disgraced Chinese turtle-blood drinkers, Marion Jones's mouth murmuring into a microphone, Marion Jones's husband testing positive for nandrolone, Michael Johnson running along a telephone and breaking records. What Jack Rhinehart had called the Divorce Olympics were hotting up, too. Solanka's ex-wife Sara Lear Schofield's antique of a second husband, Lester, died in his sleep before their final day in court, but not before he'd cut her out of his will. The bitter war of words between Sara, the Brazilian supermodel Ondine Marx, and Schofield's adult children from earlier marriages pushed the Concrete-Killer Murders off the front pages at last. Sara emerged as the clear winner of these preliminary verbal hostilities. She released photocopied extracts from Schofield's private diaries to prove that the deceased had heartily detested all his children and sworn that he'd never leave any of them so much as the price of the toll on the Triborough Bridge. She also engaged private investigators to get the goods on Ondine, the sole beneficiary of Schofield's last, hotly contested will. Details of the model's bisexual promiscuity and fondness for surgical improvement flooded the press. "She's not my type, but they say she's a great tuck," Sara commented acidly. Ondine's history of drug abuse and her sleazy porno-movie past also featured prominently; and, best of all, the Pinkertons unearthed her secret liaison with the handsome Paraguayan descendant of a Nazi war criminal. These revelations led to the model's investigation by immigration officers and rumours of the imminent cancellation of her green card. I'm still a foot soldier here but Britpack Sara commands battalions, Malik Solanka thought with a kind of admiration. I'm just a face in the crowd, but she's one of its killer queens.

PlanetGalileo.com, the Puppet Kings project, his last stab at the big time, had acquired powerful allies. The webspyders had spread their nets well. Backers and sponsors were eager to get in on the ground floor of this important new launch by the creator of the legendary Little Brain. Major production, distribution and marketing agreements with key players—Mattel, Amazon, Sony, Columbia, Banana Republic—were already in place. A universe of toys was in the pipeline, everything from soft stuffed dolls to life-size robots with voices and flashing lights, to say nothing of Halloween-special costumes. There were boxed games and jigsaw puzzles and nine kinds of spacecraft and cyborg neutralizers and scale models of the entire planet Galileo-1, and, for the real nuts, its entire solar system, too. Amazon's pre-orders for the back-story book *Revolt of the Living Dolls* were close to the Little Brain phenomenon's record-breaking fever-pitch levels. A Playstation game was close to being shipped and was already being heavily marketed; a new fashion line bearing the Galileo label was ready to show during the 7th on Sixth fashion week; and, driven by the fear of a major actors' and writers' strike in the coming spring, a big-budget movie was on the verge of being green-lit. Banks competed with each other to lend money, sending the interest rate on the huge loans required spinning daily lower and lower. The largest mainland Chinese ISP had asked to come in and talk. Mila, as the webspyders' frontwoman, was working around the clock, with extraordinary results. Solanka's relations with her remained on ice, however. Plainly, she was far angrier at being dumped than she had initially allowed herself to appear. Solanka was kept well informed by her of all developments and instructed to prepare himself for a media blitz, but as far as human contact was concerned, barbed wire might as well have stretched across the Manhattan and Brooklyn Bridges, with duplicated, three-headed versions of Eddie Ford guarding over both. In the electronic world, Solanka and the webspyders worked closely together for hours a day. Outside it, they were strangers. That was, apparently, how it had to be.

Fortunately, Neela was still in town, though the reason for her continued presence was disturbing, and greatly distracted her. There had been a coup in Lilliput-Blefuscu, led by a certain Skyresh Bolgolam, an indigenous Elbee merchant whose argosies had all failed and who accordingly detested the prosperous Indo-Lilly traders with a passion that could have been called racist if it had not been so obviously rooted in professional envy and personal pique. The coup seemed spectacularly unnecessary; under pressure from the Bolgolamites, the country's liberal president, Golbasto Gue, who had pushed through a programme of constitutional reform designed to give Indian-Lilliputians equal electorial and property rights, had already been obliged to reverse course and throw out the new constitution only weeks after it had come into being.

Bolgolam, however, suspected a ruse and at the beginning of September marched into the Lilliputian Parliament in the city centre of Mildendo, accompanied by two hundred armed ruffians, and took hostage around fifty Indo-Lilly parliamentarians and political staff members, as well as President Gue himself. At the same time, Bolgolamite goon squads attacked and imprisoned leading members of the Indo-Lilly political leadership. The country's radio and television stations and the main telephone switchboard were seized. At Blefuscu International Aerodrome the runways were blockaded; the sea-lanes into Mildendo harbour were likewise blocked. The islands' main Internet server, Lillicon, was closed down by the Bolgolam gang. However, some limited e-activity continued.

The whereabouts of Neela's friend from the New York demonstration were not known; but as news slowly filtered out of Lilliput in spite of Bolgolam's gags, it was established that Babur was not among those held hostage in the Parliament or in jail. If he hadn't been killed, then he had gone underground. Neela decided this was the likelier alternative. "If he was dead, this rogue Bolgolam would have released the news, I'm sure. Just to demoralize the opposition even more." Solanka saw very little of her during these post-coup days as she attempted, often in the small hours of the night on account of the thirteen-hour time difference, to make contact via World Wide Web and satphone links with what was now the Filbistani Resistance Movement (the FRM, or "Fremen"). She also busily researched ways and means of effecting an illegal entry into Lilliput-Blefuscu from Australia or Borneo, accompanied by a skeleton camera crew. Solanka began to fear greatly for her safety and, in spite of the greater historical importance of the matters presently claiming her attention, for his newfound happiness as well. Suddenly jealous of her work, he nursed imaginary grievances, told himself he was being slighted and ignored. At least his fictional Zameen of Rijk, arriving covertly on Baburian soil, had been looking for her man (though with what intent, he granted, was unclear). A dreadful further possibility presented itself. Perhaps Neela was looking for a man in Lilliput as well as a story. Now that history's mantle had fallen on the inadequate shoulders of the hairless, bare-chested flag-waver she so admired, was it not possible that Neela had begun to think this muscle-bound Babur an altogether more attractive proposition than a sedentary middle-aged merchant of fairy tales and toys? For what other reason would she plan to risk her life by sneaking into Lilliput-Blefuscu to find him? Just for a documentary film? Ha! That rang false. There was a pretext, if you liked. And Babur, her burgeoning desire for Babur, was the text.

One night, late, and only after he'd made a big deal of it, she came to visit him at West Seventieth Street. "I thought you'd never ask," she laughed when she arrived, trying, by sounding lighthearted, to dispel the thick cloud of tension in the air. He couldn't tell her the truth: that in the past, Mila's presence next door had inhibited him. They were both too tense and exhausted to make love. She had been pursuing her leads, and he had spent the day talking to journalists about life on Galileo-1, an unnerving, hollowing kind of work, during which he could hear himself sounding false, knowing also that a second layer of falsehood would be added by the journalists' responses to his words. Solanka and Neela watched Letterman without speaking. Unused to difficulties in their relationship, they had forged no language for dealing with trouble. The longer the silence between them lasted, the uglier it grew. Then, as if the bad feeling had burst out of their heads and taken physical form, they heard a piercing shriek. Then the sound of something shattering. Then a second, louder screech. Then, for a long time, nothing.

They went out into the street to investigate. The vestibule of Solanka's building had an inner door that could usually only be opened with a key, but its metal frame was warped at present and the lock wouldn't engage. The outer door, the street door, was never locked. This was worrying, even in the new, safer Manhattan. If there was danger out there, it could in theory come inside. But the street was quiet and empty, as if nobody else had heard a thing. Certainly, nobody else had come out to see what was going on. And in spite of the loud crash, there was nothing whatsoever on the pavement, no broken plant pot or vase. Neela and Solanka looked around, bemused. Other lives had touched theirs and then vanished. It was as though they had overheard the quarrelling of ghosts. The sash window of what had been Mila's apartment was wide open, however, and as they looked up, the silhouette of a man appeared and pulled it firmly shut. Then the lights went out. Neela said, "It's got to be him. It's like he missed her the first time but got her the second." And the breaking noise, Solanka asked. She just shook her head, went indoors, and insisted on calling the police. "If I was being murdered and my neighbours did nothing, I'd be pretty disappointed, wouldn't you?"

Two officers came to see them within the hour, took down statements, then left to investigate and never returned. "You'd think they would come back and say what happened," Neela cried in frustration. "They must know we're sitting here worried sick in the middle of the night." Solanka snapped, letting his resentment show. "I guess they just didn't realize it was their duty to report to you," he said, without making any attempt to keep the cutting edge out of his voice. She rounded on him at once, fully his equal in aggression. "What's eating you, anyway?" she demanded. "I'm tired of pretending I'm not hanging out with a sore-headed bear." And so it began, the sorry human tailspin of recrimination and counter-recrimination, the deadly accusative old game: you said no you said, you did no it was you, let me tell you I'm not just tired I'm *really* tired of *this* because you need so much and give so little, is that so well let me tell *you* I could give you the contents of Fort Knox and Bergdorf Goodman and it still wouldn't be enough, and what does *that* mean, may I ask, you know damn well what it means. Oh. Right. Oh okay then, I guess that's it. Sure, if that's what you want. What *I* want? It's what you're forcing me to say. No, it's what you've been dying to spit out. Jesus *Christ* stop putting words in my mouth. I should have known. No, I should have known. Well, now we both know. Okay then. Okay.

Just then, as they stood facing each other like bloodied gladiators, giving and receiving the wounds that would soon leave their love dead on the floor of this emotional Colosseum, Professor Malik Solanka saw a vision that stilled his lashing tongue. A great black bird sat on the roof of the house, its wings casting a deep shadow over the street. The Fury is here, he thought. One of the three sisters has come for me at last. Those weren't screams of fear we heard; they were the Fury's call. The noise of something shattering in the street—an explosive sound, such as a lump of concrete might make if hurled from a great height with unimaginable force—wasn't any goddamn vase. It was the sound of a breaking life.

And who knows what might have happened, or of what, in the grip of the revenant fury, he might have become capable, if it hadn't been for Neela, if she hadn't been standing a whole head taller than him in her high heels and looking down like a queen, like a goddess, on his full head of long silver hair; or if she had lacked the wit to see the terror flooding across his soft, round, boyish face, the fear quivering at the corners of his Cupid's bow mouth; or if in that last of all possible instants she had not found the inspired daring, the sheer emotional brilliance, to break the last taboo that still stood between them, to go into uncharted territory with all the courage of her love, to prove beyond all doubt that their love was stronger than fury by stretching out a long scarred arm and beginning, with great deliberation, and for the very first time in her life, to ruffle his forbidden hair, the long silver hair growing out of the top of his head.

The spell broke. He laughed out loud. A large black crow spread its wings and flew away across town, to drop dead minutes later by the Booth statue in Gramercy Park. Solanka understood that his own cure, his recovery from his rare condition, was complete. The goddesses of wrath had departed; their hold over him was broken at last. Much poison had been drained from his veins, and much that had been locked away for far too long was being set free. "I want to tell you a story," he said; and Neela, taking his hand, led him to a sofa. "Tell me by all means, but I think it may be one I already know."

* * *

At the end of the science fiction film *Solaris*, the story of an ocean-covered planet that functions as a single giant brain, can read men's minds and make their dreams come true, the spaceman-hero is back home at last, on the porch of his long-lost Russian dacha, with his children running joyfully around and his beautiful, dead wife alive again at his side. As the camera pulls back, endlessly, impossibly, we see that the dacha is on a tiny island set in the great ocean of Solaris: a delusion, or perhaps a deeper truth than the truth. The dacha diminishes to a speck and vanishes, and we are left with the image of the mighty, seductive ocean of memory, imagination and dream, where nothing dies, where what you need is always waiting for you on a porch, or running towards you across a vivid lawn with childish cries and happy, open arms.

Tell me. I already know. Neela, with her heart-wisdom, had guessed why, for Professor Solanka, the past was not a joy. When he saw *Solaris*, he'd found that last scene horrifying. He'd known a man like this, he thought, a man who lived inside a delusion of fatherhood, trapped in a cruel mistake about the nature of fatherly love. He knew a child like this one, too, he thought, running towards the man who stood in the role of father, but that role was a lie, a lie. There was no father. This was no happy home. The child was not itself. Nothing was as it seemed.

Yes, Bombay flooded back, and Solanka was living in it once again, or at least in the only part of the city that truly had a hold on him, the little patch of the past from which whole infernos could be conjured forth, his damned Yoknapatawpha, his accursed Malgudi, which had shaped his destiny and whose memory he had suppressed for over half a lifetime. Methwold's Estate: it was more than enough for his needs. And, in particular, an apartment in a block called Noor Ville, in which for a long time he had been raised as a girl.

At first he couldn't look his story in the eye, could only come at it sideways, by talking about the bougainvillaea creeper climbing over the veranda like an Arcimboldo burglar, or like your stepfather at your bedside in the night. Or else he described the crows that came cawing like portents to his windowsill, and his conviction that he would have been able to understand their warnings if only he weren't so unintelligent, if only he could have concentrated a little harder, and then he could have run away from home before anything happened, so it was his own fault, his own stupid fault for failing to do the simplest thing, namely to understand the language of birds. Or, he spoke about his best friend, Chandra Venkataraghavan, whose father left home when he was ten. Malik sat in Chandra's room and interrogated the distraught boy. Tell me how it hurts, Malik begged Chandra. I need to know. That's how it should also hurt for me. Malik's own father had disappeared when he was less than a year old; his pretty young mother, Mallika, had burned all the photographs and remarried within the year, gratefully taking her second husband's name and giving it to Malik as well, cheating Malik of history as well as feeling. His father had gone and he didn't even know his name, which was also his own. If it had been up to his mother, Malik might never have known of his father's existence, but his stepfather told him the moment he was old enough to understand. His stepfather, who needed to excuse himself from the accusation of incest. From that if nothing else.

What had his father done for a living? Malik was never informed. Was he fat or thin, tall or short? Was his hair wavy or straight? All he could do was look in the mirror. The mystery of his father's looks would be solved as he grew, and the face in the glass answered his questions. "We are Solankas now," his mother rebuked him. "It doesn't matter about that person who never existed and who certainly doesn't exist now. Here is your true father, who puts food on your plate and clothes on your back. Kiss his feet and do his will."

Dr Solanka was the second husband, a consultant at Breach Candy Hospital and a gifted composer of music in his spare time, and he was indeed a generous provider. However, as Malik discovered, his stepfather required more than just his feet to be kissed. When Malik was six years old, Mrs Mallika Solanka—who had never conceived again, as if her absconding first husband had taken the secret of fertility away with him—was declared incapable of further childbearing and the boy's torment began. *Bring clothes and let his hair grow long and he will be our daughter as well as our son. No but, husband, how can it be, I mean, is that okay? Sure! Why not? In privacy of home all things decreed by paterfamilias are sanctioned by God.* Oh, my weak mother, you brought me ribbons and frocks. And when the bastard told you that your frail constitution, all wheezes and colds, would benefit from daily exercise, when he sent you away for long walks at the Hanging Gardens or Mahalaxmi Racecourse, did you not think to ask why he did not walk by your side; why, dismissing the ayah, he insisted on caring for his little "girl" alone? Oh, my poor dead mother who betrayed her only child. After a whole year of this, Malik had finally screwed up enough courage to ask the unaskable. *Mummy, why does Doctor Sahib push me down? What push you down, how push you down, what nonsense is this? Mummy, when he stands there and puts his hand on my head and pushes me down and makes me kneel. When, Mummy, he loosens his pyjama, when, Mummy, when he lets it fall.* She had hit him then, hard and repeatedly. *Never tell me your evil lies again or I will beat you till you are deaf and dumb. For some reason you have a down on this man who is the only father you have ever known. For some reason you don't want your mother to be happy, so you tell these lies, don't think I don't know you, the wickedness in your heart; how do you think it feels when all the mothers say, your Malik, darling, such imagination, ask him a question and who knows what he'll come out with? Oh, I know what it means: it means you are telling whoppers all over town, and I have an evil liar for a child.*

After that he was deaf and dumb. After that when the pushes came on the top of his beribboned head he thudded obediently to his knees, closed his eyes, and opened his mouth. But long months later things did change. One day Dr Solanka was visited by Chandra's father, Mr Balasubramanyam Venkataraghavan the important banker, and they remained closeted together for more than an hour. Voices were raised, then swiftly lowered. Mallika was summoned, then swiftly dismissed. Malik hung back at the far end of a corridor, wide-eyed, speechless, clinging to a doll. Finally, Mr Venkat left, looking like thunder, pausing only to pick up and hug Malik (who was dressed for Venkat's visit in a white shirt and shorts), and to mutter, with high colour burning in his face, "Don't worry, my boy. *Quoth the raven: nevermore.*" That same afternoon, all the dresses and bows were taken away to be burned; but Malik insisted on being allowed to keep his dolls. Dr Solanka never laid a finger on him again. Whatever threats Mr Venkat had made had had their effect. (When Balasubramanyam Venkataraghavan left home to become a *sanyasi,* ten-year-old Malik Solanka had greatly feared that his stepfather might revert to the old routine. But it seemed Dr Solanka had learned his lesson. Malik Solanka, however, never spoke to his step-father again.)

From that day on Malik's mother was different, too, interminably apologizing to her young son and weeping without restraint. He could barely speak to her without provoking an awful howl of guilty grief. This alienated Malik. He needed a mother, not a waterworks utility like the one on the Monopoly board. "Please, Ammi," he scolded her when she had embarked on one of her frequent hug-and-sob fests. "If I can control myself, so can you." Stung, she let him go, and after that did her weeping privately, muffled by pillows. So life resumed its air of surface normality, Dr Solanka going about his business, Mallika running the household, and Malik locking his thoughts away, confiding only in whispers, only in the hours of darkness, to the dolls who crowded around him in bed, like guardian angels, like blood kin: the only family he could bring himself to trust.

"The rest doesn't matter," he said, the confession over. "The rest is ordinary—getting on with it, growing up, getting away from them, having my life." A huge burden had fallen from him. "I don't have to carry them around any more," he added, full of wonder. Neela put her arms around him and moved in even closer. "Now it's I who have imprisoned you," she said. "I'm the one asking you to go here, do that. But this time it's what we both want. In this prison, you're finally free." He relaxed against her, even though he knew there was one last gate he had not unlocked: the gate of full disclosure, of absolute, brutal truth, behind which lay the strange thing that had happened between Mila Milo and himself. But that, he persuaded himself catastrophically, was for another day.

Everywhere on earth—in Britain, in India, in distant Lilliput—people were obsessed by the subject of success in America. Neela was a celebrity back home simply because she had got herself a good job—"made it big"—in the American media. In India, great pride was taken in the achievements of U.S.-based Indians in music, publishing (though not writing), Silicon Valley and Hollywood. British levels of hysteria were even higher. British journalist gets work in U.S.A.! Incredible! British actor to play second lead in American movie! Wow, what a superstar! Cross-dressing British comic wins two Emmys! Amazing—we always knew British transvestism was best! American success had become the only real validation of one's worth. Ah, genuflection, Malik Solanka thought. Nobody knew how to argue with money these days, and all the money was here in the Promised Land.

Such reflections had become germane because in his middle fifties he was experiencing the superlative force of a real American hit, a force that blew open all the doors of the city, unlocked its secrets, and invited you to feast until you burst. The Galileo launch, an unprecedented interdisciplinary business enterprise, had gone intergalactic from day one. It turned out to be that happy accident: a necessary myth. LET THE FITTEST SURVIVE T-shirts covered some of the finest chests in the city, becoming a triumphalist slogan for the gym generation that acquired mass public currency overnight. It was proudly worn, too, over some of the flabbiest bellies around, as proof of the wearers' sense of irony and fun. Demand for the Playstation video game accelerated past all predictions, leaving even Lara Croft floundering in its wake. At the height of the *Star Wars* phenomenon, spin-off merchandising had accounted for a quarter of the toy industry's worldwide turnover; since those days, only the Little Brain phenomenon had come close. Now the saga of

Galileo-1 was setting new records, and this time the global mania was being driven not by films or television but by a website. The new communications medium was finally paying off. After a summer of scepticism about the potential of many massively unprofitable Internet companies, here at last was the prophesied brave new world. Professor Solanka's surprisingly smooth beast, its hour come around at last, was slouching towards Bethlehem to be born. (There were rough edges, though: in the early days the site often crashed under the sheer weight of hits, which seemed to grow faster than the webspyders' ability to increase access by replication and mirroring, the spinning of new threads of the shining web.)

Once again, Solanka's fictional characters began to burst out of their cages and take to the streets. From around the world came news of their images, grown gigantic, standing many storeys high on city walls. They made celebrity public appearances, singing the national anthem at ball games, publishing cookbooks, guest-hosting the Letterman show. The leading young actresses of the day vied publicly for the coveted leading role of Zameen of Rijk and her double, the cyborg Goddess of Victory. And this time Solanka felt none of the old Little Brain frustration, because, as Mila Milo had promised, it really was his show. He marvelled at his own excitement. Creative and corporate meetings filled his days. The e-mail standoff with the webspyders was over. Regular "face time" had become essential. The continuing, possibly even growing, anger of sexually spurned, father-fixated Mila was the single fly in this rich, even Croesus-worthy, ointment. Mila and Eddie arrived stone-faced at the crucial meetings and left without offering Solanka a friendly word. However, her hair and eyes spoke volumes. They changed colour frequently, burned like a flame one day and glowered blackly the next. Often the contact lenses clashed violently with the hair, suggesting that Mila was in an exceptionally bad mood on that particular day.

Solanka had no time to deal with the Mila problem. The Galileo project's ground-floor partners were bursting with ideas about diversification: a restaurant chain! A theme park! A giant Las Vegas hotel, entertainment centre and casino in the shape of the two islands of Baburia, to be set in an artificially created "ocean" at the desert's heart! The number of businesses hammering on the door, pleading to be let in, was almost as hard to set down as the full decimal expression of π. The webspyders created and received new proposals for the future of the property almost every day, and Malik Solanka lost himself in the ecstasy, the *furia,* of the work.

The intervention of the living dolls from the imaginary planet Galileo-1 in the public affairs of actually existing Earth had not, however, been foreseen. It was Neela who brought Solanka the news. She arrived at West Seventieth Street in a state of high excitement. Her eyes shone as she spoke. There had been a countercoup in Lilliput. It had begun as a burglary: masked men raided Mildendo's biggest toy store and made off with its entire, just-imported supply of Kronosian Cyborg masks and costumes. Interestingly—given the name of Neela's shiny-chested flag-bearing pal—no Baburian outfits were taken. The FRM radicals, the revolutionary Indo-Lilly "Fremen" who had orchestrated the raid, as was afterwards revealed, identified strongly with the Puppet Kings, whose inalienable right to being treated as equals—as fully moral and sentient beings—was denied by Mogol the Baburian, their deadly foe, of whom Skyresh Bolgolam was accused of being an avatar.

So far, the news sounded merely quaint, an exotic, unimportant aberration in the faraway, and therefore easily dismissed, South Pacific. But what followed was not so readily ignored. Thousands of well-disciplined "Filbistani" revolutionaries had made co-ordinated armed assaults on Lilliput-Blefuscu's key installations, taking the very largely ceremonial Elbee army by surprise, and engaging the Bolgolamites occupying the Parliament, the radio and TV stations, the telephone company, and the offices of the Lillicon Internet server, as well as the aerodrome and seaport, in fierce and prolonged fighting. The foot soldiers wore the usual hats, shades and kerchiefs to hide their faces, but some officers were more grandly attired. The cyborgs of Akasz Kronos led the way in what, Malik Solanka realized, was no less than a third "revolt of the living dolls". Many "Dollmakers" and "Zameens" were seen, confidently directing operations. "Let the fittest survive!" the Fremen were heard to shout as they charged the Bolgolamite positions. At the end of this bloody day, the FRM had gained the victory, but the price was high: hundreds dead, hundreds more seriously injured or classified as walking wounded. The medical facilities of Lilliput-Blefuscu were having great difficulty in caring for the casualties with the urgency that their injuries made necessary. Some of the wounded died while waiting to be treated. The noise of pain and fear filled the little nation's hospital corridors throughout the night.

As Lilliput-Blefuscu resumed contact with the outside world, it emerged that both President Golbasto Gue and the leader of the original and now failed coup, Skyresh Bolgolam, had been taken alive. The leader of the FRM uprising, who was dressed from head to foot in a Kronos/Dollmaker costume and who referred to himself only as Commander Akasz, went briefly on LBTV to announce his operation's success, to praise the martyrs, and to announce, with clenched fist, "The fittest have survived!" Then he announced his demands: the restitution of the ditched Golbasto constitution and the trial of the Bolgolam gang for high treason, which, under Elbee law, was punishable by death, although no executions had occurred in living memory and none would be expected in this case. He further stated that he, "Commander Akasz of the Fremen," demanded the right to be consulted about Lilliput-Blefuscu's next government and had his own slate of candidates for inclusion in that administration. He specified no post for himself, a piece of false modesty that fooled nobody. Bal Thackeray in Bombay and Jörg Haider in Austria had proved that a man didn't have to hold public office to run the show. A genuine strongman had emerged. Until his demands were met, "Commander Akasz" concluded, he would "invite the respected president and the traitor Bolgolam to remain in the Parliament building as his personal guests".

Solanka was troubled; the old problem of ends and means again. "Commander Akasz" didn't sound to him like the servant of a just cause, and while, Solanka granted, Mandela and Gandhi weren't the only models for revolutionaries to consider, bully-boy tactics needed always to be called by their right name. Neela, though, was elated. "The incredible thing is that it's so unlike Indo-Lillys to be like this: militarized, disciplined, taking action in their own defence instead of just weeping and wringing their hands. What a miracle he's worked, don't you think?" She was leaving for Mildendo in the morning, she said. "Be happy for me. This coup makes my film really sexy. The phone's been ringing off the hook all day." Malik Solanka, standing at one of the high peaks of his life, feeling, like Gulliver or Alice, like a giant among pygmies, invincible, invulnerable, suddenly felt tiny invisible fingers tugging at his garments, as if a horde of little goblins were trying to drag him down to Hell. "It is him, you know," Neela added. "Commander Akasz, I mean. I've seen the tape and there's no doubt. That body: I'd know it again anywhere. He really is quite a guy."

The speed of contemporary life, thought Malik Solanka, outstripped the heart's ability to respond. Jack's death, Neela's love, the defeat of fury, Asmaan's elephant, Eleanor's grief, Mila's hurt, the contemptuous triumphalism of the plumber Schlink, summer's end, the Bolgolam coup in Lilliput-Blefuscu, Solanka's own jealousy of the FRM radical Babur, his quarrel with Neela, the shrieks in the night, the telling of his "back-story", the high-speed development of the Galileo-Puppet Kings project and its gigantic success, the countercoup of "Commander Akasz", Neela's imminent departure: such an acceleration of the temporal flow was almost comically overpowering. Neela herself felt none of this; a creature of speed and motion, a child of her hopped-up age, she accepted the current rate of change as normal. "You sound so old when you talk that way," she chided him. "Stop it and come here at once." Their farewell lovemaking was unhurriedly, deliriously prolonged. No problems there of excessive postmodern rapidity. There were evidently still a few areas in which slowness was valued by the young.

He slipped into dreamless sleep but awoke, two hours later, into a nightmare. Neela was still there—she was often happy to sleep over at Solanka's place, although she continued to dislike waking up beside him in her own bed, a double standard that he'd accepted without demur—but there was a stranger in the room, there actually was a large, no, a very large man standing by Solanka's side of the bed, holding up—oh, awful mirror of Solanka's own misdeed!—an ugly-looking knife. Coming fully awake at once, Solanka sat bolt upright in bed. The intruder greeted him, vaguely waving the blade in his direction. "Professor," Eddie Ford said, not without courtesy. "Glad you could be with us tonight."

Once before, some years ago in London, Solanka had had a knife pulled on him by a flash young black kid, who leapt out of a convertible and insisted on using a phone booth that Solanka was just entering. "It's a woman, man," he reasoned. "It's urgent, right?" When Solanka said that his own call was important, too, the youth freaked out. "I'll cut you, you bastard, don't think I won't. I don't give a fuck, me." Solanka had worked hard on his body language. The thing was not to act too scared or too confident. A fine line had to be walked. He also fought to keep his voice level. "That would be bad for me," he'd said, "but also bad for you." Then came a staring match, which Solanka was not stupid enough to win. "Okay, fuck you, you cunt, okay?" the knife man said, and went in to make his call. "Hey, baby, forget him, baby, let me show you what that sad sack could never know." He began crooning into the telephone receiver lines that Solanka recognized as Bruce Springsteen's. *"Tell me now, baby, is your daddy home, did he go and leave you all alone, uh-huh, I got a bad desire; oh, oh, oh, I'm on fire."* Solanka walked quickly away, rounded a corner, and fell back, trembling, against a wall.

So here it was again, but this time it was personal, and body language and voice skills might not suffice. This time there was a woman sleeping beside him in his bed. Eddie Ford had begun to walk slowly back and forth at the foot of the bed. "I know what's in your head, man," he said. "Big fuckin' movie buff like you. Lincoln Plaza, et cetera, sure, sure. *Knife in the Dark,* you got it right off, second Pink Panther movie, featurin' the lovely Elke Sommer, am I right." The film had been called *A Shot in the Dark,* but Solanka decided not to correct Eddie for the moment. "Fuckin' knife movies," Eddie mused. "Mila liked Bruno Ganz in *Knife in the Head,* but for me it has to be the old classic, Polanski's first feature, *Knife in the Water.* A man starts playin' with a knife to impress his wife. She fancied that fuckin' blond hitchhiker. That was a bad fuckin' mistake, lady. That was grievous."

Neela was stirring, crying softly in her sleep, as she so often did. "Shh," Solanka caressed her back. "It's okay. Shh." Eddie nodded sagely. "I expect she'll be joinin' us soon, man. I fuckin' eagerly anticipate it." Then he resumed his ruminations. "We often rank movies, Mila an' me. Scary, scarier, scariest, like that. For her, it's *The Exorcist,* man, soon to be re-released with previously unseen material, uh-huh, but I retort, no. You have to go all the way back to the classical period to my man Roman Polanski. *Rosemary's Baby,* man. That's the fuckin' baby for me. Now, babies are somethin' you'd know about, am I right, Professor? Babies sittin' for instance on your fuckin' lap day after fuckin' day. You didn't answer me, Professor. Allow me to rephrase. You've been foolin' with what wasn't yours to touch, and the way I see it the fuckin' wrong-doer shall be punished. Vengeance is mine, saith the Lord. Vengeance is Eddie's, ain't that so, Professor, wouldn't you *concede* that as we face each other here, that is totally the fuckin' reality of the case? As we face each other here, you defenceless with your lady there and me with this enormous murderin' motherfucker of a blade in my hand waiting to cut off your balls, wouldn't you fuckin' accept that the Day of Judgment is fuckin' nigh?"

The movies were infantilizing their audience, Solanka thought, or perhaps the easily infantilizable were drawn to movies of a certain simplified kind. Perhaps daily life, its rush, its overloadedness, just numbed and anaesthetized people and they went into the movies' simpler worlds to remember how to feel. As a result, in the minds of many adults, the experience on offer in the movie theatres now felt more real than what was available in the world outside. For Eddie, his movie-hoodlum riffs possessed more authenticity than any more "natural" pattern of speech, even of threatening speech, at his disposal. In his mind's eye he was Samuel L. Jackson, about to waste some punk. He was a man in a black suit, a man named after a colour, slicing up a trussed-up victim to the tune of "Stuck in the Middle with You". None of which meant that a knife was not a knife. Pain was still pain, death still came as the end, and there was unquestionably a crazy young man waving a knife at them in the dark. Neela was awake now, sitting up beside Solanka, pulling the sheet around her nakedness, just the way people did in the movies. "You know him?" she whispered. Eddie laughed. "Oh sure, pretty lady," he cried. "We have time for a little Q-and-A. The professor and me, we're *colleagues.*"

"Eddie," a disconcertingly scarlet-eyeballed, blue-haired Mila said reprovingly from the open doorway. "You stole my keys. He stole my keys," she said, turning to Solanka in the bed. "Sorry about that. He has, like, strong feelings. I love that in a man. He in particular entertains strong feelings about you. Understandably enough. But the knife? Wrong, Eddie." She turned back to her fiancé. "W-r-o-n-g. How are we supposed to get married if you end up behind bars?" Eddie looked crestfallen, and like a scolded schoolboy stood shifting his weight from foot to foot, diminishing in an instant from mad-dog killer to yelping pet. "Wait outside," she ordered him, and he shambled dumbly off. "He'll wait outside," she said to Solanka, completely ignoring the other woman in the room. "We have to talk."

The other woman, however, was not accustomed to being erased from any scene of which she was a part. "What does she mean he stole her keys?" Neela demanded. "Why did she have your keys? What did he mean you're colleagues? What does she mean, 'understandably enough'? Why does she have to talk?"

She has to talk, Professor Solanka answered silently, because she thinks I think she fucked her father, whereas in fact I know her father fucked her, this being an area of enquiry in which I have done much fieldwork of my own. He fucked her every day like a goat—like a man—and then he left her. And because she loved him as well as loathing him, she has looked ever since for cover versions, imitations of life. She is an expert in the ways of her age, this age of simulacra and counterfeits, in which you can find any pleasure known to woman or man rendered synthetic, made safe from disease or guilt—a lo-cal, lo-fi, brilliantly false version of the awkward world of real blood and guts. Phoney experience that feels so good that you actually prefer it to the real thing. That was me: her fake.

It was seventeen minutes past three in the morning. Mila, in a trenchcoat and boots, sat down on the edge of the bed. Malik Solanka groaned. Disaster always arrived when your defences were at their lowest: blindsiding you, like love. "Tell her," Mila said, at last allowing Neela to exist. "Explain why you gave me the keys to your little kingdom here. Explain about the cushion on your lap." Mila had prepared carefully for this confrontation. She unbelted the trenchcoat and slipped it off, revealing, of all things, an absurdly short baby-doll nightie. This was an example of the use of clothing as a lethal weapon: wounded Mila was undressed to kill. "Go on, Papi," she urged. "Tell her about us. Tell her about Mila in the afternoon."

"Please do," Eleanor Masters Solanka added grimly, switching on the light as she came in, accompanied by that heavy-set, grizzled, bespectacled, blinking Buddhist owl, his ex-buddy Morgen Franz. "I'm sure all of us would be fascinated to hear." Oh fine, Malik thought. Seems there's an open-door policy around here. Please, come on in, everybody, don't mind me, make yourselves at home. Eleanor's flowing chestnut hair was longer than ever; she wore a long black high-necked cashmere coat and her eyes blazed. She looked amazing for three A.M., Malik noted. He also observed that Morgen Franz was holding her hand; and that Neela was climbing out of his bed and coolly getting dressed. Her eyes, too, were on fire, and Mila's, of course, were already bright red. Solanka closed his own eyes and lay back, putting a pillow over his face on account of the sudden glare in the room.

Eleanor and Morgen had left Asmaan with his grandmother and flown in to JFK that afternoon. They had checked into a midtown hotel, intending to contact Solanka in the morning to acquaint him with the changed circumstances of their lives. (This, at least, Solanka had intuited in advance: or, rather, Asmaan had filled him in.) "Anyway, I couldn't sleep," Eleanor said to the pillow. "So I just thought, fuck it, I'd come and wake you up. I see, however, that you are already entertaining; which makes it a good deal easier to say what I came to say." The softness was gone from her voice. Her fists were clenched, white-knuckled. She was fighting hard to keep her voice under control. Any moment now she would open her mouth and, instead of words, unleash a Fury's deafening, world-destroying shriek.

He should have known, Solanka thought, pulling the pillow down more firmly over his face. What chance did mortal man have against the devious malice of the gods? Here they were, the three Furies, the "good-tempered ones" themselves, in full possession of the physical bodies of the women to whom his life was most profoundly joined. Their external forms were all too familiar, but the fire pouring out of these metamorphosed creatures' eyes proved that they were no longer the women he had known but rather vessels for the descent into the Upper West Side of the malevolent Divine. . . . "Oh, for goodness' sake get out of bed," Neela Mahendra snapped. "Get up right now, so that we can knock you down."

Professor Malik Solanka rose naked to his feet under the flaming eyes of thc women he had loved. The fury that had once possessed him was now theirs; and Morgen Franz was caught up in its force-field, Morgen, who had so little to be proud of in his own behaviour, except that he too had learned what it was to be the servant of love. Morgen, to whom Eleanor had granted the gift of her wounded self and the stewardship of her son. Crackling with the energy flowing into him from the Furies, he moved towards the naked man like a puppet on lightning strings and swung his non-violent arm. Solanka dropped, like a tear.

17

Three weeks later he stepped out of a long-haul Airbus at Blefuscu International Aerodrome, into a hot but balmily breezy Southern Hemisphere spring day. A complex bouquet of odours filled his nostrils—hibiscus, oleander, jacaranda, perspiration, excrement, motor oil. Now the great folly of his actions hit him, even harder than the blow from his wife's pacifist lover, the haymaker, the pacifisticuff that had put him out for the count on his own bedroom floor. What did he think he was doing, a respectable and now extremely wealthy man of fifty-five, chasing halfway around the world after a woman who had literally left him flat? Worse still, why did it agitate him so that the revolutionaries here, Filbistanis, FRM, Fremen—why couldn't they make up their minds what they were called?—had taken on the identities of his fictions, like firefighters or workers at nuclear power plants donning protective clothing against the dangers of their work? Puppet King costumes may have become a feature of what was going on in these parts, but that didn't make any of it his responsibility. "You are not a party to these events," Professor Solanka rebuked himself for the umpteenth time, and himself replied, "Oh yeah? Then why is that hairless flag-waver Babur hanging out with my girl, wearing a moulded-latex mask of my face?"

The mask of "Zameen of Rijk" had been modelled after Neela Mahendra, that was obvious, but in the case of "Akasz Kronos", it seemed to Solanka, the opposite was true: as time passed, he had come to resemble his creation more and more. The long silver hair, the eyes made mad by loss. (He'd always had the mouth.) A strange piece of mask theatre was being played out on this remote island stage, and Professor Malik Solanka had been unable to shake off the notion that the action intimately concerned him, that the great or perhaps trivial matter of his perhaps significant, more probably rather pitiful life—but, still, his life!—was arriving, here in the South Pacific, at its final act. This was not a reasonable idea, but he had been, ever since the slightly tragic but mostly farcical events of the Night of the Furies, in an unreasonable frame of mind, having regained consciousness with a broken molar giving him considerable trouble, and a broken heart and wounded life that gave him more grief even than the pounding tooth. In the dentist's chair, he tried to shut out the tape of early Lennon-McCartney tunes and the pleasant prattle of the New Zealander quarryman delving deep inside his jaw—it came back to him from somewhere that the Beatles had begun life as the Quarrymen. He concentrated on Neela: what she might be thinking, how to get her back. She had demonstrated that in affairs of the heart she was very like the man that women had always accused him of being. She was there until she wasn't. When she loved you, she loved one hundred per cent, with no holds barred; but plainly she was also an axe-murderer, capable at any moment of severing the head of a suddenly rejected love. Confronted by his past—a past that in his opinion had no bearing whatsoever on his love for her—she had reached her snapping point, pulled on her clothes, exited, and almost at once embarked on a twenty-four-hour plane journey across the globe without a solicitous phone call about his jaw, let alone a word of loving farewell or even a guarded promise to try and work things out later, when history let up and gave her a bit of time. But she was also a woman familiar with being pursued. She might even be a little addicted to it. At any rate—Solanka persuaded himself while the New Zealander's babbling road-drill hammered at his jaw—he owed it to himself, having found so remarkable a woman, not to lose her by default.

To fly east was to hurtle towards the future—the jet-propelled hours rushed by too fast, the next day arrived on wings—but it felt like a return to the past. He travelled forward towards the unknown and towards Neela, but for the first half of the journey the past tugged at his heart. When he saw Bombay below him, he pulled on a sleep mask and closed his eyes. The plane stopped in the city of his birth for a full hour, but he refused a transit card and stayed on board. Even in his seat, however, he was not safe from feeling. The sleep mask was no use. Cleaners came on board, chattering and clattering, a platoon of women in shabby purples and pinks, and India arrived with them, like a disease: the erectness of their bearing, the loud nasal intonation of their speech, their dusters, their hard workers' eyes, the remembered perfume of half-forgotten unguents and spices—coconut oil, fenugreek, *kalonji*—that lingered on their skin. He felt giddy, asphyxiated, as if suffering from motion discomfort, though he was never airsick and the plane was, after all, on the ground, refuelling, with all its engines shut down. After take-off, as they headed east across the Deccan, he began to breathe again. When there was water down below again, he began, a little, to relax. Neela had wanted to go to India with him, was excited by the idea of discovering the land of her forefathers with the man of her choice. He had been the man of her choice, he must hold on to that. "I hope," she had told him, with great seriousness, "that you are the last man with whom I will ever sleep." The power of such promises is great, and under their enchantment he had even allowed himself to dream of return, had permitted himself to believe that the past could be—had been—stripped of its power, so that in the future all things could be achieved. But now Neela had vanished like a conjurer's assistant, and his strength had gone with her. Without her, he was convinced, he would never walk the Indian streets again.

The aerodrome, as its outdated name forewarned, was what a tourist determined to put a brave face on catastrophe would call "olde-worlde" or "quaint". In fact it was a pigsty, decrepit, malodorous, with sweating walls and two-inch roaches crunching like nutshells underfoot. It should have been torn down years ago, and had indeed been scheduled for demolition—it was after all on the wrong island, and the helicopters that linked it to the capital, Mildendo, looked worryingly down-at-heel—but the new airport, GGI (Golbasto Gue Intercontinental), had beaten the old place to it by falling down completely a month after it was finished, owing to the local Indo-Lilly contractors' overimaginative, if financially beneficial, rethink of the correct relationship, in the mixing of concrete, between water and cement.

Such creative rethinking turned out to be a feature of life in Lilliput-Blefuscu. Professor Solanka walked into the Blefuscu Aerodrome's customs hall and at once heads began to turn, for reasons that, flight-exhausted and stupid with heartache though he was, he had anticipated and immediately understood. An Indo-Lilly customs officer in dazzling whites bore down on him, staring hard. "Not possible. Not possible. No notification was received. You are who? Your goodname, please?" he said suspiciously, holding out his hand for Solanka's passport. "As I thought," the officer finally said. "You are not." This was gnomic, to say the least, but Solanka merely inclined his head in a gesture of mild assent. "It is unseemly," the officer added mysteriously, "to set out to mislead the public of a country in which you are only a guest, dependent on our famous tolerance and goodwill." He made a peremptory gesture to Solanka, who duly opened his cases. The customs officer gazed vengefully upon their contents: the neatly packed fourteen pairs each of socks and underpants, fourteen handkerchiefs, three pairs of shoes, seven pairs of pants, seven shirts, seven bush-shirts, seven polo shirts, three ties, three folded and tissued linen suits, and one raincoat, just in case. After a judicious pause, he smiled broadly, revealing a set of perfect teeth that filled Solanka with envy. "Heavy duty payable," the officer beamed. "So many dutiable items are there." Solanka frowned. "It's just my clothes. Surely you don't make people pay to bring in what they need to cover their nakedness." The customs officer stopped smiling, and frowned far more ferociously than Solanka. "Avoid obscene utterance, please, Mr Trickster," he instructed. "Here is much that is not clothe. Video camera is here, also wristwatches, cameras, jewellery. Heavy duty payable. If you wish to lodge protest, that is of course your democratic privilege. This is Free Indian Lilliput-Blefuscu: Filbistan! Naturally, if protest is desired, you will be welcome to take a seat in interview room and discuss all points with my boss. He will be free very soon. Twenty-four, thirty-six hours." Solanka got the point. "How much?" he asked, and paid up. In the local sprugs it sounded like a lot, but it translated into American as eighteen dollars and fifty cents. With a great flourish, the customs officer made a large chalk *X* on Solanka's bags. "You come at great historical moment," he told Solanka portentously. "Indian people of Lilliput-Blefuscu have finally standed up for our right. Our culture is ancient and superior and will henceforth prevail. Let the fittest survive, isn't it. For one hundred years good-for-nothing Elbee cannibals drank grog—kava, glimigrim, flunec, Jack Daniel's and Coke, every kind of godless booze—and made us eat their shit. Now they can eat ours instead. Please: enjoy your stay."

In the helicopter shuttle to Mildendo on the island of Lilliput, the other passengers stared at Professor Solanka as incredulously as the customs officer had. He decided to ignore their behaviour and turned his attention instead to the countryside below. As they flew over the sugarcane farms of Blefuscu, he noted the high piles of black igneous boulders near the centre of each field. Once indentured Indian labourers, identified only by numbers, had broken their backs to clear this land, building these rock piles under the stony supervision of Australian Coolumbers and storing in their hearts the deep resentment born of their sweat and the cancellation of their names. The rocks were icons of accumulated volcanic wrath, prophecies from the past of the eruption of Indo-Lilly fury, whose effects were everywhere to be seen. The rickety LB Air helicopter made its landing, to Solanka's immense relief, on the still-intact apron of the ruined Golbasto Gue Intercontinental Airport, and the first thing he saw was a giant cardboard representation of "Commander Akasz", that is to say of the FRM leader Babur in his Akasz Kronos mask and cloak. Contemplating this image, Solanka wondered with a pounding heart whether, in making his transglobal journey, he had acted as a lovelorn fool and political naif. For the dominant image in Lilliput-Blefuscu—a country close to civil war, in which the president himself was still being held hostage, and a high-tension state of siege existed, and unpredictable developments could occur at any moment—was, as he had known it must be, a close likeness of himself. The face looking down at him from the top of the fifty-foot cutout—that face framed in long silver hair, with its wild eyes and dark-lipped Cupid's bow mouth, was his very own.

He was expected. News of the Commander's lookalike had raced ahead of the helicopter shuttle. Here in the Theatre of Masks the original, the man with no mask, was perceived as the mask's imitator: the creation was real while the creator was the counterfeit! It was as though he were present at the death of God and the god who had died was himself. Masked men and women carrying automatic weapons were waiting for him outside the shuttle's door. He accompanied them without protest.

He was led to a chairless "holding room", whose single piece of furniture was a battered wooden table, watched by the unflinching eyes of lizards, with thirsty flies buzzing at the moisture in the corners of his eyes. His passport, watch and airline ticket were taken from him by a woman whose face was concealed behind a mask bearing the face of the woman he loved. Deafened by the strident martial music that was incessantly being played throughout the airport at high volume on a primitive sound system, he could still hear the elated terror in the young voices of his guards—for guerrillas weighted down with weapons were all around him—and he could also see evidence of the situation's extreme instability in the shifting eyes of the unmasked civilians in the terminal building and in the jumpy bodies of the masked combatants. All this brought vividly home to Solanka that he had stepped a long way out of his element, leaving behind all the signs and codes by which his life's meaning and form had been established. Here "Professor Malik Solanka" had no existence as a self, as a man with a past and future and people who cared about his fate. He was merely an inconvenient nobody with a face that everyone knew, and unless he could rapidly parlay that startling physiognomy into an advantage, his position would deteriorate, resulting, at the very best, in his early deportation. The very worst was something he refused to contemplate. The thought of being expelled without having come close to Neela was upsetting enough. I'm naked again, Solanka thought. Naked and stupid. Walking right into the approaching knockout punch.

After an hour or more, an Australian Holden station wagon drove up to the shed in which he had been detained and Solanka was invited, not tenderly, but without undue roughness, to get in the back. Guerrillas in combat fatigues pushed in on either side of him; two more got into the baggage hold and sat facing the rear, their guns sticking out of the raised back-window hatch. On the drive through Mildendo, Malik Solanka had a strong sense of déjà vu, and it took him a moment to work out that he was being reminded of India. Of, to be specific, Chandni Chowk, Old Delhi's troubled heart, where the traders crowded together in this same hugger-mugger style, where the shop fronts were as brightly coloured and the interiors as crudely lit, where the roadway was even more densely thronged with walking, cycling, jostling, shouting life, where animals and human beings fought for space, and where massed car horns performed the daily unvarying symphony of the street. Solanka had not expected such crowds. Easier to predict but unnerving nonetheless was the palpable distrust between the communities, the muttering clumps of Elbee and Indo-Lilly men eyeing each other unpleasantly, the sense of living in a tinderbox and waiting for a flash. This was the paradox and the curse of communal trouble: when it came, it was your friends and neighbours who came to kill you, the very same people who had helped you, a few days earlier, start your spluttering motor scooter, who had accepted the sweetmeats you distributed when your daughter became engaged to a decent, well-educated man. The shoe-shop manager next to whose premises your tobacco store had operated for ten years or more: this was the man who would put the boot in, who would lead the men with torches to your door and fill the air with sweet Virginia smoke.

There were no tourists to be seen. (The flight to Blefuscu had been more than two-thirds empty.) Few women were on the street, apart from the surprisingly large number of female FRM cadres, and no children. Many stores were closed and barricaded; others remained warily open, and people—men—were still going about their daily tasks. Guns, however, were everywhere to be seen, and in the distance, from time to time, sporadic shooting could be heard. The police force was collaborating with the FRM personnel to maintain a measure of law and order; the Ruritanian joke of an army remained in its barracks, although the leading generals were involved in the complex negotiations taking place behind the scenes for long hours every day. FRM negotiators were meeting with the ethnic Elbee chiefs, as well as religious and business leaders. "Commander Akasz" was at least trying to give the impression of a man looking for a peaceful resolution to the crisis. But civil war bubbled just beneath the surface. Skyresh Bolgolam may have been defeated and captured, but the large proportion of Elbee youths who had backed the failed Bolgolamite coup were licking their wounds and no doubt plotting their next move. Meanwhile, the international community was moving quickly towards declaring Lilliput-Blefuscu the world's smallest pariah state, suspending trade agreements and freezing aid programmes. In these moves Solanka had seen his opportunity.

Motorcycle outriders surrounded the station wagon, escorting it to the heavily defended perimeter walls of the parliamentary compound. The gates opened and the vehicle passed through, proceeding to a service entrance at the rear of the central complex. The kitchen entrance, thought Solanka with a wry private smile, was the true gate of power. Many people, functionaries or supplicants, could enter the great houses of power through their front doors. But to get into a service elevator, watched by white-hatted chefs and sous-chefs, to be borne slowly upward in an unornamented box with silent masked men and women all around you: that really was important. To emerge into an undistinguished bureaucratic corridor and be led through a series of increasingly unpretentious rooms was to walk down the true pathway to the centre. Not bad for a dollmaker, he told himself. You're in. Let's see if you get out with what you want. In fact, let's see if you manage to get out at all.

At the end of the sequence of interconnecting, blank backrooms came a room with a single door. Inside were the now-familiar spartan furnishings: a desk, two canvas chairs, a ceiling light, a filing cabinet, a telephone. He was left alone to wait. He picked up the phone; there was a dialling tone, and a small label on the instrument told him to dial 9 for an outside line. As a precaution, he had researched and memorized several numbers: that of a local newspaper, the American, British and Indian embassies, a legal practice. He tried dialling these, but each time heard a woman's recorded voice saying, in English, Hindi and Lilliputian, "That number cannot be dialled from this telephone." He tried dialling the emergency services. No luck. "That number cannot be dialled." What we have here, he told himself, is not a telephone at all but only the outward appearance or mask of a telephone. Just as this room is only wearing the costume of an office but is in fact a prison cell. No doorknob on the inside of the door. The single window: small and barred. He went over to the filing cabinet and pulled at a drawer. Empty. Yes, this was a stage set, and he had been cast in a play, but nobody had given him the script.

"Commander Akasz" swept in four hours later. By this time Solanka's remaining confidence had all but evaporated. "Akasz" was accompanied by two young Fremen too lowly to be in costume, and followed into the room by a Steadicam operator, a boom-carrying sound recordist and—Solanka's heart bounded with excitement—a woman wearing camouflage fatigues and a "Zameen of Rijk" mask: concealing her face behind an imitation of itself.

"That body," Solanka greeted her, striving for lightness. "I'd know it again anywhere." This didn't go down especially well. "What are you here for?" Neela burst out, then disciplined herself. "Excuse me, Commander. I apologize." Babur, in the "Akasz Kronos" outfit, was no longer the crestfallen, abashed young man Solanka remembered from Washington Square. He spoke in a barking voice that did not expect disagreements. *The mask acts,* Solanka remembered. "Commander Akasz", the great man-mountain, had become a big man in this very small pond, and was acting the part. Not so big, Solanka noted, as to be immune from the Neela effect. Babur walked with a long, sweeping stride, but after every dozen steps or so, his foot somehow managed to come down on the hem of his swirling cloak, forcing his neck to jerk awkwardly back. He also managed to collide, within a minute of entering Solanka's cell, with the table and both the chairs. This, even when her face was hidden by a mask! She never failed to exceed Solanka's expectations. He, however, had disappointed hers. Now he must see if he could surprise her.

Babur had already acquired the royal we. "We are familiar with you, naturally," he said without preamble. "Who right now is not cognizant of the creator of the Puppet Kings? No doubt you have good reasons for presenting yourself," he said, with a half turn of his body towards Neela Mahendra. No fool, then, Solanka thought. No point denying what he already knows to be true. "Our conundrum is, what shall we do with you? Sister Zameen? Something to say?" Neela shrugged. "Send him home," she said in a dull, uninterested voice that shook Solanka. "I've got no use for him." Babur laughed. "The sister says you are useless, Professor Sahib. Are you so? Jolly good! Shall we throw you in the bin?"

Solanka launched into his prepared spiel. "My proposal," he said, "which I have come a long way to make, is this: allow me to be your intermediary. Your connection with my project needs no comment from me. We can give you a link to a mass global audience, to win hearts and minds. This you urgently need to do. The tourist industry is already as dead as your legendary Hurgo bird. If you lose your export markets and the support of the major regional powers, this country will be bankrupt within weeks, certainly within months. You need to persuade people that your cause is just, that you are fighting for democratic principles, not against them. For the repudiated Golbasto constitution, I mean. You need to give that mask a human face. Let Neela and me work on this with my New York people, on a complimentary basis. Consider it pro bono work on a freedom movement's behalf." This is how far he was prepared to go for love, his unspoken thoughts said to Neela. Her cause was his. If she forgave him, he would be the servant of all her desires.

"Commander Akasz" waved the idea away. "The situation has developed," he said. "Other parties—bad eggs, the lot of them!—have been intransigent. As a result we also have hardened our stance." Solanka didn't follow. "We have demanded total executive authority," he said. "No more nambying or pambying. What is needed in Filbistan is for a real chap to take charge. Isn't that so, sister?" Neela was silent. "Sister?" repeated Babur, turning to face her and raising his voice; and she, lowering her head, answered almost inaudibly, "Yes." Babur nodded. "A period of discipline," he said. "If we say the moon is made of cheese, then of what, sister, is it made?" "Cheese," said Neela in the same low voice. "And if we tell you the world is flat? What shape is it?" "Flat, Commander." "And if tomorrow we decree that the sun goes round the earth?" "Then, Commander, the sun it will be that goes around." Babur nodded with satisfaction. "Jolly good! That is the message for the world to grasp," he said. "A leader has arisen in Filbistan, and it is for everyone to follow, or suffer the needful consequences. Oh, by the by, Professor, you have studied ideas at the University of Cambridge in England, isn't it. Therefore be so good as to enlighten us on a vexed point: is it better to be loved or feared?" Solanka did not answer. "Come, come, Professor," Babur urged. "Make your good effort! You can do better than that." The FRM cadres accompanying "Commander Akasz" began to fiddle meaningfully with their Uzis. In an expressionless voice, Solanka quoted Machiavelli. " 'Men are less hesitant about harming someone who makes himself loved than one who makes himself feared.' " He began to speak with greater animation, and looked directly at Neela Mahendra. " 'Because love is held together by a chain of obligation which, since men are a sorry lot, is broken on every occasion in which their own self-interest is concerned; but fear is held together by a dread of punishment which will never abandon you.' " Babur brightened. "Good egg," he cried, thumping Solanka on the back. "You aren't useless after all! So, so. We'll think about your proposal. Jolly good! Stay awhile. Be our guest. We already have the president and Mr Bolgolam in residence. You, too, will witness these first bright hours of our beloved Filbistan, upon which the sun never sets. Sister, be so kind as to confirm. How often does the sun go down?" And Neela Mahendra, who had always carried herself like a queen, bowed her head like a slave and said, "Commander, it never does."

The cell—he had stopped thinking of it as a room—did not contain a bed, and lacked even the most rudimentary toilet facilities. Humiliation was the stock-in-trade of "Commander Akasz", as his treatment of Neela had amply demonstrated. Solanka perceived that he was to be humiliated, too. Time passed; he lacked a watch by which to measure it. The breeze faded and died. Night, the ideologically incorrect, nonexistent night, grew humid, thickened and stretched. He had been given a bowl of unidentifiable mush to eat and a jug of suspect water. He tried to resist both, but hunger and thirst were tyrants, and in the end he did eat and drink. After that he wrestled with nature until the inevitable moment of defeat. When he could no longer contain himself, he pissed and shat wretchedly in a corner, taking off his shirt and wiping himself with it as best he could. It was hard not to fall into solipsism, hard not to see these degradations as a punishment for a clumsy, hurtful life. Lilliput-Blefuscu had reinvented itself in his image. Its streets were his biography, patrolled by figments of his imagination and altered versions of people he had known: Dubdub and Perry Pincus were here in their sci-fi versions, also mask-and-costume incarnations of Sara Lear and Eleanor Masters, Jack Rhinehart and Sky Schuyler, and Morgen Franz. There were even space-age Wisławas and Schlinks walking the Mildendo streets, as well as Mila and Neela and himself. The masks of his life circled him sternly, judging him. He closed his eyes and the masks were still there, whirling. He bowed his head before their verdict. He had wished to be a good man, to lead a good man's life, but the truth was he hadn't been able to hack it. As Eleanor had said, he had betrayed those whose only crime was to have loved him. When he had attempted to retreat from his darker self, the self of his dangerous fury, hoping to overcome his faults by a process of renunciation, of *giving up,* he had merely fallen into new, more grievous error. Seeking his redemption in creation, offering up an imagined world, he had seen its denizens move out into the world and grow monstrous; and the greatest monster of them all wore his own guilty face. Yes, deranged Babur was a mirror of himself. Seeking to right a grave injustice, to be a servant of the Good, "Commander Akasz" had come off at the hinges and become grotesque.

Malik Solanka told himself he deserved no better than this. Let the worst befall. In the midst of the collective fury of these unhappy isles, a fury far greater, running far deeper than his own pitiful rage, he had discovered a personal Hell. So be it. Of course Neela would never return to him. He was not worthy of happiness. When she came to see him, she had hidden her lovely face.

It was still dark when help came. The cell door opened and a young Indo-Lilly man entered, bare-faced, wearing rubber gloves and carrying a roll of plastic refuse sacks as well as a bucket, pan and mop. He cleaned up Solanka's mess unflinchingly and with great delicacy, never seeking to catch the perpetrator's eye. When he had finished, he returned with clean clothes—a pale green kurta and white pantaloon pyjamas—as well as a clean towel, two new buckets, one empty, one full of water, and a bar of soap. "Please," he said, and, "I am sorry," and then left. Solanka washed and changed and felt a little more himself. Then Neela arrived, alone, unmasked, in a mustard-coloured dress, with a blue iris in her hair.

It obviously preyed on her mind that Solanka had witnessed her timorous responses to her treatment by Babur. "Everything I've done, everything I'm doing, is for the story," she said. "Wearing the mask was a gesture of solidarity, a way of earning the fighters' trust. Also, you know, I'm here to look at what they're doing, not to have them look at me. I could see you thought I was hiding from you behind it. That wasn't so. Similarly with Babur. I'm not here to argue. I'm making a film." She sounded defensive, taut. "Malik," she said abruptly, "I don't want to talk about us, okay? I'm caught up in something big right now. My attention has to be there."

He went for it, gathered himself and made his play. All or nothing, Hollywood or bust: he would never get another chance. He might not have much of one anyway, but at least she had come to see him, had actually dressed up for it, and that was a good sign. "This has become much more than a documentary film project for you," he said. "This really goes to the heart. There's a lot riding on it—your uprooted roots are pulling hard. Your paradoxical desire to be a part of what you left. And, no, I didn't really think you were wearing the mask to hide your face from me, or at least that wasn't the only thing I thought. I also thought you were hiding from yourself, from the decision you've made somewhere along the line to cross a line and become a participant in this thing. You don't look like an observer to me. You're in too deep. Maybe it started out with a personal feeling about Babur—and don't worry, this isn't jealousy speaking, at least I'm trying hard not to let it be—but my guess is that whatever your feelings about 'Commander Akasz' were, they're a lot more ambiguous now. Your problem is that you're an idealist trying to be an extremist. You are convinced that your people, if I can use so antiquated a term, have been done down by history, that they deserve what Babur has been fighting for—voting rights, the right to own property, the whole slate of legitimate human demands. You thought this was a struggle for human dignity, a just cause, and you were actually proud of Babur for teaching your passive kinsmen and kinswomen how to fight their own battles. In consequence you were willing to overlook a certain amount of, what shall we call it, illiberalism. War is tough and so on. Certain niceties get trampled. All this you told yourself, and all the while there was another voice in your head telling you in a whisper you didn't want to hear that you were turning into history's whore. You know how it is. Once you've sold yourself, all you have left is a limited ability to negotiate the price. How much would you put up with? How much authoritarian crap in the name of justice? How much bathwater could you lose without losing the baby?—So now you're caught up, as you say, in something big, and you're right, it deserves your attention, but so does this: that you only went this far because of the fury that possessed you all of a sudden in my bedroom in another city in another dimension of the universe. I can't articulate exactly what happened that night, but I do know that some sort of psychic feedback loop established itself between you and Mila and Eleanor, the fury went round and round, doubling and redoubling. It made Morgen punch me out and it blew you clean across the planet into the arms of a little Napoleon who will oppress 'your people' if he comes out of this on top, even more than the ethnic Elbees, who have been, at least in your eyes, the villains of this piece. Or he'll oppress them just as much but in a different way. Please don't misunderstand.—I know that when people pull apart, they usually employ misunderstanding as a weapon, deliberately getting hold of the stick's wrong end, impaling themselves on its point in order to prove the perfidy of the other.—I'm not saying that you came here because of me. You were coming anyway, right? It was our big farewell night, and as I remember, it had gone pretty well until my bedroom turned into Grand Central Station. So you'd have been here, and the pulls and pushes of being here would have worked on you whether I existed or not. But I think that what pushed you over the edge was disappointed love. You were disappointed in me and by me, which is to say by love, by the great untrammelled love you were just allowing yourself to begin to feel for me. You had just begun to trust me enough, to trust yourself enough, to let yourself go, and then suddenly the prince turns out to be a fat old toad. What happened is that the love you'd poured out went bad, it curdled, and now you're using that sourness, that disenchantment and cynicism, to push you down Babur's dead-end road. Why not, eh? If goodness is a fantasy and love is a magazine dream, why not? Nice guys finish second, to the victor go the spoils, et cetera. Your system is fighting itself, the bruised love is turning on the idealism and battering it into submission. And guess what? That puts you in an impossible situation, where you're risking more even than your life. You're risking your honour and self-respect. Here it is, Neela, your Galileo moment. Does the earth move? Don't tell me. I already know the answer. But it's the most important question you're ever going to be asked, except for the one I'm going to ask you now: Neela, do you still love me? Because if you don't, then please leave, go meet your fate and I'll wait here for mine, but I don't think you can do that. Because I do love you as you need to be loved. You choose: in the right corner there's your handsome Prince Charming, who also, by a small mischance, turns out to be a psychotic megalomaniacal swine. In thc wrong corner there's the fat old toad, who knows how to give you what you need and who needs, so very badly, what you in turn know how to give him. Can right be wrong? Is the wrong thing right for you? I believe you came here tonight to find out the answer, to see if you could conquer your fury as you helped me conquer mine, to find out if you could find a way of coming back from the edge. Stay with Babur and he'll fill you up with hatred. But you and me: we just might have a shot. I know it's stupid to make this kind of declaration when just an hour ago I was stinking of my own shit and I still don't have a room with a doorknob on the inside, but there it is, that's what I crossed the world to say."

"Wow," she said, after allowing a suitably respectful moment of silence to elapse. "And I thought I was the big mouth on this team."

She fished a heat-softened Toblerone bar out of her purse and Solanka fell upon it greedily. "He's losing the men's confidence," she told Solanka. "The boy who helped you out tonight? There are plenty more like him, maybe as many as half the total, and for some reason they whisper to me. *Khuss-puss, khuss-puss.* It's so sad. 'Madam, we are decent persons.' *Khuss-puss.* 'Madam, Commander Sahib is acting strange, isn't it?' *Khuss-puss.* 'Please, madam, do not mention my thoughts to anyone.' I'm not the only idealist around here. These kids didn't think they were going to war to flatten the earth or abolish the hours of darkness. They're fighting for their families, and all this green-cheese material unnerves them. So they come to me and complain, and that puts me in a very dangerous place. It doesn't really matter what advice I give—being a second focal point, a rival centre, is quite dangerous enough. One rat—one mole—is all it would take, and speaking of toads, yes, I do love you, very much. Meanwhile, what I saw on the outside before I brought the team in here was an army that's pretty sick of being a laughing-stock. My information is they've been talking to the Americans and the British. The rumour says that the marines and the SAS may already be in Mildendo, in fact, I've been feeling pretty foolish for weeks about running out on you like that. There's a British aircraft carrier just outside territorial waters, and Babur doesn't control the military airfields on Blefuscu, either. The truth is I've been thinking for a while now that it's time to leave, but I don't know how Babur will take it. Half of him wants to fuck me on national television and the other half wants to beat me up for making him feel that way. So now you know the real reason why I've been wearing the mask: it's the next best thing to putting my head in a paper bag, and you came all this way for me and walked into the lion's den. I guess you must really dig me too, huh. I'm working on an out. If I can get the right Fremen in the right places, I think it can be done, and I have contacts in the army that can at least get us out to the British boat or maybe a military plane. In the meanwhile I'll make sure you get looked after. I still don't know about Babur, how far gone he is. Maybe he thinks you're a valuable hostage, even though I keep telling him you're not worth the trouble, you're just a civilian who blundered into something he didn't understand, a little fish he should throw back into the sea. If you don't kiss me soon, I'll be forced to kill you with my own bare hands. Okay, that's good. Now stay put. I'll be back."

In Athens the Furies were thought to be Aphrodite's sisters. Beauty and vengeful wrath, as Homer knew, sprang from the selfsame source. That was one story. Hesiod, however, said that the Furies were born of Earth and Air, and that their siblings included Terror, Strife, Lies, Vengeance, Intemperance, Altercation, Fear and Battle. In those days they avenged blood crimes, pursuing those who harmed (especially) their mothers—Orestes, long pursued by them after he killed bloody-handed Clytemnestra, knew all about that. The *leirion,* or blue iris, sometimes placated the Furies, but Orestes wore no flowers in his hair. Even the bow of horn that the Pythoness, the Delphic Oracle, gave him to repel their assaults proved to be of little use. "Serpent-haired, dog-headed, bat-winged," the Erinnyes hounded him for the rest of his life, denying him peace.

These days the goddesses, less regarded, were hungrier, wilder, casting their nets more widely. As the bonds of family weakened, so the Furies began to intervene in all of human life. From New York to Lilliput-Blefuscu there was no escape from the beating of their wings.

She didn't come back. Young men and women attended to Solanka's daily needs. These were some of the weary, immured fighters who, fearing their own leader, Babur, as much as the enemy outside the compound walls, had gone to their dark Aphrodite for advice; but when Solanka asked about Neela, they made dumb don't-know gestures and went away. "Commander Akasz" didn't show up, either. Professor Solanka, forgotten, washed up on the edge of things, dozed, talked aloud to himself, drifted into unreality, lurching between daydreams and panic attacks. Through the small barred window he heard the noise of battle, growing more frequent, coming closer. Pillars of smoke rose high into the air. Solanka thought of Little Brain. *I'd have set his house on fire. I'd have burned his city down.*

Violent action is unclear to most of those who get caught up in it. Experience is fragmentary; cause and effect, why and how, are torn apart. Only sequence exists. First this then that. And afterwards, for those who survive, a lifetime of trying to understand. The assault came on Solanka's fourth day in Mildendo. At dawn the door of his cell was opened. There stood the same taciturn young man—now carrying an automatic weapon, and with two knives stuck in his belt—who had so uncomplainingly cleaned up his mess a few days earlier. "Come quickly, please," he said. Solanka followed him, and then it was into the labyrinth again, the bleak interconnecting rooms with masked fighters guarding the way, approaching each door as if it were booby-trapped, turning each corner as if an ambush lurked just beyond; and in the distance Solanka heard the inarticulate conversation of battle, the chatter of automatic rifles, the grunts of heavy artillery, and, high above it all, the leathery beating of bat-wings and the screeches of the dog-headed Three. Then he was enclosed in the service elevator, manhandled through the ruined kitchens, and pushed into an unmarked, windowless van; after which, for a long time, nothing. High-speed motion, alarming halts, raised voices, the motion renewed. Noise. Where was that shrieking coming from? Who was dying, who was killing? *What was the story here?* To know so little was to feel insignificant, even a little insane. Thrown this way and that in the hurtling, swerving van, Malik Solanka howled aloud. But this, after all, was a rescue. Somebody—Neela?—

had decreed him worthy. War erases the individual, but he was being saved from the war.

The door opened; he squinted into the blinding daylight. An officer saluted him—an exotically mustachioed ethnic Elbee wearing the absurdly braided uniform of the Lilliputian army. "Professor. So happy to see you safe, sir." He reminded Solanka of Sergius, the stiff-backed officer in Shaw's *Arms and the Man.* Sergius, who never apologized. This fellow had plainly been assigned to chaperone Solanka, a task he fulfilled briskly, marching ahead like an overwound toy. He led Solanka into a building bearing the insignia of the International Red Cross. Later there was food. A British military aircraft was waiting to carry him, along with a group of other foreign passport-holders, back to London. "My passport was taken," Solanka told Sergius. "None of that matters now, sir," the officer replied. "I can't leave without Neela," Solanka went on. "I don't know anything about that, sir," Sergius said. "My orders are to get you on board that aircraft double-quick."

All the seats on the British plane faced towards the tail. Solanka, taking his allotted chair, recognized the men across the aisle as Neela's cameraman and sound recordist. When they stood up and embraced him, he knew the news was bad. "Unbelievable, mate," the soundman said. "She got you out, too. Amazing woman." Where is she. None of this matters, your life, mine, he thought. Will she be here soon. "She did the whole thing," the cameraman said. "Organized the Fremen who were sick of Babur, contacted the army on shortwave radio, arranged the guaranteed safe-conducts, the lot. The president's out. Bolgolam, too. That bastard tried to thank her, called her a national heroine. She cut him short. In her own eyes she was a traitor, betraying the only cause she ever believed in. She was helping the bad guys win, and it killed her. But she could see what Babur had become." Malik Solanka had grown very still and quiet. "The army got tired of the jokes," the sound engineer said. "They called up all reservists and dusted off a lot of old but still serviceable pieces of heavy artillery. Helicopter gunships from the Vietnam era, bought secondhand from the United States years ago, ground-based mortars, a few small tanks. Last night they took back control of the compound perimeter. Still Babur wasn't worried." The cameraman indicated a silver box. "We got it all," he said. "She arranged incredible access. Just incredible. He never believed they would use the heavy stuff against the Parliament building, and certainly not while he was holding his hostages. He was wrong about the building. Underestimated their determination. But the hostages were the key, and Neela turned that lock. The four of us came out together. And then there was the whole second route, which she set up just for you." After that nothing was said. The terrible thing hung between them like a fierce light, but it was too bright to look at. The soundman began to cry. What happened? Solanka finally asked. How could you leave her? Why didn't she run with you towards safety? Towards me. The cameraman shook his head. "What she did," he said, "it tore her apart. She betrayed him, but she couldn't run. That would have been desertion under fire." But she wasn't a soldier! Oh God. God. She was a journalist. Didn't she know that? Why did she have to cross that goddamn line? The soundman put his arm around Solanka. "There was something she had to do," he said. "The plan wouldn't have worked if she hadn't stayed behind." "To distract Babur," the cameraman said, dull-voiced, and there it was, the worst thing in the world. To distract him: how? What did that mean? Why did it have to be her? "You know how," the soundman said. "And you know what it means. And you know why it had to be her." Solanka closed his eyes. "She sent you this," the cameraman was saying. Helicopter gunships and heavy mortars, authorized by the freed President Golbasto Gue, were blasting holes in the Lilliputian Parliament. A bomber shed its load. The building was exploding, crumbling, on fire. Dirty smoke and clouds of masonry dust climbed high into the sky. Three thousand reservists and front-line troops assaulted the complex, taking no prisoners. Tomorrow the world would condemn this ruthless action, but today was for getting it done. Somewhere in the wreckage lay a man wearing Solanka's face and a woman wearing her own. Not even Neela Mahendra's beauty could affect the trajectory of the mortars, the bombs like deadly fishes swimming downward through the air. Come to me, she murmured to Babur, I am your assassin, the murderer of my own hopes. Come here and let me watch you die.

Malik Solanka opened his eyes and read the handwritten note. "Professor Sahib, I know the answer to your question." Neela's last words. "The earth moves. The earth goes round the sun."

18

From a distance the boy's hair was still golden, although the new growth beneath was darker. By his approaching fourth birthday the yellow hair would have mostly gone. The sun was shining as Asmaan rode his tricycle with great attack down a sloping path on the flowering springtime Heath. "Look at me!" he shouted. "I'm going really fast!" He had grown, and his diction was much clearer, but he was still clothed in childhood's radiance, that brightest of cloaks. His mother ran to keep up with him, her long hair twisted away beneath a large straw hat. It was a perfect April day at the height of the foot-and-mouth epidemic. The government was simultaneously ahead in the polls and unpopular, and the prime minister, Tony Ozymandias, seemed shocked by the paradox: what, you don't like us? But it's *us,* folks, we're the good guys! People, people: it's *me*! Malik Solanka, a traveller from an antique land, watching his son from the privacy of a grove of oaks, uncomplainingly allowed a black Labrador to sniff at him. The dog moved on, having established that Solanka was not suitable for his purposes. The dog was right. There were few purposes for which Solanka felt suitable right now. *Nothing beside remains.*

Morgen Franz did not run. He didn't "do running". Beaming myopically, the publisher lumbered down the slope towards the waiting woman and child. "Did you see that, Morgen? It was very good driving, wasn't it? What would Daddy say?" Asmaan's tendency always to speak at top volume carried his words up to Solanka's hiding place. Franz's reply was inaudible, but Malik could easily write his lines. "Far out, Asmaan, man. Really nice." The old hippie shit. To his eternal credit, the boy frowned. "But what would Daddy say?" Solanka felt a little surge of fatherly pride. Good for you, kid. You remind that Buddhist hypocrite who's who.

Asmaan's Heath—or at least Kenwood—was studded with magical trees. A gigantic fallen oak, its roots twisting in air, was one such enchanted zone. Another tree, with a hole at the base of its trunk, housed a set of storybook creatures, with whom Asmaan carried out ritual dialogues each time he passed this way. A third tree was the home of Winnie-the-Pooh. Nearer Kenwood House were large spreading rhododendron bushes inside which witches lived and where fallen twigs became magic wands. The Hepworth sculpture was a sacred spot, and the words "Barbara Hepworth" had been a part of Asmaan's lexicon almost from the start. Solanka knew the route Eleanor would take, and knew, too, how to follow the little group without being noticed. He wasn't sure he was ready to be noticed, wasn't certain he was ready for his life. Asmaan was asking to be carried along the next part of the path, not wanting to ride the trike uphill. This was an old laziness, entrenched by habit. Eleanor had a weak back and so Morgen hoisted the boy up on his shoulders. That had always been one of Solanka and Asmaan's special things. "Can I ride on my shoulders, Daddy?"—"*Your* shoulders, Asmaan. Say, 'your shoulders'. "—"My shoulders." There goes everything I love on this earth, Solanka thought. I'll just watch him awhile. I'll just watch over him from here.

Once again he had withdrawn from the world. Even checking his voicemail was hard. Mila had married, Eleanor left tight, miserable messages about lawyers. The divorce was all but done. Solanka's days began, passed, ended. He had given up the New York sublet and taken a suite at Claridge's. Most days he only left it to allow the cleaners to get in. He contacted no friends, made no business calls, bought no newspaper. Retiring early, he lay wide-eyed and rigid in his comfortable bed, listening to the noises of distant fury, trying to hear Neela's silenced voice. On Christmas Day and New Year's Eve he ordered room service and watched brainless television. This expedition by taxi to North London was his first real outing in months. He had been far from sure he would even see the boy, but Asmaan and Eleanor were creatures of custom, and their movements were relatively easy to predict.

It was a holiday weekend, so there were funfairs on the Heath. On their way back to the house on Willow Road—it would be on the market any day now—Asmaan, Eleanor and Morgen wandered through the usual rides and stalls. Asmaan was thawing towards Franz, Solanka observed: laughing with him, asking him questions, his hand disappearing inside Uncle Morg's great hairy-knuckled fist. They went in a bumper car together while Eleanor took photographs. When Asmaan leaned his head against Morgen's sports coat, something broke in Malik Solanka's heart.

Eleanor saw him. He was lounging by a coconut shy and she looked right at him and stiffened. Then she shook her head vehemently, and her mouth silently but very emphatically made the word "no". No, this was not the right time; after such a long gap it would be too much of a shock for the lad. *Call me,* she mouthed. Before any future meeting they ought to discuss how, when, where and what Asmaan should be told. The little fellow needed to be prepared. This was how Solanka had known she would react. He turned away from her and saw the bouncy castle. It was bright blue, blue as an iris, with a bouncy staircase at one side. You climbed up the stairs to a bouncy ledge, slid and tumbled down a wide, bouncy slope, and then, to your heart's content, you bounced and bounced. Malik Solanka paid his money and slipped off his shoes. "'Ang about," the enormous woman attendant cried. "Kids only, guv. No adults allowed." But he was too quick for her, and with his long leather coat flying in the breeze, he leapt up on the wibbly-wobbly stairs, leaving astonished children floundering in his wake, and at the top of the stairs, standing high above the fairground on the wibbly-wobbly ledge, he began to jump and shout with all his might. The noise that emerged from him was awful and immense, a roar from the Inferno, the cry of the tormented and the lost. But grand and high was his bouncing; and he was damned if he was going to stop leaping or desist from yelling until that little boy looked around, until he made Asmaan Solanka hear him in spite of the enormous woman and the gathering crowd and the mouthing mother and the man holding the boy's hand and above all the lack of a golden hat, until Asmaan turned and saw his father up there, his only true father flying against the sky, *asmaan,* the sky, conjuring up all his lost love and hurling it high up into the sky like a white bird plucked from his sleeve. His only true father taking flight like a bird, to live in the great blue vault of the only heaven in which he had ever been able to believe. "Look at me!" shrieked Professor Malik Solanka, his leather coat-tails flapping like wings. "Look at me, Asmaan! I'm bouncing very well! I'm bouncing higher and higher!"

Also available in Vintage

Salman Rushdie

THE MOOR'S LAST SIGH

Winner of the Whitbread Novel of the Year Award

'A triumph...affectionate and masterly'
New York Times Book Review

'A wonderful book, gorgeous in colour and texture, magnificent in scope, wildly funny'
Independent on Sunday

'Salman Rushdie's latest and – so far – greatest novel...held me in its thrall and provided the richest fictional experience of 1995'
Antonia Fraser, Books of the Year, *Sunday Times*

'Rushdie is still our most exhilaratingly inventive prose stylist, a writer of breathtaking originality'
Shashi Tharoor, *Financial Times*

'Endlessly inventive, witty, digressional and diverting'
Michael Ratcliffe, *Observer*

Also available in Vintage

Salman Rushdie

THE GROUND BENEATH HER FEET

'Quite simply the most absorbing, the most entertaining book you are likely to read all year'
Mail on Sunday

'This is Rushdie at his absolute, almost insolently global best – his adroit mastery of language serves brilliantly imagined characters and a mesmerizing narrative. Completely seductive'
Toni Morrison

'Here is a great novelist operating as a master of metamorphosis – transforming life, art and language in the subterranean maze of his imagination'
Don DeLillo

'This is a fabulous, glowing, witty and brilliant epic...This is the *Ulysses* of rock 'n'roll...glittering writing – humane and very funny'
Ruth Padel, *Independent*

'The first great rock 'n' roll novel in the English language'
Nigel Williamson, *The Times*